Soulmates

DISCLAIMER: This book contains content of an adult nature. This includes explicit sexual content and characters who may not conform to your religious, political, or world view. The content is inappropriate and in some cases illegal for readers under the age of 18.

PLANNED 2025 SIGNATURE COLLECTION RELEASES

The Art and Science of Love, April 2025. D.R. Peters, 'Doc' to his friends, is an artist. He paints portraits of women. Doc loves women. Many of the women he paints love him. Then smart and sexy Rita, his next door neighbor, asks him to teach her the art of love, which Doc is all too happy to do. He's not quite so sure, though when Rita, a research scientist, decides to start experimenting with the effect his relationship with his models has on his art. Doc is about to learn all about the science of the art of love.

Things I Never Told My Wife, June 2025. Actor, director, and admitted cad, Terry Reichert has led a life filled with colorful-and-beautiful-women. From his deflowering while skinny dipping to holding the love of his life as she died, from actresses to students, from stage crew to strangers—Terry never met a woman he wasn't interested in taking to another level. And during all this, he is a respected professor, industry professional, husband, and father who can honestly say, "I never went hunting for it."

Strange Art, August 2025. Words just don't come easily to Art Étrange, if they come at all. His slow speech, self-consciousness, and shyness all combine to keep him isolated from his peers. He can only let his frustrations out on canvas. If it wasn't for his sister, Morgan, Art would not have survived school, but her love holds Art together through his toughest times and expands his horizons. This special Signature Collection Edition contains all three Strange Art books, ***Art Something,*** ***Art Project,*** and ***Art Critic.***

Adams' Apples, October 2025. World War III was fought in outer space. It was over in an hour and no one won. Except Jack Adams, who was the only male of the species not caught in the viral fallout of the war that sterilized all the men on earth. Jack was the orbiting satellite repairman who inadvertently triggered the war. Now every woman in the world wants one of Jack Adams' Apples.

Drawing on the Dark Side of the Brain, December 2025. Artist Jett Blackburn's paintings reveal the soul of his subjects. They have the power to change the viewer, the model, and the artist. Sometimes emotionally, sometimes terminally. Join this digital native and his accumulation of girlfriends as they break the ties with their parents and move off to college and self-discovery.

Schedule and Releases Subject to Change

Soulmates

Devon Layne

ELDER ROAD BOOKS
LYNNWOOD, WA

<h1 style="text-align:center">1
FROM BIRTH</h1>

Jaime

EVERYONE HATED JAIME. He tried and tried to get people to listen to him, but they just ignored him. He could hear them clearly, even when they were cluttering up what they were saying with noises from their mouths. But no one would answer him when he spoke.

The reason might have been because Jaime never opened his mouth. No one had ever heard him speak. He heard people better in his head than in his ears, but no one responded in his head. They just ignored him.

Understandably, Jaime thought everyone hated him.

Not everyone, perhaps. Jaime knew his parents loved him and worried about him all the time. The words that came out of their mouths were accompanied with warm feelings of love and acceptance. But in their heads, Jaime heard words like 'slow to develop' and 'autistic.' Of course, those words never came out of their mouths when they were around Jaime. The words were always accompanied by feelings of fear and anxiety. Words Jaime hadn't learned the meaning of, but knew the feelings.

Jaime didn't understand most of what people said in their heads. That was a problem from the moment he was born.

APPARENTLY, BEING INSIDE his mom shielded him from most thoughts, but once he was outside her protective womb and people were all around, he was bombarded with thoughts from everywhere. They were all strange and other. He couldn't understand the thoughts. Everyone was shouting all at once in a language he didn't understand.

It was frightening. Jaime started trying to close out the thoughts—to shut his mental ears—but didn't know what to do. His body began to respond without his own volition. It started shutting down. He was overwhelmed by the sensations and thoughts he couldn't understand. The noise in his head was too much for him. Jaime had so much input into his infant mind that he forgot important things—like breathing.

He was abruptly torn from his mother's arms. People thinking urgent things put tubes in his nose and kept his heart beating. He was put in a plastic box that cut out much of the cacophony of thoughts.

He slept.

"I'd have to say the birth trauma did some permanent damage," the doctor told Jaime's mother and father. "I don't know how much and at this stage, it's hard to run any qualitative tests."

"What should we do?" Nola asked. That was Mama to Jaime, but she never responded to him when he said the word in his head.

"The rest of his development seems normal. Growth. Motor skills. Weight gain. All well within the standards. I'd say continue to love him and don't try to force speech development on him. Talk to him. Play with him. Just make sure he is confident in your love for him."

"We can do that," David said. That was Dada to Jaime.

Jaime heard the words in his head, but at three years old, he didn't have a large enough vocabulary to understand what they meant. That was part of what was normal with him. His language development was par for his age group. He learned far more from listening in people's heads than by listening with his ears. Some people didn't use words in their heads and Jaime struggled to learn the words they said with their mouths. It was very complicated.

People who used fewer words and more pictures in their heads were easier to understand. It was people who only used feelings and intentions in their heads who were difficult to understand. Jaime didn't understand all the pictures he saw in other people's heads, either, but he learned from them, nonetheless. There were some things people thought and then immediately tried not to think. Some of those pictures seemed exciting to the thinker, but they were just pictures Jaime silently filed away in the back of his mind to understand later.

He could usually tell when a person was excited or happy or sad or angry or worried. He could understand emotions more easily than some words. He could tell what people felt when he felt them. But he seldom understood why they felt what they did. There didn't seem to be words to match the feelings.

As Jaime's fourth birthday approached and he had still never spoken a word, his parents grew even more concerned that something serious was wrong.

2
MOMMY

Jaime and Mommy (Nola)

IN FACT, JAIME'S mother *did* offer some shielding from the onslaught of mental voices pounding at his head. Her soft and loving caresses soothed him and helped block out the cacophony. She was calm and all her thoughts were about him. He instinctively reached out with his mind to share his love for her, but she didn't seem to be aware that he was talking to her. He simply clung to her more closely than ever.

He was uncommonly quiet, even in instances where he was hurt and crying, he made no noise. Nola had to be ever more attentive to him, mindful of danger and injury, since he never cried out. She and David were increasingly concerned, and Nola's full-time job became caring for Jaime.

She played with him and read to him, pointing out words as she spoke them. In this way, Jaime learned rapidly, but even when he laughed, the sound was little more than a squeak. Nola and David became more and more convinced that the birth trauma had somehow damaged the connection from his brain to his voice box. They gave him constant words of encouragement, asking him to select the blue block or the red crayon—tasks Jaime always completed with ease. They praised his accomplishments. Sometimes, Jaime thought they were talking to him in his head, but when he responded there was nothing. They never responded directly when he tried to ask a question.

Jaime withdrew even further into himself. When he was taken to a play group with other children his age, none of them would respond to his thoughts, either. He sat off to the side and watched children laughing and talking, unable to comprehend why they didn't like him. He had so many questions and all he could do was listen and wait, hoping the answer would come. He pointed to things and his parents responded, but they often ran down a litany of what his gesture might mean before they arrived at the right conclusion.

He became more and more frustrated. People just didn't listen, no matter how he shouted at them in his mind. He found himself sitting alone with a book or a toy, obsessed with some intricate detail. He was pleased when his mother began teaching him the alphabet and showing him how the letters went together to form words.

Jaime gradually became aware of another phenomenon. People often didn't say the same thing with their inside voice as their out-loud voice. As time went by, even his mother talked aloud to him in comforting and caring tones, while her inside voice was filled with anxiety. Words like 'slow developing,' and 'autism' were in her inside vocabulary—words Jaime didn't know the meaning of but knew they were bad things about him. That was why no one would talk to him in his head, he thought. He was bad. He was an autism. No one liked an autism.

When guests came to their house or when they visited elsewhere, Jaime hid and found places where people's inside voices didn't reach him as relentlessly.

JAIME WAS FIVE years old and had resigned himself to never being listened to and being a bad person no one liked. He was playing on the floor with a toy xylophone he'd learned a tune on. His parents were very proud that he didn't just hammer on the keys. His mother was finishing the dishes from their quiet lunch together.

He hardly ever tried to reach his mother with his thoughts any longer because she never answered him. He simply couldn't understand why people bothered with their out-loud voices when they were perfectly clear with their inside voices. They never said what they meant.

The peanut butter sandwich he'd had for lunch left bits of gummy bread stuck in his mouth. He wanted another glass of milk.

«Milk, Mommy,» he thought as clearly as he could.

His mother continued washing the dishes. Jaime was getting more and more flustered as time went by. He thought perhaps if he was more polite, his mother would pay attention. He organized his thoughts and directed them to his mother again.

«May I have milk please, Mommy?» he thought as clearly as he could.

Still no response. Maybe it was all a game people played that he didn't understand. He organized his words again and did his best to speak with a squeaky little out-loud voice.

"Mother, may I please have a glass of milk?" he said, mimicking people he'd heard being polite.

Nola spun in place, dropping a glass that shattered on the kitchen floor. Her mouth opened, but no sound came out as she seemed not to be able to get air in her lungs. She stared at her son, then her eyes rolled back in her head and she collapsed to the floor, landing on the broken glass. Blood flowed from her arm and her head where they were cut and Jaime couldn't understand the jumbled thoughts that seemed to crowd each other out in her mind.

"Mommy?" he squeaked again. «Mommy!»

She didn't respond at all.

He considered getting a Band-Aid from the high cabinet in the bathroom. Mommy had fixed all his cuts and scrapes growing up with dinosaurs, Mickey Mouse, and fire trucks. He never bled as much as his mother was, though. He didn't think a Band-Aid would help. There was only one thing to do. His parents had taught him carefully to dial 9-1-1 in an emergency.

He'd heard his father's thoughts when they taught him how to use the phone.

«I don't know what good it will do if he can't talk. Maybe just making the call and leaving the line open will be enough.»

Jaime went to the phone on the table, crawling up on his chair. He carefully dialed the three numbers.

"This is 9-1-1 emergency. State the nature of your emergency, please."

Jaime thought really hard, trying to get the person on the phone to see his mother lying on the floor bleeding. There was no response. In fact, Jaime couldn't hear her in his head at all.

"Hello? Can you speak?" the operator asked.

Jaime took a deep breath. Maybe no one could read thoughts over the telephone.

"Yes," he squeaked.

"What is the nature of your emergency?"

"Mommy fell on broken glass. Lots of blood," Jaime squeaked. Tears were welling up in his eyes.

"Can she speak to me?"

"Not awake."

"I have located your address as 571 Crescent Drive and have alerted an ambulance. Help is on the way," the operator said. "I'm transferring you to a nurse who will ask you some questions. Please stay on the phone, little girl."

«Girl? I'm a boy!» Jaime thought at her. Then decided the telephone must change people's out-loud voices, too. So, he just stayed on the phone staring at Mommy. He still couldn't make sense of any of her thoughts. Then another voice came through the phone.

"This is Nurse Janet," the voice said calmly and gently. "What is your name?"

"Jaime," he said, trying to use the same calm tone through his tears.

"Jaime, can you see your mother?"

"Yes."

"Tell me where she is bleeding."

Jaime couldn't tear his eyes away from his mother, constantly calling to her. «Wake up, Mommy. Nurse Janet wants to talk to you!»

"Her head and her arm."

"Oh, dear. What part of her arm is bleeding?"

"Near her hand."

"Jaime, this is very important. Some people are on their way to help your mommy, but she needs your help right away. Can you reach her and still talk on the phone?"

"Not supposed to take the phone off the table."

"I'll explain it all to your mommy. Right now, you need to take the phone close enough to touch her."

The woman had a very nice voice, but Jaime wished she would just show him what he should do. The telephone didn't let any thoughts come through.

"Is there a long cord on your phone?"

"Mmmhmm."

"Jaime, this is very important. You need to wrap the cord around Mommy's arm between her elbow and where she is bleeding. Do you know where her elbow is?"

"Mmmhmm."

"Wrap the cord around her arm and twist it as tight as you can make it."

"Mommy won't like it," Jaime complained. "Hurt Mommy."

"Jaime, we need to do this so Mommy can wait for the ambulance. Please do what I've told you to do. I'll explain to Mommy."

She sounded urgent, even though he couldn't hear her inside voice. He knew sometimes people tried to stay calm when they were very frightened. He did. And he was very frightened right now. It didn't seem right, but Jaime picked up his mother's bloody hand and wrapped the cord around and around her arm. There wasn't as much blood coming out any longer. He couldn't hear the phone as well now.

"The ambulance is almost there, Jaime. Tell your Mommy you love her. That will help her on the ride to the hospital," Nurse Janet said.

"I love you, Mommy," Jaime squeaked. Then he doubled it in his mind and screamed, «I love you, Mommy.»

Then the most remarkable thing happened. Jaime heard his mother speak in his mind.

«I love you, too, baby boy.»

Then her thoughts sort of disappeared.

There was a noisy whining sound outside and, in a minute, two men crashed through the front door. They ran into the kitchen talking fast and thinking faster than Jaime could comprehend. He dropped the phone and ran to his room. More people came into the house, bringing things the men needed and shouting in their minds.

Jaime was overwhelmed by the thoughts. He held his hands against his head and hid beneath his bed where the thoughts weren't so noisy. In minutes, the ambulance drove away with Mommy. Jaime stayed hidden, quietly crying.

He'd spoken exactly fifty-two words in his life, and men came to take his mommy away in a red truck that made lots of noise.

Jaime and Daddy (David)

JAIME SPENT THE rest of his day crying and calling out mentally to Daddy. Other people came in the house, jabbering with each other about helping repair things and who should bring meals. No one thought about Jaime.

David returned to the house late, frantically calling out for his son and searching the house.

"Jaime! Jaime! Where are you, son? Come here to Daddy. Please don't be lost, baby boy."

Jaime came out of his room and ran to his daddy's voice. He was still crying and didn't know what to do. David was just as relieved to see his son, but he continued to talk as he tried unsuccessfully to soothe Jaime.

"I can't believe they just left you here! The stupid people! They couldn't even keep Nola alive. And they left you here alone. I'm so glad you're okay! I'll sue the city and the hospital and every fucking one of them! Oh! Thank God, you're okay."

Jaime was thankful his daddy was home and holding him, but his father's thoughts were a worse jumble than what he was saying.

We're alone. How will we survive. Nola is dead. How can we go on? Everything is bad!

Jaime tried to ask him what dead meant, but his father, too, refused to respond to his thoughts. He was afraid to use his out-loud voice because when he used it Mommy fell down and they took her away. Everything was wrong and Jaime was hungry.

David finally understood that and managed to stop crying a little.

"My God! You've been here all afternoon alone. You must be starving. Don't worry, son. We'll get through this somehow. It's just you and me now. We'll manage. I don't know how, but we'll manage."

He carried his son out of the room, even though Jaime was perfectly able to walk. Daddy seemed to need to hold him, so Jaime lay his head against his father's strong shoulders and relaxed. He carried Jaime downstairs and out the broken door. In the kitchen, there was still broken glass and blood and the telephone on the floor.

They drove to the food place with Jaime in his car seat. At the restaurant, his father ordered Jaime's favorite pancakes and syrup with a glass of milk. While Jaime ate, he kept trying to figure out what his father was thinking. His thoughts were a jumble, asking questions Jaime couldn't answer.

What am I going to do without you? Who can I get to help? I need to call the office and tell them. How can I tell them? What can I tell them? How can I ever raise our son by myself? What made you fall? Nola, please don't go!

Jaime ate pancakes while Daddy just drank coffee and made phone calls. When they got home, some neighbors were there with Uncle Kenny. He wrapped his big arms around both David and Jaime and held them for a long time. Jaime needed the bathroom, though, and began to squirm. David put him down. He ran upstairs to the bathroom so he wouldn't wet his pants.

There were women in the kitchen cleaning up the glass and the mess. Uncle Kenny was working with men to repair the door the red truck men had broken in. Everyone's thoughts were as jumbled as his father's.

It's too bad. Poor Jaime. How will David cope? We'd better get some food organized. I can watch Jaime while David makes arrangements. Did anyone check to see if things were all still here and nothing was stolen? Why didn't we think to check on Jaime when they took Nola?

Daddy took Jaime to bed. After he was in his pajamas and snuggled under his blankets, David read him a story and turned out the light. There was still a lot of racket in the house with people talking and thinking. Jaime slipped out of bed to turn on his music. If he focused on listening to the music, he could block out the noise from people shouting in his head.

Eventually, he covered his head with his pillow and went to sleep.

Jaime understood one thing clearly: His out-loud voice was bad—even worse than being ignored. He'd spoken once and Mommy was never coming home again. He would never use his out-loud voice again.

Sadly, everyone still refused to answer him when he spoke to their heads with his inside voice. They just ignored him, unless he physically got their attention and pointed to what he wanted. They couldn't ignore that and made a big fuss about all he needed to do was tell them.

It was frustrating. People talked about everything in their heads, including about Jaime, as if he wasn't even there. A nice woman came to stay with him while Daddy went to work, but before too many days passed, Daddy's work changed and he was at home a lot, working on his computer in the basement.

Jaime liked hanging out there with his father. The basement was quieter. And when his father was working, his mind was quieter and calmer. He got Jaime earphones so he could play his music without making noise in the 'office.' Jaime was happy there.

He did have to learn when he could and couldn't interrupt his father. If his father was using his out-loud voice on the telephone, for example, Jaime was not to interrupt. Jaime knew where most things were in the house, so he could find where snacks were in the kitchen—he liked pudding—and could get his own plastic glass of water. He could use the bathroom and knew he had to stand on the stool to wash his hands afterward. He knew which handle was hot water and which was cold.

Sometimes, when he had his earphones on and wandered upstairs, he went to his room to read a book or get a toy. It wouldn't be long before his father rushed in to see where he'd gone and breathed a sigh of relief when he found his son.

And David began to understand his son better all the time. He took time from his busy day to read Jaime stories and give him paper and crayons. He even set up an art place in a corner of his office. Jaime liked drawing and sometimes copied words or pictures from his books.

David spent time reading and practicing letters. He taught him how to spell his name. Jaime was a fast learner. He could see in his father's mind what was wanted. It was easier to pick things out of his mind than it was to wait while he talked.

David began to think about school, something he would have left to Nola before. She'd been teaching him letters and numbers at home and Jaime would often sit quietly 'reading.' David didn't know if he understood what he read or if he was just looking at pictures. He wondered how Jaime would do in a world where everyone talked. He read up on education for children with selective mutism and discarded most of it. Jaime wasn't selectively mute. He *never* spoke. David read articles for communicating with the deaf, but Jaime heard just fine. It appeared the doctors' diagnosis of autism was the only answer.

Then the question was whether to try mainstream education or to get him into a special education program. The problem with special education was that the operating assumption was that the child was slow at learning and had difficulty understanding instructions. Jaime had no problem understanding and learning. His responses were unorthodox, ranging from pointing and gesturing to occasional printed words as Jaime began to understand more language.

It was time to think about school.

DAVID TOOK JAIME to meet with a kindergarten teacher. The conversation was strained.

"He's never spoken at all?" the teacher asked. She'd introduced herself as Miss Judy. Jaime and his father sat across from her at a little table on chairs that were much too small for the grownups. Miss Judy had immediately set paper and crayons in front of Jaime.

"Not a word," David said. "He scarcely makes a sound even when he cries or laughs. When Jamie was born, his whole body shut down. He was rushed to intensive care and put in an incubator with breathing and feeding tubes. He was there for several days before he began to respond to stimuli. Doctors have proposed that the intense trauma after his birth resulted in a form of autism. Then last spring, he saw his mother bleed to death after a fall. That redoubled the trauma. We've been told not to try to get him to speak. If he can speak, it will come naturally. Eventually."

"Oh, my. I'm not sure what to say, Mr. Stackhouse. I'm not usually a special ed teacher. Have you checked other programs?" Miss Judy asked.

"I don't believe my son needs special education. He already knows his numbers and letters and can spell some words. He's very intelligent. He just doesn't talk, and I don't want a well-meaning special education teacher trying to get him to talk," David said.

"Hmm. In kindergarten, a substantial part of the curriculum is socialization. Children come from all backgrounds and this is an opportunity for them to learn about and from others. Much of that is through communication. If you would give me a couple of days to do some research, perhaps I can come up with a way to integrate Jaime into the class. I support your goals and my research is simply to see if I can find a way to advance them."

"I will accept that and thank you for your efforts," David said.

Jaime heard a very different conversation, though neither of the adults acknowledged what they were thinking. Miss Judy was very nice, but was at a loss for what to do. Jaime decided she really did want to have him in her class and was thinking of all the ways she could teach other children about something called 'mutism.' She didn't seem to have any doubts that Jaime could learn in her class—perhaps faster than others his age.

Daddy was barely holding back his frustration. He was very protective of Jaime and wondered if he could believe Miss Judy or if this was just a wasted effort. Jaime decided he needed to help.

He drew a picture of Miss Judy. It wasn't a Renaissance portrait, or even a good likeness. It was a woman with a ponytail and flowers on her dress. That much was clear. Under the picture, he carefully printed the word 'NICE.' He pushed the picture between his father and Miss Judy.

"It seems you have Jaime's vote," David laughed.

"That may be all that is necessary," Miss Judy said. "Thank you, Jaime. May I keep the picture?"

Jaime could see she wanted to show it to another teacher when she 'sorted things out.' He nodded.

"I'll be in touch on Wednesday afternoon," Miss Judy said. "Thank you both for considering me as a possible teacher for Jaime."

They left the school and Jaime could tell his father was feeling much better. They stopped for ice cream on the way home.

3
SCHOOL

Miss Judy and Emily

JUDY DUNLAP HAD not been a kindergarten teacher long enough to become jaded and calloused to the ideals that brought her to the profession. She was twenty-four years old, had one year of experience behind her, and had nearly finished her master's degree in education.

She looked at the drawing young Jaime had done of her and traced the word 'NICE.' She could not help but think the child had understood every word in the conversation between her and his father. And printing a word at just five years old, with no formal schooling, was advanced. If it weren't for his muteness and lack of socialization he could probably have moved directly to first grade.

But how was she going to teach him in a class of twenty children, half of whom lived in non-English-speaking homes. She sat, sipping a glass of wine with her best friend and handed her the drawing.

"Done by one of your new students?" her friend signed. Emily Hearst had been deaf from birth, but it didn't stop her from becoming best friends with Judy in college.

"He will be my student in two weeks," Judy signed back. "He is mute— either psychosomatically or physically. I don't know how to integrate him into the system. He hears and understands just fine, but how will he communicate with me or with other students?"

Emily looked at the picture again and finger-spelled N-I-C-E. Then she held her left hand palm-up in front of her and passed her right palm over it.

"Yes," Judy signed. "He wrote that while his father and I were talking. I'm just so…"

Emily brought her fist to the side of her head, rapping gently as she scowled at her friend.

"What?" Judy asked. Emily repeated the sign.

"Dumb!"

"Why would you say such a thing?"

"You have the tool in your hands. Half your class doesn't know English. Teach them all sign language at the same time."

"Sign language! He's not deaf!" Judy began. Then she realized she wasn't deaf either. She signed to her friend to be understood. "Oh!"

Judy shook her head and repeated the sign for 'dumb.' She sometimes taught songs that had gestures or signs because the children found them fun. It involved more ways to learn than just listening. Why shouldn't she teach sign language at the same time she taught English? Or any other subject for her kindergartners to learn.

"It makes so much sense!" Judy signed. "I have to make lesson plans!"

Emily laughed at her as Judy gathered her things and headed home. She had two weeks to prepare.

Jaime and Miss Judy and Juan

When Jaime and David arrived for the first day of kindergarten with all the other parents and children, the room looked much different than it had when they visited. The first and most obvious thing Jaime noticed was the alphabet characters posted in a neat row on one wall. When he'd been in the room before, the posters had capital letters and small letters. Now a hand image was beneath each letter.

The other thing that was unavoidable to notice was the chaos of thoughts flying around the room. He couldn't tell who was thinking what and wished they would all just be quiet. He put his hands over his ears but that didn't do anything for the inside voices. He repeated the sign to his father and then buried his face against his father's chest. It wasn't as effective as sheltering in his mother's embrace, but it helped. He was soon able to filter out all the intruding thoughts.

The problem was that when he shut off everyone, he couldn't hear Miss Judy's thoughts either. She was the only one talking with her out-loud voice and her hands moved as she spoke. She said they would learn both English and sign language in the class.

Some of the adults who came with their children to the first day of school looked confused, but their thoughts weren't in any words Jaime could understand. Then Miss Judy told the grownups they could leave now. David had talked to him about this and Jaime was prepared to stay with Miss Judy for a couple of hours.

Some of the other children were not prepared for this. They clung to their mothers—David was the only father in the room—and some began to cry. Miss Judy began singing a song and some of the children joined in. She signed as she went. Jaime tried to copy the gestures.

"Bye-bye, Mommy. I will see you soon. Don't worry, Mommy. You'll pick me up at noon. I'll tell you all about my day, and all the things I learned to say. Bye-bye, Mommy. I will see you soon."

Jaime wondered if the sign for Mommy and Daddy was the same. He would ask Miss Judy when he could understand more. Then she caught his eye as she changed the song to "Bye-bye, Daddy…" She brought her open hand from where it had tapped on her lower lip to tapping at the side of her forehead. Jaime grinned and copied the gesture, earning a smile from Miss Judy.

He worked hard on blocking out all the noise of the other children's thoughts as their parents left them in the classroom. He had to listen carefully with his ears for Miss Judy's instructions, as she led the class in other activities. She had two helpers in the class who explained things quietly to some of the children.

Miss Judy led the class in saying her name. She pointed to the letters in her name that were displayed on the wall, then wrote them on a whiteboard. She pointed to each letter on the board and made the letter sign for it while saying the name of the letter. Then she circled her whole name and made a new gesture. She brought her fingers and thumbs together and pointed to either side of her head, then brought her hands down in front of her. Jaime figured out that meant Miss Judy, since that's what she kept saying.

Miss Judy led the class in the alphabet song, signing the letters as one of her helpers pointed at the letter and sign hanging on the wall. They sang the song several times and the class worked hard at copying the signs.

The other helpers had names, too, but Jaime was looking at the letters on the wall and trying to figure out what his name would look like. J-A-I-M-E. He practiced spelling his name and almost missed the class being divided into groups. One group went with each of the teachers to a different part of the room. Jaime's group went to Miss Judy.

A boy sat alone sniffling. Jaime could tell he was upset with the day. Maybe he missed his mommy. Jaime still missed his mommy. He decided the boy needed a hug and went to him. The boy looked at him, but Jaime couldn't understand anything the boy was thinking; just that he was very sad and upset. Jaime put an arm around the boy's shoulders and gave him a hug while he led him to the group in front of Miss Judy. They sat together and Jaime could tell the boy felt a little better.

The next thing Miss Judy taught them was how to spell their names. She started by putting a hand on her chest, then tapping her index fingers together like a flat x. She repeated the signs saying, "My name is." Then she spelled "Miss Judy" again. She finished that with the gesture she created for her name. Jaime could read her thoughts clearly now that everyone was in a different part of the room paying attention to the book one helper was reading and to the blocks the other helper was building with. He raised his hand.

"Yes, Jaime?" Miss Judy said, finger spelling his name.

Jaime copied the hand on chest and tapping his fingers together, then spelled his name. Miss Judy caught her breath and smiled broadly at him. She turned to the other children and repeated what Jaime had said and asked him to demonstrate. He introduced himself to his classmates. He thought only one had understood him, but soon his new friend raised his hand.

"Can you spell your name, Juan?" She wrote his name on the whiteboard.

Juan repeated the introduction gestures and said, "My name is Juan." He got the 'J' correct, then hesitated over the next letter. Miss Judy held up two fingers close together and said, 'U.' Juan nodded and then completed the 'A' and 'N.'

Jaime could feel the happiness of his new friend and now he knew his name. He nodded vigorously. He pointed at Juan and then fingerspelled J-U-A-N. Next, he put his hand on his chest and spelled J-A-I-M-E. The two were so involved in talking to each other, Miss Judy had to call their attention back to the class as the others in their group introduced themselves. Some were better or faster than others and some were much slower, but by the time his group moved to the helper reading a story, everyone in his group could fingerspell his or her name.

JAIME WAS PROUD of his accomplishment. He had learned how to sign his name and he had made a new friend. When his father picked him up at noon, he gladly signed his name. David was a little perplexed without the words accompanying the signs. Miss Judy intervened and spoke as Jaime signed.

"He is saying, 'My name is Jaime.' We're learning sign language as we learn the alphabet."

"That's… That's wonderful!" David said. "Where can I learn sign language?"

"Hmm. I didn't think about that," Judy said. "I'll ask the school if I can hold a class for parents in the evening once a week. It's a good idea. I'm so thankful Jaime has brought this new experience into our classroom."

Jaime's education had begun and his father began studying sign language at once.

AFTER THE FIRST remarkable breakthrough day, kindergarten was kindergarten. Miss Judy and her helpers did all the regular kindergarten activities. They sang songs accompanied by sign language. Each day a child was invited to put the calendar day on the board. Disputes over toys and books were resolved. Discipline was exercised when necessary. Everything was accompanied by sign language.

The classroom volunteers were often no further ahead in sign language than the students were, but the results were so pleasing to Miss Judy that they applied themselves to learning as much as they could. The school approved Judy offering parents a class one evening a week. Many of the volunteers and other teachers attended when they could. Her friend Emily often joined her on those evenings to hold conversations with the parents, getting them acclimated to reading and responding in sign language.

While Jaime was a little ahead of his class, it was not noticeable since he never spoke. He liked to draw and even to print words. His friend, Juan, was often found at his side as they built with blocks, drove trucks around their little cities, and learned ever more English and sign language. Jaime learned Juan was from Mexico and soon developed a name sign that was faster than fingerspelling. He held his fingers in a v-shape and saluted with them. Before too long, his classmates had made up a name sign for Jaime, too. They simply passed their fingers over their lips in a zipper motion. David was alarmed with the sign, but Jaime, who had read his classmates' thoughts when they started signing his name that way, seemed happy with it and introduced himself to people using the sign.

ONE OF THE most important things Jaime learned in kindergarten—though it wasn't taught as a subject—was filtering out the thoughts from around him.

Miss Judy stopped to talk to David one day after the evening sign language course.

"I don't know what the exact problem is, but I've read a bit about autism and it seems many autistic children are easily overwhelmed by the amount of activity around them," she said. "I've noticed Jaime enthusiastically participating one moment and seeming to draw into himself the next. It's as if he is trying to hide from the class. Sometimes, he even goes behind the whiteboard or behind one of the assistants to hide. Do you have experience in handling this?"

"Yes," David admitted. "I hoped it wouldn't become an issue in school. He seems hyper-sensitive to noise and commotion around him. Sometimes it catches up with him after the fact. He comes home from school and immediately goes to hide in his room. He puts on headphones I originally got him so he could watch TV or listen to music while I was working. Now his headphones are programmed for classical music that I download for him. The music seems to let him calm down and breathe."

"Hmm. Headphones might create a problem in the classroom. He might not be able to hear instructions," Judy said.

"That's true, but he understands more sign language than I do already. I'm sure he can read your signs as you are instructing," David said.

"Let's try it. If it becomes a distraction to the other students, we might need to curtail their use. But it's worth a try. I don't want to lose him into some inner cavern where I can't reach him."

David explained the use of the headphones to Jaime before school and stressed how important it was to only use them when he was feeling overwhelmed. Jaime agreed and was happy to have his music when he needed it.

It was the beginning of Jaime's quest to block out the mental sounds around him. He had used it in his home and sometimes when he was with his father shopping or going out to dinner. The music itself did not block out all the thoughts around him. It was focusing on the music that let him escape from the ever-present cacophony he was subjected to.

Solid objects had often been a refuge as it seemed most people did not have much range to their thought broadcasts. The whiteboard in his classroom was made of metal that the teacher could attach magnets to. Jaime found it was effective at blocking other people's thoughts. When he hid behind a teaching assistant, she seemed to absorb the thoughts of others and he could only hear her thoughts.

But music was different. If he broke his concentration on the music, the thoughts of others were right there waiting for him. But as long as he let the music occupy his mind, the thoughts were kept at bay.

What was most puzzling and heartbreaking for Jaime, though, was that no matter how he thought to another person—any other person—that person ignored him. The only person who had ever spoken in his mind had been his mother, just moments before he lost her. He felt his father sometimes thinking love or pride to his son, but he never used words to express himself inside. He always spoke out-loud, and now used sign language with his son.

Even Jaime's new friend, Juan, didn't talk to him when he thought to him. Jaime wrote much of that off to Juan's inability to communicate in English, though he was learning slowly. Jaime was learning some Spanish, too. As Juan learned English, he associated the Spanish word and Jaime learned from that.

Nor was Juan the only Spanish speaker in the class who was learning English. That group became close friends, separate from the kids who came to kindergarten knowing and speaking English.

Jaime missed his friends during the summer and David tried to arrange a

meeting with one or more of them each week. He sent Miss Judy a thank you note.

Jaime

FIRST GRADE WAS another new experience for Jaime. His teacher only knew a smattering of sign language and used it irregularly. While some of Jaime's classmates understood sign language, many more did not. He was forbidden to use his earphones in class and it was frowned upon at recess and lunch. His teacher talked through her class, so students had to stay focused on what she was saying or what she assigned them to do. Many found that beyond their ability.

At least the uniform activity of the class kept most of the randomness of students' thoughts at bay. There were those in the class, though, who simply could not maintain focus for more than a few minutes at a time and their chaotic thoughts disrupted Jaime's concentration. He had to focus harder on blocking out their thoughts.

When his teacher found out he didn't talk, she started badgering him to say something. David came to the school and put the teacher straight with the help of Miss Judy. Mrs. Connelly did not appreciate it. By this time, Jaime could print out responses quickly and had even begun to learn to type, so Mrs. Connelly pretty much ignored him from that point onward.

As if I don't have enough problems to deal with in this class, Jaime heard her thinking.

He tried not to be a problem. He passed the tests she gave him and that was all that was required to advance him to the next grade. Her final report, however, stated that he lacked socialization and should be in a special needs class.

With the number of friends Jaime had, it wasn't obvious that he lacked socialization, but the school responded with an assessment. The State of Oregon required that the school accommodate all special needs and the Federal Government provided funding. They hired a sign language interpreter, not to interpret to Jaime, though she signed everything in the class, but to interpret

Jaime's sign language to the teacher.

This teacher was more accommodating and called on Jaime in class, waiting for the interpreter to tell her what he was saying. Jaime didn't need the interpreter's signs to understand the teacher, but paid attention to them anyway. Other students began picking up signs and occasionally asked the interpreter what a sign meant or how to sign something. By the end of the second month of second grade, nearly everyone used Jaime's name sign and spoke his name as Zipper Lips, or just Zip.

As juveniles often do, they frequently asked for the sign for naughty words. The interpreter declined to give them the sign, but Jaime was now proficient enough on his computer at home that he could look up signs for anything he didn't know in the internet. He often supplied the requested sign to his classmates. He was happy his friends who had been in his sign language kindergarten class had continued to use sign—at least when around him—and learned more sign language as they progressed in school. Only Juan and four others from his kindergarten were still in his class by the time he reached third grade.

4
STRANGER

Jaime and the Stranger

JAIME'S ABILITY TO block out others got better as he got older. He couldn't avoid some of his classmates' thoughts and by the end of the day, he was tired of blocking things and let much more slip through.

David still worked from home with occasional daytime visits to his office. He'd changed jobs to have a more flexible schedule so he could be with his son when needed. He was happy Jaime had made some friends and visited them at their houses or invited them to his house. David noted that all Jaime's friends had been ESL students in kindergarten and were fluent signers.

One day after school, the two went to the grocery store for their weekly shopping trip. Jaime was tired and immediately put his headphones on to begin playing music and blocking out the thoughts of others. He wasn't really paying attention to much else and wandered up an aisle in the store without his father.

Oh, yes. There's a good one, he heard in his mind. It so shocked Jaime that he came to a dead stop and looked around him. At the end of the aisle he saw a man in a dark suit staring at him.

We have to get the house set up. And I can't handle a little kid yet. But he's perfect. I can tell by his eyes and the headphones. He has trouble blocking people out. I'll have to let him pass for now, but I'll be back. He's one of the gifted ones. Together, we'll rule the world.

Jaime wanted to shout at the intruder with his mind, but instead, he

23

reflexively clamped down on all his own thoughts, burying them in the music that played through his headphones. He turned and ran back up the aisle, looking for his father as the stranger seemed to laugh in his head.

He was blinded to reason, not knowing where his father was. He saw the heavy door of the meat department ahead and rushed through it. The thoughts of the man, and everyone else in the store, were immediately muted. He decided to stay there until he could locate his father.

That presented a problem. He couldn't hear anyone in the store and the cooler he'd rushed into was cold. Packages and haunches of meat lay on shelves and hung from hooks. And once the door was closed, it was dark.

He thought the man would probably leave the store once he'd disappeared. He would wait a few minutes and then push open the latch from the inside of the cooler to find his father.

By the time Jaime had managed to throw his entire weight against the plunger that would open the cooler door, his lips were blue and he was shivering. He stumbled out of the cooler and practically into the arms of a butcher.

"Here he is! I've got him!" the butcher called out. A flood of voices erupted in Jaime's mind. Many were calling his name in his ears. Then he located his father and called out to him in his head. His father ran toward the meat department and caught his son in his arms. Jaime quickly scanned the thoughts he could hear in the store, but found no sign of the man he had heard in his head.

Had the man been talking to him? Or was he just thinking? Jaime couldn't tell.

Jaime

JAIME HID IN his room. The man in the grocery store had frightened him. Jaime's closet offered some refuge from intruding thoughts, especially when he put on his headphones and concentrated on the music. He knew metal walls were the most effective at blocking others' thoughts. When he rode in the car, he only ever heard his father's thoughts beside him. With the creativity of a nine-year-old, he had 'borrowed' aluminum foil from the kitchen drawer and taped it to the walls of his closet. He believed it helped.

In the sanctuary of his closet, he slowed his speeding heart and thought about what had happened.

He had read a stranger's thoughts in the store. They frightened him. But Jaime had to wonder how those thoughts had cut through the barrier of the music he was using to block others. Either the man simply broadcast his thoughts more loudly than most people, or…

Jaime's heart nearly stopped beating. Or he had been broadcasting specifically to Jaime.

In all his life, he had experienced only one time that a person spoke to him in his head. His mother had directed her thoughts in response to his declaration that he loved her, just before she died. He had certainly experienced people thinking *about* him. It wasn't that unusual. When he was introduced to teachers and other students who were told he didn't speak, they always wondered what kind of kid he was and what caused his muteness. But no one tried to inside-voice speak *to* him.

As long as he could remember, Jaime had thought this was simply because other people didn't like him and wouldn't acknowledge him when he spoke to them in his head. When he began to learn sign language, he realized that other kids spoke to him in sign while their brains thought about what they were saying. Their thoughts were focused on their hands, though, and not on Jaime.

Jaime slowly came to the conclusion that other people were deaf in their heads. If he hadn't learned sign language, he would eventually have had to use his out-loud voice or people would continue to just ignore him. At least now he had friends and could talk to them. They still ignored him in their heads, but they spoke with their hands.

What shocked him to silence when he heard the man in the store was the direction of his thoughts and the malevolence behind them. He was not a nice man. If the man had been 'ready' and Jaime had been older, Jaime knew he would have been kidnapped. But why? What did he need to be ready for?

And had the man been able to hear him?

Jaime had closed out most of the world with his headphones but he'd been thinking his own thoughts, mostly about school and Halloween coming soon. He'd already begun to meet new people in classes, but most of his classmates didn't know sign language. Had the man heard his thoughts? Jaime had automatically closed himself off to other people when he heard the man in his head. He'd never felt the need to do that before. No one had ever heard him. He realized now that it was a skill he needed to practice regularly. He just needed to figure out what he had done to block anyone else from hearing him. What was it?

This problem occupied Jaime until his father found him for dinner.

Kenton

KENTON DESPERATELY WANTED to be a telepath. He knew it was possible. He'd run all kinds of tests on students at the university. So much so that he'd gained a bit of a reputation as a crackpot. He'd only verified one actual telepathic case, but she had insisted on complete anonymity. He couldn't use her data in any summary paper. He'd decided to carefully alter his findings in other instances for his dissertation.

It was real data, after all. It simply wasn't the data from the subjects he cited. He felt justified in it. He barely passed his defense. His professors acknowledged his research but were all of the opinion the evidence cited was an outlier. He'd couched the material in an investigation of inner monologue and inner dialog. He explored some new data indicating that some people could not recognize their own inner monologue and *believed* they heard voices from outside their own head.

He speculated on all kinds of reasons for this, but his firm conclusion was that it was dangerous in the treatment of a person to ignore the idea that they might actually hear voices that emanated from external sources. The university had granted his doctorate, though there were committee members who still considered his study to be paranormal and not within the realm of real science.

What he needed was more examples, and there was no better place to get them than in his counseling practice. It was slow to gain momentum, but eventually he would get there.

Part two of his plan was to create a refuge where he could study people he identified as legitimately hearing voices in their heads without the interference of outside influences. This was sped along by two external factors.

The first was a visit he received from two men who identified themselves only as Smith from the FBI. They had read and studied his dissertation! Kenton immediately tensed up when they began discussing the possibility of his participation in studies they were conducting themselves. It was soon obvious they were not considering him as a researcher, but as a subject.

Kenton immediately left the country. He stayed in seclusion in India for two years, pretending to be a monk. He believed, rightly, that having this on his resume would shield the seriousness of his research. No one had seriously come to India to study the paranormal since the Beatles found enlightenment sixty years earlier.

He returned to Portland and immediately rented an office that was in the build-out stage. He had very specific requirements regarding the materials to be used, and special features to be added. He told the contractors that he wanted his office to be fully shielded so that clients could not be distracted by cell signals or WiFi. The contractor considered this reasonable for psychological counseling and built the Faraday cage-like structure around his entire office. The only access to the outside world was a wired internet connection and a landline phone.

The other thing that happened at that time, and was the reason he was able to afford the extraordinary adjustments to his office, was his inheritance. A rich old aunt had passed away and when all was said and done, Kenton discovered he was the sole heir to both her fortune and her property.

The property was a historical residence and he was able to update the interior, but was forbidden from altering the appearance of the property in any way. He did all the modifications internally, hiring subcontractors to follow his plans.

He wondered why there was only spotty cell phone service in the old buildings when it was fine and strong outside. His discovery was that the original lath and plaster walls were covered in chicken wire to help hold the plaster. It created a natural Faraday cage and inspired Kenton to enhance that feature throughout the renovation.

Only the upgrades to electrical and plumbing lines and the heating system needed to be permitted and inspected. And he had plenty of money and time to get things done over the course of a few years. Soon now, he would have his refuge of absolute silence where he could both study his subjects and be free of spying by the government's microwaves.

Jaime and Mrs. Chapman

FOR JAIME, THIRD grade was an important year of self-discovery. He learned arithmetic, conducted science experiments, read interesting stories, used a keyboard, and learned to read maps. With his best friends still in his class, he learned more sign language, Spanish, and handwriting.

Oregon did not require the teaching of cursive handwriting in elementary school, but their teacher felt it was a valuable skill and invited her students to stay in the classroom during recess one day a week to practice the skill. The six friends took advantage of the class and soon were writing in a beautiful script.

Cursive writing, Mrs. Chapman felt, had several benefits. She wished it was taught in elementary school, or even kindergarten when letters were taught. Writing in cursive was more natural because it made each letter a single continuous stroke. Printing disrupted the pattern recognition for children. The strokes were separate and children often forgot what stroke came next when their hand stopped still. It prevented much letter reversal. In printing, for example, both 'b' and 'd' began with a single vertical stroke. Then students had to stop and determine whether the circle belonged on the left or the right for the letter they wanted. With cursive, the flow of the two characters was different, one starting with the vertical loop and the other starting with the circle.

She'd also noted improved motor skills and word recognition when students learned cursive writing. Cursive writing required students to cross the midline of the body with their hands, improving their coordination. Words were connected together and were not seen as a string of individual letters.

Of course, students had to learn to read printed words, but she felt something vital was lacking in their education if they did not learn to write in cursive.

A key element was fostering artistry, and that is how Mrs. Chapman positioned teaching script. The six friends who took advantage of the class were soon writing in a beautiful script. Unlike the standard script that had been taught in schools until the twenty-first century, Mrs. Chapman taught her students to write Spencerian script. She called the class 'calligraphy' and her students worked hard to create the artistic letterforms.

At the end of the school year, half a dozen students had mastered the careful shaping of letterforms into the elegant script. And their classmates, who had not taken the one recess a week instruction, couldn't read what the six had written! It was like they were a secret club.

Of course, they already had a secret language as few of the students knew sign language. Mrs. Chapman used her instruction time in handwriting to learn more sign language in the absence of the interpreter. She was soon able to hold basic conversations with them in sign. She wasn't sure what set these students apart from others. Five were ESL students who spoke better English than most of her native English speakers. And one was the strange boy who didn't speak at all, but constantly showed his intelligence in his writing, math, and science skills.

Jaime liked Mrs. Chapman. His first and second grade teachers mostly ignored him and his ESL friends in the classroom and let the interpreter take care of including them. Mrs. Chapman actually talked *to* him and waited for the interpreter to speak his signed response. She made sure the rest of the class paid attention to each person who was called upon to speak.

When he and his friends were promoted to fourth grade, they all missed Mrs. Chapman. While they were still in the same class, the teachers paid less attention to the group. They continued to meet once a week to practice their calligraphy, and often sent notes to each other that no one else could read.

Jaime and David

THINGS CHANGED DRASTICALLY in middle school. Students came from three different elementary schools and were thrown together in a mix that did not acknowledge existing friendships. With three times as many students, the clique of six friends was broken up into different home rooms and then moved between classes. They did not always stay with the same group of students all day.

For Jaime, this created even more issues. The school had two deaf students in Jaime's grade. The school was legally obligated to provide an interpreter, but to economize, they lumped Jaime with the two deaf students so they would only require one interpreter. They were told they needed to take the same classes because the interpreter could not be in two places at once. More of their instruction was delivered by computer to cut the costs of the interpreter even further.

One of the deaf students was considerably behind their class in just about everything and really didn't care. If Jaime had thought everyone ignored him, it was nothing compared to Samuel. Even his sign language was sloppy. Jaime didn't think he'd ever handed in an assignment and he didn't pay attention to the interpreter.

The other deaf student, Belle, was bored to tears by the classes. She'd already studied many of the things they were learning on her computer and was way ahead of the class. But, like Jaime, she was held back in the slow learners class by virtue of the other student.

The number of students running and laughing in the halls and trying to focus on classes created a non-stop mash-up of thoughts bombarding Jaime's head. It taxed all his skills for blocking out the thoughts of others. The first two weeks of classes were exhausting for him, not because of the workload, but because of the effort it took to block so many voices. In middle school, he was not allowed to use his headphones at all—even during breaks. Neither teachers nor the administration would budge on the policy.

The operating assumption among most students and the faculty alike was that the deaf students and the mute boy were stupid. No one bothered learning sign language and other than the scattered few who had shared his kindergarten class, students shouted at them, if they bothered to recognize them at all. Jaime didn't need the increased volume and the two deaf students still couldn't hear them, so it was a wasted effort.

Jaime also recognized that the interpreter they were assigned was not very good. She frequently simplified things too much, did a lot of fingerspelling, and just got things wrong. Since all three of the sign language students had to sit together for the convenience of the interpreter, Jaime often got their attention and corrected the signs. Since he could hear the thoughts of the teacher, he could clarify some of the things he or she said.

By the end of the first term, however, it was difficult for any of the teachers to deny Jaime and Belle had established themselves at the head of the class in all areas except class participation. It was obvious that something had to be done.

Jaime and David were called into the principal's office with the interpreter to discuss the problems he was creating in class by signing to the other deaf students during class.

"I've talked to my son about the classroom situation," David said. "He has explained that the sign language interpreter is really not very good and he has to clarify what she has signed for the deaf students. He can hear the teacher and knows when it is not being interpreted correctly."

"I beg your pardon," the interpreter said. "I do a perfectly fine job of signing and he can't possibly understand more of what the teacher says than I do!"

"You don't understand it either. That's why you get it wrong so often," Jaime signed. David interpreted for the principal.

"Okay. Let's calm down. Gladys, I don't think you are needed in this discussion. I don't want you feeling like you need to defend yourself in a discussion that is really about Jaime's progress. Mr. Stackhouse can interpret for his son. We'll talk about the arrangements later," the principal said.

The interpreter huffed and left the room. Everyone else breathed a sign of relief.

"Jaime, I'm aware that you are a hearing student, and that you are attempting to help. Your deaf classmate, Belle, has transferred to an all-online learning program. Samuel is not improving even with your help. So, I don't think you are needed as an interpreter and I don't think you need an interpreter. Your grades from the previous semester are superb. You should be very proud of them."

"Thank you," Jaime signed.

"We will have an independent evaluation of the interpreter who has been in your classes to determine if she is doing the job she says she is. But that will take a while. I know the classes you've been in are not challenging you any more than they did Belle. But if you are transferred into the classes you'd like to be in, you will have to depend on your ears for instruction."

"That's fine," Jaime signed. "I like that better. The interpreter was a distraction."

"There is a downside for this. Any communication you have for your teachers will need to be in writing. That will limit class participation."

Jaime carefully penned a note on a pad of paper in elegant Spenserian script.

I can write well enough to communicate.

The principal read the note and laughed.

"You may need to print your communications. I'm not sure your teachers can read this script—lovely as it is."

"It seems the school system is not living up to its legal responsibilities," David said. "I'm not sure that passing notes is the same assistive technology as having a competent sign language interpreter."

"It's okay, Dad," Jaime signed.

The principal sighed.

"I'm not an enemy here," the principal said. "I want Jaime to succeed. He is at the head of his class in terms of his grades this term. Belle chose to move to all computer-delivered instruction because she works so far ahead of her class. I would guess she will graduate a year or possibly two years ahead of her class. I can offer the same alternative to Jaime. I have to say, though, my personal observation is that Jaime does quite well in the classroom environment. Most of his teachers agree, though not all teachers are as effective as others. How about if we try this for a term and I'll hand-pick the instructors to match Jaime's subject matter. They will be instructors who are the most open to a diverse student body. Perhaps the whole class will learn something new."

"This is great, Dad," Jaime signed. "Let's try it!"

"My son believes it is a good opportunity. He's willing to try it."

"Let's take a look at your requested classes," the principal said.

5
LISTENING VS. HEARING

Jaime

THE NEW ARRANGEMENT worked well for Jaime. To start with, he was no longer deposited into the slowest learning class. He could understand why Belle had chosen computer instruction, but Jaime often got more from the teacher's thoughts than he did from the words. He was becoming better at filtering out thoughts from his classmates, while letting the thoughts of his teacher through.

Selective hearing, he thought. In the early days of his education, some teachers had determined that he had selective muteness and tried to force him to talk aloud. He read up on the subject online and one search led to another.

His research showed that selective hearing was practiced by almost everyone who could pay attention to one aural input while ignoring all or most others. People often did it in environments where several people were talking, but they were only paying attention to one. People let themselves get so absorbed by movies or television or even music that they didn't hear anything else. In fact, that was the technique Jaime had used when he put on his headphones.

He had to practice selective hearing in his head as well as his ears.

Of course, sometimes a stray thought caught his attention. It wasn't intentional, but he found himself suddenly listening to another person. At first, it was difficult to zero in on who he was listening to. By the end of middle school, he was able to identify the thinker almost as readily as his ears could identify a speaker.

Everyone had what he considered a different *head taste*. It was like the pitch, tone, and accent of an out-loud voice that would distinguish between one person and another. He made a practice of sampling the head taste of the people around him so he could tell quickly who was thinking when he heard something in his head.

His last year in middle school, Jaime had become painfully aware of the physical changes taking place in nearly everyone around him—and, indeed, in himself as well. He might not have noticed it so soon had it not been so loudly thought about by so many of his classmates—male and female. Girls were developing secondary sexual characteristics and the boys around him had begun to notice. Their shapes were changing and the boys were reacting to the visual stimuli—like breasts and butts.

At the first mention of the subject through a stray thought from one of the boys in his social studies class, Jaime was suddenly fascinated with the subject and found changes in his own body that were making themselves known.

Girls, as well, were noticing changes in the boys. A girl might thrill to the sound of a boy's voice that had shifted from a soprano to a deep baritone. Boys who grew taller than the girls were noticed. All through their schooling, most of the girls had been taller than most of the boys. Muscle mass increased on some boys and that was noticed as much by girls as breasts were by boys. Some boys were already shaving before they reached their teens.

Jaime tried not to be a head voyeur, but it seemed the thoughts of sex were the ones screamed loudest by the pubescent boys and girls alike. He was amazed at how confused most were about the actual biology that was involved and determined to educate himself online.

David did not believe in restricting Jaime's internet access through parental controls. He felt children in general self-regulated what they looked at through their own interests. If Jaime saw something like a discussion of transsexuality, he would read it if it interested him and would not read it if he found it uninteresting. They talked about what was online a lot. Jaime recognized the dangers of social media and really didn't use it much. He found talking to people he couldn't read mentally was exhausting and undependable.

When it came to sex, his education took several late nights on his computer. He was enlightened about great swaths of human sexuality. He found how the parts were supposed to fit together, what the major stimuli were, and the risks in engaging in sex. It was almost more than he wanted to know and he was thankful he could not ride in the heads of those he saw on the computer.

It took much more effort to block the thoughts of others as he moved to high school and began encountering people who actually did have experience, or at least imagined they did. Apparently, some had watched the same videos he had because their imagined exploits matched those he'd seen online remarkably closely.

WHILE HOME WAS a refuge in the evening after a day of filtering out thoughts, Jaime still sought out ways to make his filters easier and more automatic. He'd practiced using music as a means of filtering out extraneous mental input since he was very young. As a result, he'd fallen in love with orchestral music. When the music didn't have words, he was free to just float on its melody and release his thoughts. It was like meditation to him.

He also discovered that anything that focused people's thoughts on a single subject tended to quiet a room full of noisy minds. He wondered if teachers knew how few people in their classroom focused on what they were saying. There were a couple of classes that were really interesting and people's minds were occupied with a single thing. Most classes left students' minds scattered to the wind, so to speak.

Whenever a group of people were caught in a single experience, like a movie, they focused on that experience to the exclusion of all other thoughts. Or at least of most other thoughts. The movie theater was a place of mental quiet for Jaime as he merely rode the waves of people's emotions as they watched the movie.

He spent at least one afternoon or evening each weekend at a concert or a movie. But once back in school on Monday, he would be bombarded with the typical thoughts of teenagers. Here he found sporting events were almost as good as concerts. The day of a school sporting event, most thoughts ran in the same channels—some deeper than others. It was like listening to people speaking in unison instead of all speaking about different things at the same time.

Jaime found himself at a movie one Saturday afternoon, anticipating a relaxing time with the audience—of which there weren't too many people anyway—focusing on one thing and leaving his mind relatively free. A row ahead of him, he recognized a burly boy from the football team, which had won an important game the night before. He didn't recognize the girl he was with, but she seemed tense. As soon as the lights went down and the movie started, her thoughts started to intrude on his own. They ran contrary to the thoughts shared by most of the movie audience.

I can't believe I agreed to a date with Tom. All the girls warned me he was an octopus. If he tries to feel me up again, I'll leave. I swear I will.

At the same time, Jaime became aware of the boy's, Tom's, thoughts.

I am definitely going to bust a nut in this virgin. She plays hard to get, but Dan said he got to second base just by kissing her. She is so hot!

The thoughts of the two continued to run counter to the movie for a while and Jaime was able to shut them out until a quiet and sweet scene in the movie left everyone sighing together. Suddenly the girl had an alarming thought.

Oh, my God! He's got his hand on my breast! When did that happen? I didn't even feel it! I don't want it there. What should I do? It would be stupid to make a big deal about it now that it's done. I don't even know how long he's been squeezing me. And it feels kind of good. No! I don't want this! I'll wait for a scene with action and shift my position so he can't reach it. Damn! I wish it didn't feel so good!

I knew it, the boy thought. *She's hot. Dam! Her nipple popped up hard as a rock. I can't wait to suck on it. She's got such smooth legs and a short skirt. Like she was just ready for this all along. This cherry is going to pop tonight!*

When did he put his hand on my leg? God! That kiss on my ear was just too much! I should have worn tights or pantyhose. And jeans instead of a skirt. What was I thinking? Oh, shit! I'm gonna kiss him!

Jaime observed all this from behind the couple. It was truly distracting from the movie. He watched her turn her face toward the boy and kiss him. He was surprised but got right into it. The thoughts were less orderly as the kiss progressed.

Little silk panties.

When did I put my hand on his cock?

Yeah. You like me pinching your little nipple, don't you?

I'll just relax my legs a little. His hand feels so good there.

She's wet already. Her panties are soaked.

Rub! Rub right there!

The movie was far from over, but Jaime got up and left the theater.

Jaime had never encountered another person who could communicate in their head. At least, no one but his dying mother had ever spoken to him. He often tested his theory that people were generally head deaf by speaking in his head to someone. Occasionally, a person would pause, but then would continue on their way without acknowledging the idea. Jaime modified his opinion to believing there were people who weren't originally head deaf but had trained themselves not to accept mental communication.

He would have been surprised to find a teen in a school across town who had a different experience.

Trayce

Trayce had an active imagination. She was very creative and had begun writing little stories when she was in elementary school. In middle school, her imagination had been lit on fire. She discovered web sites where people posted fan fiction for some of her favorite stories. She began writing stories herself and posting them online.

Of course, biology caught up with her in middle school as well. Her mother told her it was all just part of becoming a young woman and had given her hygiene instructions and talked to her lovingly about how her body was changing. Trayce caught overtones from her mother that said she was very concerned about her daughter maturing and would talk to her father about whether she was handling it right. Trayce thought it was odd how she had those impressions from her mother, but she often got them from her father as well. She always knew what kind of mood he was in and what he wanted to do on the weekend.

One day she had decided to ship a story about a relationship between two boys in her favorite fantasy novel. 'To ship,' she had found out the year before, was to create a story about a relationship between two characters in a story who didn't have that type of relationship in the original.

She was in her study hall and had finished her math assignment, so decided to start writing the story about the two boys. She hadn't gone far when one of her characters came to life in her head and began talking to her.

I really like him. Yeah, we compete on the football field, but it's a game. Trash talking is just part of the game. I don't really hate him. But what can I do about it?

If the guys found out I liked him, I'd be finished. As it is, I have to leave the showers when he walks in or I'd be rock hard in an instant. I think I might love him.

Trayce scribbled the words down as quickly as she could. She'd heard of people who had characters so real they dictated the story, but this was the first time she'd heard one of her own. Of course, that was when the class bell rang and everything was disrupted. She put away her writing and went to her next class.

Trayce was sad that all of her characters didn't talk to her like that. And sometimes when she sat to write about one thing, another character she hadn't even invented yet would intrude on her thoughts and she had to change everything to accommodate the new character. That was even more exciting—a character who took over the story and all she had to do was write down what she said.

The ideas came to her so fast that she despaired of being able to ever complete a story before her mind jumped to another.

Discipline, she thought. I need to teach myself to focus on one thing at a time and ignore the other things.

It was a difficult process, but gradually she learned to separate herself from the characters and treat them as things she could control. And if she couldn't control a character, she could shut them off and not think about them. Sometimes they would return to her and sometimes she would lose them, but she decided that was just part of the creative process and if she thought of them once, she could probably think of them again.

"You bitch," snarled a girl with a locker near hers. "It's taken me three months to find you, but I'm going to rip you apart."

Trayce did not recognize that she was the one being talked to until the girl grabbed her shoulder and spun her around.

"Don't ignore me, you little whore. How did you get hold of my journal? I know it was in my bag. When I saw that story on Willow Works, I made sure it was safe. It's never been out of my room since. But you wrote a sequel and it's word for word what I put in my journal. You don't have the right to steal my things and put them up where everyone can see them."

"I don't know what you mean," Trayce said. "I didn't steal anyone's journal.

Really! My stories are just things that pop into my head and I write them down. I don't know what story you're talking about."

"Oh, yes you do. I read it three times to be sure it was the same as my journal. It's the one you shipped about Janey and Alexandra getting stranded in the forest."

"That's about characters from the *Dreamboats* saga. I just made it up."

"You mean you disguised it. It's what I did last summer. I met Sally at summer camp and we hit it off. We snuck off into the woods one night to be together."

"That's not what happened in that story."

"I said you disguised it. And then you wrote a sequel and had them getting together in school. When she read it, she refused to have anything more to do with me! She accused me of being you. She thought I'd posted our private thing for everyone to see. I hate you!"

"But I didn't!" Trayce complained. "I don't even know who you are. All I know is you are in the same study hall. I don't have any idea what you are talking about with your journal."

"I'll get hold of you someday. I'll find you where no one can see us and I'll make you pay. I loved Sally and you made her run away from me. I'll kill you."

Waves of hot anger radiated off the girl. Trayce still didn't know her name. She could just see the ways the girl thought of killing her and it made her physically ill. Trayce ran to the restroom and threw up. She didn't want to go back to class, but there were still two periods left in the day.

When she got home that night, she went to the Willow Works story site and removed the two stories. It made her sad because they were the highest scoring stories she'd written so far. She didn't realize writing could be so dangerous.

Trayce didn't write for a couple of weeks after that. Whenever a new character popped into her mind, she vigorously shut it off.

No. I'm not going to write about you! You'll just get me in trouble!

Of course, the more she tried to shut them off, the more characters clamored for her attention.

Finally, she gave in and began writing stories again. Each time she imagined a new character for a story, or imagined an existing character who found his or her voice, she was elated and began furiously writing down what was said. But in the quiet of her bedroom when she transcribed her story to the computer, she would often realize how scattered her character was and how ridiculous it seemed. She would keep the voice and rewrite for consistency and storyline.

Trayce started participating in online writing groups and contests, talking about the voices she heard when thinking about a character. She was pleasantly surprised at the number of other young writers who agreed. They critiqued each other's work and called Trayce's stories 'character driven.' Her writing friends advised her to write 'by the seat of her pants' and let the characters tell the story.

The problem with all this was that the people giving her advice had no more—if as much—experience than she had. When she actually took a class in high school in creative writing, she was shocked to find her stories were really quite shallow and had no plot or real storyline. Her fans were other writers like her and a limited number of readers who were specifically into the fan fiction she posted online.

The class exposed her to plot development, story arcs vs. character arcs, planning, and outlining. She also learned about The Hero's Journey and was encouraged to find and develop her own stories—perhaps based on the experiences of her own life.

It was while she was deeply involved in the process of plotting a new story in her room that tragedy struck.

Trayce was shaken from her deep concentration and jerked herself upright screaming. Her mother rushed to the room, finding Trayce's laptop on the floor as the girl sobbed in the middle of the bed, crying "Daddy! Daddy! Daddy!"

It was not long after that police arrived at their door to ask Mrs. Lombard to come and identify the body of her husband, killed in a drunk driving accident earlier in the day.

Trayce quit writing.

6
SPEECH

Jaime

FOR JAIME, HIGH school proved to be more complicated than all his schooling before. It was good that he got to choose a portion of his own classes and tested into more advanced levels in others. He especially liked math. He was moved directly into an advanced algebra class, having already completed algebra and geometry in middle school.

The core curriculum in high school was dictated by the state. This included English language, biology, human geography, Spanish, and physical education. Jaime chose computer science for his special four-year emphasis and, because he was already proficient with computer basics, moved straight to the second level honors course.

Some teachers objected to having a student who could not participate verbally. David helped Jaime navigate the high school enrollment process by interviewing teachers for each of his classes. Math, science, and computer science classes were the easiest to enroll in. Taking a formal Spanish language course was the most difficult. The teacher was uncertain how she could assess his language skill without hearing him speak the words.

Jaime showed he was able to type his answers to questions in Spanish and the teacher agreed to assess him on written skills instead of verbal skills. Ultimately, the teacher was inspired to study Spanish sign language and began including it in her lessons. Jaime was pleased with this course because four of his friends from kindergarten were in it with him. They were all fluent

41

in ASL and the four had taught Jaime many Spanish phrases over the years.

Focusing on his own thoughts was an effective means of blocking the thoughts of others. When he was particularly focused on a geometry problem, for example, or researching the circulatory system for biology, other mental voices faded away and all he could hear distinctly were his own thoughts.

If, however, he found himself daydreaming, he could become caught up in the thoughts of another person. He didn't want to become a head voyeur, but some people were difficult to turn away from. He heard a student speaking enthusiastically about playing a basketball game, for example, and at the next game, rode in the mind of that student as he played. He found a new appreciation for the sport as the player focused on the game and devoted all his energy single-mindedly to playing his best and winning.

Jaime realized he had depended on his telepathy or mind reading all his life, but had never spent time studying it or improving it. Riding in the mind of the basketball player had shown him that it was just as possible to shut out everyone else by focusing on this one person as it was when he focused on his own thoughts. He thought of it as fine-tuning a radio when there were other stations nearby that interfered with the signal. It required a great deal of thought to develop the talent further.

On the other hand, he had encountered the thoughts of a person that was so strongly directed toward him that Jaime believed at first he was actually in a mental conversation with the boy. It didn't take too long, however, to realize that even though the thoughts were *about* him, the speaker didn't *hear* him respond.

God, I'd like to tap that! I wonder if I could make Zipper Lips scream if I fucked his ass. Shit. I'm getting hard. I need to get out of the shower. Fuck!

«Hey! Cool it man! I'm not interested!» Jaime thought to him.

I don't dare say anything. I'm not out and the other guys would crucify me if they knew. I wonder if he's a little bit gay. Or bi?

«I'm not either. I don't care if you are. Really. I'm just not interested.»

Jaime was getting angry when he realized he was figuratively talking to thin air. The boy with the lustful thoughts couldn't hear him. Jaime really had no right to police other people's thoughts, even when they were about him. He untangled his mind from the other's thoughts and dressed.

'Zipper Lips.' By the end of his freshman year, many students he had classes with had figured out his name sign and referred to him as Zipper Lips. It didn't really amount to an insult. He'd chosen the name sign himself. Even his friends called him 'Zip' when they spoke aloud to him. A fond nickname, he supposed, just as he sometimes called Juan 'Mex.' Of course, Jaime only did that in his mind and in the sign, but he quickly equated the two.

The two boys and two girls he'd maintained friendship with from kindergarten on, often met to study together. Their only shared class was Spanish, but they studied other subjects at one or another's home as well. During their time studying together, Jaime became aware that Mex and Cheery were acting strangely. It took a few minutes to realize the two had begun hanging out together and were thinking loving thoughts about each other. Jaime quickly separated himself from their thoughts. He was determined not to become a voyeur on his friends.

Cheery's real name was Letitia Rodrigues. They were not allowed to study at her house while her mother was at work, but Mex always walked her home after their study sessions. Letitia meant 'Joy' in Spanish. It was an appropriate name for the bubbly girl. Her name sign was the sign for 'cheerful.' Jaime was kind of fond of her, too, but he would never interfere in his friends' relationship. He didn't find any of the same kinds of thoughts toward him in Cheery's head as she had of Mex. His other two study partners held no such thoughts about anyone.

Jaime had to constantly practice shielding his own thoughts from others. If he could hear people's thought without them knowing it, it seemed likely that someone else could possibly do the same thing. He began to define his own set of words to explain what he experienced.

Out-loud voice was what other people used to talk to each other with their mouths. Inside voice was what people used in their heads. Most people had an inside voice, but he didn't think anyone was aware that it could be heard by a head talker, like him. They were head deaf and didn't hear anyone else's thoughts, so why would they even consider that someone else could hear their thoughts.

He'd long ago begun to identify the thoughts of individuals from each other, just as his ears could tell the difference between people's out-loud voices.

Sometimes, however, it took him a bit to figure out who a new or different head taste belonged to.

And finally, when Jaime read another person's thoughts, he considered himself a head voyeur. He wondered if everyone was born with the ability to talk in their heads, but learned to shut it out so effectively and so quickly they never realized they had it to start with.

That was the start of Jaime's investigation of whether it was even possible to awaken a person's head sense if the proper trigger could be found. Jaime imagined himself teaching his friends to communicate with their heads like they did with their hands. He started reading everything he could find about telepathic science and theory.

Jaime and Wendy

"How was your date with Donny?" Jaime overheard in the school hall. The girls were right behind him, so he couldn't help but hear them talking.

"I swear, all boys ever think about is sports. And probably sex, but the only thing they talk about is sports. And if that's all he can talk about, he can forget about sex," Wendy Anderson, a girl in Jaime's sophomore chemistry class said. She was one of his lab partners, so he could recognize her voice anytime. She never seemed to shut up. He wondered how she knew what Donny could talk about. Jaime was sure she never listened.

"Told you so," Cheryl, the friend, chided her.

"I don't know how a boy ever expects to get to first base if he can't open his mouth without quoting a sports statistic. 'Brock Moore ran for 218 yards in last Sunday's game.' 'Mason Graham passed for three touchdowns.' 'They should trade worthless Grady O'Brien and get a good tight end.' Can you imagine listening to that crap all through the movie? No thanks."

"See you at lunch. Maybe we can spot a good one if we go hunting together," Cheryl said as they parted ways at the chemistry lab.

They joined their other two lab partners as Mr. McConnell gave them the experiment they were to conduct and told them to be sure to wear their safety glasses. Jaime found it hard to focus on the teacher's words because he became caught up in Wendy's internal monologue.

Safety glasses! There goes everyone's sex appeal. Damned Donny. If he'd listened to me, he'd have gotten more than a goodnight kiss.

Jaime could see in her replay of the Saturday night events that Wendy never had any intention of letting Donny have more. He was willing to pay for the movie and popcorn, so she was willing to grace him with her presence.

With the help of their lab partners, they managed to get the experiment set up and listened to the next set of instructions.

I need the strong silent type, Wendy thought. The image in her mind was of a movie star with a ripped body who didn't say much.

Maybe I should try Zip. He's certainly silent. Not particularly ripped. Not bad looking, though. Wonder what he packs in his pants.

The team paused in their experiment to each write down the steps in their composition books. Jaime noticed his lab partners all printed their notes in block letters of varying neatness. His precisely penned Spencerian script was a stark contrast.

Look at the way he writes. I wonder if he's an alien. Maybe he's hiding tentacles down there. Like that toy Cheryl showed me a picture of. I really need to figure out how to get one of those without my parents finding out.

Jaime saw a clear image of what looked like a severed octopus tentacle, then a not quite so clear picture of Wendy putting it between her legs and pushing. That caused him to catch his breath at the exact same moment Wendy did.

Oh, yeah. I'd definitely let him get to second base. Maybe further if he really never said anything.

She imagined a completely unrealistic picture of a much stronger and physically fit man than Jaime, but with Jaime's head and the tentacle thing protruding from his groin.

The test tube they were heating began to bubble over the top and Mr. McConnell rushed to their table to cap it and direct the clean-up. He looked at their notes and tapped "step three" which clearly stated when to mix in the last ingredient. He gave the group a 'C' for the day. Jaime's three lab partners frowned at him as though he had been the one who brought their grade down.

The class bell rang and they gathered up their books and left. Jaime hastily scrawled a note in his book and tore it out. He tapped Wendy on the shoulder as they were getting ready to leave. She spun, ready to defend herself from… something. He handed her the note.

"How am I supposed to read anything you write? It's pretty, but can't you print like everyone else, Zip?" she said. Jaime took the note and quickly printed on the other side of the paper.

"Would you like to go out Saturday night?" she read. "Seriously? Oh, God! No. Thank you, but no thank you."

She handed the note back to him and rushed out the door to meet Cheryl coming up the hall.

Ew! Yuck! Why would that weirdo ever think I'd go out with him. Not in a hundred years. He was looking at me all through class. What was he thinking? Oh, yuck!

She disappeared down the hall toward the lunchroom and from Jaime's head.

Jaime and the Voice

«Don't be a dummy,» a girl's voice said in his head at lunch.

Jaime was certain the thought had been directed at him as he sat alone and pondered what had happened in chemistry. Wendy had definitely been thinking about him and imagining a date with him. He'd felt a tingle in his chest, centered around his nipples. *Her nipples,* he thought. Just at the time she was imagining that tentacle thing between her legs.

He quickly looked around the cafeteria for the source of the mental voice. There were too many people to see where she was located. He was certain it was a she and that she had spoken directly to him.

«If everybody acted on their fantasies, there would be an orgy in the main hall. Don't go confusing fantasy with reality. Geez!»

Then the voice was gone. He looked and listened, but there was only the usual cacophony of students' thoughts. He'd know if she ever spoke to him again. This confirmed in his mind there were others like him in the world— even right here in his school.

Jaime and Andrew and Linda

JAIME KEPT A lookout for the girl, but didn't recognize the head taste of any girl he encountered. It was frustrating. But it was also a valuable lesson. Someone had eavesdropped on his internal conversation in the cafeteria with ease, and he didn't even know she was there. He needed to work on blocking his thoughts from being broadcast.

In an effort to learn to block his thoughts, he began practicing meditation. He had no idea if he was really doing things right, but he watched a lot of videos on YouTube until he thought he knew the principles. Thinking of nothing was difficult. It was much easier to focus on just one or two non-important things than on nothing. This improved his focus in class. He concentrated on what his teachers were saying, and on what he read in his textbooks. Of course, his train of thought was continually being derailed by random thoughts of his classmates—especially late in the day when he was getting tired.

2:15. Like clockwork. It happens every day at 2:15, a boy's thoughts echoed in Jaime's mind. *Thank God it's just twenty minutes from the final bell. Damn, it's hard today!*

Jaime realized the boy two seats over from him in US History was thinking about his erection. That wasn't enough, though.

Linda could just slip down under my desk and suck me, he continued, thinking about the pretty girl who sat between them.

Suddenly, Jaime could see the image of the girl naked on her knees in front of him, pulling his cock out of his pants to suck. He sneaked a quick look at his classmates to convince himself she wasn't actually on her knees between the desks. Nonetheless, the fantasy was very real and Jaime felt himself hardening, too.

Sucking is good but fucking is better, the boy thought. *Bring those sweet titties up to my face and settle down on this pole. Oh God, yes! Just like Friday night. You are so hot, baby.*

The scene shifted in the boy's mind. He and Linda were no longer in the classroom, but were in the backseat of his parents' car. They were both very naked. Jaime realized this was no longer a fantasy, but a memory. They'd had sex on their date Friday night.

Jaime shifted his awareness to see if Linda was having any part of the same memory. It was in her mind as she struggled to focus on the War of 1812.

He'll want to do it again this weekend. Mom said that once you give in to a boy, that's all he thinks about. It just felt so good when we started. It hurt a little when he shoved it in. I wanted to stop, but he was already inside me and said he couldn't stop until he came. I guess. He's a good boyfriend. I don't want to lose him. Maybe we can go someplace more comfortable where I'm not hitting my head on the roof of the car. I did like being naked with him, but I wish I didn't have to keep looking around to spot anyone who could see us.

"Andrew Martin. The class attention is up here," Mr. Tollefson said, tapping the map behind him. "Who was the president during the War of 1812?"

"Um… Uh… I think… Um…"

Andrew's erection suddenly went limp. Linda was tittering a little in her head.

"I'll simplify the question a little. What year was the War of 1812 fought?"

"Uh… uh… 1812, sir?"

"Is that your final answer?"

"Um… um… Yes, sir. I think so."

"Good. Now try to stay awake for the last fifteen minutes of class. Linda, can you tell your boyfriend who was president during the War of 1812?"

"Oh. Yes, sir. It was… um… James Madison, I think."

"Yes. James Madison. He was only the fourth president of the United States and for a while, it looked like he would be the last. The British burned Washington, DC. Now…"

The class went on for another fifteen minutes until the final bell and Jaime returned to filtering out the thoughts of his classmates.

Later that night, though, the image of Linda naked and riding her boyfriend returned and he soon found himself soaked in his own emissions.

Jaime and Emerson

Jaime's work in computer science during his junior year yielded a voice generator that he could use in classes. He and his lab partner, Emerson Flaherty, created a simple text to speech engine using existing public domain AI software. Then they'd worked together to sample the voices of several of their classmates to get different tonality, accent, and gender when it was fed through the AI voice generator.

Emerson was great to work with. She'd latched onto the project enthusiastically when Jaime suggested it and the two spent a lot of time in the computer lab together working on it.

In their American Literature class, they demonstrated the device and for the first time, Jaime was able to participate in class discussions. The voice generator could interpret his tone almost as fast as Jaime could type. Emerson introduced him and Jaime interacted with his classmates.

The entire class applauded and wanted to hear the device change voices. They guessed who in the school each voice belonged to. Jaime said his goal was to create a voice that was unlike any of his classmates so it would be uniquely his own.

He regretted losing his partner in the second semester as she had the opportunity to study overseas for a term. It was less fun working on the project alone, but his participation in classes made it worthwhile.

Of course, the possibility of actually sampling his own voice was always in the back of his mind, but if he did that, he would have to explain whose voice the generator was using. Over the summer, he worked on blending multiple voices into a single intonation by sampling segments from several students and manipulating the sound waves to make them into a single unique voice. The hardest part was convincing the AI that the voice was a single voice and not a chorus. He didn't want a robotic voice that sounded like a dozen voices speaking together, though he guessed that would also be pretty cool.

7
SENIOR MOMENTS

Jaime and Emerson

WHEN CLASSES STARTED in the fall, Jaime was pretty proud to be a senior. He'd already begun making applications to colleges where he could continue his computer science study and also explore some of the psychological aspects of mental communication. It looked like he wouldn't need to go far from home as both Oregon and Washington had schools with great programs.

He was happy to have his friend Emerson back in his advanced computer science class and she was intrigued with the improvements he'd made on his text to speech engine. The voice was unique and the intonations were clear and insightful.

"How did you manage to get the voice to sound so natural?" Emerson asked. "I've never heard a text to speech app sound like a person was actually speaking."

"Music," Jaime typed on his computer. The voice was a little loud, so he reduced the volume. He didn't want to disturb other classmates. "I like classical music and I discovered that Wagner intended to be a dramatist, but was unhappy with how actors interpreted his words. So, he wrote music for them and became a great operatic composer."

"So, you set it all to music? It isn't singing."

"No. I just used notes to indicate relative tone and length. Then I fed it a few hundred phrases and sentences. I had it read the entire *Dark Love* series

50

aloud so I could tune the voice. It probably has a more romantic sound to it than is strictly necessary," Jaime typed.

"I like it. It's really… sexy. Nice job. What do you plan for this year's project?" Emerson asked.

"Mr. Perkins kind of shot down my idea as needing more research than could be accomplished in this class," Jaime said. The computer voice sounded sheepish and Emerson was amazed at that.

"What was it?"

"I'm interested in people being able to speak to each other mentally," he typed.

"Mental telepathy?"

"Technically, all telepathy is mental. But Mr. Perkins pointed out that people have tried and failed to do it for years."

"It's a cool idea, but I guess I see his point."

"Besides, last year's major project was mine. This year we should focus on a project you choose," Jaime typed.

"Oh. Well, I had a really great time in Paris this spring and summer. You know I'm kind of into fashion," Emerson said.

That was something that couldn't be told from her looks, Jaime thought. She was a nice-looking girl, but always dressed in kind of shapeless clothing, wore no makeup that he could tell, and seemed to have no sense of style at all. He was surprised when she opened her bag and pulled out a stack of fashion magazines, some in English and some in French.

"When you look at these magazines, you see that a major theme all the way through is predicting what will be in style in the next season. Some of them follow the big style advances from the major designers and runway shows, while others are more localized or seasonal. My grandmother said that when she was a girl, 'in' meant 'in the JC Penney catalog.' But I think I could use AI predictive algorithms to predict things like the most popular color for next year."

"Cool! I'm in."

Jaime and The Voice

EVEN THOUGH JAIME had conceded the idea of his thought broadcasting software as too complicated for his computer science class, it still fascinated him and he continued to work on it—mostly at home. He wanted to either broadcast thoughts through the synthesizer, or awaken the inner ear of someone so they could hear his thoughts.

He had a favorite tree on the school grounds that was located far enough from where most students hung out that he often went there with his lunch. It had been a fairly mild fall, so he decided to put on his jacket and go there, even though it was near the end of October and getting chilly. He settled under the tree and opened the notebook in which he was keeping track of his ideas to explore for mental communication. He didn't think anyone could make sense of his writing since he still used the elegant Spencerian script that only a few of his classmates could read.

He'd decided there might be an element of actual physical contact involved in mental communication, as he was touching his mother when she spoke to him just before she died.

«Be quiet! You're broadcasting your thoughts all over. Anyone could hear you. Stop thinking so loud!»

Jaime slammed his book shut as though someone was reading over his shoulder. He recognized that voice. She had once told him not to believe people's fantasies.

«Who are you?» he thought frantically. «Where are you?»

Only silence answered.

Keira and Aunt Rose

"NEED TO TALK. Coming from school," Keira texted Aunt Rose. She boarded the crosstown bus from in front of the school and shut herself off from the world. She was pretty good at that now. She could usually go a whole day in school without being consciously aware of anyone's thoughts.

Unless that boy was shouting. She couldn't believe the whole city didn't hear him.

There were kids in school who talked loudly with their mouths all the time. She wondered sometimes if they had a hearing problem and couldn't tell how loudly they spoke. They could be heard across the cafeteria at lunch. If they whispered to the person next to them in class, everyone in the room could hear them.

This guy, Zipper Lips, was like that in her head. If she stopped to think about him in school, she could hear him over all the others in the building. She'd had two classes with him and had sworn not to ever speak mentally to him.

But he was so stupid! How could he possibly have thought it was a good idea to ask a girl out just because she had a momentary fantasy about his tentacle dick. Keira had been irrationally upset about that and yelled at him. Then realizing what she'd done, she quickly shut down her inner voice and ears. She'd promised herself never to do that again.

Until today. He was actually working on a computerized thought amplifier that could force other people to hear his thoughts. What a catastrophe that would be! If he could force his thoughts on someone, they'd be as torn up and confused as she'd been when she first got her inner ears. That was her term for being able to listen to other people's thoughts.

Being able to listen. Hah! More like being *forced* to listen. What a terrible time that had been.

Her first menstrual cycle and all of a sudden, she was hearing voices. She thought she was going crazy! She couldn't tell her mother. She'd either pooh-pooh the whole idea, or she'd rush Keira to a doctor. Her only logical choice was to talk to crazy Aunt Rose. If Aunt Rose told anyone Keira could hear other people's thoughts, no one would pay any attention. Aunt Rose was a psychiatrist.

She wasn't her 'real' aunt. At least neither Keira's mother or father claimed her as a sister. But they'd been friends forever and Keira grew up calling her Aunt Rose. When it came to getting advice about hearing voices in her head, there was no one better to talk to than Aunt Rose.

Aunt Rose's house was peaceful, too. Keira wasn't sure, but she thought it might have something to do with the aluminum siding. She just knew that when she went into the house, it was quiet. There were no voices in her head, and Aunt Rose was like a blank. Keira's parents had once laughed about Rose, saying she didn't have a thought in her head. Keira could verify that. She could not read anything from her aunt.

"Hearing voices? Hmm. That's an interesting side effect of getting your first period. Let's have a little tea and talk about it." No judgment. No panic. Just acceptance and a cup of tea.

While neither acknowledging nor denying that Keira heard people's thoughts, Aunt Rose had taught Keira how to block them out and how to keep her own thoughts from being read by others. Keira was terribly afraid of that because she often had 'uncharitable' thoughts about other people. She didn't need them hearing those thoughts.

Like that stupid boy. She'd told him to stop broadcasting so loudly and he'd *answered* her! It wasn't like he couldn't hear others, but he almost got her name before she managed to shut him out.

Keira got off the bus a block from her aunt's house and hurried to the door. Rose let her in immediately. Everything went silent.

"Hearing voices again?" Rose asked as soon as they sat at the kitchen table with a cup of tea.

"Yeah," Keira said.

"Did you do the exercises I taught you?"

"Yes. They usually work just fine, but this one boy was shouting. He always shouts," Keira said. She stirred a full teaspoon of sugar into her bitter tea.

"Hmm. Lonely people often do that," Rose said. "They get louder and louder to get people's attention. Maybe not anyone in particular, but anyone. Have you met him?" She offered Keira a tin of cookies and Keira grinned as she took three.

"Sort of. I had a class with him last year and have one with him this year. He doesn't know me, though. I've just shut him out. But I yelled at him today and told him to stop broadcasting so loudly. It's dangerous."

"How so?"

"He's really smart. I know I said he's stupid, but that's only about people. Last year, he created a text to speech application for his computer and the voice sounds pretty normal. But now he's trying to figure out how to force other people to hear his thoughts."

"That sounds sinister."

"I think… I believe he's benign. But if someone who wasn't got hold of his invention… Do you think someone could force another person to do something by talking in his head?" Keira paused with a soggy cookie halfway to her mouth as she contemplated the idea.

"According to *Psychiatry Professional* magazine, around 10% of people hear voices in their heads at some time or another. About half have an active inner dialog. Some portion of the remainder—number unspecified—can't identify inner dialog and believe someone else is speaking to them. That is often malicious. Do you remember Dottie Brown? She's doing okay now as long as she stays on her meds. She caused a serious accident a few years ago when a voice in her head told her to turn her car the wrong way on a freeway exit. Several people, including Dottie, were rushed to hospitals after the collision and one died. That evidence suggests that an unknown voice could plant a malevolent thought in a person's mind."

"I'm not paranoid about it, but I believe there are people in the world who would use that ability to try to get people to do things against their will," Keira said cautiously. "I think I met one once."

"Oh, if such technology were truly available, I would guess that every government in the world would be trying to get hold of it, and they'd be outbid by every billionaire," Rose laughed. She made light of it, but Keira could see her shiver.

"I think I should meet him," Keira sighed.

"You spoke to him about it?"

"Not yet. But he's so hungry to meet someone like him. I think maybe I could show him some of the ways you taught me to control my own mind."

"Ah. I see. Well, if he is open to the idea, I don't see that it would hurt. Just take care of yourself first. Don't take him to a secret meeting place without letting someone know where you are. You know how to protect yourself."

"Yeah. I don't think I need to worry about him. He's mute."

"You don't say! That *is* an interesting thing. Deaf?"

"No. People talk to him and he uses sign language to communicate. That's why his text to speech app was so cool. It was the first time he's been able to participate in class without an interpreter."

"You kind of admire him, don't you?" Aunt Rose said as she cleared the teacups from the table and put them in the dish washer.

"Um… I… Maybe… a little. I don't really know him *that* well. There's something about him. He seems to have a few good friends and there are others who just automatically seem to trust him. Not everyone. There are plenty of kids who just think he's weird. Some are jealous, I think. You know, you hear a lot of things in the school halls. Even when you aren't listening." Keira stood and gathered her coat and school pack.

"I see. Let me know how it goes. If he has trouble controlling voices in his head, I might be able to cook up some more exercises."

"Thanks, Aunt Rose. You always make me feel better. Sort of normal," Keira said as she hugged her aunt.

"Well, as long as you are only sort of normal and don't take it to extremes, I guess that's okay."

The two looked at each other and spluttered in laughter. Keira went home to a late dinner. When she told her parents she stopped to see Aunt Rose, they asked no more questions.

Keira and Jaime

IN FACT, KEIRA had been watching Jaime since school started in August. She'd seen some pretty remarkable things. One of the school's star athletes, Gene Evans, had approached Jaime at lunch one day. One never knew how a jock was going to respond to a quiet and rather isolated kid and Keira steeled herself to rush to the rescue if it was necessary. This one was okay. He called Zipper by name and asked if he could join him for lunch. Zip had been alone in his corner of the cafeteria, much like Keira stayed alone in the corner she'd selected. Keira was curious about the conversation because it didn't look like the athlete could sign, but he wanted to talk to Jaime.

"Hey, Zip. I know you can hear but not talk. Seems kind of strange, but I'm good with that. I'm afraid I don't read sign language, but you really don't need to say anything. This guy I know, Mex… um… Juan, said if something was bothering me, I could always talk to you and know it wouldn't go any further. Is that okay?"

Jaime nodded at him and made a gesture that was interpreted as 'go ahead.'

"Remember Mike Collins? You might not have known him because he was a year ahead of us. He died last year. Stupid jerk got kicked in the head by a horse. God, I hated him. I know, I shouldn't speak ill of the dead, but the bastard stole my girlfriend. And when he died, she couldn't do anything but talk about how wonderful he was. I *wanted* to kill him."

Gene fell silent and focused on the unidentified meat of the day. Jaime just listened, but Keira knew he was reading more than what Gene was saying verbally. She couldn't read Gene from this distance, but she could listen to Jaime. Nothing that went into his mind wasn't shouted out.

Gene had actually plotted a way to kill Mike. The hatred made Jaime cringe.

"Don't ever fall in love, man. He totally ruined a good thing between Shelly and me. I didn't just *want* to kill him. I'd decided I'd do it. Damn horse got to him first. It's not that I'm upset because he's dead. It's just that I still keep imagining that *I* killed him. I can't shake the feeling that my hatred just somehow spilled out and a horse executed my desire. I didn't *do* it! If I had, maybe I'd feel better about it. I just can't get rid of the feeling that I wanted to kill him and now he's dead. It's my fault."

Gene stared at his empty plate, wondering when he'd eaten the food. Jaime put a hand on the big athlete's shoulder and gave a squeeze. Keira could hear him speaking in his head to Gene, even though he couldn't be heard.

«You didn't do it. You don't have to live in guilt. Let go of it. There's nothing you could have done.»

Keira wished Gene wasn't head deaf and could hear how calm and encouraging Jaime was. Maybe he got a little of the message from that squeeze on his shoulder. Perhaps there was something to Jaime's theory that contact opened channels.

"Anyway, thanks, man. I know I brought a bunch of shit to the table. I appreciate you listening. I just had to… tell someone. Just… um… forget I ever said anything, okay?"

Gene got up and left the table, clearing his tray and Jaime's. Jaime continued to sit there, quietly crying inside over the hurt the athlete had shared with him. He wished he'd spoken, but knowing that if he ever spoke, no one would come to him like that again. Besides, if he'd spoken, Gene might have died.

Keira sensed it wasn't the first time something like this had happened. She *did* admire Jaime a little.

«I'm on your left,» Keira thought to Jaime as she approached his tree. He immediately turned to his right, where she actually was. «Sorry. Had to make sure you were really hearing me.»

«You're like me!» Jaime shouted in his mind.

«Shh. You're broadcasting everywhere. Others could hear.»

She sat on the ground across from him, aware of his scanning of her appearance. Maybe she shouldn't have worn such nice clothes today. But she found she wanted to look nice when she met him for the first time. He paused in his assessment to watch her breasts rise and fall before shaking his head and signing, "Hi."

«I'm sorry. I'm so used to shouting, trying to get anyone to hear me that I got carried away. I'm eighteen years old and have never had anyone answer me.»

«I thought so. That's why your thoughts are so loud. You're used to no one hearing them. You're like all the other students, but louder. You don't have any filters. Thank you for thinking I'm… pretty.»

Jaime clamped down on all his thoughts and focused on a blade of grass. His thoughts weren't all just that she was pretty.

«I'm sorry,» he whispered in his mind.

«Don't go away. We need to talk. I'm used to what boys think. I guess you know what girls think, too. You thinking about my boobs was pretty tame, compared to most guys.»

«I've heard some pretty gross things. I try not to think about people like that—except sometimes when I'm alone. You took me by surprise. Are we really having this conversation?»

«Yeah. We should probably make some signs to each other so people don't think we're just having a stare-down.»

"You're in my English lit class first period, aren't you?" he signed.

"Yeah. I think we had the same physics class last year," she signed.

«Why didn't I ever notice you?»

«I try to stay invisible. If there's no noise coming from your brain, no one will notice you're there.»

"Eighteen years old and I just met you," he signed. Inside he continued,

«I've never met anyone like us.»

"Did you get the assignment for lit? I'd like to borrow it," she signed. «Don't be too sure of that. It's a big school. There are others. Most are just voyeurs and hang around eavesdropping. A lot of them don't even believe what they're hearing is more than their imagination. You were more obvious because you never use your out-loud voice.»

«Do you?» Jaime quickly signed that he'd get the assignment for her and asked for her number.

"That was clever," she said, while texting him. «Yeah. I'd been talking all my life until I started hearing people's thoughts. I couldn't just stop talking. I just put a cap on broadcasting my thoughts. I don't think anyone in school knows I can head talk.»

«When you started? Didn't you always?»

«No. It happened… um… you know… when I became a woman. When did it start for you?»

«Always. I mean, I never talked at all because I thought everyone could hear me like I could hear them. Then…» Jaime broke the thought, trying not to think of the day his mother died.

"You okay?" she signed.

"Yeah, thanks." He went on with his thought. «The only time I ever used my out-loud voice, my mother died.»

«Oh, God! That's awful!»

«So, I never used my out-loud voice again. I think I've forgotten how.»

«Oh, Jaime, I'm so sorry!»

«It's okay. I've never told anybody.»

The class bell rang and they headed inside the school.

"Let's talk again tomorrow," Keira signed.

"I'd like that," he signed back.

"You can text me later, too," she whispered.

When Keira got home, she already had a text from Jaime. She looked at it hesitantly, but it was only the English lit assignment, which, of course, she already had. Then her phone was silent for the rest of the afternoon. She wondered if he was going to ghost her and just disappear.

Her phone vibrated just after nine.

"I enjoyed meeting you today. Same time tomorrow?" Jaime texted.

"It was fun. See you at the tree. Figure a plan from there," Keira responded.

"Plan?"

"Somewhere we can talk"

"OK"

"Nite"

"Nite"

8

REMOTE CONTROL

Jaime and Keira

KEIRA APPROACHED JAIME carefully the next day, but as excited as he was to see her, he kept his thoughts down to a low hum.

"Hi, Keira," he signed, spelling out her name.

"Hi."

"Do you have a name sign?"

"I only started signing so I could talk to you. I'm not in Advanced ASL like *some* people."

«How did you know that?» he thought to her.

«You're kind of proud to be in that class and talk about it loudly.»

«Oh, crap!» "Can I create a sign for you?" he signed.

"Okay."

Jaime looked at her intently and Keira felt very vulnerable. Jaime pulled his index finger across his lips and then down to his chin in an x-sign with the fingers crossed. Keira huffed.

"Really? You focused on my hair and just called me 'Red?' Is there nothing else about me?" she spoke aloud. A rapid succession of thoughts crossed Jaime's mind as he fought to control them. Keira was thankful he used the sign for red.

«I like redheads,» he spoke in his head. «Dad says…»

«I've heard it all. It's not true. I got my freckles from the sun, not from eating souls. I just chew them up a little and spit them out.»

61

They looked at each other grinning and burst out laughing. Jaime's laugh was a strange kind of squeak.

"I'm pleased to meet you, Red," Jaime signed as he thought to her, «Why did you decide to reveal yourself to me now?»

«I got worried,» she whispered in her mind. Jaime leaned in closer. «You've been broadcasting your ideas about an invention to make others hear your thoughts.»

«It's not much. I just started sketching out the network requirements. Wouldn't it be cool to be able to communicate with others like we are?»

«Shh! You don't get it. Not everyone is as innocent as you are. I know there are people who would like to order others around with their thoughts.»

«That would be silly. Who'd listen?»

Jaime suddenly thought of his encounter with a man when he was nine. Had the man been trying to make Jaime hear him?

«Who'd have a choice? Um… Look. I know you've noticed Debbie Burk. She's another one who broadcasts loudly and if you aren't filtering, you have to hear at least some of her thoughts. Imagine what it would be like, though, for her to discover you could *hear* her thoughts.»

Keira had plunged into one of Debbie's fantasies and was shocked by her thoughts. On the outside she acted pure as the driven snow—the perfect preacher's daughter. Inside, though, it seemed all she ever thought about was what she could put in her vagina. She'd die of embarrassment if she thought either Keira or Jaime knew about what her fantasies were. Even though they were sometimes sort of 'inspiring.'

«I'd never let her know!»

«Of course not! But imagine what it would be like if someone like her suddenly heard a strange voice in their head telling them to run a stop light. If a person was unaware that you were communicating with them, they might be so shocked and surprised that they run the light and crash into another car before they tried to figure out why they had that sudden urge.»

«That would be terrible!»

Keira listened to Jaime clamping down on his thoughts about his own mother. He'd been so calm and reassuring to Gene Evans about not being at fault for Mike Collins' death. But he still blamed himself for his mother's death. She wondered what had caused him to speak out-loud at just that moment.

«It's okay, Jaime. It was an accident. And I didn't mean to eavesdrop on you just now. I think I can help you filter your thoughts so you aren't broadcasting all the time. It will also help filter out random thoughts from others so you can really focus on one thing or another. Want my help?»

«Yes! Um… See you here tomorrow?»

«Sure. Text me goodnight again tonight. I liked that.»

Jaime grinned at her and they parted to go to their afternoon classes.

Jaime and Debbie

JAIME WAS CAUGHT up in his thoughts and trying to keep them silent at the same time, when he walked into his psychology class—the last class of the day. It wasn't an interesting class and he was a little surprised at some of the students who were in it. They were people he didn't usually think of as being that smart.

"Hey! Watch where you're going!" a guy said to him as they both hit the door of the classroom at the same time. Jaime let him pass. *What a freak. He should be in some special ed class and not be taking up time in classes for normal people.* The guy wasn't very nice in his thoughts, but compared to some of the people Jaime met, he wasn't that bad, either.

«I'm not a freak,» Jaime said in his mind. Just then, Debbie Burke walked into the classroom and sat in front of Jaime, taking her sweater off to drape on the back of her seat. The guy was immediately caught up in the girl's looks and what he'd like to do to her.

Sexy girl. Come with me. I want to see those pretty tits and get you wet and ready. The boy was instantly caught up in a fantasy about Debbie that included a graphic depiction of having sex with her.

Jaime didn't think they'd ever actually *had* sex, but that didn't stop the boy's fantasy. And Jaime was responding to it, too. He shut it down, hoping to preserve his own modesty and not have to endure class with a boner. But when he snapped closed on the boy's fantasy, he inadvertently opened a channel to Debbie.

God! Can Todd be any more obvious? He's practically drooling. Not that I don't fantasize about him, too. We wouldn't be studying psychology. I'd be naked and pulling his dick out to suck on. Shit. Not today. I've already started on a different one today.

Mr. Wilson called the class to order and began reading from his notes. Jaime supposed that was why so many people took this class. All you had to do was study the notes he put on his website and you could pass any test he gave. Jaime had once tuned into Mr. Wilson's thoughts while he read his notes to the class, but his mind was elsewhere—fishing. Mr. Wilson was bored with teaching, bored with psychology, and bored with his students. Yet he found fishing fascinating. Go figure.

I sat in front of the mute boy on purpose, Debbie thought. *I've been thinking about him all day. Has he noticed how visible my bra straps are? Does he think he can figure out how to unhook it and take it off me? Yeah. That would be so hot. Do it without taking my blouse off. He could run his hands up under my shirt and play with my boobies.*

Jaime was suddenly acutely aware of the bra straps moving under Debbie's slightly see-through blouse.

Daddy would crap if he knew my underwear could be seen from the back. The blouse is opaque in front. After all, that's where it counts, right? Of course, if it were up to my stick-up-the-butt father, I'd still be a virgin and would be till I'm fifty. Don't have to worry about that, thanks to Ray. Safe from discovery there. He's too frightened of my father to ever say anything. And it was fun doing him at the church retreat. Making him sin.

Jaime received a surge of memory from Debbie: Ray from her church making out with her in the woods before each prayer meeting and finally going all the way. He was surprised to realize Ray was not a teen, but was nearly her father's age. But her thoughts weren't really on Ray. Jaime came back into focus in Debbie's mind.

Mute boy wouldn't say anything, either. How could he? I wonder if his cock is huge. Not that it would make that much difference. It has to be bigger than the carrot I used last night. God! I'm getting juicy just thinking about it. I need my fingers in the pie. I'm on the pill thanks to the clinic that doesn't tell parents. I just need mute boy to step up to the plate and hit a home run. How about if I strip off all my clothes and run around the classroom naked? Would he take me on Mr. Wilson's desk? Then all the boys would line up for their turn.

Debbie's image of Jaime was lacking a lot of detail. She did a pretty good job with his face, but the rest of his body was kind of a mishmash of pictures from health and this guy Ray. The cock she had in mind was definitely not an image of the erection Jaime couldn't control in his pants. The image of herself running around naked, though, was like she was looking in a mirror.

He hears okay, so I could just tell him to lick and he wouldn't argue, right?

When I had a couple comes on his tongue, I'd let him put his cock in me. Yeah. Right there. I can just feel him pushing it in. And he'd still be silent, even when he comes in me. He'd never be able to tell anyone. We could meet in the janitor's closet next to the locker rooms after gym in the morning. I always get so hot showering with the girls. God! If I could just touch myself a little, I'd have a good come right now.

Jaime was struggling to extract himself from Debbie's fantasy, but having no luck. The images of herself were like looking at her in the flesh. And her thoughts of the girls in the shower after gym were overwhelming. He hadn't really seen that image of girls before. Not from her perspective. Debbie liked girls as much as she liked boys. Jaime was breathing deeply and hoped he wasn't being loud enough for Debbie to hear.

Debbie thought her breasts weren't big enough and they seemed to swell in her mind. She thought Jaime's dick would grow to twice its size and she'd have to stretch obscenely to accommodate it. She returned to the reality of Jaime sitting right behind her in class.

Is he thinking of me with my bra straps on display? How about if I shake my hair a little? Hey, mute boy. What's your name? Oh. You can't speak? That's okay. I don't need to know your name. I just need your help taking my clothes off. Suck on my nipples and put your cock in me.

The end of school bell rang and startled all the students and Mr. Wilson out of their various daydreams. Jaime took his time getting his books together to allow his cock to relax a little. Then he rushed out of school to his bus home.

Jaime tried to think about what had happened objectively. Why was he so caught up in his classmate's fantasy? He'd learned his lesson a couple of years before when he asked a girl who fantasized about him on a date. That was a disaster. She had no interest in him at all. Keira had spoken to him then in his head, but he didn't know who she was. Regardless, he'd never approach insatiable Debbie.

He thought, in fact, that it had been Keira who brought their classmate up in their discussion under the tree. That probably left him open to hearing her. The images remained fresh in his mind.

His father wouldn't be home for a couple of hours. David got a new job during the previous summer and was going to the office more frequently than working from home. Jaime was glad he was getting more interaction with people his own age. He was a great father.

Jaime decided that with the images of Debbie fresh in his mind, it would be a good time to rub one out. He stripped and flopped on his bed, making sure tissues and lotion were nearby, and began thinking of the vivid images of Debbie naked.

As soon as he closed his eyes, it was as if he was reliving Debbie's whole fantasy. They kissed and he sucked her nipples, working his way down her slim stomach and burying his face in her trimmed snatch. Then she was pulling him up her naked body until his cock nestled into her pussy lips. From that point, it took about two strokes for Jaime to erupt all over himself. It was the hardest come he'd had since he started masturbating.

Yes, keep pumping. Make me come again. Come in me again. You feel so fucking good!

It was like Jaime was still hearing her fantasy while he continued to stroke his cock. Then he realized he *was* hearing her fantasy! He didn't know where Debbie lived, but somehow, she was broadcasting and he was receiving loud and clear.`

Jaime could feel himself inside her. Except it wasn't his feeling of being inside her, it was *her* feeling of being stretched and approaching her orgasm. This was going to be bigger than his first come.

I must be feeling her orgasm as well as my own. I feel so wet and so full in places I don't even have.

He tightened his grip, trying to mimic what he felt from Debbie. It was incredible and he wanted to build her up more. He tried slowing his pace, but she started to race ahead and he lost control. He could feel Debbie coming as he erupted again.

Jaime lay there panting and trying to catch his breath as he felt Debbie using her fingers to make lazy circles around her clit, hanging onto the euphoria just a little longer.

Yeah, he was good, she thought. If I thought he was really that good, I'd make a play for him. Guys are never as good as the fantasy, and mute boy would be no different. It was a good day though. Tomorrow… No, Monday, I'll do Bob Ames. Ever since Patrice told me about building a fantasy all day, I've been having the best after-school orgasms ever. And the guys are always much better than they would be in real life. Clumsy idiots who can't tell what's exciting from what hurts. Yeah. I think I'll nap a while before everyone else gets home. Maybe there's another come lurking down there if I just leave my fingers in the swamp.

Jaime withdrew from Debbie and left her to her own manipulation, so to speak. If he let himself stay in her mind while she napped and masturbated again, he might never get to the kitchen to fix dinner. Besides, she was a little disappointing now that he thought about it. He'd had a couple of good orgasms—stellar comes—but she just chose a random guy each day and built a fantasy around him. Jaime happened to tune in on the day he was featured. It didn't mean anything.

Jaime and Keira

Friday seemed to crawl as Jaime waited to rush to his tree and meet Keira.

«Oh, geez! I'm glad you're here. That Richard Privy was broadcasting so loud in PE, I couldn't shut him out. I hated what he was thinking about me, but it still made me twitchy. Does that ever happen to you?»

«I had that problem in psychology yesterday. Debbie Burke was really getting herself worked up. I was her featured fantasy of the day.»

They looked at each other and both started giggling.

"I think the kids in our classes spend more time thinking about sex than about school," Jaime signed. "If we were tuned into everyone's thoughts all the time, we'd be real perverts."

«So, I know you can block other people's thoughts. You need to routinely block yourself from broadcasting everything, too,» Keira said in his mind.

Jaime had a fleeting image of him and Keira naked and squashed it immediately. He didn't want to scare away his new friend.

«I'm sorry if I think anything that offends you,» he thought to her. He looked down so he wasn't looking straight at her. *Maybe some of those fleeting images weren't just mine.*

«Right. So, anyway, I wanted to show you a couple of ways you can filter what you're thinking without clamping down on everything. I learned the hard way,» Keira thought.

«What happened?»

«There was a boy in my eighth grade class who thought some of those things and knew when I responded. It was soon after I started hearing people. It was really embarrassing. At first, I clamped down on everything, like you do. Then there was a thought that I heard that said, *I know what you're thinking. You can't hide from me.* It scared me when he basically told me he knew I was blocking him and could read me anyway. I started letting stray thoughts through that were really benign. You know? They sounded just like what everyone else was thinking around me. Instead of connecting with him, I just got lost in the crowd. It was a close call.»

«What did you do about *his* thoughts?» Jaime asked.

«I mostly filtered him out, only allowing things that were really important to him. That's how I avoided getting raped.»

«Geez, Red! He was going to rape you?»

«No. But he'd heard some other boys planning to trap me on my way home. He warned me and I just took a different way home that day,» Keira said.

«That's a relief.»

«No, it's not,» Keira sighed audibly as well as inside. «He was actually a nice guy, but with typical hormonal teenage thoughts. I was having the same kinds of random uncontrolled thoughts. He took my usual route home that day and when the boys who were lying in wait for me saw him, they blamed him for me not being there. They beat him up.»

«Is he okay?»

«He moved away. I'm just really careful now.»

«You know I wouldn't do anything like that, don't you?»

«I know you wouldn't try anything physical with me if you weren't invited. The important thing is to let your mundane thoughts flow freely so others can see them, but keep your deep thoughts—the important stuff—filtered out.»

«I've never thought about having two kinds of thoughts before. I see what you mean, though.»

«It requires a higher level of consciousness at the start. You have to really be conscious of everything you're thinking. You know, there's a theory that you can only hold six thoughts in your mind at the same time. So if you don't want to think about a big floppy fish in a polar bear's mouth, you need to come up with six other things to think about and the bear will disappear.»

«Crap! Now I'm thinking about a big floppy fish in a polar bear's mouth!»

«It requires practice, but I'll work with you if you'd like,» Keira suggested. «Having a reserve of images like the fish you can call up anytime helps to block other thoughts. … It means we'll be in each other's minds a lot. You don't need to filter those… stray thoughts from me. I mean, I understand all about normal… kind of sexy thoughts. I have them, too. I won't get upset with you as long as you promise not to get upset with me. I'll let you know for sure if one of those thoughts is deliberate.»

«I'll try not to be too embarrassed by them or dwell on them,» Jaime said with a silent sigh. The image of Debbie flashed across his mind and Keira grinned at him. «Red, how far do your thoughts reach? I mean how far away can you hear a person?»

«I guess a couple hundred feet if there are no obstructions in the way. I know you've figured out how to put physical barriers between you and other people. Metal works best. But don't worry about it. You were sitting right behind Debbie and she was specifically fantasizing about you.»

«Yeah. I wasn't too worried about that, though, I felt like a… What did you call them? A voyeur. It was later that was the real surprise.»

«What happened?»

Jaime grimaced a little. They'd agreed to talk about embarrassing things, though, and this was a real puzzle to Jaime.

«When I got home yesterday… the images from Debbie were still pretty fresh and… compelling.»

«I can imagine—especially with as explicit as Debbie gets in her imagination. It's okay to take care of your urges when you're in private.»

«Yeah. That's okay. It happens. I'd guess I'm a pretty normal guy in that regard. But when I… relaxed and started to enjoy the fantasy, I suddenly realized I was listening to Debbie again. Not remembering what she was thinking in class, and not developing my own fantasy. She was doing the same thing I was and I could hear her thoughts and feel what she was feeling.»

«Shit! How far does Debbie live from you?»

«I don't know, but we sure aren't neighbors. It has to be more than a mile.»

«Zip, I've never experienced anything at all like that. Do you think she could hear you?»

«I don't think so. She was pretty wrapped up in herself. She just dragged me along with her.»

«That's really powerful and a little scary.»

«Please don't be afraid of me.»

«Yeah. No. I just… Would you… Just in case… Could you not think about me when you… you know? Grab any other girl's thoughts who's convenient. Just not me.»

«I can do that. I don't want to disrespect you. You're my friend.»

«Yeah. Well, it's just that if we ever really become intimate, I'd want it to be in physical proximity—not just in my head.»

The thought of actual physical intimacy with Keira almost derailed Jaime's thoughts. He quickly focused on a polar bear with a big floppy fish in its mouth.

«Maybe we could… like… go out sometime,» Keira suggested. «I mean if you wanted to talk some more, you know.»

«You are the most important person in the world to me. I've never known anyone like me before. I'd love to go out with you. Tomorrow? We could see a movie and talk in the dark. No one could see when we forget to sign.»

Keira smiled and Jaime could see more than just the thought of going out. He could see she was happy.

9
DANGER AVERTED

Jaime and David

DAVID HAD WORKED hard at learning sign language, even though he knew his signing was sometimes pretty sloppy. Jaime was proud of him and never had trouble understanding him. Usually, David could understand his son's signs. Nonetheless, Jaime practiced what he wanted to say to his father as he prepared dinner that evening.

Jaime had taken on the responsibility of preparing dinner during the week since his father had returned to office hours most days. They planned menus together and went shopping together. Both were pretty basic in their tastes, but Jaime was a good cook.

Friday night was one of David's favorite dishes—breaded porkchops with applesauce, butter beans, and mashed potatoes. It wasn't really difficult to make. Jaime completed the preparations and practiced what he wanted to say. When his father got home, they sat down to the meal and David made sounds of appreciation. Before they got up from the table, Jaime held up a hand to stop his father.

"Dad, I'd like to go on a date," Jaime signed. "Would that be okay?"

Lord, Nola. I knew this day would come. Why am I not prepared? David thought.

"Do you… have someone in mind?" he asked aloud.

"I met a really nice girl named Keira Nolan," Jaime signed. "I'd like to take her to a movie tomorrow if it's okay."

"I take it she signs?"

"We don't have any trouble communicating," Jaime signed as he nodded.

"Are you planning to go by bus or would you like me to drive?" Jaime had not yet gotten his license, though he had a permit and often drove with his father.

"I was thinking you'd want to meet her, and I'm sure her parents would want to meet me. How about if you drive so I could pick her up and then we can catch a bus or streetcar coming home?" he signed.

David had so many thoughts going through his mind so rapidly, it was hard for Jaime to pick out what he was really thinking. It was all confused with fear… *Of what?* Jaime wondered. *Of me being on my own?* He realized then David was worried his son would get hurt.

"If you're sure you're ready for this, then I'll plan on it. Do you know the timing yet?" David said.

"I need to check the movie times and confirm with Keira," Jaime signed.

"Then I think it would be okay," David sighed. *I hope I've prepared him for this. Does he know to be respectful? Will he try to push things too fast? Will he get hurt? Or hurt her?*

Jaime carefully avoided responding to his father's thoughts.

JAIME SENT A text message to Keira and they agreed upon the movie and the time. Jaime checked the bus and streetcar schedule to be sure they could get home from the theater. Then he gave his father the information.

"My parents have a million questions," Keira texted him later. "Mostly want to know how we communicate."

"Sign. Only way Dad understands"

"Yeah. Wish I was better at it"

"I'll share meanings with you"

"Thanks"

"See you tomorrow"

"Nite"

Jaime's dreams were filled with thoughts of Keira. His mind wandered to the possibilities of what they might do together if they were dating steadily. He remembered his promise to Keira, so switched his thinking to the shared fantasy with Debbie as he put himself into deep sleep the usual way. Fortunately, he didn't connect with Debbie this time.

Jaime and David and Keira and her parents

"KEIRA'S NEVER DATED much either," Jaime signed to his father. "Her parents want to meet both of us."

"I have to agree with that," David said aloud with his hands still on the steering wheel. "Is this the place?"

Jaime pointed in the direction of Keira's house to guide David to a parking spot. It was a nice quiet neighborhood, not unlike where Jaime lived and only a few streets over. Jaime decided at once that he could bike to Keira's house if they wanted to just hang out.

«What do you mean by hang out?» Keira shot back from the front door.

«You know! Like go over to Ground Beans for a coffee,» Jaime explained, blushing. He could hear Keira giggling in her mind.

"Hi, Jaime. Hi, Mr. Stackhouse. I'm Keira. Please come in and meet my parents," Keira greeted them aloud at the door.

"Lovely to meet you, Keira," David said.

"Mom, Dad, this is Jaime and Mr. Stackhouse. These are my parents, Mr. and Mrs. Nolan," Keira spoke aloud automatically signing to practice interpreting.

"John and June," Keira's father said, extending a hand. David shook it and then June's hand.

"David," he said.

"Come in for a cup of coffee. Do you have time, Keira?" June asked.

«We're good for, like ten minutes, right?» she asked Jaime.

"No problem. Dad expected it," Jaime signed

"We've got, like ten minutes before we need to head to the movie," Keira said.

"Nice to meet you, Jaime," John said as they sat in the living room and June got the coffee she had already prepared. "Is this okay, Jaime? Just speaking normally? Keira said you hear fine."

"It's good." Jaime signed. David started to interpret at the same time Keira did and then shut up quickly. He was as interested in Keira's sign language ability as her parents were.

"Keira tells us you invented a text to speech engine last year, Jaime. David, is that part of your background, too?" June asked.

"I'm in product management," David answered. "It's more of a marketing job than a technical job, but I need to understand the technology. Jaime and I consulted a little on establishing what his product requirements were, but the design and programming were all his own."

"That's interesting. Jaime, do you plan to release the product to the public? Seems like it could be useful," John said.

"There are other text-to-speech engines which are very good," Jaime signed. Keira interpreted, reading Jaime's mind as much as his signs. "I wanted one that would be uniquely my voice. I haven't even put it online for others to experiment with. I don't want everyone speaking with my voice."

"I never thought of that being an issue," John said. "Very clever."

"Well, we need to get going if I'm to get these kids to their movie on time," David said. "Perhaps we'll get together again sometime."

"You kids be good. You know the rules, Keira. Home by eleven. The street-cars stop running at eleven-thirty," June said.

"The movie's at six-thirty," Keira answered. "We should have plenty of time to grab a soda and get home afterward."

Why didn't I think to set a curfew for Jaime? David thought. *Well, at least with Keira having a curfew, he'll have to come home then. It's just a formality. They're both eighteen.*

Twenty minutes later, David dropped the couple at the theater in plenty of time to get popcorn before the movie started.

Jaime and Keira

«Was meeting my parents too painful?» Keira asked.

«No. It was funny, though, when Dad decided you interpreted my sign language better than he did. That was when he decided we wouldn't have any trouble communicating.»

«I was embarrassed when my dad started thinking all those protective thoughts about what he would do to you if you hurt me,» Keira said as they found seats in the theater. «I know you wouldn't hurt me.»

«My dad had the same thoughts at home today. He constantly asks my mom if he's doing the right thing.»

«Does she answer?»

That brought Jaime up short as he thought about his father's mental conversations with his mother. Sometimes he thought he did hear her answer.

«I think there is a place in Dad's brain where his memories of Mom live and he consults that. So, even when he imagines he hears her response, it's coming from someplace inside him.»

«Wow. You've thought about it. Did she ever speak to you? I mean inside?»

«Once. I think. It was the first time I thought she was actually trying to think a message to me and said she loved me. It was… right before she died.»

«Zip, that must have been so painful for you.»

«I didn't understand what was going on. I was only four—almost five. It was later that I began to understand that she was never coming home. I'm better now.»

«I'm so glad you can share things like that with me.»

Lights came down in the theater and previews started. The auditorium was about half full and they thought this wasn't going to be a very popular movie. Still, it sounded like a decent premise and it was likely people would be so wrapped up in it that they wouldn't be broadcasting other thoughts.

The Summoned was about a group of high school girls who believed one of their number had been cursed. So, they decided to have a ritual and summon a demon to find out who had cursed her and to remove the curse. It was all fun and games until the demon actually appeared. It started off with a cartoonish animation of a red creature with horns, but that image soon dissolved into a high school girl like those who summoned her. She said it would make it easier to relate in that form. The newly summoned demon set off to remove the curse on the friend and to find the source.

Jaime and Keira soon tuned out both the movie and the audience so they could continue talking with each other, head-to-head.

«The hardest part is not letting other people's thoughts affect you,» Keira said. «I guess it's okay to camp on someone's fantasy or even a favorite memory. I mean, high school is probably the most fertile head space in the world for picking up a fantasy and running with it. Like you did with Debbie. I've done it, too. I never had the contact carry over to when I got home and decided to enjoy it, though.»

«I didn't even realize girls had that kind of thoughts until we got to high school,» Jaime said. «I thought all the fantasies I overheard were from guys. They weren't all that interesting until I happened on a guy's memories of actually doing it. I realized then that there was a wide gap between fantasy and memory.»

«I think it's natural to tune into people of the same sex at first,» Keira said. «We all go through that developmental phase when the opposite sex is icky, then vaguely interesting, then possibly attractive. Maybe everyone starts life gay and we learn to be hetero or bi or something.»

«Well, when I got caught up in Wendy's fantasy a couple of years ago, it was the first I realized that girls had some really creative fantasies. And they have actual experience with some of the parts guys find most interesting.»

«Sorry I yelled at you. I couldn't believe you were responding to a girl's inner fantasy in real life.»

«I got caught up in it. Isn't that what you were talking about in not letting others' thoughts affect you? I avoided girls entirely for a month after that, but when Mex and Cheery started dating and making out, it was hard to shut them up. I made a concentrated effort not to listen to their thoughts. They're my friends and it seemed like a real invasion of privacy. You know?»

«Yeah. That's probably smart. When I eavesdrop, it's mostly only on girls I don't know now.»

«Not boys?»

«You… need to… understand that boys' fantasies are a little frightening to girls. At least to me. They fantasize the same way they play football. Line up and crash into her. Pin her to the ground and start humping. As soon as they come, they huddle up and call another play.»

«Yuck.»

«Yeah. I know you don't really do that, though, I'll bet your encounter with Debbie was the first time you ever experienced it from the girl's side.»

«It seemed a lot like a boy's fantasy to me. Except the visuals and some of the feelings were more intense. I'd never really seen a naked girl through someone's eyes before. Including her.»

«The same as a boy, except she was in charge. She told you when to kiss, when to suck, when to lick, and when to fuck her. It was all based on her control. When I listen to a boy's fantasy, he is in control. He's going to do something to me or to her. And most especially, he doesn't care how she feels about it, as long as he comes.»

«Hmm. It seems Debbie didn't really care if I was having fun or not in her fantasy. It was just an assumption that whatever she wanted, I'd do.»

«And you did!» Keira laughed. «The thing is that you knew all along that you could stop her from doing anything like that to you unless you wanted it. When I see a boy's fantasy, I know there isn't anything I could do to stop him from just raping me.»

«Oh, geez, Red!»

At that point, the movie reached a scene in which a truly ugly and powerful demon suddenly appeared before the human-looking demon hunting down curses, and the entire audience screamed. Keira and Jaime reached out automatically to take each other's hand.

And the world shifted.

Their mental perception multiplied to such an extent, they were instantly aware of every thought in the auditorium. Not the overwhelming cacophony they had each struggled with in times past, but individual voices they could easily distinguish. They could look at any person in the theater and read exactly what was going through their mind. In fact, every glance one of them made was instantly duplicated by the other as if one set of senses governed them both.

Of course, most of the thoughts were of surprise and fear at the sudden image and stab of music accompanying the demon's appearance. They were focused more tightly on the ensuing battle. A few were disappointed that something else had been interrupted and tried to regain the intimacy they were sharing with each other.

And one emerged as simply evil.

Scream, little girl. Scream. It's good practice. By the time I'm through with you, you'll have screamed so much you won't have a voice. And then I'll make you wish you could scream some more.

The images accompanying the thoughts were so graphic and gory, Jaime and Keira both gagged and turned away from each other to keep from throwing up. Their contact broken, the inner voices in the theater returned to a general cacophony, but both could readily identify the man ahead of them who had been thinking of what he would do, and the girl two rows beyond to whom he intended to do it.

«What was that?» Keira panted.

«I've never experienced anything like it!» Jaime exclaimed.

«Those images…»

«That wasn't just a fantasy. It was a memory. He was… He's done it before!»

«And he plans to kidnap her and do it all to her!»

The sheer terror of what they'd experienced brought their hearts to a stop before they were able to concentrate once again on the movie as it reached its conclusion.

«What are we going to do?»

«What can we do? You just lectured me on not letting others' thoughts affect me.» *I'll have to get Red home and then go after him. I hope I'm not too late.*

«He's going to rape and torture and kill her!» Keira screamed at him. «They weren't random thoughts. He's going to do it. And he's done it before. Don't you dare go someplace without me!»

«We saw it together. I can't see his thoughts right now, but I know which one he is. We'll have to follow him and keep him from kidnapping that girl. Together.»

«Together.»

THE MOVIE ENDED and people started leaving before the credits had played. The girl headed toward the exit on their right and the man toward the exit on their left.

«You follow her and keep her in sight,» Jaime said. «I'll follow him.»

«I don't like being out of touch with you.»

«I can reach you. I know it now.»

They split, Keira following the girl and Jaime following the evil man. Once he was moving, the man's thoughts came into clear focus. He was taking his time because he had left his van parked where the girl usually walked on her way home from the neighborhood theater. He'd been planning this for a long time, but now he was ready to act. He'd been denying himself any relief at all for a week, just so he would be primed for this night.

«Can you hear me?» Jaime sent.

«Yes,» came the startled response from Keira. «We're just leaving the restroom.»

«Follow her outside. He's parked in a white plumbing company van a block away. He's going to grab her and knock her out. Nothing subtle-like either. He plans to club her with a wrench.»

«How are we going to stop him? I'll tell her to go a different route.»

«We can't catch him if he doesn't try to get her. When you see the van, dial 9-1-1 and report a suspected attempted kidnapping. Start streaming video to them. I'll try to rescue her somehow.»

«Jaime, be careful!»

Jaime followed the man at a distance until he got into his van and then Jaime circled behind it. The van was metal, of course, so he couldn't get a good read on the man inside, but could tell when he moved to the passenger sliding door to watch for the girl.

His heart was hammering when he saw the girl round the corner and Keira a dozen yards behind.

«Make the call and start recording,» Jaime said. «Stay against the building.»

The side door of the van was open slightly and just before the girl came parallel with it, the bad guy dropped a quarter out of the van that rolled into her path. She was startled and bent down to pick up the coin. The door slid all the way open and the guy jumped out to grab her. Just as he spun to shove her into the van, Jaime reached the door and slammed it shut.

"Let her go!" Keira shouted as she came running toward them.

The guy looked at Keira with her phone held up and at Jaime, still standing by the closed door and raising his phone to record. He shoved the girl to the ground and ran for the driver's side of the van to jump in and drive away. By that time, Jaime was recording the van's license plate.

Keira ran to the fallen girl and knelt beside her.

"What's going on?" the girl demanded, watching the van squeal away. Jaime stayed away, recording the progress of the van as Keira tried to speak reassuringly to the girl.

"That guy tried to grab you and haul you into his van. My boyfriend realized what he was doing and slammed the door on him. You're safe now. Are you injured?"

"Scraped up. Who are you?" the girl shot at Keira.

"I'm Keira. Luckily my boyfriend heard him muttering about getting you as he was leaving the theater. I've still got 9-1-1 on the line."

"Thank you, I guess. It was so fast. I didn't know what was happening." The girl started shaking and sobbing, clutching her knees in her arms as she sat on the pavement.

At that moment, a police car screeched to a stop beside Jaime and Jaime pointed toward the girls. The officer ran to assist Keira. Another cruiser pulled up and the officer started to talk with Jaime. Jaime made a sign of his lips being zipped and held up his phone. He played the video of the man getting into the van, the license number, and the direction he was headed. The officer didn't delay, but requested backup, an ambulance, and pursuit. He motioned Jaime to join him as they approached the girl who was still sobbing. Keira's eyes were leaking, too.

"My boyfriend can't speak," she said. "He can hear, but not use his voice. I can interpret his sign language."

"An ambulance is on the way. How's the girl doing?" the officer escorting Jaime asked the one kneeling.

"Shaken up. Possible shock. Hasn't said anything but 'No' since I got here. Miss, we need identification. Did he take your wallet? We need to notify your parents."

The ambulance arrived and the EMTs rushed to the girl who finally managed to say her name was Heidi Schvaneveldt. She begged them not to call her parents, but her school ID indicated she was only sixteen years old, so the parents were called and Heidi was transported to the hospital for evaluation. The police finally turned to Jaime and Keira. Jaime sank down on the sidewalk beside her, realizing he was shaking as well.

"Okay," said the officer who had been the second to show up. The other pulled out to follow the ambulance. "You streamed the whole incident to 9-1-1. What tipped you off?"

"He followed her out of the theater where we were on a date. He muttered that she'd soon be his, and that got me suspicious. She stopped to use the restroom and Keira followed her while I followed him and saw his van," Jaime signed and Keira interpreted.

"How did you coordinate your actions? You followed the girl and you followed the man?" the officer asked.

"Yes, sir. As you can see, we know ASL. Sign language. We could make arrangements across the theater."

"Handy thing. And your solution to stopping the kidnapping was to slam the door shut in the perp's face?"

"I'm not so big that I could attack him directly," Jaime signed. "He's a big guy and was carrying a wrench of some sort."

"Okay. Let's get your names and contact info so we can get in touch when we catch the guy and need you to identify him. That was a dangerous thing to do, you know. It worked out okay this time, but don't risk it again, okay?"

"Yessir."

The policeman took down their information from Keira's license and Jaime's permit. They were both eighteen, so the officer was satisfied that he didn't need to call their parents.

"Can you get yourselves home?" he asked.

"We were going to stop at the café over there for ice cream, but I've got an eleven o'clock curfew. I don't think we have time now." Keira looked at her watch. It was almost ten-thirty. "We'd better catch the next streetcar home."

"That's a good idea. We'll be in touch as soon as we have anything."

The officer left and Jaime and Keira headed for the train stop that would get them to Keira's neighborhood.

«We stopped a kidnapping!» Keira shouted as they boarded the train. «We're heroes!»

«Do you think we need capes?» Jaime asked.

He looked at Keira and they both burst out laughing.

10
THOUGHT POLICE

Jaime and Keira

«WHAT HAPPENED BACK there anyway?» Keira asked as they walked to her door. They had reached for each other's hand, but withdrew before they touched.

«I don't know… Can we leave this conversation for later? I'm really drained… and a little overwhelmed,» Jaime responded.

«Yeah. I get it. Maybe we could get together tomorrow and just go for a walk?»

«I think Dad will agree to letting me bike over in the afternoon,» Jaime grinned. «We should exchange videos. You know we'll have to explain.» They sent each other the videos from the night.

«Okay… Until we figure out what happened, maybe we'd better not touch or… kiss goodnight.»

«Right. Okay. Nite.» Jaime hadn't considered the possibility of a good-night kiss. That would be awesome. But delayed.

«Nite… boyfriend.»

Keira and Her Parents

OF COURSE, NEITHER Jaime's nor Keira's night was over. Both knew they needed to talk to their parents about what happened. Otherwise, when a policeman showed up to have them testify, it would be completely unexpected.

"How was your date?" June asked Keira as soon as she walked in the door. Both parents were uncharacteristically up late on this Saturday night, pretending to watch TV and doing a good job of eating popcorn while they waited for their daughter.

"Um… Mostly good," Keira ventured. "We had… or I should say we encountered some problems after the movie."

"What did he try?" John growled. "I just knew he'd pull something."

"Please, Dad. It wasn't about Jaime. Let me describe the whole thing. When the movie ended and we headed toward the exit…" Keira had to go through the entire story, just as Jaime was doing with his father.

Jaime and David

"So, WE WANT to get together tomorrow afternoon to talk about it and to kind of end our date properly, without the police or anything," Jaime signed to his father.

"I can imagine," David said. "I'll call John and June to verify it's okay. You *are* okay, aren't you?"

"Yes, Dad. We were scared and shaken, but neither of us got hurt." Jaime shared the videos that he and Keira had exchanged. The parents were all terrified for them.

"Okay. You might text Keira and make sure it's all right for me to call her parents at this hour."

Jaime sent a text to Keira and received a quick response that her parents were waiting for the call. Jaime nodded at his father and headed to his bedroom.

Jaime and Keira

AFTER A FLURRY of late-night text messages between Jaime and Keira, mostly detailing how much fun they had and hoped to repeat the best parts of the evening again soon, they finally said their goodnights and went to bed.

He could feel Keira still thinking of him. It wasn't as strong a connection as when they were close and communicating, and it was nowhere near the connection they'd shared for a minute while holding hands. That had been unreal!

Jaime cut his thoughts off with a picture of a polar bear holding a big floppy fish in its mouth. He'd promised not to try to connect with Keira when they were alone and feeling… horny. He just couldn't call another girl to mind at the moment. He wondered if polar bears actually fished through the ice like cartoons showed. He was pretty sure grizzly bears feasted on the fish they caught from rivers and streams. Probably black bears, too, but he couldn't think of having ever seen an image of a black bear with a fish.

He puzzled over the conundrum until he faded off to sleep.

«Did you sleep okay last night?» Keira asked when he bicycled up to her house.

He didn't go in, but Keira came out and they began a silent walk to the park. Both were wearing winter jackets and risked holding gloved hands. There was a frisson of excitement there, but nothing like what had overwhelmed them the night before.

«Thanks to the polar bear,» Jaime chuckled. «All night, though, I had images from the theater flashing through my dreams. Some were just the movie or people going 'Oh, shit!' when we all got surprised. Others were a little disturbing.»

«Like the kidnapper?»

«Yeah, of course. But there were at least fifty people thinking about things other than the movie. I remember flashes from all of them. Why did we zero in on the kidnapper?»

«Maybe we should back up a little and figure out what happened.»

«We were startled and reached for each other's hand, I guess,» Jaime said.

They both looked down at their joined hands.

«I don't feel the same thing now,» she said.

«Maybe it has to be skin to skin.»

«Let's wait to try that. Why did we reach for each other's hand? And why did we start holding hands as soon as we left the house this afternoon?»

«It seemed… sort of natural.»

«Yeah. Natural. Like it was perfectly normal for a boyfriend and girlfriend to hold hands, right?»

«I guess that's… Red? Are you my girlfriend?»

«If I wasn't before, I sure am now. Zip, I've never felt anything like that ever before. It was like…»

«Yeah. Like I was *in* you.»

«More. Like I *was* you.»

«That's it. Like there wasn't any part of me that wasn't open to you nor any part of you I couldn't feel. It was too much to comprehend all at once.» Jaime was excited and then stopped suddenly in embarrassment. He grabbed for the polar bear.

«We both had… thoughts. Since we both had them, we shouldn't need to be… embarrassed by them.»

«Aren't you ever embarrassed by your own thoughts, even knowing no one else can hear them?» Jaime asked. «A lot of times I catch a stray thought from someone and they are immediately embarrassed by their own thought and try to shut it down.»

«Well, yeah. But… I don't feel like I should be embarrassed because *you* heard my thoughts. It might take a little work to get to that point, though.»

«Yeah. Red, are all girls afraid all the time? I mean, that girl Heidi was just as scared of us and the policeman as she was of the kidnapper. And… I can see you are… cautious.»

«I'm probably not as fearful as most girls because I can hear the thoughts of people around me. But yeah. We… It's kind of programmed into us, or taught to us repeatedly from the time we're babies. All men are trying to touch us, look at us, see through a gap in our blouse, or up our skirt. All men notice a nipple pop if we don't have enough layers of clothing between their eyes and us. I know… you do it, too.»

«I'll never look at a girl like that again!»

«I think it's as ingrained in boys as it is in girls. And that being said, I appreciate the sentiment. It tells me a lot about the kind of guy you are. For most girls, it wouldn't make a difference if you looked or didn't look. They can't read your mind. Girls will assume you look—even when your eyes dart away as we look at you. You know the popular meme: Girls would rather meet a bear in the woods than a strange man.»

«Preferably one with a floppy fish in its mouth,» Jaime sighed. The breath was audible as well as internal.

«The thing is, even though I think most boys reflexively look at girls that way, the majority of them are decent enough to shift their thoughts away and would never act on those thoughts. Unfortunately, head deaf girls don't know which ones are a danger and which are just… guys.»

«I still don't understand, though,» Jaime said. «When we touched, I felt us… expand, I think is the word. I could hear a hundred times more than I usually hear when I'm completely unfiltered. And it wasn't just crowd noise, like with everyone talking out-loud at once. I could hear each of them individually.»

«Wow! That was more than I got,» Keira said. «I mean, I heard more, but I could only filter out a few distinct thoughts. As soon as I heard the kidnapper, everything else just went away.»

«The girl, Heidi, has a very unhappy homelife. Her mother often sends her out to the movies while she entertains at home. She was afraid if the police called her mother, she'd be punished. She was thinking of running away. That was before the movie ended. After the attack, she was thinking maybe she'd have been better off if he took her.»

«Wow! You got that all in the minute we were holding hands?»

«More. There was a guy hoping his date would really appreciate him going to a chick flick with her. He figured it should at least be worth a blowjob. Another guy was worried he wouldn't get out in time to meet his dealer. And a guy was thinking that if anyone saw him at the movie alone, he'd get outed as gay and he would kill himself.»

«I guess I'm glad you heard more guys than girls,» Keira said.

«I think most of the girls were in the 'Oh, shit! No!' crowd.»

«I was at first,» Keira said. «I don't know if it was because of the movie or because of the crowd reaction, or because I was holding your hand.»

«You didn't want to hold my hand?»

«I *did* want to hold your hand! I *do* want to. It just surprised me that it happened all at once and then everybody else flooded in.»

Jaime looked at their gloved hands, still clenching each other firmly.

«We could…» Jaime's thoughts outpaced his conversation as he imagined the tingle of contact when they held hands.

«Yeah. We could try again. But we should prepare ourselves. I mean, we're pretty isolated here in the park with just a few people around, not like all the people in the theater. Still, touching might send us into each other again and we might… It scares me a little, Zip.»

«Me, too,» Jaime said. He led her to a picnic table. «How about if I just lay my hand flat on the table and you put yours on top of it. Neither of us will grip. That way, either of us can pull away if it's too much.»

«Jaime, you're really kind. That's one of the things I like about you. Thank you.»

«I just don't want to be like all those guys girls are afraid of.»

«You're succeeding.»

They sat on opposite sides of the picnic table and took their gloves off. Jaime extended his hand palm up across the table. Keira took a deep breath and softly laid her hand on his.

They were both prepared for a rush of sensations, but even that preparation was not enough to stem the feelings of pure joy that flooded them both. They smiled across the table as each opened more to the other. Awareness of other people in the park played around the edges of their senses, but they were completely focused on each other.

«Do you really think I'm that pretty?» Keira said in his mind. Only to Jaime, he was asking the question himself and his answer was «How could I think anything else?»

Both teens blushed and mirrored each other biting their lower lips. Something told them that if they stayed like this for long, they might never want to let go. They slowly withdrew their hands.

«I don't know what love is,» Jaime said deliberately. «I don't have a frame of reference. But I know I've never felt so happy in my life.»

«Then let's only use the words we understand,» Keira said. «I *joy* you.»

«And I joy you.»

They put their gloves back on and held hands all the way back to Keira's house. They were still filling each other with happiness.

When Jaime saw Keira in school Monday morning, his heart leapt. He knew he was grinning from ear to ear and tried hard to clamp down on his exuberance. Keira was smiling broadly, too.

«It's okay,» Keira shot to him. «I don't mind people knowing we're a couple. Do you?»

«No! We *are* a couple, aren't we?»

«Definitely. I hereby declare you my boyfriend.»

She reached out her hand and Jaime prepared himself for the sensation. Keira took his arm, though, and while the thrill of contact was there through his shirt and sweater, the resulting multiplication of talents was muted.

«Nice,» he said.

«I don't think it's a good idea to actually touch in school. There's too many people in range.»

«It could be pretty overwhelming. I like this, though. Sit next to me?»

They found seats next to each other in their first period English lit class and settled in for the lecture. Jaime opened his laptop so he could participate in the class discussion. Then a sharp stab of thought entered his mind.

For every freak, there's an equal and opposite re-freak. What does she see in him?

For an instant, Jaime thought the boy two rows back and a seat over was actually talking to him, but it was soon obvious he was overhearing the boy's internal monologue.

I'm so much better than him. But she wouldn't go out with me. Now she holds his arm in the hallway and sits beside him in class. I could show her what she's missing.

Jaime glanced at Keira, but she was focused on Ms. Henderson and the exposition of *Ulysses*. He tried to raise more filters, but not even a floppy fish could block the boy's angry thoughts. They became more violent and Jaime could see the boy beating him up and raping Keira. The kid imagined himself with a cartoon-sized dick, so large that when he shoved it into his cartoon image of Keira, she bulged outward. Everything he was thinking looked like a badly drawn cartoon. He couldn't even see a realistic face, but just an image of her pussy and his dick ripping into it.

Jaime was breathing heavily when Ms. Henderson handed out a discussion sheet and asked the class to start making notes on examples of foreshadowing, flashback, symbolism, irony, and characterization. It was like a switch was thrown in the kid's head and all thoughts of Jaime and Keira vanished.

«See you at lunch?» Keira asked when class was dismissed.

«Too cold to go outside. In the cafeteria?»

«Okay.»

Jaime was still clamped down on his thoughts about the boy in class. They parted for their second period classes and Jaime forced his attention to not getting hit in the head in a game of dodgeball in PE.

"WHAT'S THE PROBLEM?" Keira asked aloud as she joined Jaime in the cafeteria.

They took a table together as far from others as they could get. They still needed to be careful about who could overhear them. Jaime had learned early on, though, that people often said things with their mouths that they weren't thinking in their minds. He could do the same with his hands.

"Stupid *Ulysses* assignment. I don't get it," he signed. «Brad Johnson,» he said in his mind.

«They guy who always thinks in cartoons? I've put up a permanent filter not to hear anything he thinks. He asked me out once and showed me a sketchbook of manga-style drawings he carries around. I said no. It's too hard to figure out if what he's thinking at any given time is an actual thought or if it's a story he's thinking of drawing. Poorly.»

«He wanted to beat me up and rape you!» Jaime said, trying to calm down so he wasn't shouting.

«Take it easy, hon,» Keira said. «We need to be careful about letting thoughts like that affect us. Remember? Not many people are disciplined in their thinking. If we let them in, every stray thought comes out of their heads into ours.»

«It was gross. I wanted to punch him. He couldn't even call your face to mind. All he could see was a cartoonish image of your… privates… that he could rip up. Then he just quit thinking about anything except the worksheet Ms. Henderson handed out.»

«Well, he certainly couldn't have any ability to see a realistic image!» Keira laughed. «Really, Jaime. That stuff goes on all the time. But it's just like Brad in class. The thoughts occupy their minds until something else demands their attention. Then they evaporate. I don't worry about it unless I hear the same guy repeating things incessantly and not dropping the thought when something else comes up. They're the dangerous ones.»

«So, that's been on my mind a lot. How do we tell the difference between someone truly malicious and someone having a vivid fantasy?» Jaime asked. «I mean, there was no doubt in my mind that the kidnapper Saturday was going to kill that girl if he got hold of her. But there was a guy preparing a drug buy a few seats over and that didn't faze me at all. It's still illegal.»

«I don't think we responded to whether it was legal or illegal,» Keira said. «It was evil, pure and simple. That's the way I interpreted it. But even then, if we hadn't been connected to each other so… completely, I don't know if I'd have done anything. I mean, I might have tried to delay her in the restroom or to walk home with her, but that would have just delayed him. It wouldn't have stopped him like you did.»

«They caught him. Dad checked the news reports this morning and said it was on the police bulletin.»

«Thank God! Still, the point is we knew he was really going to kidnap and kill her. You acted because we absolutely *had* to stop him. He had actual memories of having done it before.»

«It's too bad we can't supply *that* information to the police,» Jaime sighed.

«I guess. We have to be careful, Jaime. We aren't the police. We can't just raid people's minds and turn them in.»

«Wow! That would be pretty awful. What if we reported a fantasy as having actually happened?»

«You get it. There was a movie once that portrayed some kind of thought police who could get a person arrested for a crime they intended to commit in the future. Of course, it backfired and they accused someone who was innocent,» Keira said.

«Just accusing someone of something could cause them to do it, too,» Jaime said. «I read that somewhere.»

«The bell is about to ring for class,» Keira said. «…Would you like to hold hands for a minute?»

«You know the answer to that,» Jaime grinned.

They quickly glanced around to be sure they couldn't be observed and to note who they were likely to hear when they touched. Then they reached their hands toward each other under the table. The contact was simultaneously more controlled and more intense than their previous contacts. The blending of their minds took their breath away. Before they could get carried away with the emotions or lose themselves in the thoughts of those near them, the class bell rang and they withdrew.

«Keira, you make me so happy!»

«I joy you, Jaime!»

THEY HADN'T MADE a plan, but Keira intended to meet Jaime outside school at the end of the day and possibly stop for ice cream on the way home. But when she exited, she saw Jaime in a close conversation with another girl. She thought she recognized the girl, but Jaime put an arm around her. The blow was almost physical to Keira. She jolted back away from the scene and ran back into the school building as if she forgot something. When she re-emerged ten minutes later, both Jaime and the girl were gone.

Jaime and Cheery

"ZIP, YOU HAVE to help me. I don't know what to do," Letitia 'Cheery' said when she caught up with Jaime outside of school. They'd been friends since kindergarten and she'd been in an actual couple relationship with Mex since the past spring.

"What's up?" Jaime signed.

"It's Juan. He…" Cheery stopped and looked around. Jaime heard what she was thinking before she leaned in and whispered. "He wants to go all the way. I can't do that!"

"I know Mex will respect you. You just need to tell him you don't want to," Jaime signed.

"That's just it. I *do* want to. I'm just so scared. I love Juan. The nuns say a girl will never be respected by her husband if she gives in. And I might get pregnant. And the priest says it's a sin."

Cheery's thoughts were flowing in such a confused mass that Jaime put his arm around her shoulders to comfort and calm her down. He began to get a clearer picture of the problem. There were so many mangled bits and pieces it was hard to pin down. He was surprised Mex wasn't right there beside them, but Mex had football practice before the last game of the season. Otherwise, he followed Cheery around like a lovesick puppy. He'd been thinking about marriage.

Cheery was genuinely afraid, and genuinely in love with Mex. She wanted desperately to make love. But between the restrictions of the church—very important in the Latina's life—and her fear of getting pregnant and having to raise a child by herself—just as her mother had—Cheery was scared half to death of intimacy.

Jaime could see in her memories, though, that she and Mex had already progressed to stages that would lead to the next step. He really didn't need the images of Mex's erect penis just before Cheery put it in her mouth. Or her feelings while Mex sucked on her nipples while he played in her panties. No wonder both were ready to have sex!

"I can talk to Mex," Jaime said. "But you need to *really* be up front about your worries and talk to him about them. Without making out at the same time. If you believe the church and think it is sinful and wrong, you have to tell him that and start thinking about marriage. If you are just afraid of pregnancy, there are ways to prevent that. The church doesn't even frown that heavily on condoms anymore. But you both have to talk it out and respect each other's feelings."

"I know, Zip. I know it in my head, but when I see him, I just want to do whatever he wants to make him happy. He's my forever man."

In Cheery's mind, she already had a wedding dress picked out. They were both seventeen, but Jaime knew their parents would agree to a marriage, even if they didn't wait to graduate first. He had no opinion on that. Whatever made them happy.

"I'll go around to the team entrance and talk to Mex after practice," Jaime signed.

"Thanks, Zip. I owe you one." She stood on tiptoe and kissed him on the cheek, then took off down the street toward her home.

11
RESOLUTION

Jaime and Mex

JAIME SENT A text to Mex asking him to meet after practice. It was too cold to wait at his tree, so he selected a bench near the locker rooms as the meeting place. He was still tired from his weekend adventure. The added stress from his friends' crisis was more than he wanted to deal with. He should have talked to Keira after school and reached out to her from his bench. She was a long way away and then disappeared altogether.

Jaime didn't worry about it. They were both new at this boyfriend/girlfriend thing and needed to work out when they'd communicate. He hadn't made a plan with Keira, so she might be anywhere or with anyone. She was really good at hanging out a mental 'Do not disturb' sign. It was something Jaime needed to practice and he set his mind to blanking out everything. As soon as the peace settled in on him, so did sleep.

That was where Mex found him after football practice.

"HEY, ZIP! YOUR text sounded urgent. You going to make me watch you sleep?" Juan said.

Jaime's eyes popped open and he looked at his friend. That had been a deep sleep! He hadn't even sensed Mex approaching.

"Hey. Busy weekend," Jaime signed. "Didn't hear you come up."

"I want to get over to Lettie's house as soon as I can," Juan said. "We'll have an hour to ourselves before her momma gets home."

"That's what I want to talk about," Jaime signed. "I talked to Cheery. She thinks you're pressuring her to have sex."

"And she doesn't want to," Juan sighed. "Damn. I didn't think she'd bring you into it."

"That's the problem," Jaime signed. "She *does* want to. She's scared."

"Man! What's she scared of? I love her!"

Jaime could see the truth in that statement. He thought Mex was as much in love as Cheery was. At least they had that going for them.

"How important is the church to you?" Jaime asked.

"I go to mass every week. We go together. The priest kind of got after me for having touched Lettie. I don't tell him about that in confession anymore."

"That's one thing that's bothering Cheery. I mean, what you say in confession is between you and the priest, but she's afraid she's sinning."

"I don't think either of us really believe that," he said. "We talk, you know."

"Good. Has she told you she's afraid she'll get pregnant and end up like her mother—a single mom trying to scrape together enough to survive on?"

"No! She'd never have to deal with that! Man, I love her. I would never abandon her. We can use a condom. I don't mind."

"Well, you need to deal with those two big issues before you push her into something she isn't ready for. You're only seventeen. Try to keep it zipped a little longer until you're both on the same page," Jaime signed.

"It's so difficult! She's the absolute sexiest girl I've ever met. We grew up together. I get crazy if she even looks at another guy and I don't look at other girls. I know you don't understand all that about love and stuff, but this is the real deal."

Jaime's mind was flooded with images from Mex that featured every sexy thing he'd ever done with Cheery. Jaime had to catch his breath.

"I *do* understand. I've got a girlfriend, you know?" he signed.

"You what?" Mex was taken completely off-guard. "When did you get a girlfriend? You've never even been on a date!"

"Keira," Jaime fingerspelled. Then he used her name sign. "We were out this weekend."

Juan contemplated the name and the sign and came to a resolution.

"The red-haired girl in our class? We were all in physics together last year?

Wow! That's unreal. Still, you've only dated this weekend. You can't possibly know what's inside her. I tell you, man, love is like every waking thought and most of your sleeping thoughts are about that person. It's hard to concentrate in class. I even messed up a play in football practice because she flashed across my mind. I'm just…"

Mex cut himself off in mid-sentence as he thought of something else.

"Geez! A baby! We need to be *really* careful, don't we? The Ducks are recruiting me. You know what that means? Full ride to the university. I need to do something quick. I need to make sure Lettie is with me. Shoot, man. I need to get moving. I'll talk to you later. Good luck with Keira."

Juan turned and bolted from the school, but Jaime saw that he was headed toward the mall, not toward home. He planned to get an engagement ring for Letitia!

Keira and Rose

Across town, another conversation was taking place.

"Okay. So, you had a great weekend date with this guy. Zip, right? You had a big adventure. I should have known when I saw the news about that guy the police arrested that you were involved somehow. So, you had an intense weekend with this guy. Scare you?" Aunt Rose asked after Keira had told her story.

"A little. It was really overwhelming. Almost like we were sharing the same… um… body, I guess. I mean, we didn't do anything, you know? Well, we held hands for a couple of minutes. I felt so connected to him. And then seeing him put his arm around that girl after school… I thought he really liked me!" Keira had been sniffling ever since she got to Rose's house and the tears threatened to break free again.

"And without talking to him or trying to connect like you say you did at the movie, you jumped to the conclusion he was involved with someone else and you ran away," Rose said.

"I guess."

"Keira, we've talked about jumping to conclusions based on things no one else can see. You're lucky the adventure with that kidnapper turned out well.

I'm sure you'll be called on to identify him and testify about how you knew he was going to try to snatch that girl. You can't count on every intuition being spot on. Sometimes, just seeing something isn't enough. You don't know what this Zip and the girl were talking about. You don't know what their relationship is. For all you know, he was comforting her because he'd just told her about you and she was heartbroken. Honey, you have to investigate."

"It's… We were so connected. I was happy when I saw him and I know he's happy when he sees me.» Keira sobbed. «But it was so hard to see him with her and I just knew there was something really… um… sexy passing between them." She'd been too far away to really hear what was going on, but she had felt the sexual tension being communicated.

"So, are you going to just be miserable and avoid him for the rest of your life? Or are you going to use that joy you have in each other to confront him and find out what's really going on?"

"I… I'll talk to him. Do you think I can believe him? I never experienced anything like this before."

"Only you can answer that. You won't have anything to believe or disbelieve if you don't talk," Rose admonished her.

Keira sniffled as she finished her tea. She hugged Aunt Rose and went home.

Jaime and Keira

IN FACT, HER contact with Jaime was destined to come sooner than expected. When she got home, her parents said a detective from the police department had been by to see her and would come back soon. They wanted to compare her story to Jaime's.

«Calling Jaime,» she said using as much volume as her inner voice could manage.

«Wow! You got me loud and clear,» Jaime responded. «I wanted to see you after school, but something came up.»

«I could see that,» Keira snapped. «It looked like you and that girl needed some private time.»

«That girl? Oh! Cheery. After I talked to her, I had to hang around school until football practice was over so I could talk to her boyfriend for her.»

«She wanted you to tell him she was breaking up?»

«What? No. She wanted me to talk to him about why she was scared to go all the way. It was kind of funny. Mex was torturing himself and ran off to buy an engagement ring for her. He was knocked off his feet to find out *I* had a girlfriend!»

«Who?» The response was curt.

«You!… Keira, is something wrong?»

«I saw you hugging her! We can't even do more than hold hands for a minute and you had your arm around her!»

«I was trying to get a clearer picture of what she was going through! Her thoughts were pretty muddled and I thought the contact would help me sort them out.»

«Can I believe you, Jaime?»

«Believe me? I… I don't think it would even be possible for me to lie to you about something. You'd know in an instant. You can look inside right now. I'll come over and you can hold my hand and probe everything I've ever thought.»

«No!… Tomorrow. We can hold hands for a minute and you can tell me all about it.»

«It's pretty intense. She and Mex both had really graphic thoughts about each other.»

«We've got other problems tonight. A police detective is on his way to compare my story with yours about how we knew the kidnapper was going to grab that girl.»

«Wow! I just got home and have to get dinner ready. Uh-oh. There's someone at the door. He's broadcasting 'police.' I need to concentrate on what he wants.»

«Contact me as soon as he's gone. I want to be sure our stories match.»

«Will do.»

Jaime and the Detective

Jaime had his laptop out and was using his text-to-speech app to talk to the detective. It had taken a few minutes to figure out how to communicate, but the detective was surprisingly patient. His thoughts said he dealt with teens all the time.

"So, you don't speak at all?" he asked.

"Never have," Jaime typed.

"So how did you and your girlfriend make a plan to follow the alleged kidnapper so quickly?"

"We both heard him muttering about how he was going to make her scream. I signed to Keira and she went to follow the girl while I followed the guy."

"You're pretty good at sign language, huh?"

"I've been using it since kindergarten. Keira is newer, but she does pretty good. It's amazing how much of a conversation we can have without anyone realizing we're talking to each other."

"The guy, Alex Rames, claims he never said anything in the theater, but someone was telling him he had to grab the girl… to protect her."

"I can't swear I've quoted him word for word. Maybe Keira picked up more than I did. But we knew he was going to try to grab her."

"Okay. The officers at the scene had you send your video to them and I've reviewed it. We recorded the video your girlfriend streamed to the 9-1-1 operator. I don't think there's any problem with the two of you, though I'm sure the attorneys will want to depose you. You shouldn't talk about this with anyone—least of all your girlfriend. If they think you colluded on the story, it will damage the testimony."

"We never thought about that. We told our parents the whole story and talked about it on Sunday. I'm glad you caught the guy," Jaime typed.

"We've linked him to three other missing persons. That girl, Heidi, doesn't know how lucky she is that you were there. Have a good evening."

The detective turned to leave just as David got home. They chatted for a few minutes and then the detective left. Jaime apologized for not having dinner ready.

"Let's go grab a pizza," David suggested. Jaime quickly agreed.

Jaime quickly contacted Keira before they got to the car and played back the entire conversation with the detective, stressing his warning about collaboration. Then he got in the car with his father.

Keira and the Detective

"He kind of had to shove people out of the way in order to keep Heidi in sight," Keira said. "Jaime was closer to him, so he might have heard more than I did. I just heard, 'Make her scream like the others.' It wasn't hard to tell who he was talking about because he was looking right at her. Jaime signed to me to follow the girl and he took off after the guy."

"Did she know you were behind her?"

"I don't think so, but I'm not sure. It's not like I follow people a lot. Maybe she knew. I'm pretty sure she saw Jaime cross the street just before she was attacked. You'd have to ask her. She didn't want to talk to us after she was shoved to the ground. It was all I could do to convince her to just stay where she was until the police got there."

"Okay. I warned your boyfriend not to talk about this. You will undoubtedly be deposed by the prosecution and the defense if it comes to trial. I can't overemphasize this. A suspicion of collusion on your testimony could mean he walks scot-free."

"Yessir. I understand."

As if those two could keep secrets from each other, the detective thought as he left. *They'll be talking about it before they sleep. Wonder how they do that. We could subpoena their text messages, I suppose.*

His train of thought disappeared when he got into his car.

Jaime and Keira

«Are you still mad at me?» Jaime asked as he held Keira's hand and transferred all the memories of his encounters with Cheery and Mex from the previous day.

They'd stepped behind a dumpster before school to block out the thoughts of the other students arriving. Some of those memories were really graphic as both of the teens had thought about their relationship and what they had done together.

«No,» Keira said. «I'm sorry. When I saw you put your arm around her, it was like someone punched me in the stomach. I couldn't breathe! I should have come to talk to you right then. I'm sorry.»

«My whole mind is open to you, Red. I give my whole being to you. Does that make sense? I know we're not ready for some things because we've only known each other a week. But it's all on the table for you. I will never… I *could* never lie to you.»

«They did have some really sexy thoughts,» Keira giggled.

«I try hard not to think of my friends like that.»

«I'll bet it's hard. So was he.»

«I really didn't mean to plant that in your brain.»

«Well, let's replace it with something.»

«Big floppy fish?»

«That'll do for now. I was thinking of ice cream after school.»

«Oh, heck, yeah.»

They quickly pulled their hands away from each other before the conversation became too personally graphic. Nonetheless, the seed had been planted.

Jaime and Keira decided to see an afternoon matinee of an animated feature on Saturday. They spent the entire movie holding hands and after taking a while to just enjoy being in touch and 'in' each other, they tuned into the thoughts of those around them.

«Children's thoughts are so random!» Keira said.

«Only about one in ten is actually involved in the movie. The rest see something and it reminds them of something else and they're off on their own story,» Jaime said.

«Pretty much like we are!»

«This is really fun. But that poor kid is trying to figure out why her mom keeps sniffling in a funny movie. Her mom brought her to the movie, but her dad… Shit! Her mom's full of how to tell her daughter that Daddy was killed overseas. Those poor people!»

«I wish there was something we could do to help,» Keira said.

«Red, this is one of those cases where there isn't anything that can help. We can sympathize and even empathize, but there's no way to make it better for them. The little girl knows her mommy has been crying and is unhappy, but doesn't know why. It makes her sad, even when she laughs at the movie. The woman's lost her husband and her daughter's daddy. She doesn't know how to tell her little girl that Daddy will never come home again,» Jaime said.

«Zip, you're crying.»

«It just reminds me so much of when I lost my mom. I was about the same age and just didn't understand why she was never coming home.»

«I know I can't make it better, but lean on me, baby. Let me share your sorrow.»

They ignored the rest of the movie, just sharing the sadness, both of Jaime and of the woman and her daughter.

There were a lot of sympathetic mental kisses that went on between the two of them and they reached out to the mother and daughter with the same, but didn't know if it really had any effect.

«Third date,» Keira whispered in his mind as he walked her to her door later that evening. «We can kiss then.» They'd had dinner at a little Mexican restaurant after the movie and realized they actually *needed* a break from the heightened sensations resulting from holding hands. Keira took both his hands in hers and pulled his gloves off when they reached her front porch. They held their bare hands together and just enjoyed the bliss of sinking into each other.

«Isn't *this* the third date?» he asked.

«The walk in the park doesn't count. Nor does tomorrow's,» she giggled.

«Okay. So next weekend. What about it?»

«That's when we can kiss. Just a little, until we find out how it's going to affect us,» she said.

«Wow! It's going to be a long week,» he sighed.

«Yeah, I know. We'll have to play a game to make the time go faster.»

«What kind…?»

«I'll tell you tomorrow. See you then, boyfriend.»

«Yeah,» he smiled. «You definitely will!»

Trayce

ON THE OTHER side of town, Trayce was having a different problem. She'd begun writing again as her mother sank further into depression after her father's death. It had been almost a year and her mother hadn't gone back to work. She had a drink in her hand most of the time. She sat in front of the television, staring blankly until she went to sleep.

Trayce was fighting the depression as well. It was almost as if she'd lost both parents. Her only outlet had been to open the computer and start typing. This fall, she'd managed to enroll in her first ever creative writing class at school and she was more committed to writing as a career than ever.

But the teacher, while giving good advice and exercises, didn't think much of fan fiction. She cited a play by Tom Stoppard titled *Rosencrantz and Guildenstern Are Dead*. She said that, like the common cuckoo, Stoppard had chosen to lay his literary eggs in someone else's nest. Then she went on to cite several other authors who wrote in other people's universes or even took over series from previous authors, starting with Nancy Drew and working her way into contemporary television series that featured multiple writers for different episodes.

"Excuse me, Ms. Dorn," Trayce had asked, "but isn't that exactly what we do when we follow your writing prompts for class?"

That stopped her teacher's rant about fan fiction short.

"Okay. I was using prompts as a way to get you into the flow of writing, but I see you are far beyond that," she said sarcastically. "So, your next assignment is to write a short story between 5,000 and 20,000 words in length. It is *not* to be fan fiction or written in anyone else's universe, but must be completely original. Let's find out if you are really ready to become a writer. First draft is due next Friday."

Trayce could feel the animosity of the other members of her class. No one was happy about the assignment. Including Trayce.

"I really thought she'd just stop knocking fan fic," she muttered. "Not force us into something else."

She sat in her room all day Saturday and suddenly had a vague notion for a story. She would write about a woman who just received the news that her husband had died overseas. It was definitely a stretch for Trayce. It wouldn't be a happy story. How could it be? She'd lost her own father and knew how it hurt. She would write about how the woman received the news and then took her five-year-old daughter to see a funny movie before telling her that Daddy wasn't coming home again. She could feel the intense emotion of the characters. She just needed to get an effective resolution so it was a story instead of a slice of life.

She opened her laptop and started writing the notes she would need.

12
FANTASY GONE WILD

Jaime and Keira and Angus

JAIME AND KEIRA spent most of their afternoon walking together, holding hands, and staring into each other's eyes. They were completely lost in each other for a long time before the presence of others around them began to impinge on their awareness.

First, they focused on a woman walking a tiny fluffball of a dog and daintily picking up the poop.

Oh, my baby. That's such a good girl. Are you ready to go home now? You want to be carried? Come to Mommy.

«I think the dog understood all that,» Jaime said.

«Don't tell me you could read the dog's mind!»

«No, not at all. I don't think. It just seemed like she responded to what the woman was thinking more than to her voice.»

«I get it. There's an argument going on. It sounds serious. Over there.»

The people Keira identified were too far away for their hushed voices to be heard, but their thoughts were racing together. The guy had gray hair and beard. He wore a bowler hat and a utility kilt. One woman was tall and strong, the other only slightly shorter and elegant. The conversation was heated.

Old man, you've done this one too many times. How long do you think we'll let you just walk all over us. Your days are numbered, said Kate.

You're farting in the wind. We should grab the bag as soon as we see it and be away before anyone knows it's gone, Angus replied.

Right. Like the last time we tried that kind of move and were almost killed, Thursday (the younger woman) said. It was really too cold out for the short skirt and bare legs she was sporting.

We couldn't just leave them, Angus said. *They were sitting ducks. If you'd just taken off your top like I told you to, the muggers would have dropped everything to stare.*

In the club or on the beach, Angus. Not on the street, Thursday said.

Jaime and Keira could see that all three shared very familiar images of each other nude. Apparently, both women worked in nude clubs nearby.

Hold it. No, that's where you have to slug him, Kate said. *It starts the fight and he draws the sword.*

«What?» Keira asked.

«They aren't fighting, they're rehearsing something. I wondered what was going on. They didn't look all that angry. But that cane he's got with the dragon head? It really is a sword!» Jaime said

«Is that legal?»

«Hey, you two!» Angus shouted in their heads. «If you're going to eavesdrop, be quiet about it.»

«You're a head talker!»

«Shh! Don't tell the girls. We get into too many scrapes to have them thinking all they have to do is think to me and I'll rescue them,» Angus shot at them.

«Are you actors?» Keira asked.

«Amateurs. I'm a detective and these are my sidekicks,» Angus said.

«Cool! Um… What are you picking?»

«Dandelion leaves and raspberry leaves. For the rabbits. Are you done prying into my affairs?»

«Sure. Sorry. Didn't mean to be nosey. We just don't know many people like us,» Jaime said.

«There aren't many. I haven't had a conversation like this in years. Kind of refreshing.»

«Maybe we'll see each other again sometime," Keira offered.

«Maybe. I come here often. Little chilly these days, but there are still leaves on the raspberries.»

«Nice to meet you, Mr. Angus,» Jaime said. «Maybe we'll see you on Sundays.»

Jaime and Keira withdrew and felt Angus putting up some mental defenses he hadn't used in years. They could hear the women getting ready to start the scene again and decided they should take their eavesdropping elsewhere.

«That was weird,» Jaime said.

«Yeah. It shows though, how wrong we can be when we overhear people's thoughts. They were rehearsing a play!» Keira said.

«Yeah. He's a detective? He has to be at least seventy-five.»

«Yeah, but the ladies with him weren't more than forty or so. And man, could they strut their stuff,» Keira said.

«Really! I'm too young to go to those places!» Jaime said.

«Yeah, but you can fantasize about them. Or not. I've got another idea.»

«I'm all ears. Or whatever this is,» Jaime said.

«I think we really need to go slow and grow into our relationship a little at a time,» Keira said. «We haven't even kissed yet and I know we're both thinking about going all the way.»

«I didn't mean to let that out,» Jaime said.

«We were so deep in each other, I'm not sure you could have kept it in. You had to have heard the same thing from me.»

«I kind of thought it was just me being reflected in you.»

«No. Jaime, I want to be your lover. It just scares the shit out of me. That's why I think we should really take it easy. It's why I said no kiss until next week. We're only just getting comfortable holding each other's hand and look where that took us today! What's going to happen next? I don't think I'm ready to find out.»

«Yeah, I agree. It's just hard is all.»

«I could feel that.»

They both snorted.

«We shouldn't go without any relief,» Keira said. Jaime looked at her with a thousand questions. «I said I thought we could play a little game this week, right? Well, what if we kind of open ourselves to hearing fantasies this week—you know in school. Then we could just take a fantasy home and enjoy it. Individually, not together. But then we could share what happened.»

«Isn't that kind of voyeuristic?»

«No one gets hurt by it. We just have to be sure we don't act differently toward anyone, okay?»

«Yeah. I mean, it's not like we've never done anything like that before. It would be like going to sleep with the image of that Thursday girl in our heads. She was really…»

«She sure was. Let's see where it takes us this week.»

Jaime and Keira

Jaime typically found girls' fantasies and the occasional memory to be more inspiring than those of boys. He was fascinated by girls' bodies and the thoughts they sometimes had. Keira also preferred girls' fantasies because they were less graphic. Boys' *memories* were often better, in her opinion. Imagining herself on the receiving end of a boy's attention—one who had actually experienced sex—was breathtaking.

Still, as much as their contemporaries *thought* about sex, most of it was in fleeting bits and lustful reactions rather than anything to really build on. There was so much going on at school that took attention away from daydreams, it was rare to find someone with as well-developed a fantasy life as, say, Debbie Burke. Jaime had decided to stay well away from Debbie's fantasies in the future.

By Wednesday, neither had found a likely subject for a good fantasy and they were contemplating just taking one of their own memories when they sat at lunch in the cafeteria. It was raining out and they sat near each other, sometimes allowing their hands to brush against each other for that momentary expansion that allowed them to distinguish individual thoughts from the crowd.

Juan and Letitia stopped by their table to show Cheery's new engagement ring. She was beaming and Mex couldn't stop grinning. They were headed out for a little alone time away from school. They could hardly keep their hands off each other.

«There was enough fantasy material there to last a week!» Keira said.

«I can't think that way about my closest friends,» Jaime answered. «It just wouldn't be right. I blocked out everything they were thinking.»

«I understand that. I'll skip them, too.»

Jaime glanced over by the windows where he spotted his computer lab partner, Emerson Flaherty. He liked her, but didn't consider her to be a *close* friend. She sat alone, looking out at the rain.

«I see her,» Keira said to him. «She's awful mousy, isn't she?»

«To most people. It isn't how she sees herself.»

Keira focused on Emerson.

«Wow! I should say not! Do you suppose she's really that way? Why would she hide that around school?»

Keira returned her attention to a guy who had caught her eye.

«What do you think of that guy at the table straight across the room from us?»

Describing where the guy was sitting wasn't really necessary. Jaime could instantly zero in on him from Keira's thoughts with a mere brush of his hand against hers.

«He's slept with how many girls?» Jaime thought in shock.

«He doesn't even remember. It's been going on for years. And not just girls. Adult women. College women. Mothers and sisters of his friends. He didn't know what he was doing at first, but now he fancies himself a born seducer.»

«And he thinks they're all happy about it. Is he just making all this up in his head?»

«I don't think so. I'm going to pick a couple of memories as they come through his mind this afternoon. I'll think about them later.»

«It's hard to think of you imagining somebody else… you know… doing it with you.»

«Don't. Focus on Emerson. If we don't choose other people for when we want to… masturbate, we'll end up thinking about each other and… You told Mex to keep it zipped a while. We need to do that, too. This is just as important for us. If we rushed home after school and made love today, it would blow my mind. Yours, too, I think. I'm not sure I'd recover. We're getting better at controlling things when we hold hands, but even that… I come close to losing myself every time we do it. We need to go a little at a time and when we make love, it will be phenomenal.»

«When we… Do you think we'll make love, Keira?»

«I'm counting on it. This weekend, I want to kiss you after our date. Just a little. We have to be disciplined about it. But I'd really like that.»

«So would I. You know, it's easier to tap into the way someone imagines having sex than the way they imagine kissing.»

«Strange things. I think it's because people stimulate their own… sex organs when they masturbate. It's really hard to stimulate your lips… or… tongue.»

«Wow!»

The bell rang and they shared a quick hand squeeze under the table before heading off to class.

Jaime and Emerson

JAIME KEPT A light connection with Emerson all through the afternoon, waiting to see if she returned to the sexy thoughts she was having at lunch. She had been his computer lab partner for over a year and they were currently working on her concept for using predictive AI for color trends. He found the subject as fascinating and absorbing as she did, though her application concepts were drastically different. He'd never really spotted her active fantasy life. This day was different.

Rain always makes me think of Dom and Raquel, she thought as she puzzled over a design problem the teacher had assigned. She glanced out the window and picked up her fantasy where she'd left it in the cafeteria. *It was Paris on an afternoon just like this.*

Emerson's carefully maintained image at school was as a quiet intellectual, slightly aloof and uninteresting. She was a computer nerd and the previous year had created her own search engine that was customized to her interests without flooding her with advertising and irrelevant links. It was simple, but it always gave her the results she wanted.

In Paris as an exchange student the previous spring and summer, she was anything but the mousy girl she appeared to be in Portland. She'd dressed sexily, talked differently, and acted outgoing. She wore makeup and was downright flirtatious. Talk about living a different life in her fantasies! Only Jaime soon realized this wasn't a fantasy. Her alternate personality was real, and so was her exchange term in France.

The images she remembered as she sat near Jaime were vivid and detailed. She'd made love to both a boy and a girl! The memories could easily fuel Jaime's time alone after school.

After school, Jaime and Keira met up to walk to the bus stop.

«I don't know about you, but I'm ready for a little relaxation with my vibrator,» Keira said.

«Wow! Now I'll have to focus harder on Emerson to keep that image from taking over!»

«You plucked some great content, too. She really did that? Hot! I'm hanging out my 'Do not disturb' sign as soon as I get home. You need to, too.»

«Yeah. When I did that yesterday, I fell asleep.»

«Oh. Well, better luck today,» Keira giggled. They touched hands again and went their separate ways.

"I'm soaked!" Emerson said to her companions. All three of them were drenched through to the skin after being caught in the sudden downpour. They'd taken quick shelter at Dom's apartment.

"I like this," Raquel said, looking at Emerson and then reaching out to stroke the pointed tip of Emerson's nipple, tenting the fabric of her almost sheer blouse.

"You know, you are just as exposed as I am," Emerson said, playfully returning the attention to Raquel's nipple.

Just like now, Emerson thought, looking at herself in the mirror. *I'm glad I took my bra off before I left school.*

Jaime suddenly realized he was not simply replaying Emerson's schooltime memory of her rain-drenched afternoon in Paris. Emerson was reliving it as she looked at herself in the bathroom mirror. She stood differently than she did in school—not slouched, but upright with her shoulders back. And her very prominent nipples poking out the thin T-shirt she had worn to school.

"Do you like them?" Raquel asked.

"Oh, yes," Emerson said to her reflection as she stroked her breasts.

"Oh, yes," Jaime repeated in his mind as he felt Emerson's fingers on her nipples. She paused in her memory a moment to play with the sensitive points, bringing Jaime's cock to absolute rigidity.

Then an image of Dom, shirtless, appeared in her memory.

"Do you girls want a T-shirt or something to put on so you can get out of those wet things?"

"If we take off our shirts, I don't see any reason to put something else on, do you, Raq?"

Emerson stroked Dom's chest and Raquel followed suit, paying attention to Dom's nearest nipple.

Though he couldn't feel what Dom had felt, he could feel the memory of Emerson's nipples being stimulated by her two friends.

All this time, while the images played in the back of his mind, Jaime was looking out Emerson's eyes as she looked at herself in the bathroom mirror. She got as turned on by watching herself as by the memory itself. Jaime could feel the tingling in her pussy as she reached for the hem of her T-shirt and slowly pulled it up off her wet skin. She pulled it over her head and off, feeling the cool air against her tender nipples. The image in the mirror was very different from how Jaime had imagined the girl would look when he saw her in school. She pressed her hands against her breasts, remembering those of her girlfriend pressed against her as they came together for a kiss.

Jaime's mind filled with a vision of Keira pressing her lips against his, her mouth opening to touch his tongue with hers.

He snapped his eyes open and jumped out of his bed, locking up his mind and hanging his mental 'Do not disturb' sign on his thoughts. He pulled on sweats and went to the kitchen to begin preparing dinner while he tried to sort out his thoughts and feelings. Maybe another time he might satisfy his aching groin, but not now. Not today. Not tonight.

Jaime and Keira

Jaime had never been conflicted about his ability to read others' thoughts. It had always been natural—the way his world worked. But only once before had he ever connected 'live' with another person's sexual fantasy. With Debbie Burke, it was almost as if she *wanted* the connection—*invited* it—and he was helpless to break it. But something was very different about connecting with Emerson's relived memory of her time in Paris.

«Did you have a good time last night?» Keira asked at lunch. She was shifting back and forth at the table as if she needed to say something but hadn't decided what.

«I… didn't do anything,» Jaime responded. It seemed both teens had other things on their minds and weren't sure how to share them.

«Why? I thought you were into it when you left school.»

«Like you were into Seth Thomas?»

«That… didn't exactly go like I planned. I started sorting through the memories I grabbed from him, you know? None of them were the least bit exciting.»

«What do you mean?»

«Like, I can't believe anyone falls for his lines. He's so… empty. The women he thinks he leaves satisfied are more like hollow images that are just vacant of any emotion at all. I'd like to read one's memories to compare it to his someday, but it's really not that interesting.»

«I get it.»

«Why didn't you go ahead with Emerson? Even the brush of her memories I got felt exciting,» Keira said as she unwrapped her sandwich. Having said her piece to him, she was less antsy. It was easier knowing Jaime hadn't followed through either.

«Yeah. They were exciting. Some of the most exciting I've experienced. But there were two things. Maybe three, but I can't separate them all.»

«You want to just share them?»

«Yes, but I want to try to sort them out first. I don't know if sharing them intact would transfer the impact they had. Or maybe you'd get the impact without getting the reasons. Does that make sense?» Jaime asked as they kept their hands busy with their lunches.

«Tell me then.»

«First… Remember what happened with Debbie Burke?»

«Oh, yeah! You mean you connected with Emerson the same way?»

«Yeah, sort of. There was a big difference. Debbie was fantasizing about me. It was like I was invited to participate. But Emerson… she's a very private girl who keeps her life here in Portland very separate from the way she lived in Paris. When I fell into her mind, she wasn't fantasizing, exactly. She was reliving something that was very personal and very special to her. She didn't deserve to have someone spying on her. You know what I mean?»

«I think I see the difference. You felt more like a peeping Tom with Emerson than with Debbie.»

«Yeah. Like I was violating her private space. I guess that's all part one of the two things.»

Jaime hesitated in sharing the other thing—the more important thing to him. He still wasn't sure how Keira would take it.

«Do I have to beg you to tell me? You know, I won't think badly of you, no matter what.»

«The other thing was you.»

«What?»

«I couldn't take part in Emerson's memory without thinking about you. When I felt her kiss, I felt you. I couldn't take you out of the scene. And since I promised—we promised—not to fantasize about each other like that, I had to shut it down and hang out a 'Do not disturb' sign.»

«Oh, Jaime! That's so sweet!»

«I'm glad you think so, because… because you're the only one I want.»

«Oh! Oh, wow! That's like… Well, I didn't have the kind of connection with Seth that you had with Emerson, but still, it was just that I didn't find him interesting.»

The end of lunch bell rang and they scooped up their garbage to discard. Their hands brushed against each other and both were filled with the calm and yet exciting synergy of their relationship.

«We really have to continue this talk. I mean, really. It's important to both of us and we can't let it just be a surface conversation,» Keira said.

«Let's take the bus to your house after school and I'll walk home from there,» Jaime said.

The warmth suffused both of them as they went to their classes.

13
FIRST KISS

Jaime and Emerson

IN COMPUTER SCIENCE class, Jaime had a hard time looking at Emerson. No matter what his response had been, the visual of her taking off her shirt in front of the mirror was vivid in his memory. He couldn't look at her without blushing.

"Hey, Zip, you okay?" she asked as they sat next to each other going over the initial diagram for her project.

Emerson was tackling an interesting concept of using AI predictive techniques for sociological phenomena. She was starting with color theory and thought she could use historic data regarding color trends over the past twenty years to predict what the popular colors would be in the next year's fashions.

"Oh, I'm fine," Jaime signed, quickly recovering his composure. "Your project reminded me of something in Isaac Asimov's *Foundation*."

"Isn't that an old science fiction book?"

Jaime quickly switched to his laptop so he could use text to speech. He had to keep the volume really low so they didn't disturb anyone else in class. Emerson leaned in close. She smelled good, which was distracting to Jaime.

"Yeah. Almost like a hundred years. But it's pretty good. I read it when I was a freshman and was really into anything that had to do with mind reading," he typed.

"So, what reminds you of my project?"

114

"Well, in the book, Hari Seldon establishes what he calls 'psychohistory.' It's a new field of science and psychology that allows for the probabilistic prediction of the future. But one of the things he says is that it might not be possible to predict the behavior of an individual person, but the mob was always predictable. Hence, whenever you are dealing with a mass event in history, it is possible to predict what will happen, even though you can't predict what any individual will do."

"So, I'm predicting a mass event and not what an individual designer will do?" Emerson asked.

"I think that's the parallel."

They started listing out the variables that Emerson's algorithm would need to consider. The list started getting long.

"Did you ever have someone just randomly cross your mind?" she asked hesitantly.

"Oh, yeah. Happens all the time," Jaime typed. He laughed his odd little squeak.

"I suppose so. You just happened to cross my mind after school yesterday. It was odd. Then whatever it was I was thinking of at the time disappeared and I forgot all about it until just now."

Jaime opened his senses just slightly and was flooded with Emerson's memory of her afterschool session the day before. She'd been about to kiss her Paris lover when Jaime's face flitted across her memory and she kissed him. Then it was gone and she was back with her lovers.

«Can you hear me, Emerson?» he asked, projecting to her.

"I think it's weird how the mind works and random thoughts hit us. I guess that's how dreams are made. The synapses in our brain fire and suddenly there's a happy dog running across a field that turns into a hideous monster under the bed and disappears in a lullaby or something. I think that's why I liked your original project description of tech for transferring thoughts from one person to another. It was a little… uh… tinfoil hat-ish, but it was interesting."

"I have a lot of studying to do before I can tackle that one. And even if I figured it out, I'd never be able to convince anyone I was serious about it," he typed.

"I suppose."

The class period ended and both closed their computers to head for the last class of the day.

"Thanks for all the help on this project, Jaime. It seems a little less daunting, knowing that you're thinking about it, too. Let me know if I can help on your thought machine. See you tomorrow."

Jaime signed "later," and went to his psychology class.

Jaime and Keira

«Do you think she can hear you?» Keira asked when they got off the bus at her house.

«I don't think so. The image I got, though, is that she thought of me at the exact same moment as her remembered kiss, which is when I suddenly saw you there and shut her off. Is there some stage between? Like when someone receives the *impression* of something, but didn't actually hear it?"

«That would sure cover a lot of situations like 'premonitions.' Someone thinks of a loved one and says, 'Be careful on that road tonight.' That person doesn't hear what they said, but something tells them to slow down right before the curve where a car is stalled in the road.»

«That's logical. I don't know if that's what happened with Emerson. And I don't want to run any experiments on people without their knowledge. It's just… It never used to scare me that I could hear people's thoughts. I thought everyone could and just chose to ignore me. But now, there are all kinds of issues and… ethics to deal with. I'm afraid I'll implant something into someone's mind unintentionally and they'll do something terrible.»

They stopped on Keira's front porch before going inside.

"I love you," she said, taking his hand.

«What?»

«I had to say it out-loud before I could say it inside. I love you, Jaime.»

«Yes. I mean, yes! Love! So much love!»

They were of one mind when their lips came together and they kissed for the first time. And time stopped. That's not unusual when lovers kiss for the first time. The world seems to go away as they are lost in the first sensation of lips to lips. It was more than that for Jaime and Keira.

The world dissolved away from them as their minds melded in that touch.

Every conscious thought in each other's mind was transferred between them. The emotion of their attachment to each other overwhelmed them and they swam at the border of consciousness as they felt the first rush of acknowledged love through their combined nervous system. It threatened to completely overwhelm them.

And then the kiss was over. It only lasted an instant, but in that instant their lives had changed.

They felt a happy sigh in the backs of their minds.

«I… I… You… We…» Jaime's thoughts stumbled over each other as he tried to catch the breath that had been knocked out of him.

«We need to do that again, soon!» Keira said. «No! Not yet! I need to… How did we…? This might take a while.»

They sat on the porch on either side of the door and just looked longingly at each other, still holding hands.

«You were jealous of Emerson?»

«Oh, God! I didn't want that to come out. I didn't mean it. I mean, it was just a flash when you described her image of you just as she was imagining the kiss in her fantasy. I didn't want another girl doing what I wanted to do so badly.»

«It's okay. She imagined that. It was right when I imagined you. But nothing in my imagination compared to the reality of you.»

«Did you ever think that when we kissed it would be like that? I mean this?»

«I could never have imagined what we just had. Not in a million years. It felt like I stuck my lips in a light socket and flipped the switch.»

«Wow! That's expressive,» Keira giggled. «Shocking!»

«I mean… Yeah! I felt so much energy and power and immensity that I thought I was flying. I thought for an instant, I'd died and my mind was completely released from my body.»

«Yes. We were like one person for that instant. Soulmates. Do you think it will always be like that?»

«I don't know if I should hope it is or hope it isn't.» Jaime squeaked his laughter. «I mean, if it's always like that, we won't ever be able to kiss for more than a second. You know? I kind of hope that we'll be able to control it a little so we can do it more often. Like…»

«Holding hands.»

The teens looked at their hands, held tightly together. There was a flow of energy between them—a resonance in their thoughts. They could see the automatic controls that had kicked in so that holding hands didn't continue the overwhelming input to their brains.

«But it's there. I can see it. If we opened ourselves a little, we'd be able to hear everyone near us, like we did in the theater, or the park the other day,» Jaime said.

«Lucky there aren't any people near us right now. I'm not sure I could hold them back. And I don't want to stop holding your hand.»

«Did you mean it, Keira?»

«That I don't want to stop holding your hand?»

«No. I can feel that. When we said, 'I love you,' was it more than a spike in our hormones? Was it more than a flash of jealousy, or a stab of lust? The only real love I've ever known was from my parents. It was… is… nothing like this. This sense of wanting to be with you always—to share everything in my life with you. I have to define love by these feelings.»

«Yes, Jaime. I'm sure of it. I've been fond of people. I've certainly had lustful thoughts about some who caught my attention with their daydreams. But I've never experienced anything with the depth and passion I feel for you. I love you.»

«I love you, Keira.» Other thoughts ran uninvited through Jaime's mind and he tried unsuccessfully to quash them before Keira picked up on them.

«Yes!» she said. «But no. I mean… I *want* to make love to you. I want to give you my all and take from you all you can give. I want to feel us naked together, kissing and… everything. I just can't. Not right now.»

«I didn't mean now now. I just meant that… now I really want to make love to you.»

«It scares me,» Keira whispered in her mind.

Jaime had a discussion with Cheery just a few days before and that was exactly what she said. He remembered her fears vividly.

«I will never abandon you,» he said. «I know it's sudden and we've only been dating a couple of weeks, but I pledge my life to you.»

« Oh, yes. Really, Jaime, we're on the same page about all that. I'm on birth control, so I'm not worried about pregnancy. I have faith in your loyalty and constancy and honesty and love. All the things girls are usually afraid of, I'm not. I'm not afraid of it hurting. I'm not ashamed of how I look. I'm not afraid of what you'll think of me. I love you and the natural thing to do is to make love. I want to.»

«It sounds like…»

«I'm still scared.»

«Okay. I have a lot to learn, I guess.»

«We both do. Think about our kiss a few minutes ago. In fact, let's walk to the park and do it again so we aren't right here on the front porch.»

Still holding hands, the two left their backpacks on the porch and walked the block to the park, sharing little observations—a dog chasing a ball, a breeze that threatened snow, the smell of the air. The sharing was automatic. They caught the thoughts of people passing them and recognized them as a kind of universal hum that was always in the background now. Still, they could open their senses a little more and quickly identify which of a dozen thoughts was coming from which of as many people.

Love's in bloom. I always thought fall was the best time for love, not spring, thought a woman glancing at their held hands. *That night, September ninth, when Dev took me home from practice and we made out in the car while it rained outside. I wonder how long it took him to unfog the windows. All the windows in my apartment fogged over when I went inside. That will always be the first day of fall for me. The first day of love.* There was a kind of wistfulness in her imagining that whispered, *Those days are gone.*

Jaime and Keira glanced at each other and leaned closer together, both relishing the sweet memory of the woman they had passed.

«We shouldn't shock anyone here,» Jaime said as Keira led him behind a bush near the path.

«I'm ready,» Keira responded. «Let's try it again.»

They moved closer together, holding each other in their eyes as their lips finally made contact. Jaime had once heard there were 10,000 nerve endings in the lips and he was sure all 10,000 points were linked to Keira. The sounds around them changed and instead of wind and leaves and passing people, they heard their heartbeats. They felt the chemicals released into their bodies as the kiss lingered.

Keira could feel the pressure against her breasts where they pressed against Jaime, but she could feel it from his perspective as well. A completely different level of excitement from the same stimulus. On the other hand, she felt the growing pressure of Jaime's erection as it ballooned between them and that gave her a much different kind of arousal. Jaime mostly ignored the erection. He was used to them. She was not and relished the feeling.

And beneath it all, beneath the heart throbbing excitement, beneath the absolute joy of their kiss, Jaime felt what he could only describe as terror from Keira. And he recognized that he shared it in some measure, but had never acknowledged it in the excitement of his new discoveries.

«What is it?» he dared ask her.

«Everything is so much more than anything I've experienced before,» Keira said. «Sharing thoughts and emotions with you makes me *feel like* you.»

«I feel that, too. Like I don't really exist any longer. I feel like you. Like, I understand now about all kinds of things that were a mystery. A female mystery, if you will. Is that what we are afraid of?»

«I'm afraid that I'll lose myself, Keira sobbed. She broke the kiss and pressed her face against Jaime's chest as she cried.

«Lose myself? As if I really didn't exist any longer?» he said.

«Yes. We'll become so close together that we'll lose what was uniquely individual. I'll never know if a thought was my own or yours. I'll never know if this…» She pecked him quickly on the lips then returned to the way he was holding her. «…is what I wanted or what you wanted.»

«It sounds like a fantasy… I mean a fairy tale. Like they became one person and lived happily ever after. Maybe we would even forget that we once were individuals. We'd be like those aliens who assimilated everyone. Resistance is futile.»

«Is it, Jaime? Should we just give in and let it be what it will be?»

The two gave in to one more kiss in the park.

Mmm.

Jaime and David

"Dad, does Mom still talk to you when you ask her questions?" Jaime signed.

David was taken aback. Might know his son would have picked up on the silent conversations David had with his dead wife. Jaime had been the subject for most of fourteen years. *Did she answer? That was a good question.*

"I think it's a little more complicated than that. It gets harder and harder to actually remember her voice. I know you agree, but I'd give anything to have her back with us again." *Oh, Nola. It's true, you know. I still love you so much.*

"It's hard for me to remember, too," Jaime signed. In fact, he'd heard his mother's voice when he was a child, but they'd never really had a conversation. He just didn't have the frame of reference his father had.

"You were so small. I guess it's always been that I ask a question and my memory pulls together what I think she would say and I hear that in her voice. Only, I have more and more difficulty remembering her voice and it sounds more like me talking to myself all the time. I don't even know for sure if I'm recalling what I think she would say or if I'm just fantasizing what I'd want her to say. Does that make sense, son?"

Jaime nodded. It was almost what he and Keira had talked about. His father added another dimension to the discussion: What if they could no longer tell if the other was thinking something or if they were making it up out of what they wanted the other to think? Part of the excitement of those lovely moments as they kissed was seeing inside Keira, understanding her more, and identifying what she thought apart from what he thought.

He began to understand their fear better, though they'd put it aside long enough to have one more long delicious kiss at her door before he came home to make dinner. Simply put, he didn't want to *become* Keira. He treasured what she felt and what she thought. He didn't want to start wondering if what he *thought* she felt was only what he *wanted* her to feel.

It had been difficult for them to part after such an intense discussion and the overwhelming experience of kissing each other. Holding hands had seemed to open the world to them. Their senses had been multiplied when it came to hearing others and identifying who specifically they were listening to. They decided to experiment more with the phenomenon during their date on Saturday. They were going to the symphony.

Kissing had opened them to a deeper experience of each other. Jaime had called it being soulmates, though he wasn't completely sure what that meant. He'd actually felt a little physically bloated and Keira had explained that it happened to her every month and her period was about due. She felt his pleasure in simply having an erection grow as they kissed, even though he knew they wouldn't go any further. He just enjoyed getting hard.

Those were two things that had emerged during their kissing conversation. They also dictated how important it was for them to progress as slowly as they could manage in their relationship. What other couples feared was nothing compared to the enormity of losing themselves totally in the other person. Had it been Keira's deep subconscious that had sighed in the background when they kissed? It seemed so wistful.

They needed to explore the various aspects, learn to back off, and learn to share just portions of what they were feeling. The place they selected as a 'quiet minds' location was the symphony. Afterward, they would find a quiet place and practice kissing some more.

That would all come on Saturday.

14
PRACTICE MAKES PERFECT

Jaime

THURSDAY EVENING, JAIME finished his homework after dinner and sat in his room to make some notes on Emerson's prediction concept. He opened his composition book and happened to see his diagram of the proposed thought transfer computer. He hadn't thought about it the past week or two after he and Keira started dating. Emerson had mentioned it in class as they were working and called it a little tinfoil hat-ish. Jaime smiled at the term and nodded as he traced some of the paths in the concept. He jotted down the words 'skin contact' next to one of the boxes.

Everything he'd ever read or researched on the subject was an expose of people who claimed the ability to telecommunicate or had devised a way of doing it. They'd all proved to be frauds. Now, some of the most popular magic shows in talent competitions had some element of 'mind-reading' in them. Jaime thought they looked interesting and wondered how the magician was accomplishing the mentalist feat. He'd like to be in the audience sometime to hear what was really going through their minds.

He studied his diagram a minute longer and drew a secondary box below and to the right that simply held the word 'proof.' He could not even prove to a third party that he and Keira spoke telepathically. It would immediately be assumed they were intimate with each other and had worked out signals, like so many other acts had done.

It takes a minimum of three. I'm sure of it now. It's logical that three with the talent would have enough synergy to broadcast in a way that would demand attention. I just need to find them.

Jaime slammed his book shut and closed his mind to all input and broadcasting, hanging out his 'Do Not Disturb' sign and going silent. That had not been his thought!

He recognized that voice—that head taste—as if he was still the nine-year-old who had heard it in the grocery store. The man had said he was too young then and they weren't ready. It had frightened Jaime so much he'd hidden in a walk-in refrigerator in the grocery store until one of the staff had discovered him. The voice—that particular head taste—still frightened Jaime.

Had the man been broadcasting? Trying to get Jaime to expand his concept?

He turned off his computer and cell phone. For the first time in a long time, he retreated to his closet where the walls were still lined with aluminum foil. He drew into himself and began to shut down all his senses. He couldn't let the man find him. Whoever it was, he was as evil as the kidnapper they'd stopped on their first date.

Jaime and David

Jaime had managed to shut off all his senses, hiding in the closet, when his father found him.

"Jaime! Jaime, come back!" his father shouted as he shook his son.

David pulled him out of the closet and held him as he worked to make sure he was still breathing and his heart was still beating. When Jaime began to regain consciousness, his father was on the phone to 9-1-1.

"He seems to be waking up. He was completely unconscious and unresponsive. His heartbeat was faltering. I just went in to tell him goodnight and found him."

The operator connected David to the duty nurse.

"EMTs are on their way, sir. Estimated arrival is five minutes. Please stay on the line and keep me updated as to his progress. Do you see any signs of drugs in the vicinity? Needles? Packets? Pills?"

"No, there's nothing like that around. I don't think Jaime would ever touch anything like that. He's even more conservative than I am."

"Has anything like this happened before?" the nurse asked.

"No. Well, that's not right. It was just like this when he was born. Doctors never figured out what went wrong with his system then. He just shut down a few minutes after birth and was placed in an incubator, even though he was full term. Once his breathing and heartrate stabilized, he still didn't wake up for two days. I'm afraid that's what caused his autism."

"Your son is autistic?"

"Yes. Sorry, I should have mentioned that. It's the term we were given. He's never spoken. He hears fine, and he's fluent in sign language. He's smart and has never had problems with learning in school. If anything, he's a little faster than others in his class."

"The type of shutdown you are describing has been observed in autistic children who become over-stimulated or who are severely frightened. Was he engaged in any activity that might cause intense emotions?"

"I don't believe so. He sometimes plays video games, but there were none running. His phone and computer were shut down. He's awake now. Jaime, can you hear me?"

Jaime nodded his head and then signed, "I'm fine. Sorry, Dad."

"He says he's fine now," David said.

David got up off the sofa where he'd been sitting cradling his son to answer the door and let the EMTs in. The 9-1-1 nurse disconnected to talk to the EMTs while they examined Jaime. David interpreted his sign language for them. They tested his heartrate, blood pressure, blood oxygen level, and even ran a breathalyzer to determine if there was any intoxication at play. Everything tested normal.

"We can take him to the hospital for more tests," one of the techs suggested. "I honestly don't know what they'd find. The staff recommends that you visit your doctor and have a full battery of tests run. I'm sure he'd want to run an electroencephalogram—that's an EEG—and possibly follow up with an MRI to be sure no abnormalities have developed or gone undetected."

"Abnormalities?"

"I'm not suggesting any specific possibilities. Often MRIs are just a routine exam that verifies everything is normal. Rarely, an MRI will detect things like tumors, inflammation, blood flow, and obstructions to blood vessels. There are really too many possible things an MRI could detect or verify to list them all for you. You should read up on them before you talk to your doctor."

"Okay. Thank you," David said. "Jaime, do you think we need to go to the hospital now, or should we just call Doc Roberts in the morning?"

"I feel fine now, Dad," Jaime signed. "Let's leave it until tomorrow. I don't think anything will happen again tonight. It must have been the stress of working on my class project. I'm fine."

"Okay. Thank you for getting here so fast, guys," David said to the techs as they packed their gear and headed back to the ambulance. *I wish they'd been as fast when Nola needed them.*

Jaime and Keira

«WHAT HAPPENED? ARE you okay?» Keira demanded Friday morning as she grabbed his hand at school. The warm flood of assurance she received from him helped to calm her down, but she was still frightened.

«I had a kind of incident last night. We need to talk about it, but we don't have time at school. It's really important. I sort of shut everything down.»

«No kidding! I was kind of getting used to feeling you… you know… way in the background of my thoughts. But all of a sudden, you were just gone. It wasn't like 'Do Not Disturb.' It was more like 'Moved. No forwarding address.' You scared the fucking shit out of me! I must have sent you a dozen texts!»

«Oh, shit! I should turn my phone back on. When I started shutting down, I turned off my phone and computer, too. It was unreal. I've never been so scared. Dad called 9-1-1.»

«My God! Zip, we should cut school and go somewhere.»

«I don't want to do anything out of the ordinary. Dad's already making an appointment with my doctor to have an EEG and MRI run. I haven't had those since I was a lot younger.»

«Okay. But I love you. I didn't realize how much until you were just not there.»

«After school. We'll find someplace quiet and I'll share the whole thing with you. Share it, not just tell you. Um… We might have to kiss.»

«Sneaky. Of course we'll have to kiss. Call out to me anytime you are feeling like that again. Okay?»

«Okay. Geez. Brad Johnson's at it again with his imagining you as an anime girl. Why do they all have such huge boobs?» Jaime asked as they sat in English class.

«Shh. At least it's not a gross one yet. Shut him out!»

They managed to focus on Ms. Henderson as she led a discussion about why so many 21st century English language books were focused on revisiting the past instead of dealing with the present.

«WHERE ARE WE going?» Jaime asked as Keira led him onto an unfamiliar streetcar across town.

«My aunt's house,» Keira said. «I called and made arrangements at lunch. It's private. But we can't mess around there. I mean besides a little kissing. She didn't offer us a bed.»

«You had me convinced we should go slow the other day, but I'm really convinced we need to be cautious now. I want to kiss you. I want to do so much, sometimes my mind overflows with it. But I'm scared of other things besides losing myself if we go all the way now.»

«Last night?»

«Yes. You know, I love holding your hand. I bet most teens don't get any-where near the amount of pleasure from this that we do.»

Keira took the hint and the change of subject. They shared news about their day at school until they got off the streetcar a block from Aunt Rose's house.

As soon as they walked through the door, Jaime could feel the quiet in the house.

«What is it about this house?» he asked.

«I think it's the aluminum siding. She also had the whole house insulated with something that has metal fibers in it. I don't know what it was.»

She led him to the sofa. They dropped their backpacks and sat close, still holding hands.

«It works. Is she one of us?»

«She's a psychiatrist and never lets anything leak out of her mind. I think the absence of thought from her when I visit is an indication that she *is* one of us, but I've never heard anything from her and never felt her listening to confirm it. She just gave me a ton of helpful suggestions when I came to talk to her after I started hearing voices.»

«Is that what you thought was happening?»

«I didn't have any idea. Yes. I heard voices, but they were coming from everyone around me. Anyway, tell me about what happened last night.»

«Kiss,» Jaime said.

That sounded like a good idea to Keira. The two touched each other lip to lip and Jaime's world opened to his girlfriend. He shared what had happened the night before, but then went on about his fear of the voice he heard in his head and the extremes he went to in blocking the intruder's thoughts.

Jaime included his assessment that this was what had happened when he was a baby, as well. It made sense and now that he had been through it as an adult, he could see how to prevent it from happening again.

His sharing of the event was so complete that Keira felt the fear as well.

They went on to share more than the experience of the night before. The kiss deepened and became more passionate as the two embraced and let their love flow between them. They were becoming aroused and some explorations had already gone beyond what they intended when they finally pulled away from each other.

"Oh, wow!" Keira said aloud as she pressed her legs together. She left Jaime's hand on her breast. It felt so good and so natural. Jaime squeezed a little, pressing delightfully against her hard nipple, and slowly pulled his hand away. "Yeah. We aren't going to mess around like that, remember?" Keira said.

«I didn't mean to. I was only trying to share what happened.»

«Yeah, but we were both sharing more than that. I love you and you know I want to go all the way. We just need to kiss and practice more control until we're sure we won't get lost in more intimacy.»

«That's what scared me so much. I mean, not exactly. He suggested that what was needed for him to force communication mentally was like a quorum. I think he called it a synergy and he couldn't find three people he could put together. Thankfully, we've never tried to talk to anyone else while we were united that deeply. But he might use me to get to you! I couldn't bear that!»

«What were you thinking about exactly when you heard him?»

«I was flipping through the pages of my notebook to make notes for Emerson's prediction project. Last year she assisted me on my text-to-speech project. This year, I'm helping her on a pretty cool predictive algorithm. But anyway, I happened on the diagram I was working on when you first contacted me. I was chuckling because it really was what Emerson called 'tinfoil hat-ish.' I just drew a box I labeled 'proof' because none exists outside our personal experience.»

«So, it wasn't even your project specifically that he was interested in. He's actually interested in you.»

«That's terrifying.»

«It scares the shit out of me, too,» Keira said.

Her solution was to kiss again and share encouragement with each other. They managed to keep the floodgates closed this time, with only a little petting included. They just absorbed the physical sensations that coursed through their bodies. The kiss still left them breathless.

«We should… um… pull ourselves together… before we cross the line in your aunt's house. I should go fix Friday night dinner for Dad since I didn't make a plan with him to be out tonight. We can still go to the concert tomorrow and hold hands, can't we?»

«And experiment with isolating thoughts while we are,» Keira said. «Then we need to find a place where we can kiss some more. Maybe not quite as insulated as this so we stay more aware of our surroundings.»

«Agreed,» Jaime said. «Um… Would you like to come to my house for dinner after the concert? Maybe hang out and watch a movie afterward? I don't mean alone. My dad would be in the house.»

«Yeah. If we can still kiss a little.»

«Practice,» Jaime agreed. «We need more practice.»

Jaime and David

"WELL, YOU KNOW Doc Roberts. He's concerned and interested, but doesn't think it's serious," David said, enjoying both the company and the meatloaf Jaime had prepared. "You've got an appointment at his office for an EEG and talk on Friday next week. He'll decide then whether to refer you for an MRI. I'm glad the new insurance with this company has kicked in. We're well covered."

"I'll cooperate," Jaime signed. "I just don't think he'll find anything. Didn't they do a bunch of those tests a few years ago?"

"I suspect he'll compare the results to see if there are any changes, among other things. He says every year there are advances in the technology and in the understanding of the test results," David confirmed.

"People always think if it's science it's forever," Jaime signed as he squeaked a laugh. "They forget: That's religion. Science is constantly changing as new information emerges."

"And you learned that in computer science?"

"Freshman biology."

"You really worried me last night, son. I want science to tell me something that helps, that's all."

"Uh… D-A-D," Jaime fingerspelled the word to get his father's complete attention.

"What is it, son? Is there a problem?"

"No. Not exactly. I was wondering… You see, the concert Keira and I are going to tomorrow is in the afternoon. Would it be okay if I invited her to dinner after? Here, I mean? I'll cook and we can just hang out and watch TV or something for a while before she goes home."

"Hang out? Oh, wow!" *Now what, Nola?* "This isn't one of those 'Netflix and chill' things I hear about, is it?"

"Dad! Keira and I have only been going together for a couple of weeks. We aren't like having sex or anything. I mean, I'd like to kiss her before we take her home, you know."

"Ah! Before *we* take her home. You expect me to be around to help?"

"Yeah. Why wouldn't you be?" Jaime signed the right words, even though he was pretending to an innocence he no longer had. One day he would definitely bring Keira home when his dad was not there. Just not now.

"Okay. Yeah. That would be fine if it's okay with her parents. I mean… Jesus, son! You're both eighteen. If you'd been like all the other teens we've ever known and had been dating around since you were fifteen or sixteen, I wouldn't even be concerned at this point. It's just that all this is as new to me as it is to you. Please don't blame me for not getting it right away." *Oh, Nola, please don't let me screw things up with our son. How do I let go?*

Jaime grinned at his dad and instead of answering, he just hugged him. He thought David had an opinion of teens that was a lot more sexually active than was real. Compared to the overall population at his school, Jaime only knew of a handful of teens who even had regular or frequent dating experience—with or without sex.

He went to his room to text Keira.

Trayce

Across town, Trayce was settling into her bed with her laptop. Her mother was already asleep in front of the television. Sometime in the middle of the night she'd wake up and switch it off and go to bed. Or she'd wake up, change channels, pour herself another drink, and go back to sleep in her chair. It was depressing to think of.

Trayce had turned in her short story to Ms. Dorn and didn't know whether she should be proud that she completed the assignment or scared that it wasn't any good. Once she started writing, the words just tumbled out. The vision she'd had of the little girl and her mother going to a movie while the mother figured out how to tell her daughter that Daddy was never coming home joined with Trayce's own experience of waiting for the police to arrive and standing with her mother going into shock as they told her about her father's death. Trayce remembered so clearly the feelings of that day, she could almost tell what her mother was thinking.

With her fan fic, Trayce hadn't spent a lot of time truly editing her stories. Oh, she proofread them and made sure the punctuation was correct, but she hadn't really read to see the quality of the writing itself. Was it honest? Was it said the best way she could say it? She kind of wished there was someone she could have shared the story with just to get feedback, but it really didn't fit into the conversations she had with her writing group.

Now with the story finished and turned in, there was nothing more she could do about it. She thought she might work on another fan fic, but earlier in the week, she'd had an idea that just flitted through her mind while she was editing. She'd jotted down a couple of notes so she wouldn't forget it, but now that the other story was finished, she could focus on that idea.

The old man in her idea had been so funny! He was obsessed with butts and was likely to make a fart joke at any moment. And his companions were strippers! Angus, Kate, and Thursday. They were a pretty lighthearted trio, but there was an underlying danger in them. He carried a dragon-headed cane that concealed a sword. The three were secret crime-fighters like Marvel superheroes. Except they were just an old retired detective and a couple of strippers.

Trayce began plotting a mystery for them to solve. More than a mystery. For Angus to get involved, it had to be a murder. And beneath their sexy personae, those strippers were badass. Maybe one of them got in trouble and the other two had to go to the rescue. They had to get there before she became the next victim.

Yes. She'd never written a murder mystery before, but the characters in her mind just demanded her attention.

Trayce started making notes and plotting her story.

15
THE LISTENERS

Jaime and Keira

«REMEMBER: WE NEED to keep ourselves shielded. We're just listening,» Keira said.

«Listen and identify. We aren't trying to stop kidnappers,» Jaime grinned.

«Please let there not be any!»

They found their seats in the auditorium. They'd started holding hands as soon as Jaime arrived at Keira's house and they headed for the streetcar. They'd been using the time to fine tune their filters. Or that's what they told each other. Both were just happy to be holding hands. There were a lot of mentally whispered endearments, and an occasional memory of their kisses. They tried to keep the latter to a minimum because both preferred to have the physical contact of the kiss to the mere memory.

After finding their seats, they settled in and observed the audience around them.

«Three rows down and over about halfway to the right,» Jaime pointed out. «She's not happy to be here. Usually it's men who aren't as glad to go to the symphony as the women they bring.»

«But look. She's not with a date. Not exactly. She's here with her little girl who she promised to take to the symphony. She doesn't mind being here. It's just an interruption to what she wanted to do today.»

«The little girl is excited, though. She wants to hear the big drums,» Jaime said.

«Hmm. Brahms might not be the best composer for timpani. The other two pieces are concerti for chamber orchestra. Not a lot of percussion in that, I don't suppose.»

«Here's the conductor. He really gets a charge out of the applause. Feels he deserves it.»

«It's really just one of the reasons he loves his job, though. He's already *hearing* the music.»

The audience settled after the applause and then the featured cellist arrived on stage to a fresh round of applause. He shook hands with the conductor. The chamber orchestra checked their tuning and all eyes turned to the conductor. The music began.

For a few minutes, Jaime and Keira were swept away by the pleasure and emotion experienced by the audience, and the sheer joy with which the musicians played.

«It's like they are all connected to the conductor. Even the soloist is watching for the conductor's cue. He does it all with the tip of his baton and they all understand exactly what he wants!» Keira said.

«Look at how many people are following the baton, too,» Jaime answered. «It's one of the reasons I love coming to concerts. Everyone is of one mind.»

«It's magical!»

The first concerto finished with no further deliberate thoughts passing between the two. They were happy—content to be among the listeners in the auditorium. And happy to be touching each other, physically and mentally.

During the second concerto, they began to reach out to touch those around them. Their first attempt was almost too much, as the entire audience flooded their senses. They clamped down, gripping each other's hand more tightly. They quickly looked around to see if they had disturbed anyone else, but there was no sign of anything but the enjoyment of the music.

«Too much, too fast,» Keira said.

«Let's see if we can limit the range. Maybe ten feet around us.»

«I'm not sure how to do that. You lead.»

Jaime closed his eyes and let the music wash over him. Then he began to slowly open himself to those around him. Keira closed her eyes and followed in her mind.

The man next to Jaime was nodding at the edge of sleep and his wife kept nudging him so he wouldn't snore. It wasn't that he didn't enjoy the music, but it relaxed him so that he wanted to sleep. Poor guy.

Behind them, a woman was envisioning her upcoming wedding to the tune that was being played. Of course, she didn't want that exact music at her wedding. She wanted something a little more upbeat and music that didn't demand the wedding party pay attention to it instead of her. Keira giggled a little in her mind.

They catalogued all the people within five seats of them, side-to-side and front-to-back. When they were finished, they were exhausted, having read upwards of a hundred people in the packed orchestra hall. They shut down their contact and let the music take them where it would, like most of those they'd peeked in on.

After the second concerto, there was an intermission as the stage was reset for the full orchestra. Jaime and Keira stayed in their seats, observing the people around them as some stood to stretch and others quickly made their way to the lobby bar or restrooms.

«People try to be so sophisticated at a concert,» Jaime said.

«With varying degrees of success.»

«The guy next to me really loves the concert. He can't help it that the music always puts him to sleep.»

«It might be the best rest he ever gets. What about the man in the center front who is so preoccupied with his business that he can't rest at all?» Keira asked.

«He's really stressed out. He wants to talk business with the man accompanying him with their wives, but knows he has to endure the entire concert before he can hope to get him alone. Do you really think his business will fold if he doesn't get the guy's support?»

«I don't think he'll need to worry about it for long. The only thing on the other guy's mind is how much he'll have to pay to get a piece of the action.»

«He'll be relieved.»

«I thought we'd hear a lot more um… fantasy stuff… sex talk,» Keira ventured.

«It's a different kind of crowd than the movie,» Jaime surmised. «Older. More attentive to the music than to each other. The music just supplies all the emotion they need while they are in the auditorium.»

«Well, here comes the orchestra. People are coming back to their seats. Do they tune like this every time?»

«Maybe it's partly just to loosen their fingers while they call the audience back to their seats. The noise from the instruments reminds me of the noise of the audience, now there's no music.»

The two extended their consciousness to others in the audience as they filled the auditorium again. With no music to focus their thoughts, it was far more of a cacophony in their heads, but the two soon filtered out certain individuals.

«When the music stops, the minds return to the chaos of daily life,» Jaime said.

«Did you catch that?» Keira asked excitedly. «There's someone, on the far left back. She's wishing the music would start so all the noise in her head would stop. She's interested in listening in on one person who is sitting three rows ahead of her.»

«I hear her. She wants everyone else to be quiet, but doesn't have any filters on what she broadcasts herself. Like I was.»

«The man she's interested in isn't a love interest. He's more of a competitor in business.»

«He uses the concert as a place to think out his strategy and… an invention that he's anticipating patenting.»

«She's going to tell someone all about it. Oh my! She's a corporate spy! She targets certain people to read their minds and then sells the plans to competitors.»

The conductor returned to the stage to applause and the two teens tried to focus their attention on the first bars of Brahms' Symphony Number 2. It didn't take long for the audience to settle and let the music wash away all other thoughts. As the music played, those who had other things on their minds— obsessions—came into clearer focus for Keira and Jaime.

«She'd be a terrible international spy,» Jaime said. «Everything she hears from his mind, she leaks out of hers. She has no concept of other people like her. Should we tell her?»

«I don't think she believes she's actually reading his mind. She thinks she's just really good at reading people's body language and developing stories about what they are planning. She found out a long time ago that she could sell that information, so she calls herself a professional people watcher.»

About six minutes into the first movement, the timpani rumbled and the little girl with her mother squealed in delight. It was mostly internal, but her mother quickly hushed her. She was bouncing in her seat. Jaime and Keira filtered out the surrounding mental interference and focused on the orchestra. There was another good timpani part before the end of the first movement and they tuned in on the little girl just to share her joy in the big drums.

«The blonde with the golden flute and the sparkly black dress is in love with the conductor,» Jaime suggested. They both focused on her as the second movement started.

«She has all the music memorized and automatically turns the page of her score, but she never takes her eyes off the conductor,» Keira added.

«Is it love like we have?» Jaime asked. «Or is it some connection the music makes between them? It excites her.»

«And him, but he's got so many bits to attend to. He can't be so single-minded in his attention as she is.»

«Maybe she just loves the music and he is the embodiment of it.»

«It's really hard to read the musicians. The music controls them and fills their minds. We can feel her adoration, but we can't really hear any words,» Keira said.

«Would you be quiet? I just want to listen to the music.»

Jaime and Keira instantly clamped down on all their senses, blocking out the thoughts of anyone else in the auditorium and shielding their thoughts against being read. The mental voice had come from the first row of the balcony and was gone as quickly as it had interjected itself.

Jaime could feel Keira shaking and infused their touch with all his calming energy. Discovering one person in the auditorium who was listening to the thoughts of another had been an exciting moment. But being reprimanded by another listener for making such a psychic racket had shocked them nearly as much as the voice Jaime had heard Thursday night had shocked him.

There was nothing malevolent about this new voice, though. He was irritated, but he might not have even recognized they were communicating with each other. In their intense discussion of the flutist's love for the conductor, they had allowed their thoughts to leak out. They were supposed to be practicing not letting that happen.

In the third movement, they got their fill of the flutist's solos and the little girl got all the timpani she could desire. It was an uplifting and dynamic finale.

They joined in the applause of the audience and realized when their hands left each other, the intensity of the audience input was muted. The drop in mental volume was almost like muting the television during advertisements.

They linked arms and tried not to speak to each other until they were well away from the concert hall.

«Do you think he identified who we are?» Keira asked when they were on the streetcar headed to Jaime's house.

The streetcar itself cut down on the amount of mental noise the two could hear and they immediately rejoined their hands. There were only a dozen other people in the car and the metal sides and movement served as an effective barrier from outside.

«I don't think so. He wasn't interested. He just heard a lot of mental noise and wanted it to go away. There was a note of frustration in his head taste. Like he often heard voices and the music was an escape from it. We were just voices in his head who interrupted his peace and quiet. When he told us to shut up, we did. That might have been encouraging to him.»

«How so?»

«He heard the voices in his head and was able to tell them to be quiet. And they were. I bet that doesn't often happen.»

«So, during the afternoon concert, we discovered two other people who could hear people's thoughts. Out of how many people there?»

«The concert hall holds around 2,800. I'd say it was about three-quarters full.»

«That's four head talkers in about 2,100. One for every five hundred and change. If that holds true for the general population, we're a lot more common than I ever imagined,» Keira said.

«I wouldn't extrapolate it that far. We heard two others, neither of whom really had a concept that they were literally listening to other people. Our school is about 2,800 and you are the only other head talker I've encountered there.»

«True. It's hard to do a real survey, though. We could try at lunch, but otherwise people are in fairly well insulated classrooms. We only share one class, and we don't hold hands,» Keira said.

«It calls for more experimentation,» Jaime said. «We'll have to go out on dates every weekend. Maybe twice. Like, I could come to see you tomorrow.»

The image of Jaime and Keira kissing was so plain that both of them started laughing.

«Let's find out how that next part goes this evening. You're sure your dad won't, like, hang around with us all the time? Will we even get to kiss?»

«I'm sure. We'll have dinner together and then go watch TV or play a game. He won't join us. He figures if we aren't in my bedroom, we aren't going to go too far.»

«My parents have been talking to me, you know? They want to be sure I can take care of myself, but they recognize I'm eighteen years old. They even said I don't really have a curfew. They were just trying to remind me that the trains stop running at 11:30 and didn't want me to get stranded somewhere. I'd guess what I hear from them is a lot like you hear from your father.»

«Well, you'll find out firsthand when we get inside the house,» Jaime said. «Don't forget to sign. We'll have to stop holding hands for a while.»

«I guess so. I need to cook!»

Jaime's dad tried not to be intrusive while still being sociable. He asked about the concert and they felt safe telling him about the little girl who squealed when the timpani played and the guy next to Jaime who kept falling asleep, actually snoring once.

Keira helped Jaime in the kitchen. He fixed rather simple but tasty stuffed bell peppers and she made a salad. David busied himself cleaning up the leaves that had fallen in the yard.

«Your dad's sweet,» Keira said.

«For the past fourteen years, we're all each other has had. I worry about him, especially since I've met you. I don't want him to be lonely.»

«Didn't you pick up about Olivia?» Keira asked.

«What?»

«There's a woman who works with him named Olivia and he's thinking of asking her out. He thinks she's interested, but he's worried about any sign of harassment. You know how offices are these days.»

«I try not to eavesdrop on Dad too much,» Jaime sighed. «After I figured out that he just didn't hear my inside voice, I realized he needed privacy, too. I listen for clues when we're talking, but even then, I'm careful not to answer or comment on what he's thinking.»

«Well, he might ask you how you'd feel about him dating.»

«I'd never object to him finding any of the joy I have with you.»

Keira leaned toward Jaime and gave him a quick electric kiss, jumping back almost instantly.

«I know we weren't prepared for that, but I couldn't help kissing you when you said we had joy.»

«Well, that's part of our experimenting. We need to learn to kiss without being overwhelmed. Try again?»

Jaime turned toward Keira and the two met in a sweet and gentle kiss. It still had the potential to turn explosive, but they managed to restrain their exuberance until they parted.

«Yeah. I really liked that,» Jaime said.

«Really really liked that,» Keira agreed.

"THAT WAS A good dinner, kids. I'll clean up the dishes and the kitchen. You go ahead to the family room," David said. "I have some correspondence and review of specs to do for our new project. I'll be in my office if you need me."

"Thanks, Dad," Jaime signed. "Watch a movie with us?"

"You don't need me to chaperone you. Don't get too carried away. Let's plan on running Keira home about 11:30. Earlier if you want, Keira, but I'd like to get to bed before midnight."

"Thank you, Mr. Stackhouse. We just… you know… want to spend some time together."

"I understand. I think you should start getting used to calling me David."

Jaime and Keira went to the family room and David cleaned up the kitchen.

TEMPTING AS IT was, they didn't want to spend the next four hours just making out. Neither was sure they could restrain themselves for so long. They decided to forgo the television and put on music. Then Jaime got out a game of chance.

«I don't play games of skill and strategy,» he said. «I could always tell what Dad was going to do next, so it wasn't fun. I can't control the dice, so it makes a game fair. What you decide to do on a given throw doesn't affect what I should do.»

«I had the same problem. I suddenly started winning games of chess at school and realized I needed to back off fast or someone would make a big deal out of it. I started losing them on purpose.»

«Here's a score sheet. You can roll first.»

«New rule,» Keira said. «Five of a kind and the roller gets a kiss. Just a little one, okay?»

«That really ups the stakes!»

Keira did not get a five of a kind on her first turn. Nor did Jaime. In fact, they were in their second game before Jaime managed the roll.

«Now, relax and think of what you want to share with me,» Keira instructed. «I have something to share with you.»

They moved together and touched lips before pulling back.

«I love you, too,» Keira said.

«You really like to dance? I don't think I know how. I've never danced with a girl.»

«Then it's something I can teach you when we finish playing this game.»

«Does it have bonuses, like kisses?»

«We'll see.»

The game ended with one more quick kiss and then they moved to dancing. Keira selected music that had a good beat, but didn't require touching or coordinating their steps. It was quickly obvious that Jaime didn't know what he was doing. Keira changed the music to a slow tempo piece and invited Jaime into her arms for a close dance.

This was much different. They held hands with one hand and wrapped the other around their partner. In this position, they moved close together and it was easy for Keira to give Jaime instructions and for him to follow her lead instantly.

The next song was slower and they moved closer together until their bodies were pressed tight and their cheeks touched. With this amount of contact, they began sharing more and more of themselves with each other. The basement television room seemed to shield them from any outside mental activity.

«Why would you ever wear a dress if it doesn't have pockets?» Jaime asked.

«My point exactly! You can't even carry a cell phone without occupying at least one hand. Even if it has pockets, they are usually sewn shut. A woman is helpless to defend herself. And believe me, it's not comfortable to stuff a phone in your bra!»

«I don't know what I'd do without pockets. I wouldn't know what to do with my hands—if I wasn't holding yours.»

«You know Patrice Carlisle, right?»

«Oh, yeah. She's the one who told Debbie Burke to build up a fantasy all day.»

«Well, she wasn't fantasizing Wednesday when she was attacked after school.»

«I don't have any classes with her and have been shutting Debbie out of my mind in psychology. What happened?»

«She was walking home from school alone because the girl she usually walks with was absent that day. A guy grabbed her arm and tried to drag her into the bushes. She had her phone in her hand and hit him with it, right across the face. Then she took off running and the guy gave up because he was bleeding.»

«Dang! She was lucky.»

«DO NOT go looking for him! I saw that flash in your mind. The police caught him because when she ran, she dropped her phone and the dummy picked it up and tried to make calls on it. Police tracked the call and picked him up, and the phone with the shattered screen with him.»

«Good. I'm glad, but you know if I knew about something like that and didn't do something… I don't know what I'd do.»

«Kiss me and I'll show you.»

The kiss was not a quick peck like the ones they'd had before. They stopped moving to the music as they accepted each other fully in a kiss that lingered and deepened.

«It would be like this when we're making love,» Keira whispered.

«Only no clothes between us.»

«I can imagine that, but don't start removing them right now. We were so close to each other with a hand held and our cheeks rubbing together. Just imagining more skin touching makes my whole body tingle.»

«I can feel it. When I… When I'm alone, those parts of me never feel that way. My chest and my stomach. I mean…» Jaime whispered in his mind.

«I can feel that. I didn't know how much guys… or you, at least… like to be hard. I think if my clit was this hard all the time it would drive me insane.»

«It does a little. We have parts that correspond to each other, but they feel completely different. I knew lips had a lot of nerve endings, but I never thought about how many the tongue has.»

Keira moved her hips against Jaime's cock and felt the intensity through both their bodies.

«We need to take a break for a while. We can kiss again when we settle down a little,» Keira said.

«Yeah. I'm afraid I might make a mess in my pants, just holding and kissing you.»

Wow! came a whisper in the backs of their minds.

16
SCANNING

Jaime and Keira

ON SUNDAY, THEY walked in the park and practiced quick reads on people. And of course, they kissed occasionally, just to open their senses more.

"Behave yourselves decently! There are children in the park. Find someplace private!" a woman barked at them as she walked past them. She had a dog on a leash and ignored the pile of poop it left as she was lecturing them.

«None of the children are hers,» Keira said. «She thinks if we'd had a proper upbringing, we wouldn't be making a spectacle of ourselves.»

«She's a very unhappy person because the world doesn't behave according to her idea of the way it should. We're just an example of the degeneration of the species.»

«I think we're an example of the ascent and improvement of the species,» Keira laughed. «Though maybe at one time, the entire human race could communicate telepathically and we are a step in the de-evolutionary process.»

«It makes my head hurt to try to parse that thought,» Jaime said.

«Funny. I don't feel it hurting at all.»

«Look! It's the old man, Angus. He's picking raspberry leaves for his rabbits.»

«Let's talk to him.»

They walked up near the old guy, picking the few green leaves that were left and putting them in a plastic box.

144

"Hello, Mr. Angus," Keira said aloud. "How are you today?"

"What? Who are you?" he growled.

"Um… We kind of met a weak ago. Maybe it was just in our heads."

«Oh, you're the ones who were talking so loud,» Angus said in his head.

«Yes,» Jaime answered. «Sorry if we disturbed your rehearsal.»

«Oh, the girls are in a film-writing class and I agreed to help them out by reading one of the parts. It was just a scene we did for their class a few days ago.»

«That's interesting,» Keira said. «Excuse us for asking, but do you know if there are many people around like us? We encountered a couple at a concert and didn't think we knew anyone else.»

«Hmm. I wouldn't say many. Meeting two at a concert? That's pretty high. But three of us in a scarcely inhabited park is just as odd. I don't go looking for them.»

«Thank you. I hope your rabbits are well,» Jaime said.

"You two have a good day. I'll not be around for a while. I've got a new case and I'm just collecting food for my friends before I have to leave for a few days."

"Be careful out there," Keira said. They smiled and left each other. Jaime and Keira walked back to her home.

«Keira, I want to do this every day. I don't mean just kissing, but talking to you and holding your hand. We can do other stuff, too, but probably not every day. I can live with that.»

«According to my voyeuristic survey of members of our class, I'd say about half *have had* sex, but something less than a third have had sex in the past three months. We should check that as we surf the school for head talkers tomorrow.»

«We're both going to do that?»

«When I suggested it, you jumped right in with a full intent to participate,» she said.

«There's a downside of having our thoughts so easily read by each other. We know when one of us is bullshitting.»

«And don't you forget it!» Keira laughed. They paused at her front door and gently kissed. «Seriously, though, we need to allow each other privacy when we want it. I don't want you to think you're just an open book and we don't have to actually converse about anything.»

«You're right. I love you and I want to share my life with you, but sometimes random thoughts are embarrassing and I don't want them automatically broadcast to you.»

«I agree. I'll see you in the morning, Jaime. Let's see if our investigation reveals anything.»

Trayce

"Trayce, this is really good," Ms. Dorn said on Monday in a school across town. "I'm honestly impressed. The sensitivity and understanding you wrote into this mother and daughter relationship was heartfelt. And the tragedy so sad. You see? You didn't need to camp in someone else's yard at all."

"Thank you, ma'am." Trayce was pleased with the praise and thought her story was, in fact, good. But it had really hurt to write it. The story of the little girl losing her father was too near to Trayce's experience. The mother was written as she *wished* her mother had been. The mother in the story was heartbroken, but her first concern was her little girl and how to make the transition easier for her.

Trayce's mother had held it together for only as long as it took to bury her husband. Even the night after the funeral, Trayce had seen her staring vacantly at the TV with a drink in her hand. She wondered if her mother had always had a drinking problem kept in check by her father, or if the blow had been so crippling to her that she could just no longer function.

Trayce saw a counselor, but the counselor had seemed bored by the story of losing her father. The counselor felt Trayce was a teenager now and should be able to deal with tragedy. When Trayce quit seeing the counselor, her mother quit going to counseling as well. Trayce lost herself in writing again. Her mother lost herself in booze.

Trayce had two ideas for new stories. The first featured an old man who fancied himself a detective. His imagination was filled with dangerous adventures while his reality was focused on a couple of strippers who played along with him. He used a cane and imagined it was a sword. In his world he could simply stab a villain, even if the villain was shooting at him. She'd begun making notes about what kind of mystery she might create for him to solve.

The old man was almost a comic character with a number of butt jokes and fart jokes, but he was also a sweet and sympathetic man who had a hard life and had no one else in it but the people he met in the clubs. She wanted to write him with the same empathy and sensitivity she had used for the little girl, but wasn't sure how to proceed.

Into this, another scene had inserted itself. It had begun to filter into her consciousness over the weekend when an imagined kiss had moved her so much, she'd involuntarily whispered 'Wow!' The premise for the story was a pretty simple high school romance. Except it was really sexy. So far, all she'd managed to jot down were notes about how good holding hands and kissing felt. She'd been so caught up in the fantasy that she'd laid in bed playing with herself for over an hour Saturday night. She could just feel their lips as they pressed together, the instant tingling of her privates as their tongues touched and the thrill when he caressed her breast.

I need a boyfriend, Trayce thought. That would surely cure her of the romance of having a boy touch her. She'd be fighting him off all the time.

She'd dated a few times. The boys were disgusting things who just wanted sex. At least that was her take on them. They wanted a payback for every nice thing they did. They all had a goal, it seemed, and her legs were the goalposts. They just needed to get their balls between them and score.

Maybe she was gay. She liked girls, but had a hard time imagining putting her face… *there*. Now that she was eighteen, she thought she'd just walk into Lovers Package and buy a couple of toys. She'd glanced in the window once or twice and it didn't seem like there were many men around. The clerks were women. Maybe they could give her some advice.

In the meantime, she supposed she'd try to work on the old man story. She needed to imagine what it felt like to be old. How old was he? Forty? No, she thought he was *really* old, like maybe sixty. If he was only sixty, though, wouldn't he have a job? Maybe he was ancient—like seventy-five. Did men that old still go to strip clubs? She didn't think men that old even cared about women or sex. Why would he be at a club like that?

Trayce puzzled over her problem all day.

Jaime and Keira

Keira and Jaime met before school to put a strategy in place for surveying how many people might have the 'gift' of hearing other's thoughts, and how many people regularly had sex.

«So, like we did in the park, we just sort of skim the people we meet to see if they are aware of other people's thoughts,» Keira said.

«Do you think we should try to communicate with anyone?»

«Only if you suspect they are actively receiving. And do it some really subtle way.»

«Like just make a suggestion that they look up?» Jaime asked.

«That might work. I have to work out the probabilities in my statistics class. We'd better get to lit and start checking.»

They headed to their first period class and attempted to survey the people in it, but the class was interesting and engaging. No one was actively broadcasting or apparently listening mentally.

They split up, promising to meet up again at noon.

Jaime thought he had a hit in his Design Technology class when he spotted a classmate looking up when he suggested it. In reading the kid's thoughts, though, it turned out that he was a little OCD and there was a ceiling tile that was slightly crooked. It drove the kid crazy and he couldn't take his eyes off the misplaced tile when he was in that classroom. He was not absorbing a lot from the instructor, but he did have an interesting project plan he was drawing up for the class.

At lunch, the couple was flooded by images and information from the students in the busy room. It was impossible to break in on anyone's thoughts in the room with a subliminal command.

By Thursday, Jaime and Keira had amassed a lot of data on how many in their class of 700 had sex at some time in their past, how many had sex in the past three months, and surprisingly, how many had sex over the past weekend. But neither had discovered a person who could communicate mentally like they could.

Looking into the lives of their classmates also resulted in a few images that were hard to shake. Some of those they shared with each other and enjoyed the result.

«Josie and Brent had sex six times last weekend!» Jaime said. «And all they could think about was when and where they can do it during the week before they repeat the whole adventure next weekend.»

«I think they win for most sexually active couple,» Keira agreed. «Even when you see them in the hall, they're hanging on each other. I have to think they are almost psychically linked, like we are.»

«I don't think so. But his images of her and the feelings he had when they were making love were… inspiring. And she was just as into it as he was. Neither of them wants anyone else, but they want each other all the time.»

«Did you…?»

«Yes. I couldn't help it. The experience of the two of them combined was compelling.»

«So did I. Compelling is a good word for it. I nearly had to go stroke myself in the restroom between classes after I read them!»

«I did manage to get home. And I had no live connection to them while I relived some of their memories. It was still pretty breathtaking.»

«Do you think I'll love having you in me as much as she loves having him in her?»

«I hope so. But she was on the verge of coming every time they touched. That might be distracting!»

«So, how many did we find who had sex over the past weekend?»

Jaime opened his notebook where he had inscribed a coded list of incidents they observed and the count of those who had ever had sex, compared to those who had recent sex.

«Of the people who had sex over the weekend, ten were in couples, like Brent and Josie, and it wasn't the first time they'd made it. Of the other seven, six were in relationships with people I never saw or surveyed. Only one of them had sex for the first time with their partner—not the first time ever.»

«And the seventh person?»

«He went out of town to a party at a college he's thinking of attending. He had sex with a girl he'd never met before and didn't know her name.»

«He couldn't remember who he slept with?»

«It was more like he never did find out. He didn't even have a clear image of her face in his mind; just of the two of them rutting on a sofa and then losing track of each other.»

«That blows my mind,» Keira said. «Could you ever do that?»

«I don't think so. I know I couldn't with you. If I didn't know you, I think I'd still have a really good picture in my mind of any girl I made love to.»

«Yeah. Like Josie,» Keira chuckled as the image of the intense lovers filled both their minds. «That's a hard image to shake. I mean, he saw her from absolutely every angle. I think they're pretty committed to each other.»

«So, did you find any trace of anyone who could head talk?» Jaime asked.

«No. I even checked out your friend Emerson. I wasn't spying exactly, but I wanted to make sure she wasn't just hiding from you. Negative.»

«I agree. I dropped in on her thoughts in class, just to make sure. She was not among those who had sex this weekend, but had in the past three months. She just got back from Paris in mid-August.»

«And it's mid-November.»

«Which reminds me: I have a doctor's appointment Friday. I'm getting a brain scan. Think I have one?»

«Silly. I wonder if it will show anything abnormal.»

«I doubt it, but I'll know. I can read Doc Roberts pretty well. He's run this test on me before.»

«Saturday you can fill me in. It's my turn to host you after the play.»

«You're inviting me to your house?»

«Yes. And my parents will be gone this weekend. That doesn't mean we're going all the way, but I think it means we'll have an opportunity for a little more exploration. Jaime, I feel almost as horny for you as Josie and Brent feel for each other.»

«I'm trying not to let that control me,» Jaime said. «I still think we need to go slow and easy for a while.»

«We'll make it slow. I'm not sure it will be easy.»

Jaime and Doc Roberts

FRIDAY WAS A long day in the clinic for Jaime. David accompanied him and interpreted for the technician conducting the test when Jaime needed to communicate. He'd been told that a sign language interpreter would be provided, but Jaime's quick scan of the nurse told him he'd encountered this interpreter before and did not trust her to interpret to him or for him.

David agreed when Jaime explained he'd seen the name on the nurse's clipboard. David would only be needed during the time when Jaime could not have his computer at hand. The tech was afraid the extra computer in the room might somehow alter the test results.

In addition to the EEG, there had been cognition tests that Jaime had to respond to. These were pretty elementary as far as Jaime was concerned. They were used mostly to detect learning disabilities, ADHD, and similar problems. In Jaime's case they tried to identify any errors in communication signals between the brain and the mouth. As had always been the case, since Jaime did not speak at all, the tests proved inconclusive.

"WELL, JAIME. I don't see any abnormality in your EEG at all," Doc Roberts said.

"I didn't feel anything," Jaime responded, using his computer text-to-speech engine.

"That is a very clever device. And you say you invented it?"

"Invented is too strong a word. Text-to-speech is a known technology. I programmed this engine to give myself a unique voice."

"I have to say that when I hear it, I can well imagine it is your actual voice. Want to try replicating it aloud?" Doc asked.

"I've tried. Sorry."

"Okay. So here are the results of the video electroencephalogram. I could just read the graphs, but I admit to a weakness for color pictures. The pictures reveal nothing that would be considered an abnormality. A few of your brainwaves are slightly higher than the norm, but they are still within the acceptable range. These would be considered pretty normal for a mind as creative as yours. Your intelligence is high, your school output is excellent, and your scientific inquiries are great. Those items would all point to the variance we see here,"

Doc said. *Either that or you're a mind reader. Wouldn't surprise me, but if you are, keep it to yourself.*

Jaime carefully schooled himself to ignore the thought, but quickly noted what part of the videography triggered it. He would need to study this more closely in order to determine if it was, indeed, a description of his talent. In order to do that discreetly, he would need access to the equipment himself and he couldn't see a likely path to getting that access unless he studied to become a tech himself.

That was an interesting thought. He hadn't really decided a course of study for college, but had always assumed it would have something to do with computers.

"What do you recommend?" Jaime asked through the TTS.

"Well, if I were set on getting as much of your insurance money as I can, I'd recommend we do an MRI, an MEG, a PET scan, an ambulatory EEG, and a sleep study. Frankly, unless you want to become a lab rat, I don't see the sense in any of them." *And I hope you don't really want to be a lab rat. There are research foundations out there that would jump all over the opportunity to hook you up to scanners 24/7.*

Doc Roberts' internal monologue was so targeted to Jaime that he wondered if the man was a head talker himself. Jaime carefully kept his thoughts shielded.

"The EEG technology hasn't changed much in a hundred years other than to add the video tomography to it. But it hasn't changed much because it's been dependable. MRI detection of problems undetected by EEG is only about ten percent. That could be a significant number for a patient who was experiencing an unexplained pain or had a high cancer risk, but it isn't high enough to merit automatically ordering one just because the EEG is normal."

"Well, I don't think there's any reason to order more tests. I was just really stressed out that night, working on a school project. You gave me some good exercises to relieve stress during my checkup last year. I should have been doing them more regularly," Jaime typed.

"Yes, you should. Can I share your results and our conversation with your father?"

"Sure. I just wanted to see what it was like to act like an adult managing my own medical care."

"Talk about it with him. He's always been concerned about you. He wants what's best for you." *He's always wanted what's best. What a burden to have shouldered when his wife died. He's done well, though. Jaime is a fine young man.*

17
VOYEUR

Jaime and Keira

"**W**AS IT TERRIBLE?**"** Keira asked aloud when she picked up Jaime on Saturday. With her parents away for the weekend, she had use of the car. Since the theatre was on the south side in Lake Oswego, she was happy to drive.

«Not too bad. The video electroencephalograph was interesting. There are places that could be identified as possibly contributing to the ability to hear others, but one would need access to the equipment and a huge sample of people, including known head talkers, to verify that.»

"Are you going to pursue it?"

«No. I'm trying to block it from my mind. Why are you out-loud talking instead of in my head?»

"I'm driving. I'm afraid if I got inside your head I'd lose my concentration on the road. Why did you pick a play so far away?"

«I wanted us to be someplace where we weren't near our usual environment. No interference from what we expect. And it's an interesting play.»

"So, tell me what it's all about."

«*R.U.R., or Rossum's Universal Robots*, was written by Karel Čapek in 1920. Much like Isaac Asimov's *I, Robot*, it tells of a time when intelligent robots plot to take over the world from humanity. Unlike Asimov, Čapek did not project the three laws of the positronic brain that would protect humans. It's particularly interesting today because of the advances in artificial

154

intelligence, and it asks a lot of questions about whether we are being taken over by AI.»

"Did you memorize that from a review?" Keira laughed.

«No. The play is so old that the English version script is in the public domain. The original was in Czech. I downloaded it from Project Gutenberg.»

"Your mind is filled with limitless surprises."

«Good! This is our exit.»

The GPS spoke at the same time and both laughed. Jaime quieted himself, determined not to be a passenger seat driver.

Jaime and Keira agreed on a method of surveying the audience before they started discussing anything, determined to discover if there were any other listeners present. After they were satisfied they were communicating only with each other, they would further build mental barriers against being 'overheard.'

The most important thing to both of them was that they would be holding hands. There was still a shy smile shared between them as they both experienced the pleasure of the physical contact.

«I love holding your hand. I find that I am physically pleased as much as I am emotionally pleased by the mental connection between us that it enhances. I love you, Keira.»

«I love you. Your touch makes me hungry for more. Now, let's check out the audience as they enter.»

They opened the channels that allowed them to silently observe the people entering the 200-seat theatre. It was a manageable number of people and they rapidly sifted through the thoughts of those entering. In addition to people who were avid theatre-goers and students of theatre, there was also a smattering of family and friends of the actors and crew.

Both identified a half dozen 'persons of interest' in the audience. None of them, however, seemed to be aware of what anyone else was thinking. They were simply broadcasting their thoughts loudly.

An attractive woman in a short skirt and low-cut blouse—not the usual attire for an afternoon Oregon theatre crowd—drew the attention of two men as she found her seat. A minute later, her date entered the auditorium and the attention of the other men was rather abruptly cut off as he sat beside his girlfriend.

Lucky dog, they seemed to think simultaneously.

«I think we can shut out the audience with no problem,» Jaime said. «Maybe we can spend time observing them at intermission.»

«Mmm. If the play is no good, you can spend your time mentally ravishing me,» Keira sighed, squeezing his hand.

«Don't test my resolve. I might not be able to limit it to mentally ravishing you.»

«Later,» Keira flirted.

The play began and the company president character began dictating a letter to his secretary. He was soon interrupted by the introduction of a visitor. The visitor was part of a league devoted to 'freeing the robots.' She could not accept the idea that the robots were not people, felt little or no pain, and had no emotions.

She then confused the human staff of the factory for robots and began to preach to them regarding their liberation, which they applauded. By the end of the first act, she'd agreed to marry the president because it would be a better way to influence the treatment of the robots.

«That's weird,» Jaime said. «Reading the actors is like reading the script. They don't have an identity other than the characters they are playing. Angus, Kate, and Thursday were basically themselves when they were rehearsing.»

«That's not true of all the actors. Marius and Sulla certainly succeeded in blanking out everything. I'd have thought initially that they really were robots. Others have a bit of themselves leaking in.»

«Domin and Helena certainly built a convincing relationship between them rapidly. He was really quite heartfelt in his proposal. But she was just as calculating in her acceptance. She suddenly seemed much older than she appears on stage, and genuinely saw submitting to a man—any man—as a channel to getting what she wanted. Do you think that was really her thoughts and personality coming through?» Jaime asked.

«Her list of credits in the program would indicate she is certainly older than her role's twenty-one. I don't know if it's her real personality or if she is simply drawing on other experience to create the character.»

«The more we listen to people's thoughts, the more confusing I find people!» Jaime said. The second act began.

THE SECOND AND third acts took place ten years later, the day the robots succeeded in their rebellion and killed all the humans on earth except one. This was one of the managers who was a builder and worked with his hands like the robots did. Unfortunately, he could make nothing of the process to create more robots and within a year the robots started dying out.

In the epilogue, it was revealed that two robots had been created who could love and care for each other—and presumably procreate. The last manager pronounced them Adam and Eve.

Jaime and Keira continued holding hands until they returned to the car. Keira used both hands on the steering wheel and Jaime seemed withdrawn.

"What is it?" she asked.

«It was… depressing,» he responded.

"There was a note of hope at the end. A new Adam and Eve."

«Yes. I suppose the play tried to be hopeful. It wouldn't have been very successful if it just ended with 'and that was the end of the world.' I mean that one woman in the audience. I can't get her off my mind.»

"Jaime, you need to close your mind to her. It can't be good to keep contact like that."

«I don't mean that literally. I'm not still reading her. I just keep thinking about how awful it must be.»

"Oh. Yes. I've known depressed people before. I try to actively avoid their minds."

«I couldn't. She was unquestionably beautiful and the best dressed at the play. But her mind was filled with sadness. She wished she'd stayed home in bed. She wanted to sleep and not wake up. She thought she loved the guy she was with, but was just too tired to deal with him. She believes she's ugly and doubts he loves her. She couldn't let him see her without makeup and made excuses when he called.»

"I looked. He's in love and at the same time totally oblivious to her sadness."

«Always looking happy exhausts her. I'm worried about her. She thinks she'd be better off dead.»

"What could we do about it?"

«I wanted to go up to her and tell her life wasn't that bad. She was beautiful and intelligent. She had nothing to be sad about. I shouted at her, but she's head deaf and couldn't hear me.»

"It wouldn't have made a difference, honey. She didn't need a *reason* to be sad. She's depressed. She hates herself—everything about herself. Her boyfriend tells her she's beautiful, but she assumes that means he wants sex from her, so she doesn't believe him. She still has sex with him, but the euphoria of an orgasm only lifts her for an hour or so. Then she feels guilty about using him and her mood is even darker than it was before."

«We… Keira, we have to be completely honest with each other. I'd die if you believed I only told you you're beautiful because I want to have sex with you. It would be horrible!»

"When we make love, you'll know I want it as much as you do. I do want it as much as you do. We just need to pace ourselves a little. And there's no one to help us do that but us. I know how hard it is. I just don't want to go to bed with you and never be able to get up again. I want to go to college and become a pediatrician. Don't you think that would be a good use of our talent? I'd be able to look inside and tell what the tyke is feeling and where it hurts."

«Is that what you *want* to do or what you think you *should* do because it would be a good use for your talent?»

"Yes. It would be a good use, but I've always had a fondness for children. They are so creative and so vulnerable."

«I'm not criticizing. Just asking. I want to do something meaningful, too. I'd really like it to be something that helps other people like us—assuming there are enough others like us to bother with. I'm worried about us. Someone wants to *use* us and I can't help but think he is evil. And if more people knew about us, there would be more people who wanted to cage us and use us.»

THEY STOPPED FOR dinner at a Mediterranean restaurant not far from home and took their time over their meal, touching often and listening to people around them.

«How do you deal with people who think in a different language?» Jaime asked.

«Well, I can't understand the thoughts in words. Some people have a very pictorial thought process and I can get the picture. But mostly, all I can do is feel their emotions. That's pretty informative.»

«Yes. I dealt with it a lot when I was little. My best friends in kindergarten, some of whom are still my best friends, like Mex and Cheery, didn't speak any English when we started school. We all learned sign language together and I learned a lot of Spanish as they learned English. I discovered there are a lot more emotions than I had words for. How many words in the English language? 200,000? American Sign Language only has about 10,000 distinct signs. Maybe I should work on signs for a broader range of emotions.»

«I read somewhere there are over 500 English words for different emotions, but most people aren't familiar enough with them to use them easily or to find the right word to express what they are feeling. And sometimes multiple words describe the same—or seemingly the same—emotion, or degrees of the same emotion.»

«Like?»

«I could be annoyed. If I'm really annoyed, I'd be angry. If I was really angry, I'd be in a rage. Where in that range does 'irritated' fit? Or 'indignant' or 'furious' or 'wrathful'? Think what we needed to do to find our own word for love. I joy you and I trust you. I think that means I love you.»

«Aren't there degrees of that, too? The Greeks had at least three words for different kinds of love. I know the love I have for you is different than the love I have for Dad and that's also different from the love I have for Mex and Cheery.»

«And I don't think that even scratches the surface of the kinds of love and affection people have.»

«I adore you.»

«I think it's time to pay the bill and go to my house.»

Jaime and Keira and a Voyeur

Sitting in Keira's living room with the lights low and soft music playing, the two spent a long time just holding hands and staring into each other's eyes. When other teens did that, they might wonder what their partner was thinking. It was quite clear to Jaime and Keira what each was thinking.

«Let's agree that we'll keep hands above the waist,» Jaime suggested.

«And keeping clothes on. If I got naked with you, I know I'd want to go all the way and it would be hard to stop,» Keira added.

«That idea is just breathtaking.»

«I've been dying to know what it's really like to feel our skin touching each other. I just don't want to strip and try it.»

«Anticipation,» Jaime said. «I've felt that in several people's minds.»

They kissed lightly and then a little more deeply, opening themselves to each other.

«Do you think the robots felt anticipation?»

«I don't know. You have to have a frame of reference for that. We both have knowledge, even if not experience, of what we are anticipating. I think Čapek missed something—or maybe polite society wouldn't let him go there.»

«What's that?»

«Porn. Every new technology was first used for porn.»

«Gunpowder?»

«Okay. Communication technology. If we start with cave drawings, there are pictographs that show sex and even large drawings of phalluses and things that could only be considered vaginas. I bet before that, people used drawings in the sand to communicate sexual desire. Carved goddesses that were worshiped had detailed genitalia and were often pregnant. When ancient Egyptians started writing things down on papyrus, bits of hieroglyphic erotic poetry appeared. Before Gutenberg printed the Bible, he printed pornographic handbills. Camera obscura was first used to project the images of people having sex in another room. As soon as photography and movies started, nudity and sex were portrayed. First videos? Porn. First use of the internet? Porn. If R.U.R was producing humanoid robots, the first demand would be for sex substitutes. They would have to have functional genitalia and use it on demand.»

«Oh, gee. We have that today! Robotic sex dolls with AI!» Keira said. «And the electric car guy says he'll have production quality humanoid robots within the next two years!»

«I like that term, 'the electric car guy.' It reminds me of the book *Do Androids Dream of Electric Sheep*? And you know that some of those androids in *Blade Runner* were made for sex.»

«Why are we still talking about robots and the play?»

«So we won't go too fast. Keira, I love to touch you.»

«I love to feel your hands on me under my shirt. Oh, Jaime, please. I mean, please agree now while we still have our senses about us that we promise not to go further than we've agreed, even if we both decide we want to go further later. We have to make that decision in a rational moment.»

«I do want to go further. I want to go all the way. But I don't want to do anything that might later cause regret because we didn't abide by our agreement.»

«That's it exactly. Respect and regret. And understanding that respecting our agreement builds a foundation of trust. We won't have regrets later. I love you, Jaime?»

The two were losing themselves in the sensations of kissing and touching each other. Keeping their clothes on didn't mean they couldn't get their hands under them. Jaime experienced the same thrill of having Keira's hands under his shirt as they kissed as he did with his hands under her shirt. And there were some technicalities they were both willing to exploit.

«How does this work? I've never done one. I thought you could do it with one hand,» Jaime said, fumbling with her bra.

«It takes a lot of practice. Use two hands. You have to kind of squeeze the sides together to release them. Oh, yes. That feels so good. When I get home from school, the first thing I do is get rid of my bra.»

«I don't know why girls wear them. Keira, I've never felt a girl's breasts before. They're awesome!»

A flood of images hit Jaime's mind and he caught his breath for a moment, pulling back from Keira's breasts.

«I understand now. The support thing. The modesty—enforced by the school from the time girls are little. And the protection thing. It's all three combined. Plus, a good helping of old-fashioned fear that you are vulnerable without a bra,» Jaime said.

«Push your shirt up so we can press our chests together,» Keira said. «We still have our clothes on. I need to feel your skin against mine.»

«Yes! Oh, God! I feel the vulnerability and the excitement. I guess guys don't have that feeling unless they happen to get a hard-on in school.»

«And that's not out there all day like breasts are. Oh, Jaime. If it was just the two of us together, I'd never wear a bra or a shirt. Or probably even clothes. Kiss me. Hold me. Hold me.»

Hold me.

«I didn't know my nipples were sensitive like that, too,» Jaime breathed.

Touch me. Yes.

«I love your lips on my breasts. It makes a flood of juices between my legs.»

Touch me.

«No. we agreed.»

«I want to kiss some more.»

«Your neck. Your ears,» Jaime whispered.

Touch me.

«Shh. Listen,» Keira whispered. «We're not alone.»

Yes, press there. You're so hard and I'm so soft.

«Oh, God!» Keira gasped. Both could feel the touch in their genitals.

«I'm not going to last long doing this,» Jaime moaned.

«I'm coming with you!»

Yes! I love you! Oh, touch me more!

«What?»

«You…?»

Oh, why aren't you more than my imagination? I love you so much!

«We're receiving *her*,» Jaime whispered in his mind to Keira.

«I can feel her. She's… I'm going to…»

«I feel it too. Your hands…?»

«Hers.»

«I didn't think I could do this so soon. Oh!»

«Oh!»

Yes!

«We need to pull away,» Jaime whispered again.

«One more kiss while we're touching? Kiss me and tell me you love me.»

«I love you so much. I can't live without you,» Jaime said as he lost himself in the kiss and the feeling of their chests rubbing together. When he began to get hard again, he pulled away and adjusted his cock in the sticky mess in his underwear.

Ahh! I can't take any more. What's happened to me?

«Who are you? Please tell us,» Keira projected to the unknown presence.

I'm so sleepy. I'll dream of this all night long.

Jaime and Keira sat, only holding hands as they let their breathing return to normal. Their shirts fell back into place, hiding their chests from each other's eyes, but the memory lived on.

«Do you see what I see?» Keira whispered.

«She's so satisfied,» he answered.

«I wouldn't recognize her on the street, but I'd know her touch in an instant,» Keira said.

«What do we do?»

«She thinks we're a dream. She's still dreaming of being held in our arms. Together.»

«She got feelings from us, like we got from her, but no real image.»

Jaime and Keira moved together and held each other again, this time keeping clothes between them and not letting their sexual drive re-engage, but holding each other in the afterglow of lovemaking. In their minds, the voyeur embraced them in her dream. She was happy. And so were they.

«When we were… kissing and touching… there were times I heard her voice,» Keira whispered, trying not to disturb the dreamer.

«At first, I didn't realize it wasn't you. She was pretty insistent about being touched.»

«I don't think she got the memo about keeping it above the waist,» Keira chuckled. «Her fingers… Could you feel what she was doing, love?»

«I… yeah. It was… wow!»

«Just so you know, I feel exactly like that when I touch myself.»

«Wow! How do you feel? I mean emotionally, now?» Jaime asked.

«So much in love with you. And very… affectionate.»

«For her, too.»

«Isn't that strange?» Keira asked.

«I love you, Keira. I know you and I've been intimate with you physically. But look at her sweet little dream. She's so… I don't mind that she shared this with us. Do you think she'll do it often?»

«Think of it, love. Look at her dream. We're still connected. How could I think anything but sweet thoughts about her. I don't know if we'll ever meet her in the flesh, but I think we can expect she'll be visiting us when we're making love.»

«Wow! We need to make sure she knows the rules when we're together. We still want to go slow. Having a third person's lust egging us on will make that a lot more difficult.»

«We'd better pull our clothes together and leave our sweet lover to her sleep.»

«We love you,» they both whispered before pulling away and severing the connection.

18
FANTASIES

Jaime and Keira and the Voyeur

«HOW DO YOU feel?» Jaime asked when they went for their Sunday walk to the park. Keira's parents were still away, but they felt it would be better to stick to a routine that allowed them some contact but didn't lead to shedding their clothes.

«I'm so in love with you,» Keira said. «I don't feel the least bit bad about anything we did yesterday.»

«And… *her?*»

«Yeah. That was something else! Did you think her up?»

«I'm still trying to comprehend that *you* are my girlfriend. I can't even imagine someone *else*,» Jaime sighed.

«Except she was *with* us. And we didn't imagine her. It was important, somehow.»

«Are we alone now?» Jaime asked.

Both assessed their filters and barriers.

«We seem to have good filters set up right now. I think it might take some extraordinary contact to bring her in,» Jaime said.

«Maybe some other time,» Keira said. «I'm worried about how much control she has over the contact. Even if she has any. It could be us that's drawing her in. What if she was doing something important when we made love? I mean like driving, or taking a test.»

«Or talking to her parents!»

The two walked hand-in-hand, listening to the sounds that surrounded them. That included happy children playing an imagination game in which they were hunting for dragons. Though the dragons were different in each child's mind, they were equally real.

«I was thinking about the play some more,» Keira ventured. «It was like those children playing their imaginary dragon game. The game they are playing completely fills their minds. They don't have room for any other thoughts.»

«That's like most of the actors were. They were so into their characters, they didn't have any other thoughts, either. I see,» Jaime added.

«Maybe we should select a play we can get into and memorize it. Then we could slip into the characters anytime we felt vulnerable. No one else could read what we were thinking and I'll bet we couldn't hear anyone else talking to us or just broadcasting their thoughts,» Keira suggested.

«I'm willing to try that out. It seems that control of our own broadcasting and receiving is really significant. We know there are others like us out there. At least somewhat like us. Angus is the only one we've actually had a conversation with and for all his detective work, he's really a kind guy. We should be careful about what we let out—and what we let in, as well.»

«Except…»

«Except our… what do we call her?»

«Let's say she's a satellite for now. It feels like she is just caught in our orbit.»

«Except our satellite,» Jaime agreed.

«Let's kiss and see if she joins us.»

«Do you want to go back to your house first?»

«No. I don't want to risk getting carried away. We can't go *too* far while we're here in the park.»

«Yeah. I just… Thinking about kissing you brings a hundred wonderful feelings and images to mind,» Jaime said.

«We'll see if we can keep them under control. And her.»

«I love you,» Jaime thought as their lips came together.

«I love you, too.»

I love these characters! They turn me on so much! I need to find a story for them. Maybe I should go to my room and think about them for a while.

«Not now, love. We just wanted to give you a little kiss.»

Yeah. Just a little kiss. I really don't have time right now. I need to finish this paper or Ms. Sullivan will be all over my case tomorrow.

Jaime and Keira held their kiss another moment or two and then slowly parted. They were sure they heard a sigh.

«Later,» they whispered.

They returned to Keira's house holding hands, but holding their thoughts behind barriers to the outside world.

«She thinks we're characters in a story she wants to write!» Keira whispered inside to him.

«That's an interesting take. I wonder if she knows she's part of the story.»

«And just kissing with our minds open to it brought her in with us. We need to be really careful not to interrupt something important that she's doing. Who is Ms. Sullivan?»

«At the moment, I'd say she's a clue. Our satellite is a student. Ms. Sullivan is a teacher. We can check the faculty of all the schools in town to see if there is a match somewhere,» Jaime suggested.

«Then we could go there and try to spot her.»

«Very carefully.»

«Right. This could take a while. It's a short week and I'll bet every teacher in the city has made papers due before Thanksgiving. I have two.»

«We've both got the paper for Ms. Henderson's lit class. And I've got one for Design Tech. But there's only three days of school, then Thanksgiving. It's so nice of your parents to invite us to Thanksgiving dinner. It's like… being accepted into your life,» Jaime said.

«And your father asked if he could bring Olivia!»

«I haven't even met her yet. I hope she's nice!»

«How could she be anything else,» Keira laughed.

«I love you, Keira.»

«I love you.»

They kissed softly once more and heard a sigh in the backs of their minds.

Jaime and Keira and the Families

THE TIME BOTH flew and crawled getting to Thanksgiving. The papers that were due were no small matter. As seniors, they were expected to write papers that were properly formatted, with all quotes and references cited correctly. In a way it was good that these two papers were due before Thanksgiving instead of being part of the great Christmas holiday break rush—like Jaime's psychology paper was. And he'd definitely need time to study for his Calculus final. Jaime and Keira scarcely had time to meet after school and hold hands or have a little kiss. There was no time for anything else.

While they had slowed down some of their amorous adventures, David's love life had picked up. Olivia was a little younger than David's 42, but was definitely interested in him. When they picked her up on the way to Keira's house, Jaime immediately read that she had hoped he would ask her out and was very pleased. Jaime concentrated on not hearing her because he didn't want to eavesdrop on his father and his love interest.

"I'M SO HAPPY you all included me in your invitation to dinner," Olivia said when she met June and John. "I had to get out of California because the superficial pressure there was killing me. It's all about how you look and where you live and who you know. But I don't have any family up here. David came to my rescue."

"You are more than welcome, Olivia," June said. "Jaime and Keira have drawn us closer to David. I'm glad you could join us as well."

"I thought Dad just made you up so I wouldn't feel bad about spending time with Keira," Jaime signed. Keira interpreted for him, much to David's delight.

"I'm not going to throw cold water on your relationship," David laughed, "but I don't feel like I need an imaginary friend in order to cope."

«Unlike us,» Keira shot to Jaime.

«She's not imaginary. We are!»

«Oh, yeah.»

"There was an article in *Psychology Today* a couple of years ago—maybe more—that said all our friends are imaginary," June said. "It's especially true in our era of internet communications and artificial intelligence. We have hundreds of friends online whom we have never met. We have bits and pieces that they've exposed to us, but most of our friendship is imaginary."

"Thank heavens for real people," Olivia said, taking David's hand.

"Sartre said we are beings that cause ourselves," Jaime signed and Keira interpreted.

"Did I get that right?" Keira asked. Jaime nodded.

"He also suggests that in order to exist, we must interact with others," Jaime continued with Keira interpreting.

"That's a deep subject for high school," John said. "How did you get into Sartre?"

"Oh, we had to read *The Stranger* in our lit class as an example of existentialist literature," Keira said.

"I thought it was interesting and read some other of his works. *Being and Nothingness* was really deep and I didn't comprehend more than a quarter of the book," Jaime signed.

"Most of my reading is technical, I'm afraid," David said. "How did all of you happen to get into *Psychology Today* and Sartre?"

"Well, June is a social anthropologist and I teach literature at the university. We actually met in college in psychology class," John said.

"Don't worry, though. I think we've both exhausted our knowledge on the subject," June laughed. Olivia breathed a sigh of relief.

Trayce and Lanie Lombard

ALL TOLD, THE Thanksgiving holiday was relatively painless. Even Trayce had fun with her mother, who seemed almost her old self.

"Do you want to go shopping tomorrow?" Mrs. Lombard asked her daughter?

"Really? Who can get too much shopping? That would be fun!" Trayce said.

"I've been failing as a mother," Mrs. Lombard said. "I'm sorry, Trayce. When your father was taken from us, it was like part of my being left me. I'm working on getting better. I've been attending AA meetings the past couple of weeks. I can't promise I'm there yet, but I want to be here for you. I realized I was on the brink of losing my daughter as well as my husband."

"Mom, I love you. It's been hard on me, too. I'm sorry if I haven't been a good daughter."

"Don't! Don't ever doubt that you are a good daughter. Taking care of me when I've been so depressed is not something you should ever have had to do. Your love has made a huge difference to me."

"What's changed, Mom? I mean, I'm happy we're out doing things together, but what's happened, like this week?"

"In addition to starting AA, I went back to counseling, just like we did for a while last year. Maybe you should go back, too. But you seem to be doing fine. I started hearing voices of people who weren't there and imagining terrible things happening all the time. I started seeing a new therapist a couple of weeks ago and she prescribed a new medication for me. She also told me I needed to start attending AA because alcohol would react negatively with the medicine. I can't believe what a difference it's made. I almost feel like my old self. I know I've got a long way to go, but for the first time since your father died, I feel like I have hope."

Trayce took in the information that her mother had heard voices and imagined terrible things. Perhaps it was genetic! Maybe her whole story idea was because she was schizophrenic and could be cured with her mother's magic pills! She needed to take that into consideration. And weigh the possibility against the blossoming of her writing. She'd turned in her short story called "Murder by Angus." She was pleased with it and was sure Ms. Dorn would like it, even though it had some pretty risqué bits. After all, two of the characters were strippers and everything any of the three of them said had a double entendre.

"I might see some friends over the Christmas break," she ventured, wondering where that idea had come from.

"Good. Good. I'm glad you are meeting friends. You've seemed to avoid people a lot this year."

"I think that's another aspect of missing Dad. And you. I didn't… um… feel very likable," she said.

"I'm so sorry, Trayce. You are always welcome to bring your friends to the house. I know it's been embarrassing, but I think I'll rehire that cleaning service who came in every other week. Neither of us needs the burden of keeping the house in 'company's welcome' shape."

"If we can afford it, that would be great."

"We can. I plan to start job hunting, too. Might even get a holiday job if I see something interesting at the mall this weekend. You can point out what store you'd like the best discounts at tomorrow."

"Mom! You can be so funny sometimes."

Emerson

EMERSON'S HOLIDAY WAS not as positive as the others. She enjoyed the time with her parents, her younger sister, and her grandparents. She'd always been blessed with a happy and comfortable home. For her eighteenth birthday, her grandparents had bought her a new Kia.

Her grandfather, however, was a classic homophobe. He'd taken her car shopping and saw she liked an Outback. He immediately steered her to the Kia dealer and told her he'd buy her any car on their lot if she'd just forget about the Outback. He didn't want his girl driving around in a lesbian car.

Emerson cringed at the declaration. Her grandfather was always so nice and loving otherwise. She told him if she ever had a girl lover, she'd make sure she brought her guy, too. Even at his age, her grandfather was enough of a dirty old man that the thought of two girls with a boy made him stop to think. If he knew what she'd done in Paris… Well, she wasn't a lesbian—at least all the time. She'd made love to both Dom and Raquel and loved them both. She guessed that made her bisexual. Whatever. She didn't need a label. She loved both of them and couldn't wait to return to Paris.

That was the problem. On Black Friday, she received a letter from her boyfriend and girlfriend. Only it wasn't a letter. It was a wedding invitation. The two were marrying on New Year's Day! The speed of the event was staggering. In August, they'd pledged their love to each other. She'd made all her plans to return to Paris to be with them. To be a real threesome.

> *Je t'aime, Emerson. We love you so much. But Dom and I are meant for each other and we just have to get married. Partly because I'm pregnant. He won't hear of me being a single mother. My parents wanted the wedding before I was too big to fit in the church. What could we do? We know this is*

probably too hasty for you to join us. It would be so wonderful. We hope you will still come to visit us this summer.
Your loving Raquel

Emerson had locked herself in her room for the rest of the day, crying.

We were supposed to be a threesome, not a married couple and their summer visitor! How could they do this to me?

The more she cried and the more she questioned, the more it became clear that Dom and Raquel had always been a couple and she was just a third wheel. Out of sight, out of mind.

I should have followed through with Zip, she thought. *I've been fantasizing about him all semester. I'm even learning sign language! What have I been thinking. Subconsciously I knew I'd never be with them, so I've imagined myself with my computer partner. He's always so nice to me. And sometimes when he looks at me, I think he knows what I hide at this school. I thought I'd keep up the charade until I left after graduation and then let the wild girl loose. Maybe I should let her loose now!*

Emerson continued her fantasizing about dropping her mousy persona at school and letting go with Jaime. She went so far as to get some of her Paris outfits out of her closet and try them on in front of her mirror. She danced and spun around, watching herself and building an elaborate scenario in her mind. She'd wear the red dress to school after the New Year. No! Why wait so long. She'd bring it out on the last day before Christmas and just quietly ask Zip if he'd like to take it off of her.

Zip, I've been thinking a long time about this. Remember when I told you you'd crossed my mind one afternoon? You crossed my lips that day and the kiss was delicious! I know you've looked at me and have seen that I've been hiding something. Here it is. Won't you unwrap your Christmas present?

Yes, look at my breasts. They're aching for your touch. My nipples are so sensitive! Kiss them. Suck! Oh, God, Zip! Lower, yes! I'll open my world to you. I wax my whole pubic area. Do you know why? It's so I'm perfectly smooth for your tongue. Yes, there! Suck on my clit. Take me here, right here, on the computer lab desk. I'm your Christmas present and you're mine!

Emerson was lying on her bed with the red mini dress crumpled on the floor beside it. Her fingers worked on her breasts and clit, rubbing, pinching, twisting. She slid two fingers into her slippery pussy and began pumping vigorously.

Yes, Zip. Fuck me. Fuck Dom and Raquel out of me. Let them have each other and their little brat. I don't want them. I want you! Just you!

Her fingers flew, plunging into her as her thumb strained to flick her clit in time. Soon she arched her back with only her heels and her shoulders touching the mattress.

Zip! I knew you'd be wonderful. Fuck me! Fuck me! I'm coming. I'm coming! Oh, God, yes! Fuck me again!

She tried her best to erase the memory of Dom and Raquel with the anticipation of Jaime. After five comes, she'd almost succeeded.

Jaime and Keira and the Satellite

«WE'RE IN PUBLIC,» Keira said to Jaime Friday night. They were at the movie theater watching a new Christmas release. Of course, they sat in the last row of the crowded mall cinema. «We have to be subtle. But no one will see us kissing once the lights are out.»

An advantage of the last row was that it was the least illuminated by the screen. A second advantage was that the last row was reputedly always occupied by couples who had the same thing on their minds.

They held hands and opened their minds just to those nearest to them. Indeed, those on either side were anticipating slouching down in their seats for some serious making out. They pushed the armrest between their seats up so there was nothing between them. They hadn't bothered with popcorn or soft drinks. If they got dehydrated, they'd just leave.

The lights went down and the previews played. Then the feature.

Elf 007 Is Missing! was a comic live action romance in which a female (of course) secret elf agent on a mission to protect Santa from a possible abduction is accidentally left behind in the suspect's apartment. While there, they discover each other and he attempts to hold her hostage for ransom but they discover neither one wants to let her go.

Enough about the movie.

As soon as thoughts had settled down in the theater and people focused on the movie, Keira and Jaime started with a tentative kiss. When it was apparent no one near them was paying any attention to them—or the movie—they let the kiss deepen and opened themselves to each other.

«I love you! I wish we weren't in a theater. This is going to be so difficult!»

«That's the idea, remember?» Jaime said. «It's supposed to be too difficult to get carried away. But I'm completely in love with you! I want you with all my heart and soul.»

«My soulmate. Yes, you can caress me. I'll turn toward you a little so no one can see where your hand is.»

Jaime had one arm around Keira's shoulders and the other was being subtle as he could as he caressed her breasts.

Oh, geez! I would think of you now—while I'm watching a movie with my mother. I can't let her know how hard I'm breathing. The movie isn't that exciting!

«She's with us!» Keira whispered.

«I knew she'd show up. That's why we're in a public place and can't get too carried away. We need to let her know the rules,» Jaime responded.

They opened themselves a little more so they were sure their imaginary lover could hear and feel them.

«We love you so much. We had to find a quiet place where no one would be watching but we couldn't get too carried away,» Keira said.

«We promised not to rush. I know it's difficult, but if we take it slow, it will be so much better when we finally really do it,» Jaime added.

Yes. Take it slow. I can't… I can't even touch myself. Mom would know! Oh, but kiss some more. Do what you can do in the last row of the theater. But don't come! I couldn't possibly explain that to mother if I started squealing or gasping for breath!

«Do you know why I wore this baggy Christmas sweater?» Keira asked.

«I think I can feel why.»

«You'll feel it better if you put your hand under it.»

«Oh! Yes! I love to touch your breasts!»

Why are my nipples tingling so much? I just want to rip my clothes off! You can't… can't lift it up to suck on me… her. I know people would see that.

«There's lots of room inside for your hand, but don't expose me,» Keira echoed. «Oh! Just right there. You know just how firmly to rub my nipples. Mmm. Kiss me more.»

Oh, kisses. I want kisses. My imagination is just too damn good sometimes!

«Love, you need to let go,» Jaime gasped. «We didn't make an explicit rule about staying above the waist, but if you keep that up, I'm going to come!»

«Oh, my God! I didn't realize I was doing that. It was so… handy. I just wanted to feel what you felt when you were really hard. I'm sorry. I'll pull back.»

If he came, I'd come. I think she'd come just from him exploding in her hand. Oh, please. I've got to… I've got to stop…

«If we don't take a break, we'll both come,» Keira said. «One more. One more little kiss. If we can't control ourselves, we'll have to leave the theater!»

I don't want you to go. Just… just cuddle and hold me. I mean her. Oh, I need to get home and write this all down. And take care of business.

Jaime and Keira reduced the intensity of their making out and lowered the volume of their thoughts a little. They caught up with where the movie was. The elf, who was played by a champion gymnast who was only about four feet-six inches tall, had sprung up on a shelf to replace a typical elf-on-a-shelf. She hid the doll behind a book and stayed very still. The handsome but rather dense guy walked past her several times, glancing at her and shaking his head. Eventually, he laid down on the sofa and went to sleep.

Jaime and Keira stepped up the tempo of their making out a couple of times, always backing off before they went too far, and listening to their satellite as she rose and dropped with them. After the movie, they closed down their psychic channel as completely as they could and headed for the exit. They caught the next streetcar toward Keira's house before they opened to each other again.

«That was really fun, but also really exhausting,» Jaime said.

«Think of how well we controlled ourselves. Not just because we didn't go too far at any given time, but because we were able to back off from the mental volume and focus on just one thing to hear,» Keira said.

«She was so loud and clear it was like she was actually in the same theater with us,» Jaime laughed.

«Oh, my God! Maybe she was! Did you see what movie she was watching?»

«No. I figured the one playing in front of us was too strong a visual image to imagine a different one. Can you imagine if she'd been watching *Die Hard* twenty-seven or whatever while we were watching *Elf on a Shelf?*»

«That was so funny. But what if we didn't see what she was watching because she was watching the same thing we were?» Keira asked.

Jaime was dumbstruck. No thoughts could penetrate his amazement. He eventually shook it off.

«We might have just missed an opportunity to meet her,» he sighed.

«Or at least see her. It might not have been the best time to meet her with her mother right beside her,» Keira said.

They walked from the trolley stop to Keira's house and paused on the porch.

«I'm still really turned on,» Keira said.

«Yeah. Me too. This could be a little frustrating.»

«We could… continue when you get home.»

«You mean mentally? Do you want to do that?»

«I've touched you. I want to feel it when you… you know.»

«I want to feel you, too. I almost made a move up your leg, but I was afraid that was too much like what you'd done touching me. I was afraid if you came, I'd come and she'd come.»

«I think you're right, but I'll be touching myself and letting you feel me through my fingers. And you'll be touching yourself while I feel you.»

«I'd really like that,» Jaime said. «But we have to have, like a safe word if either of us gets freaked out.»

«Elf!» they both said at once.

«Before you go, we could step over to the corner of the porch where the light doesn't shine and have another really good kiss. A *really* good one,» Keira said.

They moved to the corner and kissed, opening themselves up more to each other and soon letting their satellite join them. Jaime slid his hand under Keira's sweater and she encouraged him to get his head down there as she leaned back against the house.

"Mom! I'm really tired. Today was such fun. I think I need to go to bed now." Why did I imagine him sucking my nipples right now? I have to get undressed.

«It's okay, love. We're just fantasizing about each other. You have time. We'll wait.»

Yeah. They must be crazy horny after their date and not going too far in the theater. I bet they'll go to bed and just think about each other as they touch themselves. I'll get my teeth brushed and hang up my new dress. Then, I'll get all relaxed and have a little play time. Geez! I'm still wet down there!

19
DELIBERATE CONTACT

Jaime and Keira and Their Satellite

JAIME REACHED OUT to Keira from his bed to hers. It was almost like they were holding hands again.

«Are you sure you want to do this?»

He was lying naked on his bed and sensed Keira was also naked. She shared the image of her looking in the mirror before she lay down. He quickly got up and examined himself slowly in the mirror. He guessed he wasn't bad looking.

«Bad? You look great! I… Am I okay?»

«Honestly, the most beautiful creature I've ever seen.»

«I think your opinion is colored by our emotions,» she giggled. «Now I really can't wait to be with you like this when we're together. I want to feel all your skin touching all my skin as we make love.»

«Wow! I'm kind of leaking,» Jaime said as he followed Keira's desire to touch him. She dipped between her legs and he could feel the moisture there.

«So am I,» Keira affirmed. «No matter how close we are mentally and how turned on we are, the experience is still lacking the physical element. I can feel you touching my nipples and sliding through my wetness, but I'm feeling through my own hands.»

«I feel you stroking my cock and touching my nipples, or your nipples. But it's my own hands. I know from memory this felt… different when I was feeling myself through your hands. When we were together.»

«Do you want to stop?»

«No.»

«Me either.»

For a few moments they simply let their partner share the sensations through their own touches.

«I'm not going to last long, Keira.»

«I can feel it. It starts way up inside you.»

«Like yours does! I can feel you contracting a lot farther inside than your fingers are reaching.»

«Yes! Let it… Oh, Jaime!»

«Keira!»

Both teens felt the orgasm of the other combined with their own. It might have been slightly less intense than what they'd experienced when physically petting with each other, but neither was able to express a coherent thought for minutes.

Oh, yeah. So good, a voice sighed in their heads.

«She's here!» Keira whispered.

«Are you okay?» he asked. «Can we do some more? She's touching… Oh, wow!»

«I feel her fingers in my vagina! I'm not touching myself!»

«She's different than you, but I'm as hard as I was before.»

«It's like I have two lovers. She's playing with my clit while I'm stroking your cock.»

I'm coming!

Keira seized up with the satellite's orgasm and Jaime started spurting in her hand. His hand. None of them were physically together, but they'd just shared another intense orgasm.

«I think we'd better go to sleep,» Keira said. «'Night, lovers.»

«I'm shot. I'll see you tomorrow, love. 'Night!»

Such a beautiful time. I love these guys. What… What is the story?

Jaime and Keira

«WHAT DO YOU think?» Jaime asked as they walked in the park.

«We really need to find her. I'm irresistibly drawn to her. I want to hold her in my arms, like I hold you. Is this a side-effect of being mentally connected? If there was a man who eavesdropped on our lovemaking, would we fall in love with him?» Keira asked.

«There's something unique about our relationship with her. I feel the same way you do and I'm embarrassed by it because I didn't want anyone but you. But feeling my fingers stroking her sex and breasts, and feeling the same excitement in you, just blew me away.»

«I think the problem—and the pleasure—is that we experienced all three of our orgasms at the same time. Talk about 'double your pleasure.' Only it was a lot more than double. Or triple,» Keira said.

«When we do it… I mean go all the way… we need to make sure we are in total privacy. So, no one can eavesdrop on us.»

«Except… Maybe it won't be just the two of us. Maybe we'll all three be together.»

«I'm going to be thinking about that all the time now!» Jaime said.

«I thought about it a lot,» Keira said. «I don't think she was aware that she was in an experience with two other real people. Hers was strictly an emotional response. Remember Debbie? It was one-way. You were riding in her fantasy and experiencing what she was experiencing. But she was completely unaware of you. Emerson? That might have been a flash of awareness, but she was caught up in her own memories. But neither of them was really experiencing anything *you* were thinking. This girl, our satellite, wasn't responding to our words, but was caught up in her own experience of what we were feeling. She thinks we're just a figment of her imagination.»

«Wow! I never evolved anything like that in my imagination. She must be a real dreamer.»

«Or she has always believed everyone she heard in her head was just her imagination. I think there are others who might believe that way.»

They paused in the park to share a sweet kiss, careful to keep it just between the two of them.

«Do you think we were affected by her, too? I mean, if she was experiencing some deep emotions while she was getting herself off, did some of her excitement leak into our experience?» Jaime asked.

«Is it possible? I don't know if *anything* is impossible anymore.»

«I love you, Keira.»
«Yeah. Kiss me.»
Yeah.

Trayce

"Ms. DORN, IS it normal for an author to… um… believe in her characters?" Trayce asked in her senior creative writing class Monday morning. "I mean, like they are real people she might meet on the street?"

Trayce had relived her experience from Friday night over and over. First there was the movie when it felt as if the characters she'd been thinking of were just behind her in the theater, watching the same movie she was. She'd had such real feelings of being kissed and caressed, she was afraid her mother would ask her what was wrong.

Then when she got home, she decided to relive some of the fantasy and get herself off before going to bed. She'd hardly touched herself when the two characters she imagined in the theater were in her head again. They were so sexy! She'd never thought up characters who were so connected to each other. It was almost as if they could read each other's minds.

The girl—Keira, Trayce decided to call her—was a fiery redhead. Cute, of course. All Trayce's heroines were prettier than she was. When Trayce put her fingers to work in her coochie, she thought she was touching Keira. In fact, she no longer had a reservation about putting her face between a girl's legs if she was like Keira.

That hadn't been all. She could feel herself stroking the cock of—Jaime, she decided to name him. And the feeling of him spurting his stuff in her hand was incredible. It was the most powerful orgasm she'd ever had.

Continuing their new bonding as mother and daughter, Trayce and her mother had gone to Cannon Beach together and just sat in restaurants and went shopping for the next two days. Trayce hadn't heard a peep from her characters while she was gone.

"Are characters real people?" Ms. Dorn repeated. "I believe that real people influence what we write about characters. You have a friend who always scratches her nose when she's on the telephone and suddenly a completely unrelated character develops the habit of scratching her nose when she's on the telephone.

"In his journal, author Ash Mann once stated that the people in his head were often more real than the people he met in person. I don't know that I'd call that 'normal,' though," Ms. Dorn concluded.

"Oh, there was that movie where the guy realizes he's a character in an author's book. It was kind of the opposite way around and the character starts hearing the author narrating his life," said Kevin Border, an aspiring writer in the class.

"I think that when characters become real to you, they become real to your readers," Ms. Dorn said. "Certainly, if you hear voices in your head, it is much healthier to treat them as characters than as real people. But it's not uncommon for an author to talk about how the characters hijacked his story and took it someplace he didn't intend."

Trayce wanted to be an author as her career and planned to go to the university to major in creative writing. If Ms. Dorn's class in high school was any indication of what she could expect, it would be a great major. Her father had once told her that she should follow her passion for a career, but it might be a good idea to minor in a subject she could earn a living at while her career got started.

She'd enrolled in a class at Rose Community College that was an introductory survey of social services. She thought that might be an interesting job and a gateway to all sorts of characters for her stories. She'd be getting her term paper back this week, as everyone tried to get finished before the winter break.

Jaime and Keira

THE FIRST WEEK of December was chaotic at school for Jaime and Keira. They met at lunch Monday to touch base on their search for a teacher named Ms. Sullivan.

«Did you find anything?» Jaime asked.

«It's really hard to find a directory of the teachers in all the schools in

Portland. You have to go school-by-school and then it's buried. I haven't found a Ms. Sullivan,» Keira said.

«The only one I found was at Rose Community College. She teaches an introductory survey of social services. The description says it's designed for students who might be considering a career in social services to understand what the work is like and the kinds of professions available. From what I found, it looks like a lot of students are double credit students, getting both high school and college credit.»

«That sounds like a good possibility. I bet there would be papers due for a class like that.»

«The problem is getting to it if it meets at the same time as our school is in session. We'll need to plan a cut day. And even then, we don't know if that's the class she's taking or even if she'll attend that particular day.»

«Oh my! We could… No. I'm not going to suggest that. It would be a bad habit to get into. And we don't actually know what she looks like. She didn't give us the naked mirror look we gave each other. I wonder if she got a look at us then.»

«She might never join us again,» Jaime said self-deprecatingly.

«Don't put yourself down. I loved what I saw.»

«You know the other problem is that if she thinks we're characters in her head that she wants to write about, we should be really careful about approaching her. Last thing I'd want is to make her think she's crazy.»

«We'll have a lot to think about at the ballet Saturday,» Keira said.

«It sounds like a nice quiet place to connect. I wonder if they think about their characters like the actors did.»

«We need to get an early start so we can eat and get to the show. It's near the Old Spaghetti Factory, so why don't we go there for dinner?»

«Okay. It's a plan. I love you.»

«Yeah. And you.»

Jaime and Emerson

A SURPRISE WAS waiting in Jaime's computer science class Monday afternoon. Emerson was at their lab station, but it wasn't the Emerson he was accustomed to seeing. This Emerson looked like she'd walked into class direct from the Avenue des Champs-Élysées in Paris. She wore a black miniskirt that might have been shorter than school policy actually allowed. She had bare legs that ended in high heel black over-the-ankle boots. On top, she wore a form-fitting knit sweater that was so loosely knit that her black lace bra was clearly visible through it.

Perhaps even more startling, was the careful makeup she applied. Jaime thought she was always nice looking, but her makeup looked like it had been applied by a professional for a television appearance.

"Wow! Emerson, you look incredible today!" he signed, then quickly launched his TTS app. He handed her a Bluetooth earbud he'd thought to prepare for her.

"Thank you, Jaime," she said coyly.

"I mean, you always look really nice, but today you look like you stepped off a fashion show runway," he typed in. She smiled at him.

"Oh, I had to do a presentation in Advanced French today on Paris fashion. You know I was there all last spring and summer."

"Yeah, we missed you here."

Jaime did a quick read and discovered Emerson had not made a presentation in French just before her arrival in this class. In fact, she'd cut the class to change clothes and apply her makeup. She'd done it just to impress Jaime!

"Wow! It's really sexy."

"I'm not always a mouse," Emerson said. "I just don't like to draw a lot of attention in school. I thought… well… you might like to see it."

"Thank you, Emerson. You really are a stunning girl. I think I always knew that."

"You are one of the few people in school who treat me like a beautiful person, no matter what I'm wearing," she said. "So, I was wondering… I'm thinking of having a little party over the holiday break and I wondered if you'd like to come. With me."

God! Did I make that clear enough? I want him to be my date at my party. I've got to make sure.

"I mean… you know… like as my date for the evening. I know we've never done anything like that, but you've been so helpful with my project and I liked working with you last year, I thought we could just hang out, you know?"

By which I mean make out. And make love. And spend our lives together. Oh, Emerson, you're making such a hash of things. Don't be desperate!

Jaime paused a few seconds before beginning to type his reply. He put it on delay so he could backspace and delete things that didn't sound right.

"I really like you, Emerson. I guess we've never talked about this kind of thing, but I've got a girlfriend. You might know her. It's Keira Nolan. I'm not sure if you have any classes with her. But, we're pretty serious and I wouldn't want to mess anything up in our relationship by dating anyone else."

He finally pressed the translate button and watched Emerson's eyes get big and round.

A girlfriend? How did I not know that? Not that he's ever made a suggestive remark to me, but I thought he liked me. Oh, crap! I'm going to… No, I can't cry! I have to just… oh, dance with it, Emerson!

"Oh, that's okay, Jaime. I mean. I didn't know that or I'd never have made the suggestion. Keira? Wow! She has gorgeous red hair! Congratulations. I… um… feel a little like an idiot for not knowing that, but you're right: We've never talked about it before," Emerson said without slowing down. "I had a boyfriend in Paris and found out we'd just broken up and I was kind of at a loss. I just thought 'who is the nicest guy I know in this school?' And decided to ask you out. It's no big thing. Just forget about it, okay?"

I'm so stupid! The first time I've ever had the guts to ask a boy out—invite him to my house—and he's got a girlfriend! Why did I put these clothes on? Now everyone will look at me differently. I need to go to the restroom and change. And then I'm going straight home and wash the makeup off my face and shower while I cry over my stupidity.

"I like you, Emerson. I really like being your lab partner. We're doing some good stuff on both our projects. Don't blame yourself for not knowing my relationship status. I'm really flattered that you'd think of me like that."

"Yeah, well, um… I've, like, got a dentist appointment, so I have to leave school early today. I'll see you tomorrow, okay? 'Bye!" She laid the earbud on the table, grabbed her bag, and left.

Jaime was really sad for his friend. He should have realized she was thinking of him that way.

Jaime and Keira

«Well, do you want to date her?» Keira asked after school.

«No! She's nice and she can be really sexy, but those aren't anything that would cause me to not be with you. You are what makes me whole. Please don't think I want someone else!»

«Remember when we stood here on the porch and I told you I love you?» she asked. Jaime nodded. «We kissed and you saw that flash of jealousy. I was sorry, but it's true. When you saw Emerson with her shirt off and shared that image with me, I felt so insecure because I really love you and don't want anyone to interfere with that. I can see in your heart, though, that you don't have those feelings for her. So just love me a little harder, okay?»

«If I love you any harder, I might break you,» Jaime said, soothing his girlfriend. «Is it… like, okay? What we're doing with our satellite?»

«It's a contradiction, isn't it? I don't feel the least bit threatened or jealous of her. We have a special link, the three of us. We'll be fine. Kiss me and we'll share it with her, wherever she is.»

They kissed, thinking of the unnamed 'her' as they shared their love.

Oh, I feel so good. Like I've just been kissed. Too bad I'm getting on a bus. I'd like to spend some time with that.

«Later, love,» they whispered to her. They heard a sigh in return.

Jaime and Emerson

Jaime kept his mind open most of the week. His goal was to discover how a person would react to discovering he could talk in their heads. Of course, his earlier survey for head talkers was just his class. This time he expanded it to the whole school, paying special attention in the halls for anyone who seemed the least bit open.

He found one who had a brief pause when he spoke to him, but shook his head and went on his way. The ability to hear was there, but had been so deeply suppressed that Jaime's voice was considered just a random thought.

And there was one person who seemed to always be open to him, though he tried not to eavesdrop on her, especially after Monday. Tuesday afternoon they both went back to their projects like nothing embarrassing had ever happened. Wednesday afternoon, though, Emerson's thoughts caught his attention in the computer science class.

"What do you think of this plan?" Emerson asked.

"Why are you converting everything to this color model? Is it practical?" Jaime signed. Emerson had been studying sign language online just so she could understand Jaime more easily, she didn't always get his fluid signs. Usually, Jaime clarified when needed by printing a neat note. Emerson had as much difficulty reading his elegant handwriting as she did his signs.

"I didn't understand that last sign. Is it what?"

Jaime stopped her a second and handed her his Bluetooth earbud. He typed the question in and she listened to the voice she'd come to associate as his.

God! I wish you could just talk to me like this. We could be a lot closer. I just can't get around the idea of trying to make love without being able to hear his voice. We'd constantly have to interrupt things to sign or for him to type into his app.

"Oh. Yes, practical."

Jaime was momentarily taken aback by her suggestion that they could be making love if he could talk. He liked Emerson. He was sympathetic to her secret life and desire to return to her lovers in France. But he had a girlfriend, and as attractive as he knew Emerson to be from her image in the mirror and her outfit on Monday, he wouldn't actually have sex with her. He was sure she wouldn't either. He thought.

"The Hue/Value/Chroma color space has a better representation of what we actually see. RGB and CMY both are kind of flat spaces. Every color gets equal representation in a color wheel. But all colors are not equal. In the three-dimensional HVC system, we can immediately see that yellow, for example, is much lighter than blue. It isn't directly opposite as it would be on a flat color wheel. Once I have an HVC formula for the color, I can translate it to any other color model, like RGB, CMY, HLS, Pantone, or Munsell. So, it gives me a single color model to plot all the data into without worrying about ink colors, fabric dye colors, or the range of a rainbow."

"Wow! That's brilliant. You can grab a sample of any color and plot it, independent of its own color space. I like it."

Then kiss me. God! Emerson, get ahold of yourself. He just likes your invention, not you. It was just a fantasy.

"Thanks. Do you think it will work?"

"I think the input side is genius. If you only developed that for the class, you'd still be ahead of what I'm doing. It's the predictive output that I'm not sure of. Once you see the mass of color information, how do you predict the next hot color?" Jaime typed.

"Yeah. I've run some experiments. I enter a series of color values and have the algorithm predict what color comes next in the series. That works, but it's based on the sequence of colors. I think I still need to have a fourth input that I haven't even started yet—maybe over winter break. It's a time-value. If I have a hue of 280º, a value of 80%, and a chroma of 45%, I still need to plot that on a timeline in order to see what comes next. I'm hoping to generate a simple value first. What is the hot color of 2001? 2002? 2003? That would give me the basis for a single color pick for 2025. It's too general to be practical for a broad spectrum of uses, but if I limited it to colors in fashion, it might be useful."

Finding the hot color for each year could kill me. What do I sample?

"I see. If you collect a whole bunch of samples, how do you weight them according to their importance, even in one industry? For example, if you have one fashion designer who simply falls in love with purple for a season, how important is that compared to the color palettes of a dozen other designers, none of whom use purple?"

"Oh, crap!"

I've been paying too much attention to methods of collecting colors and a timeline for each to consider the weighting of them. This whole project is useless! How can I weight the value of a fifth variable? Shit shit shit! I must look like an idiot to Zip!

"I think your whole concept is brilliant. It's probably more than anyone is tackling for our class. I finally settled on just allowing a user of my TTS to record his own voice and change the frequencies or tone. And I didn't mean to introduce another complication. I was just thinking that this had a lot more development that could be done in the future. You could probably sell the concept based on what you've done so far. For any series of colors, you could predict the next color, but with your use of the HVC model, you could also turn that final value into an entire color scheme by using complementary and contrasting colors."

I'd fuck him right here on the desk. How can he be so encouraging while pointing out the flaws in my design? And then point out an expansion for it that is brilliant!

It's almost like he knows my own doubts. I was trying to ignore more complex inputs. I'm going home after school and… no, I have to go to the dentist right after school. Tonight, though. Tonight, I'm going to fuck myself into oblivion.

The class bell rang and Jaime was left with a vivid image of Emerson lying naked on her bed, using a huge dildo on herself.

Jaime and Keira and Their Satellite

«Emerson gave you this?» Keira asked when she took Jaime's hand to go to the bus stop.

«She was pretty vivid about imagining what she wanted to do.»

They shared Emerson's fantasy, including her thoughts that she wanted to fuck Jaime, and if Keira was part of the deal, she was okay with that, too. By the time they reached Keira's house, they were both a little shaky.

«I love you,» Keira whispered as she and Jaime kissed at her front door.

«So much! I love you more than ever. I want you more than ever. I believe I need you. You make me complete—something I've only imagined being.»

«More. Kiss me more.»

Oh, God! I didn't think I was going to imagine them this afternoon, but when they pop into my mind it's almost overwhelming. I need to get inside so I don't make a spectacle of myself at the front door!

«She's right. We're still on your front steps,» Jaime whispered in Keira's mind.

«Yes. We should stop. I want you so much!»

They slowly pulled away from the public display they were creating with each other. Then they hugged, putting their cheeks next to each other.

Now where was I? Just getting that delicious feeling when we kiss. It's… damn… I lost it.

«Bedtime tonight?» Jaime asked.

«I know it seems kind of formal to make this arrangement in advance, but we don't have another opportunity today. Make love to me tonight. Show me how much you love me.»

«Are you sure? We'll be missing the… um… physical part.»

Oh, I'll provide all the physical I could want. Bedtime is a good idea. I need to make dinner for Mom now.

«Tonight.»

20
JEALOUSY

«ARE YOU THERE, lover?» Jaime whispered to Keira when he got to bed that night. The two had become accustomed to simply whispering the other's name to connect. They didn't know the actual range, but they were each in the back of the other's mind throughout their normal day at school and home.

«I'm here. Kisses.»

They were not in physical contact with each other, but the memory of kissing on Keira's front porch, relived by each of them, brought the sensations to life. They felt closer together with a much stronger connection. Jaime noted the distant connection did not open them to their surroundings as much as being physically in touch.

«I love you so much. I wish we were together, touching and holding each other,» Jaime whispered to her.

«Like we were at my house? Jaime, I don't know if I could keep the restriction of staying above the waist next time. Or staying clothed. I want you so much.»

«Our satellite wants us to do even more. Let me kiss your breasts again,» he answered.

«Yes. Like that. I want to feel you touching me. I want to feel you in me.»

«Like this?» Jaime asked as he projected the image captured from Emerson in school earlier in the day. «God! Look at the size of that. I'm not nearly as big as that.»

«I'm glad! I'm sure I couldn't take all of that. In fact, I don't think she can. I love the feeling of it rubbing up and down through my juices, though. Can you feel it?»

«I'm really sensitive right at the tip now. Mmm. Show me how to rub it against your clit.»

«Yes. Rub me there. I'm so ready for you.»

«I want to feel me pressing inside you.»

«Yes! Just the tip. No. More. Like that. I feel you going inside me.»

«I feel you… I feel me… What are you using? It's stretching me!» Jaime cried out.

«Stretching you? You must be feeling me. I feel so full. Oh, my God! Thrust!»

«What's…» Keira? That's not our feeling!»

«Jaime! It's Emerson! She's using that thing and thinking about… us!»

«Oh, gee! She's tormenting my vagina. Only I don't have a vagina! Ah! Out! In!»

He has a girlfriend. That's okay. Dom had a girlfriend. Raquel and I shared him. Or maybe Dom and I shared her. Or they shared me. I wonder if Keira's bush is full and red like her hair? I don't care if she's a wooly mammoth! I'll eat her while Jaime fucks me. Yes! I'm so close!

«I'm being fucked! By you, but she's controlling the motion. And I can taste me on her tongue! Or someone. She was lovers with both of them. Oh, yes. Push faster, lover,» Keira gasped.

«I'm… I can only go at the speed she sets. It's like she's controlling my thrusts in her rhythm.»

«Kiss her nipples some more. Mine. Suck on me!»

Emerson touched her breast as she continued to thrust with the dildo. Keira supposed correctly that she couldn't take it all, but she thought it was the size she remembered. The pussy she'd been licking, though, hadn't had a red bush. It was shaved bare. Raquel's pussy. But it was Keira she was imagining.

«I'm not going to last much longer. Oh, Keira, I love you so much!»

«I want to wait for her, but I'm not going to… Oh, god! She's coming.»

«Oh God!»

«Oh God!»

Mon Dieu!

«What are you doing? What are you doing? Who is she?»

«Lover?»

«You can't be with her! You're mine! Send her away! Send her away!»

It took an effort on Jaime's part to completely sever the connection with Emerson, who was just getting ready to ramp up again.

«Lover? You've joined us!» he thought to their satellite.

«Of course I'm here! It's my story. I won't let you hijack it with another woman! Send her away!»

«She's gone, honey. She was only a fantasy. She wasn't with us.»

«I could hear her speaking French.»

«Her lovers are French. You came to us. We were afraid you wouldn't get here!» Jaime said.

«You're my characters! I don't even understand how I'm talking to you and hearing you so clearly in my head. I must be mad!»

Jaime and Keira began putting little kisses around their lover's face, sending her calming thoughts.

«I don't understand. Ms. Dorn said if you hear voices in your head and they are ignoring you, you must be a writer. If they are talking to you, you have a different problem. I used to hear you, but you didn't talk to me. Now I'm hearing you talking to me. I must be crazy!»

«What's your name, precious?» Keira asked gently.

«Trayce,» she moaned as she began returning Keira's and Jaime's kisses.

«We don't want to scare you, honey. You're not crazy. You are one of the few people who can hear other people's thoughts, like us. You're only the second one we've ever met. And we've fallen hopelessly in love with you.»

«I don't know what to think or what to do?» Trayce cried. «I thought you were characters I invented for my story. I have a lot of characters that are real enough that I can hear them talk.»

«You can write stories about us if you want,» Jaime said. «But we're real people and you've been with us ever since our first kiss.»

«I love kissing you. I mean, imagining I'm kissing you,» Trayce said. «How can I be in love with voices in my head? It doesn't make sense.»

«We got wrapped up with a fantasy of a school classmate, but we were really expecting to be with you tonight,» Keira said. «Isn't it cool how we can all be in different places and still hold each other and make out.»

«Wait! You aren't even together?»

«No. We're each at home. Are you at home, Trayce?» Jaime asked.

«Yes. I heard your voices this afternoon say, 'bedtime.' I was a little late to the party, I guess. You'd already started.»

«We were inviting you to join us. We just get a little carried away when we're together in our heads. There's a lot to be considered about becoming physical in our affection. It always seems to multiply the effect of being in each other and feeling what the other feels and hearing what they're thinking. So we're trying to go slow as we adjust to the whole shared experience thing,» Keira said.

«And I just say, 'Hey, let's go!' I'm sorry. Going slow is a good idea, but are we going to make love tonight? I mean in our heads? Really?»

«If you'd like.»

«Like? It's only in my head, so why not? I might be dreaming. Kisses?»

«As many as you want,» Jaime said.

He connected deeply to Keira to share the experience of kissing each other with Trayce. She responded and welcomed the sensations.

«Mmm. So good. Your kisses just make me float!»

«That's a good way to describe it. When we're actually together, you wouldn't believe how deeply we share things and how much we can read what's around us.»

«Touches?» Trayce asked.

«Wherever you'd like,» Jaime whispered, reaching out in his mind to touch her breasts. Of course, the only frame of reference he had was touching Keira's breasts and the feeling was transferred to Trayce from Keira. They were getting closer to all being in each other.

«You were… When you were with *her*, Keira, you were… licking.»

«I've never actually done it before. It was all her memories and my imagination,» Keira said.

«You have an imagination? Imagine… Imagine licking me,» Trayce directed. She still thought of them deep down as characters she was writing.

«Gladly, lover,» Keira said.

Jaime focused on kissing and sucking on Keira's/Trayce's nipples.

«Oh! Oh, yes. I feel it. You… Are you going to make love to me, Jaime?»

«Yes. We are both going to make love to you. We want you so much.»

«I want you. Oh, how I want you to be real. You could be my Christmas gifts.»

«When you're ready.»

«Touch me! Touch me more! Kisses! Kisses! Lick! Suck!»

«Aren't you glad you have two lovers?» Keira chuckled, imagining licking Trayce's clit as she flicked her own.

«Nothing could possibly be this good in real life. I'm… Oh, yes!»

Keira and Jaime were swept up in Trayce's orgasm and mentally collapsed, leaving themselves completely open.

«I never imagined you were so complex!» Trayce gasped.

«Well, people tend to be more complex than what books would indicate. We've only gotten this close when we were all having sex with each other,» Jaime said.

«You're a mess!»

«Yes. I was just making love to two of the most wonderful girls on earth.»

«That other girl you were with?»

«No. You and Keira. You are the one we're with.»

«I was so jealous. How can characters have such a grip on me that I felt betrayed?»

«You are going to have to decide,» Keira said. «If we're imaginary, you can't blame us if we go away. If we're real, you need to invite us to meet you.»

«I need counselling. I should see a doctor. How can two characters in a story I haven't even written be so complex—give me such a powerful orgasm? I know you wouldn't hurt me. It must be me projecting that on you. I want you so much!

«Talk to Dr. Rose Edmonds.»

«Who's that?»

«Look her up. You'll see.»

«I love you. I love you both so much! I don't want you to go away.»

«We love you, Trayce. We love you to the end of the world.»

Jaime and Keira and Trayce

WHEN DAVID ANNOUNCED that he had a date Friday night and wouldn't be home for dinner, Jaime and Keira decided to have a TV date.

«Want to have spaghetti tonight?» Jaime asked.

«Sounds yummy. Want to eat me for dessert?»

«What?!»

«It's just a thought. After our little adventure the other day, I've really been wondering what it would be like with the physical element in addition to the… um… Emerson's memories.»

«I'm willing. I don't know what I'm doing, but I'd love to try. We need to set boundaries, though. If we aren't going all the way, we need to know what's acceptable and agree to an ironclad rule that we won't go further,» Jaime said.

«Yeah. I didn't mean to bring it up like that,» Keira said. «I mean, it was kind of an aside to myself, but I let it escape to you. Freudian slip, I guess. But if you're willing, after we eat and choose a movie and kind of get used to being together so we can control ourselves, I think we could do more of, kind of full-body exploration. Just no penetration. Except in my mouth. If you eat me, it's only fair that I return the pleasure.»

«Keira, you blow me away.»

«Later, I'm just going to blow you.»

THE TWO TEENS were in an otherwise empty house with David not expected until well after ten. Jaime was betting he wouldn't get home before midnight, based on a quick read of his thoughts for the evening. He didn't expect to 'get lucky,' but he hoped they'd really spend some time enjoying their company and getting to know each other in a very non-work environment.

When Keira arrived, they immediately kissed, letting the feeling expand and linger. It might have been one of the most leisurely kisses they'd ever had, even though they were certainly passionate enough. In the house alone, they closed their senses to everything but each other.

«I need to stir the sauce,» Jaime said as he led Keira to the kitchen.

«I'll start the salad. Is the water boiling for the pasta?»

«Yes, my love. Don't make too big a salad. There's way too much spaghetti and meatballs.»

«It's always so difficult to stop eating that kind of meal. I don't want to get overly full, though. I'd hate to have an evening with you where we both just sat around moaning about how we stuffed ourselves,» Keira said.

«I'm so nervous, I don't know if I can eat anyway.»

«Oh, honey, there's really nothing to be nervous about. We're both going to love what we do tonight with no feelings of remorse. It's excitement, not nerves.»

«I just want to contain my excitement enough that you have plenty of time to enjoy yours.»

«Do you think *she'll* show up?» Keira asked.

«Haven't you felt her this week? Since our rather dramatic time Wednesday, I've kind of felt her humming in the back of my mind most of the time. It's almost like I feel the connection with you.»

«I have felt her. There was a time yesterday when I thought she was talking about us. I wonder who to.»

«I don't know, but I've had an uncomfortable feeling about it. I couldn't get a good reading on her and felt she must need privacy, so I didn't want to force my way in. Something just felt off.»

«I'm sure we'll find out.»

They managed to contain themselves through another kiss and dinner. After they'd cleaned up and made sure the leftovers were stored and the dishes washed, they went to the TV room. Jaime flipped on a random movie and the two settled on the couch together.

«Oh, I've always wanted to see this,» Keira said. «I might not be able to pay attention to you for a while!»

«Really? Um… Okay. We did plan a TV date.» Jaime was a little confused and disappointed.

«I'm kidding, doofus! I'm not interested in what's on TV. I'm interested in the boy I'm watching it with,» Keira laughed.

«You really managed to spring that on me. Well played! I think we're getting better at preserving our independence when we're together. It's feeling more natural.»

«Yeah. You could kiss me now,» Keira said.

«I'd love to.»

From then on, the teens let down some of the rigid barriers they'd held when making out previously. They explored each other's mind as well as their bodies. Jaime let Keira know how starved for a woman's attention he'd been, which had driven some of his voyeurism on his classmates.

Keira had her own demons to contend with, including her self-image and doubts about being lovable. It seemed they shared many of the same doubts and neuroses that their classmates did, even though they could readily see how wrong they were.

«It became, like, normal to be embarrassed about growing breasts,» Keira said. «Everybody else is embarrassed by it, so I might as well be, too. Besides, I've seen what boys actually think when they see a girl in the hall. They try to not let girls see them, but I swear, every time a boy sees a girl, he tries to see if our nipples are pushing through.»

«That's why so many layers of clothes and heavy bras, even for girls who don't need the support. And boys are always looking for a gap in your shirt buttons to see if they can glimpse the curve of your bare breast, your bra, or the bonanza: your nipple. Like now, your nipples are hard enough to see through your bra and everything,» Jaime said.

«Silly! I'm not wearing a bra. I wanted you to see them.»

«They… You are beautiful.»

«I'll accept both compliments,» she giggled. «Yes. You can touch me.»

Jaime slid his hand under Keira's T-shirt and moved upward to cup her breast and lightly stroke first one nipple and then the other. Keira settled into his embrace and kissed with even more intensity. She copied his movement and played with Jaime's chest.

«I can't tell if I'm excited by your touch on me or my touch on you,» he whispered. «It feels so good!»

«I think it's both. It's like being caressed in stereo. If I focus, I can feel your channel and I can feel my channel. When I let them blend, it's more than the sum of the two.»

«The whole is greater than the sum of its parts,» Jaime quoted. «I read that somewhere.»

«Gestalt. Or I guess in its simplest form just synergy. Aunt Rose explained it to me once. Synergy is generally used for physical things, like the production of energy from a moving object when it collides with a stationary object. Gestalt is more psychological. Like when two people brainstorm an idea, they might get results that neither one would think of individually,» Keira said. They'd discarded their shirts and were pressed chest-to-chest as they continued kissing.

«We're experiencing both at the same time,» Jaime said. «Maybe on a level no one else ever has.»

«Do you think we're the first people who ever united their minds as they united their bodies?» Keira asked.

«The mere fact we both attend the same school and heard each other would indicate a much higher likelihood of it having happened before. There are seven billion people on earth. We can't be the only two who have felt this way.»

«We're the only two *of us* who have ever felt this way. Yes. Suck! Lick. Kiss all over my chest and stomach. I love your touch—your lips. You take my breath away.»

«I think our breathing and our heartbeats are in sync. I can feel every breath you take as I fill my own lungs,» Jaime said.

«Let me kiss your chest now. You've felt the sensations in my nipples. I want to feel your sensations. Are they as sensitive as mine?»

The two were totally wrapped up in each other, ignoring the movie playing in the background as they explored their bodies and relationship on the sofa. They were unrushed and had forgotten the rest of the world. All was silent but the entwining of their being with each other.

«Yes! Touch me. Let me push them down. I want to feel you touching me.» Keira kicked her trousers and underwear off her feet and let Jaime explore between her legs.

«You're so slippery.»

«I'm so ready. Yes! Oh, my love! Is it terrible? Am I ugly there? Do I smell?»

«So beautiful. This might be the most beautiful sight I've ever seen.»

«Emerson's memory of her girlfriend? That was pretty amazing.»

«This is far more beautiful. I could live on your juices. You are *not* smelly. Don't even think that. You're divine!»

«Oh, Jaime! Again! Your tongue. Do that again. I've never felt anything like it! I want you to make love to me.»

«I'm making love to you with my tongue. As much as I want everything, we promised only oral.»

«Yes. And no remorse. Oh, love! Are you going to come when I do?»

«I'm trying to experience your orgasm without losing control of my own. I don't know if it will work.»

«We're going to find out… in… just a… second. It's so… Oh! So good!.

«Oh, God! What did you just do to me?» Trayce screamed in their heads. She was dazed with Keira's orgasm.

«Trayce? Are you with us?»

«I knew if I settled down to masturbate, you'd show up. You love watching me, don't you.»

«We were kind of too wrapped up in what we were doing to even notice when you joined us,» Keira said. «We were hoping you'd be here. Did you feel that? Wasn't it the most amazing thing you've ever experienced?»

«What did you do? I'm totally knocked out!» Trayce said.

«Jaime licked me to orgasm! And I'm about to return the favor.»

«You're going to lick him? My God! You're going to put him in your mouth? I was just going to stop to say… Oh well, I'll ride along a while first. You're really going to suck him?»

«Until he comes in my mouth and I swallow all he has to give,» Keira said. Jaime moaned.

«I can feel… I feel both my mouth getting full and I feel the sensation of me slipping in and out of my mouth! I can't believe I'm feeling both. If he comes, I might choke on it while I'm coming. You're so close,» Trayce gasped in their minds.

«I'm going to… Keira, you don't have to take it in your mouth!»

«I want it, Jaime. I want to feel it. I want to taste it. I want to drink you up.»

«And come with you. Oh! I'm coming again!» Trayce called out.

«Me, too,» Jaime moaned as he shot into Keira's mouth and she greedily swallowed. She found her own core and flipped the switch to her climax.

All three lay panting and basking in the closeness of their shared climaxes.

«That was an experience,» Trayce sighed. «It just shows the power of the mind. We can create such amazing things.»

«We're so glad you are with us, Trayce. We'd have done more to include you if we'd known you were lurking nearby,» Keira said.

«I went to my room after dinner and undressed, lay down on my bed, and started masturbating. I knew if I got close, you'd show up. You did, and that proves my point. You're a figment of my imagination. I saw that nice doctor today and he helped me.»

«He?»

«Dr. Schwartz. He got me right in when I called. He was so nice. He said it was time to put away my imaginary friends and focus on my schoolwork. He was right. Staying in my head for too long isn't healthy. I need to go out and experience real life. Maybe I'll have a boyfriend. Or a girlfriend. Experimenting with this story has led me to realize I'm not opposed to that. But I'm throwing away my story notes and kissing you goodbye.»

«You're lying to us,» Jaime growled at her. «You aren't throwing things away. You love us.»

«I love *the idea* of you. True, I might have stray thoughts about you. Maybe one day I'll dig out my notes and write the story. Until then there are many other things to do and experience. I just stopped by to say goodbye. And thank you for the powerful orgasms. That will last me for a while!»

«You know we're in the back of your mind, just like you are in ours,» Jaime pled.

«Goodbye!»

With that, Trayce began to fade away from their consciousness as she built barriers between them.

«We love you,» Jaime and Keira whispered. But Trayce was not there. She was only a whisper in the backs of their minds.

21
CATASTROPHE

Jaime and Keira

«CAN I SPEND the night with you?» Keira cried as she and Jaime held each other.

«You know I want you,» Jaime said. «But we promised. No remorse. No regrets. And I don't think it's a good idea to make love to each other for the first time when we're hurting from being rejected so callously. We'd always associate our first time with her rejection.»

«You're right, of course. I just don't want to be apart from you. We're completely naked lying on the sofa together, loving each other, reveling in our feelings of being united. But neither one of us is turned on. You're not hard. I'm drying up. Oh, hold me, Jaime! Show me how much you love me.»

«I love you to the height and width and depth of my soul, Keira. You are all the world to me. My soulmate.»

«We'll make love, Jaime. Soon. We have each other and that whole is still greater than the sum. I love you. Hold me and just let me feel you as we touch.»

«I didn't think your aunt would give her that kind of advice,» Jaime sighed internally.

«She didn't see my aunt. My aunt is Dr. Edmonds. Who is Dr. Schwartz?»

«I don't know, but I don't like him. Maybe I'll go see him myself and show him what an imaginary friend looks like in the flesh.»

«Honey, don't be upset tonight. Not over that. We have enough to be

201

upset about. Let's just have each other.»

«That's all we really need.»

Jaime and Keira stayed naked, lying on the sofa long after the movie had ended and another started. They dozed a little, sharing dreams of a life together. Eventually, their amorous thoughts returned and as they kissed, their bodies moved together and brought them once again to a climax.

A barely present sigh echoed in the back of their minds.

They managed to get dressed just before David got home at one.

Trayce

Trayce was sad. She wasn't quite miserable. It was the kind of sadness that comes when there is no joy around. She'd gotten used to having joy in her life. That her joy came from imaginary friends disturbed her and made her sad.

She lay awake for a long time that night. Even implementing Dr. Schwartz's key word triggers to block out voices in her head, she was still aware of them. They were sad, too. When they finally fell asleep, she did, too.

In the daylight the next morning, it didn't seem so bad. Her characters weren't living together, so even though she felt a stray thought or two, it wasn't as if they were actually having sex. She half-remembered sighing with satisfaction in her sleep, but that could have been from anything. *Right?* She'd written down a couple of those scenes, but there was still no story to her story.

It had been that way since puberty. She'd always been creative and made up stories, but when she started reading fan fiction for some of her favorite books, she discovered the erotic side of her stories. It was fun to 'ship' two favorite characters, putting them in a romantic relationship. And that was when her characters started talking to her.

She could be almost anywhere and suddenly a character she did or didn't recognize would randomly start talking. She would giggle a little, then rush home to write a story about the character, sometimes giving it a place in an existing fictional universe, and occasionally just setting the story in her school. She usually inserted herself as either the second party or even as a third.

But she'd never had characters as real or persistent as Jaime and

Keira—characters who talked *to* her. And they were hot! And sexy! They did things she'd never imagined before and she could absolutely feel what they were doing. Who would have thought that she could not only feel what was going on with the girl, who had the same equipment she did, but with a boy! She could feel him getting hard—could feel where in his gut the flow started and the entire passageway his come followed into his girlfriend's… mouth! She'd never seriously considered oral sex as an option like that.

When they started insisting they were real, she knew she had a serious problem. She knew she needed help. She couldn't talk to her mother about it. Even though her mother had gotten active in AA and had a new counselor, they were still light years apart, it seemed.

How long will it take until the yearning goes away? Trayce thought. That must be what her mother felt about alcohol.

Keira had told her to visit a psychiatrist named Edmonds, but she certainly wasn't taking advice from her characters. The first counselor she found who could take her for an immediate appointment was Dr. Schwartz. She didn't really want to go to a male doctor, but beggars can't be choosers, her mother always said.

He was nice. He said it wasn't uncommon for very creative women to imagine voices starting around puberty. It was just their intense creativity operating in their brains. He'd even explained what he called the bicameral brain and how one side could talk to the other. What she was hearing was actually her own internal voice.

Okay. So, I already know it's all in my head! What do I do about it?

Dr. Schwartz was understanding, if a little patronizing. But his interest reached a new high when she told him about the two characters who talked back to her and insisted they were real. That seemed to open a different chapter and he wanted to know all about them. She declined to give him their names because she'd just made those up. He wanted to know all about when and where she heard them. It was embarrassing to admit it was usually during masturbation, but had occurred at other times.

He gave her exercises she could use to block the voices and encouraged her to stay away from them if she heard them. Engaging with them could deepen her dependency. He said to simply say goodbye to them and not let them bother her again.

So, Friday night, even though she'd determined not to participate, she found herself with her hand between her legs and the characters having sex in her head. And what sex they had! Without even penetration. But she never would have thought she'd imagine taking him in her mouth and letting him spurt his stuff there. It was just so intense!

She had to force herself to part from them and say goodbye. It was a resolution she was determined to keep.

Jaime

KEIRA AND JAIME intended to go to the ballet Saturday evening. Jaime was going to drive the two of them for the first time since he'd gotten his driver's license. That had been an ordeal, but he finally succeeded in using his father as an interpreter to explain the process as described in the manual for testing deaf drivers. The tester finally agreed when he understood that he could give Jaime oral instructions but Jaime couldn't respond while he had both hands on the steering wheel where they belonged.

Before he could meet Keira, Jaime had to go grocery shopping with his father—usually, a favorite outing for the two. They stopped for lunch at a diner and then went on to the store. They usually stayed together while shopping because that was part of the fun. They had their list and the menus for the week.

"We're out of salsa!" Jaime signed. "I'll go back and get it."

"Don't forget chips," his father laughed. Jaime took off for the aisle they'd passed just a minute before.

Stupid bitch! Thinks she can just ditch me? I'll show her. Nobody tells me we're breaking up. She changed the fucking locks! I'll kill her. I know she's here somewhere.

Whoever it was, the broadcast of his thoughts was loud and clear and nearby. It brought Jaime to a stop with a jar of their favorite salsa in hand. The narrative of what the guy would do to his bitch girlfriend continued and Jaime could see he had serious intent to kill or maim the woman. He ran across the ends of the aisles until he spotted the man halfway down between the toilet paper and tissues. He turned up the aisle, not knowing what he could do.

A woman pushing a grocery cart crossed the aisle at the end and the boyfriend raised a gun.

«No!» Jaime shouted with his mind. He sprinted toward the man with the jar of salsa raised in his hand.

"Bitch! Nobody breaks up with me!" the guy shouted.

Jaime hit the man in the head with the jar of salsa, shattering it all over. His momentum carried the man to the floor as a second shot rang out. Jaime's jump carried him onto the man, but his grip on the guy's shoulders and the broken salsa jar as he struggled to deflect the shot meant his own head was unprotected and he, too, hit the floor—and a shard of the broken glass.

Jaime and Kenton

THAT'S GOT TO be him! He saw the guy in his head. Someone was watching as David ran to hold his son. Jaime was swimming in and out of consciousness.

Why didn't he yell? That would have turned the man and protected the woman. Stupid!

Jamie recognized the head taste. He'd heard that inner voice before.

«I'm not stupid. I can't out-loud talk!»

The man ignored him and continued to rant in his head about missed opportunities, but he'd know now where to find the kid. That was two parts of his needed gestalt. He just needed to get them together where he could control them.

"Jaime! Jaime, are you okay?" David screamed as he slid to the floor on the spattered salsa. He kicked the gun away from the shooter's flexing fingers and knelt to cradle his son. A store employee ran up with a tape dispenser and wrapped the shooter's hands together as the guy began spitting profanities.

I could have collected him today, but not while he's injured and has attention all around him. Damn it! So close!

Jaime exerted all his effort to focus on the outside world and shut the bastard out of his mind.

"Jaime! You're safe, just stay still." David grabbed a roll of paper towels the store guy handed him and tore off a dozen sheets to press against Jaime's head where he was bleeding. "An ambulance is on the way. Police are coming into the store now."

Jaime tried to look toward the end of the aisle where the shooter's target was lying. But she wasn't dead. She was screaming in pain. The shooter had hit her in the leg, his shot thwarted by Jaime's impact. She pushed herself to a seated position as other shoppers tried to help her. Having shut out all the thoughts of people surrounding them, Jaime was acutely aware of the rising volume of physical noise in the store.

"I heard the shot and looked up," the stock boy with the tape was yelling at a policeman. "This guy hit him from behind and knocked him to the ground. He's a hero!"

"Okay, okay. Take it easy. We'll get an official statement."

The officer snapped handcuffs on the shooter over the tape the stock boy had used. Another officer carefully chalked the outline of the gun and bagged it. The ambulance crew was rushing to take the woman out of the store as she was still screaming. An officer had chalked an outline where she had fallen.

It all seemed to happen at once, but it was actually several minutes before enough emergency responders had arrived to get the entire situation under control. Even fire trucks showed up.

"I kicked the gun over there," David said. "He was trying to reach it."

"You related?" the officer asked.

"This is my son. He was knocked out. He's bleeding. Help him."

"We've got a gurney on the way," the officer said. "Where were you when it happened?"

"I was just coming toward this aisle facing the woman who was shot. My grocery cart is around the corner over there."

The officer examined Jaime.

"He was unconscious?"

"Yes."

"Can you hear me, son? How did you know the guy was going to shoot?"

"Saw him pull the gun when I was at the end of the aisle there," Jaime signed with his eyes closed. He felt so woozy. His father interpreted.

"Jaime doesn't speak. Never has. He hears okay, but only uses sign language to speak," David said.

Jaime was focused on shutting out everything around him. All the voices in his head were going silent. He just needed to sleep.

"Okay. We'll hold the rest of the questions until we can get him to a hospital and get him checked for concussion. It looks like he'll need stitches for that cut on his head."

"What about me?" the shooter complained. "That kid knocked me out. I could have a concussion."

"We'll have a doctor check you at the station," the officer said. "Perps don't ride in an ambulance or go to the hospital." The officer looked up at Jaime. "I recognize you, don't I? You broke up that kidnapping a few weeks ago. Quite a talent for being in the right place at the right time."

"Bad timing," David interpreted.

"Don't tell that woman he shot it was bad timing," the officer said.

The second ambulance arrived and EMTs examined Jaime as David gave their contact information to the officer. Another officer dragged the shooter to a squad car and took off. As soon as he was loaded onto the gurney, Jaime let go of the last vestige of consciousness he was clinging to.

Jaime and Keira

JAIME WAS AWAKENED at the hospital. There was the usual hurry up and wait routine. A doctor arrived and immediately put three stitches in the cut on Jaime's head after cleaning the stinging salsa out of it. It took longer to get a thorough examination for concussion. They determined he should stay overnight for observation, which Jaime objected to, but his father encouraged him to follow the advice. He kept his mind utterly closed. His phone buzzed several times before he was finally able to reach it and see the half dozen messages from Keira demanding to know what had happened and if he was all right.

"Got my cape a little bloody. At Mercy Hospital," he texted her.

"OMG! I'm on my way. Please be okay!"

"Nothing too serious. Just got hit in the head."

"You think? I'll talk to you when I see you."

A POLICE DETECTIVE arrived at his room to check on Jaime and get his statement. Since Jaime didn't have his computer, he had to sign and his father interpreted. It seemed pretty clear, but the policeman was sure Jaime would be called to testify if the guy didn't plead guilty at once.

Keira waited in the lobby until David realized she was there and brought her to the room where they stashed Jaime.

"Since you have a visitor, I'll make myself scarce for a while, son. I'll be back before visiting hours are over," David said. "I can give Keira a ride home."

"Thanks, Dad," Jaime signed.

"Thank you, Mr. Stackhouse," Keira said.

As soon as he was out of the room, Keira bent to kiss Jaime.

«Please don't die. Please don't. I'll do anything. Just please still be here,» came the voice in their heads as soon as their lips touched. Jaime's channels opened at last. For an instant, he thought it was Keira, then recognized their satellite's head taste.

«It's okay, love,» he said. «I'm just a little banged up. It's nothing serious.»

«Kiss me. Kiss me. Kiss me. It feels so real!»

«It is real,» Keira said, a little exasperatedly. «Don't you just love the way his lips taste?»

«I'm losing it. I didn't mean to try and kill off my characters! How can I let you take over my mind so completely? I thought I was just pushing you away.»

«Don't worry. We'll still be here when you're ready to meet us. You won't need to make anything up.»

Jaime and Keira stopped kissing and looked at each other. Trayce faded into the distance a little.

«When it happened—whatever it was that made you lose consciousness— it knocked the breath out of me,» Keira said. «But Trayce screamed in my head. I had to keep my thoughts as calm as possible and be reassuring without knowing if I was getting through to her at all. I finally said I'd kiss you as soon as I saw you and cut her off. I've still been able to hear her crying for the past two hours or more.»

«We need to find her and show her we're real.»

«That psychologist convinced her that it's common for creative people to imagine very real people to populate their fiction. But she shouldn't be obsessed with them.»

«Great. So, she thinks she's going crazy.»

«Yeah. We need to be really careful!»

They kissed again briefly and heard Trayce's sigh in the back of their minds. They kept hold of each other's hand.

«Maybe tonight, um… when everything's quiet in the hospital, you should… you know… reach out to her and see if she'll talk to you.»

«I would feel like… That would be like… I'm not going to cheat on you, Keira. Not even in my head. You are the love of my life. My soulmate. I know we've both fallen for Trayce, but we've always been together when we talked to her or felt her with us.»

«Well, not always,» Keira said. «I mean, this afternoon… you were isolated from us, you know? First, you were unconscious, and then you kind of shut down. In the emergency room, I couldn't read you or your dad at all. During all that time, though, I was sort of in touch with her. We didn't make love or anything like that. I mean, we were both really upset. But I kept imagining us kissing a little and comforting each other. I don't see why you couldn't do that, too.»

«I'll think about it, honey.»

"Oh, look. Your dinner is here. I suppose that means your dad will show up soon. Better have one more little kiss now."

They kissed and Jaime could feel the smile whispering in his mind.

Jaime and Trayce

AFTER THE NURSES made their ten o'clock check-in, Jaime finally felt like he had the privacy to attempt a contact with Trayce. They still didn't have enough information about her. He didn't even know what direction she lived in. And the hospital might still be putting up too much interference to communicate long distance without Keira's kiss to boost the signal. He'd whispered a «Goodnight, I love you,» to Keira and she'd whispered back, so at least the two of them could be in touch.

He thought in his mind of the times they'd been together, all of which had been pretty intimate—the most recent, while he was kissing Keira in the hospital. He settled on that memory and thought of her.

«Trayce? Are you there, lover?»

«Lover? Can I really be your lover? I must be nuts.»

«You aren't crazy. We're real people and somehow we've connected in our minds.»

«You're… people? There are really two of you? I thought when I wrote the story, I'd have to write myself into her part.»

«Keira would be very hurt if you didn't continue to love her.»

«Oh, I *do* love her. I couldn't write her out of the story. She's… a really great kisser.»

«I agree. She's the first girl I've ever kissed. The only girl I've kissed physically.»

«And you're so in love. I'm terrible for putting myself in your lives. I don't want to spoil anything for you,» Trayce said.

«We like having you with us.»

«She was so sweet! She kept kissing my face and telling me it would be okay. I was too worried that putting your story away had hurt you to do anything but cry.»

«We don't have much experience. First girlfriend and boyfriend, you know?»

«You're ahead of me!»

«I don't think so. You've been there almost every step of the way. At least since our first kiss.»

«Maybe longer. I didn't know it was you. It seems you've been lurking around the edges of all the stories I've written lately.»

«May I see what you look like?»

«How?»

«Just look at yourself in a mirror.»

«Um… I guess so. I saw what the two of you looked like when you were looking at each other. So pretty and so handsome. I know what I look like. I just avoid mirrors most of the time. My mouth is too big. My eyes are too far apart. My hair is dull and lifeless.»

«I don't believe you. That's your self-image talking, not reality.»

«Yeah. Well, fine. You're just a voice in my head anyway. What difference does it make?»

An image in a full-length mirror filled Jaime's mind. Trayce was naked! He'd only intended to ask to see her face.

«My breasts are too small and my hips are too wide. My… everything…»

«Shh. Let me say it. I don't have much to compare to because I've only seen Keira like this. And glimpsed a couple of people's self-image. You're just as pretty. You have a mouth I'd love to kiss. I'd like to kiss all of you. Your breasts are perfect! I can imagine holding you close like this.»

«Oh, God! I can feel you. You're hard! For me! Are we going to…?»

«No, honey. Not tonight. I'd want Keira with us and I'm lying in a hospital bed.»

«Oh, yeah. If you are just a voice in my head, why am I thinking up all these rules?»

«You'll soon find out. We're much more than voices in your head.»

«I really wish it was all true. Like a Christmas movie where the voices in my head turn out to be real people who love me and have been looking for me all their lives,» she sighed.

«Maybe we're like the elf sitting on a shelf that you just don't see as you pass us by.»

«That was such a funny movie. No! You were there?»

«Yes. It took us a while before we figured out we were watching the same movie.»

«You were kind of distracting. But *I* was watching that movie. What else would my characters be watching?»

«How did your paper for Ms. Sullivan go?»

«Oh!… I haven't gotten it back yet, but I think it turned out okay. I almost got distracted when I was polishing it.»

«We tried to leave you alone and not distract you. Is that at Rose Community College?»

«Yeah. Monday and Wednesday at three.»

«Maybe we'll see you there. I'm really tired now. I think we should say goodnight.»

«Yeah. Yeah… Kiss?»

«You know it's really just the memory of Keira and me kissing. It will be better when our physical lips touch.»

«I was there.»

Jaime tenderly kissed Trayce in his mind.

«Oh, yes! I love goodnight kisses!» Keira said in their minds.

«Goodnight, lovers.»
«Goodnight, lovers.»
«*Lovers?* Yeah. Goodnight, lovers.»

22
CLOSE ENCOUNTERS

Jaime and Keira and Trayce

«WE NEED TO meet her,» Jaime said when Keira came to visit him at home Sunday afternoon. The doctor had released him from the hospital, but told him to just stay home and not exercise for the day. David had suggested that he just invite Keira to visit instead of going out for their Sunday walk. Keira jumped at the opportunity.

"I can't believe you got cut so badly," Keira spoke aloud, kissing the bandage on his forehead. «What do you suggest?»

«We should go to the college and meet her after her class. It's on Monday and Wednesday at 3:00. After the winter break, we might not know where she is.»

«I can't go tomorrow,» Keira said. «I committed to helping with the elementary school winter concert. The kids are so cute! You could go, though.»

«No. We should go together. She really needs to see us both and understand we are real.»

«Okay, then. We'll go after school Wednesday,» Keira said. «It really upset you.»

«Even with the evidence of hearing me cut off when I was unconscious and you comforting her and me contacting her last night, she still thinks we're characters and it's unhealthy to think we are really talking to her. That doctor really screwed things up for us.»

«Well, we can try to convince her when we're present. She still might reject the notion that we're anything more than voices in her head,» Keira said.

«There's something else we need to be aware of,» Jaime said at last. «I was a target yesterday. Not of the shooter. The guy who wants to capture head talkers had come to the grocery store to find me. He even had people in the parking lot to grab me.»

«What?!» Keira said, alarmed. «Why didn't you say something?»

«I figured this was best dealt with in person when we were at least partly shielded. It's one of the reasons I shut down after I was knocked out.»

«Jaime, that's terrible! We should call the police!»

«Keira, honey. Can you imagine how they'd respond to that? I heard a guy talking in my head who was planning to kidnap me? They'd think I was crazier than Trayce believes she is.»

«Oh, shit! We need to be really careful.»

«No kidding,» Jaime said. «It's the same guy I've heard before. Only this time he said he had two pieces to the puzzle and he was sure he could get all three if he had one of them.»

«Is he a head talker?» Keira asked. She had curled up next to Jaime on the sofa and was kissing his face as they talked. They hadn't turned to really kiss, but both knew it was coming.

«No. It's all his internal monologue. He's proud of his ability to recognize head talkers. I don't think he has a good concept about them being able to hear him. He might believe we're projecting our thoughts to each other instead of listening to each other.»

«We need to be able to hear him, Jaime. We'll have to keep our awareness open enough that we can tell when a threat is nearby. If he already knows about the two of us, we don't want him to know about Trayce.»

«Maybe she's safer if we don't try to visit her,» Jaime sighed.

«You know who would help? We happen to know a head talker who is a private detective. I bet Mr. Angus would keep an eye on things.»

«He's so old. Can he really do anything?»

«I bet he can do anything when those two strippers are with him,» Keira laughed.

They kissed deeply and, in the process, opened themselves fully to others in the vicinity.

«No! Maybe you don't have homework, but I do,» Trayce said, defiantly. «I'm writing a different story right now and I don't want to be interrupted.»

«What's this story about?» Keira asked.

«A woman who is really depressed but has to go out in public with her boyfriend and be sociable. I really want to write something meaningful about depression and its effects on a person.»

«Wow! Do you always write about people we've met?» Jaime asked.

«I used to write fan fiction, but my creative writing teacher challenged me to build a story around a character. I've done two and they were both pretty successful. One was about a little girl and her mommy who just lost their father/husband in the war. That was really part of my story, too. I lost my dad in an accident over a year ago. My teacher loved it! My last story was about an old man who fantasized about being a young detective who had two strippers as sidekicks. My teacher gave me an A, but said it was not appropriate for school.»

«We met Angus, Kate, and Thursday in the park near here,» Keira said. «The little girl and her mom were in a movie theater when we were first dating.»

«Well, of course you would have all the same experiences I write about. They're all in my mind with you,» Trayce said.

«I think you are reading the characters from our minds,» Jaime said.

«That's not possible. What day is it in your world?» Trayce asked.

«What do you mean?» Jaime asked.

«It's Sunday here. How long ago was your incident with the shooter in the store? I wrote that down so I could add some thrilling events to the story.»

«It's Sunday, Trayce. The whole thing happened yesterday,» Keira said.

«Oh.» She sounded disappointed. «Of course, we're tied closely together at the moment so our experiences are in sync. But if I wrote it and said it happened last spring, then you'd agree that it happened last spring.»

«No. You can surely write a story about it and set it in any time or place you want,» Jaime said. «You could say it happened in Seattle, for example. Maybe there's a better setting for it up there. It still wouldn't change the historical fact that it happened yesterday in Portland.»

«There's no sense arguing with myself over this,» Trayce declared. «Now let's have a little kiss and let me get back to work.»

«Really, Trayce? You're just going to eavesdrop on the two of us as we're making out. We'll try to put up some barriers so you aren't dragged into it, but Jaime and I aren't going to kiss just to entertain you,» Keira said.

«Fine. Just leave me alone while I work on my story.» Trayce abruptly closed her mind to them by reciting some ridiculous mantra they didn't completely understand.

"You know, we haven't chosen a play yet. We should spend the afternoon reading and memorizing our parts," Keira said. They did have a little kiss, but closed themselves off from contact with Trayce. They spent the afternoon with Jaime's laptop open, searching for a play they could easily memorize to slip into if someone was eavesdropping on them. They chose *A Streetcar Named Desire*.

Jaime and Emerson

AT SCHOOL, JAIME was in for another surprise from his rather surprising computer lab partner. First, while not dressed as provocatively as she'd been when she made her proposition the previous week, she was wearing a skirt that came to mid-thigh with over the knee socks and white tennis shoes. Her tailored blouse was tucked in to accent her bust and narrow waistline. And even to the casual observer, her black bra was apparent under the blouse.

"Wow! Emerson, you're letting your Paris persona shine through," Jaime typed on his TTS laptop. He handed her the Bluetooth earbud, which she put it in an ear already adorned with dangling earrings. She smiled then reached to touch his head.

"What happened? You're injured!" she said.

"I had an encounter with a piece of broken glass," he typed. "Just a couple of stitches and it will be fine. So, you do look great!"

"Thank you, Jaime. I've lived in a shell too long. I didn't want anyone in our class thinking they could date good old Emerson for a good time. You know, the girls who dress… more attractively… get hit on a lot. I kind of closed up the look in middle school, except when I travel. You're right, this is a modest edition of the Paris look. I'm glad you like it."

"You know, I've always thought you were attractive, even when you were wearing baggy jeans and sweaters," he typed. "This is a good look for you."

"Zip, I know this is going to sound like it's coming out of left field, but do you and Keira have um… like another girlfriend? I mean… I'm asking because… I'd be interested. You know? I was part of a *ménage à trois* when I was in Paris and I miss them terribly. Please don't spread that around. I trust you with the information, but that's just because I really trust you. Anyway, the other two are getting married and I'm the odd girl out. I'm sitting beside you each day in comp sci, and you're really cool. I've seen you with Keira but I don't have any classes with her, so I haven't been able to talk to her. And… God! I'm making a hash of things. You must think I'm really desperate. But I can't get the two of you off my mind. You've been so helpful on my project and Keira is so pretty and… I'll shut up now," Emerson said. She was flushed red.

"Emerson, you're really a great partner in class. I like you a lot, and I know Keira likes you, too. I don't think she'd go for adding another person in our group. Yeah. There's another girl we met… online. But you might also have the wrong idea about us. Keira and I are dating, but we're not really… like… having sex, you know?"

"Oh, shit! I mean, like, yeah. I thought you probably were because you seem so connected. That's one of the reasons the two of you are so attractive. But that wouldn't mean we couldn't hang out, you know? I mean… well, if you've got someone else, that would kind of complicate things for both her and me, wouldn't it? Please, just forget I brought it up. I was allowing fantasy to control my stupid mouth."

"Emerson, I'm really flattered that you'd think of Keira and me like that. I know she'll feel the same way. Don't be embarrassed about it. We're teens. Fortunately, most people don't realize when I've stuck my foot in it because I do it quietly! Well, Keira knows. But we can, you know, hang out a little and we'll still be working on our projects. You'll still test my voice customization app, won't you?"

"Of course I will! Um… Maybe it would be okay if Keira was around when we did the test. I'd like to get to know her better anyway."

"Sure."

Jaime and Keira

«She actually suggested that? Holy cow!»

«It was really hard not to imagine her, you know, stretched out naked on her bed. But the thing is, she's definitely head deaf. I was reading her while she was talking and she was thinking about the great come she had while masturbating to our image Friday night. There wasn't a trace of indication she was even remotely aware of our presence.»

«Still, it's interesting that she picked up on us as potential partners. I wonder if there is some kind of aura that surrounds people who are, like, into or open to a multiple relationship. There must be something about us that attracted Trayce to us, too.»

«And I'm not about to give up on her.»

«We have to let her be her. If she just can't deal with the reality of head talk, we can't let her believe she's going crazy. It's hard enough when you accept it and have someone to share it with,» Keira said.

«That's true. I… We care for her like we do for each other. How is that even possible? I love you with all my heart. And I love her with all my other heart.»

«I've been inside your heart, love. I think it's big enough to love us both. Like I love you both. Isn't that the craziest thing? We didn't know her at all until she showed up while we were kissing!»

«Maybe it's not possible to connect that way without falling in love. I was in love with you at least by the time we kissed. And even though she's fighting any possibility other than that we're characters she made up, she's shown us a lot about herself. I mean, I wanted to see her face and she stood naked in front of a mirror for me!»

«Do you think she's ever done that before?»

«She said she avoided mirrors. It wasn't just her body she was showing me. She showed me how uncertain about life she was. What her dreams were. How the two of us fit so naturally into the picture with her.»

«When I was, like, holding her while you were in the hospital, I found out a lot. She lost her father in an auto accident with a drunk driver. Her mother was in and out of touch mentally almost ever since, but is better now that she's seeing a counselor and is in AA. In some ways, I think the idea of having both you and me as lovers is a way of replacing her parents. But she's so vulnerable! I just hate to think of her facing everything all alone.»

«Wednesday, we'll convince her we're real.»

«I hope so.»

Jaime and Keira and Trayce

«WE SHOULD GET to the college in plenty of time to grab a cup of coffee before her class gets out,» Jaime said.

«You want coffee?»

«I was just thinking about something to do while we're waiting.»

«I was thinking we could find a nice spot and get warmed up. You know. Kiss a little?» Keira suggested.

«We just need to be careful not to disturb Trayce in class, but we can use the time we are kissing to survey the area for threats. I haven't heard anything from that guy so far. I want to be ready if he's going to throw a bag over my head and drag me off.»

«I love you, Jaime.»

Once at the college, they found a spot to stand about a hundred yards from the main entrance to the building where Trayce's class was held. They sat on a bench holding hands and observing the students passing by. There weren't too many of course, because classes were in session. A few were arriving early for their next class or heading to the library. Trayce's class would be out at four.

«We're going to freeze our butts,» Keira giggled.

«At least there's no snow or wet on the bench.»

They shared a soft kiss, relishing the feel of each other's lips and extending their range exponentially. They kept strong barriers up against being overheard.

«Can you tell if she's there?» Keira asked.

«I feel a hint, but it feels a long distance away, or probably just inside that building and muted by all the brick and metal.»

«We should have gotten coffee,» Keira giggled. «It's cold out here. No sign of the bad guy?»

«Nothing.»

They held hands and tried to just relax. Eventually, students started appearing, exiting the building. They clutched each other more tightly as they held their breath expectantly.

«There! That's her. God, she's beautiful!» Keira exploded.

«Wait. She's talking to someone. Don't interrupt her,» Jaime cautioned.

«Now. Kiss me.»

«Trayce, we're here. See us kissing?» Jaime asked.

Trayce's eyes snapped to Jaime and Keira. Her heartrate accelerated and she made a single step toward them.

«We won't hurt you. We just want to meet you.»

No! No! It can't be. I just saw two random people kissing and thought of them. They aren't real. I have to get hold of myself, Trayce screamed in her mind.

«We're real. We told you we'd visit. We'll wave.»

Keira and Jaime each raised a hand and waved at Trayce, but that only seemed to aggravate her level of panic.

I thought them up in my head and I'm hearing things that make them seem real. I'm projecting them onto random people and imagining they're real.

«We're real.»

«Go away. I'm not crazy. I'm not! You're characters. You aren't real. I'm not going to meet you after class. You aren't really here. Go away!»

Trayce picked up her pace and then started running toward the bus stop. The bus that had just arrived wasn't the one that would take her home, but she joined the crowd who were boarding and slouched down in a seat holding her hands over her ears.

Jaime and Keira let her go and didn't try to contact her as the bus pulled away.

«That didn't go as planned,» Keira said sadly.

«That was our bus.»

«Another will be along after a while.»

«Let's go have that cup of coffee and wait for a while. There's no reason to hurry.»

«And if she went the wrong direction, she'll need to get off the bus and get back to her line. We don't want to look like we're chasing her.»

«It didn't go at all like I thought it would.»

«I'm sorry, Jaime. I'm sorry, Trayce. It all sounded so good. I guess we fooled ourselves, too.»

Jaime and Emerson

"Hey, you okay, Zip? You look a little down," Emerson said when he got to the computer lab on Thursday.

"Fine," Jaime signed. He connected his computer and handed Emerson the earbud. "Sorry. Didn't mean to blow you off. You know how young love is. Ups and downs."

"You and Keira? Oh, no!"

"Oh, Keira and I are fine. Our girlfriend kind of rejected us yesterday afternoon. It was the first time we were to meet IRL instead of virtually, you know? When she saw us, she just took off. I guess we weren't what she was expecting."

"Was she what you were expecting?" Emerson asked. Her head immediately rushed to the possibility that there was room for her, but she quashed the idea violently.

I'm not going to be a rebound. Especially on my rebound. God! What a disaster.

"She was all that. Except for running away from us. I think we'll just cool it for a while and let our hearts heal. It's almost Christmas, after all," he typed.

"Yeah. Gotta be good!" Emerson laughed.

"Say, I didn't mean to ignore what you are wearing. Just looking at you each day, I'm thinking Keira and I might need to move to France! You look great again today."

Emerson was wearing a brown suede skirt that stopped at mid-thigh, thigh-high black socks and ankle boots, and a horizontally striped long-sleeve T-shirt. Her light brown hair, usually tied back in a ponytail or bun, hung in curls around her shoulders.

He noticed! she thought while blushing.

"Oh, um… thanks. I just figured that since I've exposed myself at school, so to speak, there's no reason not to wear the things I really like. Unfortunately, some of them don't meet school regs. Too bad. They're really cute. It's getting too cold to wear skirts, though. I've got some better fitting jeans than what I usually wear."

"I'd love to see them sometime," Jaime typed without thinking how it might sound. Emerson blushed again.

Oh, I'd like you to see them. Just before I took them off.

"Look what I did with my color picker. I took your advice. The prediction algorithm is still intact, but now when it predicts a dominant color, it displays three color schemes that it could be used in."

"I knew it!" Jaime typed. "Seeing the dominant color by itself just wasn't getting there. But seeing how it would look with other colors really makes it come alive. Nice job, Emerson."

I'd wear clothes like this every day just to have him look at me like that. I need to make an effort to get to know Keira. They're really nice people.

"I'd like you to test the improvements on the voice manipulation algorithm when you're available. I know things are crazy as we head into the last two weeks of school, but I fed it different expression algorithms, too. I'd like to see what it does with a real voice."

"Yeah. Sure. Maybe you and Keira and I can meet here in the lab after school next Monday or Tuesday."

"I'll have to check with Keira about timing. She wants to try it, too."

"Okay."

Jaime tried not to be down for the rest of the period, but then listening to Mr. Wilson read his notes in psychology class the next period almost put him to sleep.

23
RETHINKING

Jaime and Keira and Angus

ON SATURDAY, JAIME and Keira went to the ballet they'd intended to go to the previous week. They'd been feeling pretty down since their Wednesday non-encounter with Trayce. Friday night, they played games with David and Olivia, then Jaime took Keira home. Their kisses were slow and less passionate than usual, both wanting simply to be held.

Instead of scanning the audience for anything other than signs of danger, they simply sat and held hands as they were swept away by *The Nutcracker*. Like the rest of the audience, they were caught up in the music and the beauty of the dance, thinking of nothing at all but the performance.

Their parting after the ballet was more loving and caring than passionate. They sank into each other's minds and let that deep connection carry them through the night. On Sunday, both teens awoke refreshed and still in contact with each other. They headed for their usual Sunday walk in the park.

«Calling Mr. Angus,» the two united their minds. «Are you in the park today?»

«You kids? Not yet. Is it important?»

«We kind of need some help about a guy who is stalking head talkers.»

«I'll be there in twenty minutes,» Angus said. «Don't broadcast any more.»

The two just walked around the perimeter of the park, holding hands, and talking quietly. It was only fifteen minutes when they saw the bearded old man in a utility kilt, carrying a silver headed cane. They didn't call out to him, but walked toward him.

"Tell me about it," he said shortly.

«There's a guy who has…» Jaime began.

"Use your voice."

"He doesn't have a voice," Keira said. "He signs. I'll interpret."

"A guy has been close to me twice who has spotted me and intends to grab me," Jaime signed. "He's convinced that if he has enough of us together, he can use a gestalt of some kind to force people to do his will."

"The last time he was approaching Jaime, he said he needed three and knew the third would come when he grabbed Jaime," Keira continued.

"What have you done?" Angus snarled, stepping back, and clicking the release on the dragon head that would free the sword from the cane sheath. "He wants three, so you conveniently lead him to the third so we're all together?"

"He doesn't know we're here. We surveyed all around before you got here. He's not here."

"He could be shielding."

"He's not one of us," Jaime signed. "He thinks he can identify us, but he can't hear."

"I don't think he knows me, either," Keira said. "But we have a girlfriend who could be in danger because she doesn't believe in her ability. She thinks we're all just characters she's writing about. She wouldn't recognize if he was near."

"Let's go to my place and smoke a bowl. It will help me think."

"We're only eighteen, Mr. Angus. We don't smoke."

"Course you don't," he sighed. "Where were you when he identified you?"

"Grocery store," Jaime signed and Keira interpreted.

"Where's the girlfriend?"

"We don't know where she lives. She goes to Rose Community College two days a week."

"There was a guy a few years ago—well maybe twenty—who advertised for telepathic research studies. I decided to investigate. He matches your description. Wanted to use a command voice to force people to follow him. Grandiose picture of himself as the governor and then the president in his head. He had a girlfriend at the time who could hear and he was looking for more. No matter what they did, she couldn't make him hear. I thought they'd given up. If he still has her and has found a way to make him hear, he'll be dangerous."

Angus thumped his cane on the ground a few times, relatching the sword. Then he looked up at them from beneath bushy eyebrows. He pulled a business card from a kilt pocket and gave it to Keira.

"Use the number on the card to call me next time. Don't clutter the air-waves. The girls and I will do a little investigating. Send me a text message so I can reach you if I find something serious. Just try not to go shouting to everyone you see. And if you'd like to get into the stripping business, let me know. The girls will help you and it's good experience. Develops confidence."

"I'm uh… I'm not… You're really a dirty old man!" Keira said in shock.

"Ass if," he replied, being sure to project his meaning. "Butt not everyone has the wind in her sails for it. You could do well. I'm off to hunt and 1gather some treats for the lagomorphs."

Angus turned and ambled off toward the raspberry bushes that still had a few green leaves. He began pulling off the leaves and putting them in a plastic baggie.

«Wow!» Jaime said. «He's sure a strange guy, isn't he? Inviting us to share a bowl? Are you sure we should have contacted him?»

«He's a dirty old man obsessed with butts. But he's basically harmless,» Keira admitted. The two headed back to her house.

Trayce and Rose

THE WEEKEND WENT painfully slowly for Trayce as well. She had an itch between her legs she desperately wanted to scratch, but resolutely ignored it for fear she would not be able to control her encounter with the characters in her head.

Monday, she cautiously looked out a second floor classroom window at the college to try to spot if it was clear. Something told her to just stay put for a while and take the next bus. She never saw anything suspicious, but she waited just the same.

Her Wednesday class at the college was just as uncomfortable, but it was the last class of the term and she was confident she'd done well. All her end of term papers were complete and turned in. The last week before Christmas was almost a formality. No one would probably even know if she didn't show up for high school classes the rest of the week, but that just wasn't Trayce's way of doing things. Even if all they did was sleep in class, she'd still show up like a good little girl.

Once she got home and had dinner with her mother, she sat in her room idly surfing the web. She decided to prove to herself that Keira and Jaime were fiction by looking up the psychiatrist Keira had suggested. Of course, there wouldn't be such a one because she'd undoubtedly made up the name on the fly.

'Rose Edmonds, young women's counseling,' she read. Well, she must have spotted the name at some previous time when she was thinking of counseling. God knew her past year was reason enough for counseling, even if she hadn't started hearing voices. That was probably how the name entered her subconscious as a possible character name.

As unhappy as Trayce was, she decided anything was worth a try. She called the office and left a message requesting an appointment. She was surprised to receive a return call just fifteen minutes later.

"This is Rose Edmonds," the caller said. She sounded nice. "I wanted to get back to you quickly because your message sounded stressed. How can I help you?"

"Um… Hi… um… Dr. Edmonds. I… I'm… just confused and sad and lonely. I hear voices in my head and I've been trying to block them out, but it just makes me sadder," Trayce said, suddenly sobbing.

"Are you in a safe place right now?"

"I'm at home."

"That didn't answer the question."

"Yeah. I mean, no one's going to hurt me here. Mom and I already ate. I didn't expect to reach you so soon."

"I can imagine. My office hours are later than most counselors. Most of my clients are students and they find they don't have daytime hours for appointments. Would you like to come in right now?"

"Now? It's, like, seven o'clock."

"I'll be in the office until nine and have no appointments scheduled this evening. Later if necessary."

"I guess. If it's not too much trouble."

"I assure you, I'm happy to see you."

They exchanged the office information and details. Trayce was surprised that it wasn't far. Much more convenient than Dr. Schwartz. She'd had to cut an afternoon of school to see him.

Trayce was instantly comfortable with Dr. Edmonds—Dr. Rose as she asked to be called. Her voice was gentle and everything about her was calm. There were no negative vibes in her office. And Trayce was ready to just unburden herself of everything that had happened recently. A woman was much better to talk to than a man.

"What's funny is that they are the only characters who will talk now," Trayce said. "I used to have so many characters talking in my head I had to concentrate to focus on just one or two. Now all I can think about is these two. I decided to write a new story this weekend, but I couldn't think up a single good character for it."

"When did you start hearing characters talking to you?"

"Oh, I've always had a pretty active imagination. Only child, you know. I'd make up people to play with, have tea parties, talk to my stuffed animals. It was around eleven that I started recognizing that the characters could be completely independent from what I was trying to play. Then they would take off in unexpected directions. I started participating in a writing contest that let participants talk to each other online and discovered having characters take over a story and go a different direction than the writer intended was pretty common. So, I just went with the flow."

"Get some interesting stories?"

"Sort of. A lot of characters seemed to disappear quickly as far as having conversations or talking in my head. Usually, I had plenty of insight into the character by that time to finish writing the story and sometimes, the character would pop back with something interesting to include."

"That was a past tense statement. What changed?"

"My teacher in creative writing challenged me to come up with an original story that wasn't based on a fan fiction. It was hard, but I sort of heard… not a conversation exactly, but I had a glimpse inside the head of a woman who had just received word her husband had died. She took her little girl to a movie to laugh and have fun while she decided how to tell her that her daddy wasn't coming home. It triggered a lot of my own feelings about when I found out my father was killed by a drunk driver. I sort of poured myself into the little girl."

"That sounds very intense and very healthy."

"I got a good grade. Then I had this completely off the wall idea of an old man who thought he was a great detective and two strippers who followed him around making sure he didn't get hurt. It was a good story, but my teacher said it wasn't appropriate for school because it was pretty ribald."

Rose laughed at the thought.

"These sound like healthy expressions. What has you worried?"

"My two new characters, Keira and Jaime, told me that those were all real people they'd encountered and read the minds of. I mean, not only are they characters who are talking to me, they're taking credit for two of my best stories ever!"

"Ah. And when you discarded the characters, suddenly the story ideas dried up. Is that the case?" Rose was quietly scribbling notes on a pad of paper. At the mention of Keira and Jaime, the problem came into sharp focus.

"Wow! I feel like I'm getting writing counseling from a good editor," Trayce chuckled. Dr. Rose's office was really peaceful. It was like an underlying hum in her brain had been silenced. "Well, I usually listen to characters for a while and find out a lot about them, then I go away and write a story. But… I mean… The characters have always been separate from me. Like I'm just listening in on them. These two… They talk *to* me and act like they hear me answering them! That's not logical. Dr. Schwartz said it was a factor of the bicameral brain and that it is really one side of my head talking to the other."

"Perhaps. You spoke to Dr. Schwartz?" Rose made more notes on her pad. "The fact that you are seeking help and are questioning the existence of your voices tends to override any breakdown of consciousness that would lead to paranoia or schizophrenia. Bicameral communication is typically not challenged. It is also referred to as command communication. You are told by an outside voice to do something and you simply obey. You don't ask why."

"I guess that's a relief in one way, but it still leaves me with voices who insist they are real people. And I really wish they were."

"Tell me about that, Trayce. Why do you want these individuals to be real?" Rose asked.

Trayce stopped to consider the situation and how much she was willing to admit.

"They're… good people," she finally answered. "I don't mean they're perfect, but they're in love and…" Tears welled in Trayce's eyes. "I think they love me. And I love them! How can I be in love with a couple of characters I haven't even written about yet?"

"Now tell me why you *don't* want them to be real."

"Oh! I mean… That would be crazy, wouldn't it? If they were real people just walking around, and I was having these conversations in my head with them, then that would be impossible! I'd be making everything up."

"Isn't that what you want?"

"To mean I was making it up? I mean… um… If I was making them up, then they couldn't be real, right? But then… I'd really be alone… They wouldn't love me!"

"Trayce, you have obviously developed an intense emotional bond with these people. And if they are real, they've developed the same kind of bond with you. But keeping them away is causing you pain that finding out they were imaginary couldn't match. What would you do if you found out they *were* real people and the three of you could talk to each other in your heads? No one has ever been able to prove that was possible, but people have reported various levels of having a mental conversation with another for centuries. It's not beyond the realm of reason in our world, where we communicate so freely with complete strangers. How many of your online friends—say, in your writing group—have you actually met? Yet you have no difficulty considering them real, even though social scientists estimate that nearly half of our online friends are made up—some by a person and some by an AI."

"How would I know they were real and I wasn't just hallucinating them?"

"You don't seem to have a disconnect from reality in any other sense. You go to school and do your work. You write your papers and go to a college class. You write stories and you know the stories are made up. You would have to trust your external senses as well as your internal senses. In other words, touch them, listen to their voices, look them in the eye…"

"Make love," Trayce whispered.

"What?"

"We always have the best connection when we are being… intimate."

"You have sex with them in your mind? That's a pretty common fantasy for teens."

"Sort of. Only they talk about needing to go slow so they can preserve their individual identity. I thought just getting to an orgasm was the whole purpose of the fantasy, but they set up rules for how far they would progress at any one time. Then they'd do things I never imagined and I could *feel* what it felt like for them, even though I knew it was my own fingers that were actually touching me."

"What do you really want to do, Trayce?"

"I want… I want to sit down with them and have a proper date where we eat dinner and talk like normal teens. I want to touch them and have them touch me and make love with them."

"Both of them?"

"Yes."

"So, why don't you make a date? Invite them out and if they don't show up, you'll know once and for all it was just your imagination and you can relax about whether or not you are crazy. It was just a vivid fantasy."

"What if they *do* show up?"

"That's what you really want, isn't it? Think of it as a dream come true."

Dr. Rose was so sweet and caring that Trayce left feeling better about herself, whether she was crazy or not. When the subject of a date came up, Trayce immediately jumped to having Christmas dinner together. But Dr. Rose questioned whether a first meeting should have the pressures of family all around them. Trayce agreed that her mother would probably freak out.

The whole idea was proving once and for all that they either did or didn't exist. Then Dr. Rose said something that slowed Trayce down significantly.

"When you ask a question of your lovers—or of anyone for that matter—you must be prepared to accept the answer, no matter what it is. And understand there are more possibilities than you have considered—even when you've considered all of them. One possibility, we agree, is that they don't show up and you prove they don't exist. The experience is one of loss because you have already convinced yourself they're real. The second is that they exist and you have been telecommunicating with them. In that instance, you will know that things you have shared with them, believing they were imaginary, were actually shared with real people."

Trayce thought immediately of having brazenly stood naked in front of a full-length mirror to 'show herself' to Jaime. Somehow that act seemed more intimate than their sex games and orgasms.

"A third possibility," Dr. Rose continued, "is that you discover they are real, but you are not talking with each other mentally. In that case, they might not even recognize you and you will know you have simply been fantasizing about two other people and they are not a part of the equation."

"Wow! That would be extreme!" Trayce had said.

"There may be other possibilities," Dr. Rose had said. "What I am saying is that before you ask the question, be sure you are prepared to accept the answer."

Trayce contemplated that on her way home, determined to accept any answer, but deciding to write down all the possible answers to the question she could think of. That might mean she'd have to talk to them to complete the list. If she did this, she wanted to be prepared.

24
ARRANGEMENTS

"KENTON, THIS IS Rose," she said when voicemail kicked in. "I know what you are planning. Leave them alone! So help me if you harm one of them, I'll hunt you down and burn you. You know I can do it. Just don't."

She hung up the phone. Trayce had mentioned the crazy doctor which meant he knew about her ability. He'd been searching for the right combination for years and if Trayce gave him the names of Keira and Jaime, he would try to bring them all into his experiment. It had been two days and Rose had left a message each day. Kenton Schwartz seemed not to be in his office. She didn't have a cell phone number for him and doubted that it would do her any good anyway. He probably had her blocked in every way he could think of.

She'd been young and foolish when she met him in college. That had been over twenty years earlier. She was curious about her ability to read minds and had volunteered to participate in his 'study.' They'd even dated for a while. That was when she read his real intent. He had no understanding of head talk. He was amazingly effective at spotting people with the gift, but even after his study, he didn't have a clue. He still had the opinion that those who could telecommunicate 'sent' messages to other people. It was an ability he desperately wanted, but failed at miserably.

Rose had understood early on that the ability manifested itself in 'hearing' other people, not in speaking to them. It had been frustrating to her.

She'd taken up the study of psychiatry to understand the subject better. What she'd discovered was a degree of mental control. She could shut her mind in both directions, sealing off any possible leaking of her own thoughts and blocking the reception of others' thoughts. It was a valuable skill that saved her sanity.

She specialized in teen girl counseling. Girls approaching womanhood, like she had, often felt emotionally and mentally unstable. The popular notion among predominantly male psychiatrists was only a step removed from the dark ages notion that all female problems could be traced to the 'wandering uterus.' They figured that in today's 'modern' understanding, they could pre-scribe drugs that would neutralize the voices in their heads.

Rose had tried the drugs herself and discovered they didn't silence the voices, but rather made the listener not care about them. She was disgusted with the way most drugs affected the psyche. A popular anesthetic didn't actu-ally dull the pain, but made the patient forget about it. The results were still scarring.

That was why Rose had counseled young women in ways to block the voices and to keep themselves from being heard. Only rarely did a patient clearly have the ability to read others' thoughts. She was certain Trayce had some element of that ability, but not as strong as in her niece Keira. Although Rose hadn't met him, she'd gleaned enough from Keira's mind to know that Jaime was possibly the most skilled listener she'd ever encountered. It was rare to find a male with the gift.

There was an older fellow who had participated in Kenton's studies and seemed to realize quickly what he was up to. She'd wondered what had awak-ened his inner ear and discovered he'd been treated for PTSD after Vietnam with the new miracle drug, LSD. It hadn't done anything for his PTSD, but had opened his mind in unexpected ways. She never told Kenton about that—or that she'd briefly had a 'relationship' with the older guy. He was pretty irresistible. It sounded a lot like Trayce had somehow encountered Angus's thoughts as well.

Trayce's 'voices' seemed to mostly be an in-and-out kind of hearing. But somehow, she'd been caught in the orbit of Keira and Jaime. Rose would be interested in how the proposed meeting would go. She was positive Trayce would initiate contact.

Rose picked up the phone to dial Kenton again and put it down. He wasn't answering ten minutes before, he wouldn't be answering now. His experiments in college had gone further and further afield until the university pulled his funding for his study as not being scientific. But if he interfered with the three teens, she would absolutely make him pay.

Angus

"Hey, sweet cheeks," Angus said when Keira answered her phone early on Saturday.

"Mr. Angus, I'm not one of your strippers," Keira shot back.

"Of course not. You'd still be good at it," he laughed. "This is serious. You need to tell your boyfriend to switch grocery stores. We've been spot checking that Safeway location where he was injured and I believe it's being surveilled. Tell him to go to Fred Meyer instead. Or Whole Foods if he can afford it. Just don't go up to the same store today."

"I'll contact him right now!" Keira said.

"By text message. We still don't know if this guy has the ability to read minds, or has someone with him who does. When I ran into him twenty years ago, he had a girlfriend who could hear people. When she and I shared a little recreational time together, we tuned in to listen to him. He is not a nice man."

"Yessir. I'll text Jaime right away."

"We're going to hang out at the Safeway to see if we can get a positive ID. You take care."

"Thank you. 'Bye."

As soon as she hung up, Keira texted Jaime with the information. He and his dad always went grocery shopping at about 1:00 in the afternoon. But Jaime would need time to convince his father to change stores. She warned him not to contact her mentally. They'd have plenty of time that evening at the concert they were attending.

Jaime and David

"Dad, I know it's silly, but I'm just not comfortable going back to that store again right now," Jaime signed to his father.

"I don't blame you, son. Don't worry about it. I'll get the groceries," David said. He'd actually been concerned that his son was showing no emotional stress since the shooting incident in the store. The same police detective who had investigated the attempted kidnapping had stopped by to interview Jaime. He said it was likely the case would never come to trial because the girlfriend denied that her boyfriend was actually trying to kill her. He'd just wanted to teach her a lesson and she learned it. She loved him even more now than she had before. He'd be charged with discharging a firearm in the city limits and causing injury. He would lose his license to carry and probably serve a suspended misdemeanor sentence.

"No, Dad. I really enjoy going grocery shopping with you. I'm just wondering if we could maybe try a different store. Maybe Fred Meyer or even Whole Foods."

David chuckled.

"Back in the day, your mother and I loved to go to Whole Foods, but we called it Whole Paycheck. Why don't we try it. We might have to try some unfamiliar brands, but it should be fun," David said.

They went to the store and did a pretty good job of finding either what they thought they wanted or a reasonable substitute for it. For good measure they stopped at Freddie's to pick up a few things they wanted that weren't at the other store. It was another bonding experience for father and son.

Jaime was ready for his date to the concert with Keira early.

Angus

"Count this as a warning," Angus said as he pressed the butt of his cane against the neck of Kenton Schwartz. Kate and Thursday were on the other side of the van distracting the couple who were supposed to be standing guard.

"Did Rose send you?" Kenton demanded.

"That's no concern of yours. These kids are under my protection and I won't let you have them. The next time I put my sword to your neck, I won't have it sheathed. Am I clear?"

"He's eighteen. He can speak for himself."

"Which shows how much you don't know," Angus said. "Go and don't come back!"

He caught Kate's eye on the other side of the van. She and Thursday thanked the couple for their donation to the children's hospital they were collecting for. The girls were in bun-revealing short-shorts and crop tops that showed the lower hemisphere of their breasts. Raising their hands would have revealed more than was strictly allowed in public.

They quickly piled into Angus's Lexus and he pulled away. They stopped a block away and watched to make sure the van left the parking lot.

Trayce and Jaime and Keira

"If they don't show up, they were imaginary and I need to just forget about them," Trayce said as she checked her list of options. She wanted to be sure she had all the possibilities covered before she tried to make contact. *Tried!* She was actually going to conjure them up in her mind. She was pretty sure they'd be having sex this evening. That was how it always worked. She undressed and got in bed, even though it was only eight-thirty.

"If they do show up and know me," Trayce said as she reviewed the list. "Oh, fuck! Dreams come true? That sounds so trite. Maybe when we actually meet each other, we won't be interested in going on. She's so pretty and he loves her so much. They might reject me!"

Trayce was panting a little, even though her hands were busy holding her tablet and writing. The thought of Jaime and Keira rejecting her was terrifying—more terrifying than that they didn't show up and therefore didn't exist. She still wrote it down.

"If they show up and don't know me, it's been my imagination playing on two people I happened to randomly see and latched onto. We might become friends and they might not be interested."

She simply had to talk to them and lay out the plan. Somehow, she never considered that they might not agree to meet at all. After all, she was the author and controlled the storyline, wasn't she? She set her tablet and pen aside and deliberately started to masturbate while thinking of her two lovers. It always worked best when they were being intimate and nearing orgasm. She focused on rubbing her clit and pinching her nipples.

«Jaime and Keira! Let's play!»

«Whoa! Hold on!» Jaime said. «We can't play now! We're at a concert!»

«But you're always…»

«We do have lives, Trayce,» Keira said. «I thought you didn't want to talk to us again.»

«I can't help it! If you're not having sex, how did I connect to you?»

«I just told Keira I thought you'd enjoy this music. Listen with us a minute.»

«It's beautiful. What is it?»

«It's Prokoviev's Violin Concerto Number 2,» Jaime said. «Can't you just feel the tension and agony?»

«Why would you be thinking of me during a violin concerto?» Trayce asked, a little bewildered.

«I guess we were thinking that you kind of had a lot of stress and this music would let you know you aren't alone,» Keira said.

«I wish you were here with us, love. You can see through our eyes and listen through our ears,» Jaime said.

«You still call me 'love.' I… I'll just be quiet until the music finishes.»

Trayce rode along in Jaime and Keira's minds as the orchestra completed the performance. She not only heard the music, but shared in the bittersweet emotions it evoked in their minds. They… She realized it was not only in their minds, but they were reflecting or transmitting what much of the audience was experiencing. It was as if their emotions were being multiplied and Trayce let them wash over her.

«It was so beautiful! I know I've never heard that before. How can I be listening to something I've never heard before? I don't have *that* good an imagination!»

«It's intermission now and we can all reflect on it a bit if you want to,» Keira said softly.

«I… wanted to talk to you. Is it okay?»

«We're just so happy to be with you!» Jaime said. «Please talk to us. Are you okay?»

«It's been a struggle. I think I'm doing okay and then there is a whisper in the back of my mind and I think I'm hearing you. I… I went to see Dr. Edmonds this week. I have to find out… I need to know if you are real. If I don't know, I'll always think I've gone crazy. She said I had to accept the answer if I asked the question. So, I've been making a list of things that might be the answer if we agree to meet, and I want you to add to the ideas. Okay?»

«I think you already know we want to meet you,» Jaime said. «We tried to see you last week, but you ran away.»

«I just got… freaked out! I wanted you to be real, but I couldn't face the possibility that you were.»

«What are your options?» Keira asked.

Trayce began going through her list. Jaime and Keira were discarding things almost as fast as she thought of them, but they stayed on her list.

«It's always possible that something else could happen that would cause us not to show up. I mean, remember when Jaime attacked a shooter and was knocked unconscious?» Keira asked.

«Are you trying to prepare me for you not showing up?»

«No! We'll move heaven and earth to be there. Um… Where? And when?» Jaime asked.

«Wait!» Keira said. «There are other possible outcomes. These are all answers to your questions. What if we meet and you decide you don't like us? How would we handle that?»

«I… I don't know. How can I project what would happen to you? I suppose that if you don't show up, you don't exist. But I can't imagine you showing up and me not liking you. We've… already been intimate.»

«The thing is that we do exist, whether you believe in us or not,» Jaime said. «No matter what you decide—even if we were in an accident and couldn't get there—we'd still have to go on being us.»

«It would be better, though,» Keira sighed. «We'd know, at least, that our worlds simply didn't intersect. We may have followed a lovely path for a while, but you were a figment of our imagination.»

«Me a figment…? Are you aliens? How can our worlds not intersect?» Trayce asked, alarmed.

«No, we're not aliens. But you have to understand that the one time we tried to physically interact with you, you ran off and told us to go away. We go to

Washington and you go to Adams. They are like different worlds, across the river. I take AP courses and one international double credit class. You go off campus to the community college twice a week. We live in different parts of town and in many ways, just in different worlds. It's the intersection of those we are interested in. That intersection is represented by the three of us,» Jaime explained.

«Okay. I get it. We're all putting what we believe and want on the line. Are you willing to get together?»

«Absolutely!» Jaime and Keira chorused.

«Then let's meet for lunch at the B&N Café at Lloyd Center.»

«Good choice. Bookstores are nice and quiet. Almost as good as a library when it comes to hushing people talking in their heads.»

«You hear other people, too? I thought it was just us,» Trayce said.

«I guess that's something we should explore when we're together,» Keira said.

«Okay. We're on Christmas break. Should we meet this week?» Trayce asked.

«It's kind of chaotic getting up to Christmas. The mall will be a zoo!» Keira said.

«How about the day after Christmas? Boxing Day. Yes, there will be a crowd, but I can't wait any longer,» Trayce said in frustration.

«Christmas, Christmas don't be late,» Keira sang in her head, mimicking the Chipmunks.

«I want more than a hula-hoop,» Trayce laughed.

«Okay, Boxing Day it is,» Jaime said. «The bookstore should be quiet enough.»

And public so no one can grab me, Trayce thought.

«You can trust us, Trayce. People are settling for the concert. Will you stay and listen to Shostakovich with us?»

«Yeah… Will we make love later?»

THE LOVEMAKING PART of the teens' date was more timid than previous encounters. Trayce had been missing from their lives for ten days. Making out and petting between Jaime and Keira, while still intense, had been tinged with sadness that their satellite was not with them.

Now that she was back in the mix, they all felt it was necessary to take it slow and easy while they got back together. They spent more time learning about each other and asking what each liked and didn't like.

«It's been so hard to stay away from you,» Trayce said as they held each other in their minds. Jaime and Keira were providing the sensations of the physical touches they enjoyed. David was out with Olivia and wasn't expected home until much later, so Jaime and Keira were in the TV room holding each other.

«We've missed you. Maybe we haven't even progressed in our own relationship as we would have if you had been with us,» Keira said.

«If you're just my imagination, you couldn't really progress without me,» Trayce ventured.

«We were progressing pretty well before we encountered you,» Jaime said. «It's different now, though. *We* know we belong together.»

«You surprised me with the concert this evening. I've never been to a live orchestra concert—except the school orchestra. And it was nothing like this.»

«Students are still learning their instruments. Most of them aren't planning a career in music,» Keira said. «Did you see the tears on the violinist's cheeks? She wasn't *thinking* about the music. She *was* the music.»

«I couldn't have experienced that without you. You… see or hear other people, don't you?» Trayce asked.

«All the time. One of the biggest lessons we had to learn was how to block out people when we don't want to be disturbed,» Jaime said.

«Don't you hear others?» Keira asked.

«That's silly. I mean… Okay, maybe. I've been accused of stealing a classmate's journal to write one of my stories. I didn't think I was hearing her, but maybe. Maybe. Maybe. Usually, when I'm working on a story, I start to hear the characters talking and it helps me write more. But when I'm home working on the story, I don't hear them and after I finish the story, I never hear from them again. That's why I assumed you were just characters in my over-active imagination.»

«I'm so looking forward to proving you wrong on that!» Keira said.

«It might be that you've learned on your own to block out other people except when you are working on a story. That kind of makes sense.»

«Or that you have very limited range and only hear people who are close,» Keira added.

«But I couldn't block you out. Not completely. And I know we aren't sitting next to each other. I'd be working on something completely different, like advanced algebra, and I'd suddenly be aware of one or both of you and what you were thinking.»

«Sometimes… I guess a lot of the time, or most of the time, we can feel you sort of lurking in the backs of our minds. We tried to be welcoming but respectful of your boundaries. We didn't want to scare you away by being too excited about it,» Jaime said. He caressed Keira as they kissed.

«Oh, that feels good. I didn't know I liked having my breasts touched so much. Mmm,» Trayce said.

«Kiss us, precious,» Keira whispered as she kissed Jaime deeply.

«If real kisses are anything like this, I'm addicted,» Trayce sighed.

«There's definitely an additional element when we touch each other physically in addition to mentally,» Jaime said. «I hope you don't mind too much that I'd love to be touching you and Keira at the same time.»

«Oh, yeah. Right there! That's so good!»

«You need to experience the excitement of having his hand inside your clothing,» Keira said. «You were already naked during the concert.»

«I thought I had to be in order to contact you. It's always been strongest during sex.»

«We're working up to that. Who knows? Maybe you'll be with us,» Keira said. «We'd like that.»

Trayce could sense the approval in Jaime's mind as he worked his hand into her panties. Except she wasn't wearing panties. He was working his way inside Keira's panties. She spread her legs in sync with Keira and felt the touch in her private parts.

Trayce lay still on her bed. Her hands clutched the sheets at her side. She was determined not to let her own fingers stimulate her, but to simply experience Keira and Jaime. She wasn't disappointed. She rose to her peak as Keira did. Then, much to her surprise, she peaked again when Jaime did.

«Even if you aren't real, I might not be able to ever stop this,» she sighed.

25
EXCITEMENT

Jaime and Keira and Emerson

JAIME AND KEIRA were both a little cautious about going to Emerson's house on Monday. They were simply going to try out Jaime's vocal impression software, but Emerson had been pretty explicit in her thoughts regarding her desires for the two of them. Still, they figured they'd be safe enough if it was the two of them with a classmate.

Emerson's house was impressive. The neighborhood didn't look all that different than either Jaime's or Keira's, but the houses tended to be taller. Jaime's house had just a main level and a lower level family room plus garage and small office. It had two bedrooms on the main floor plus kitchen, dining room, living room, and bath.

Keira's home had a similar design, though it was slightly larger than Jaime's. Compared to Emerson's house when they went inside, both houses were tiny.

"Your home is beautiful, Emerson," Keira said.

"Thanks, Keira. I know it's kind of ostentatious. I seldom have anyone come over. It's all my mom's fault. She's the executive director of Mercy Medical Center and decided her family needed a home suited to her status. Even my little sister never invites anyone over. It's embarrassing."

Jaime could peek into Emerson's mind, which seemed always to be open to him, and tell that while she was a little embarrassed about showing her wealth, she was also rather proud of her home and that was why she'd invited

Keira and Jaime to do the test there.

They walked past the Christmas tree in the living room and through the dining room to get to the stairs down.

"I can give you a tour of the whole monstrosity, but I don't want you to think I just invited you over to get you in my bedroom. We've got a pretty big family room and space to work downstairs," she said.

"We can wait for the tour," Keira said. "We should probably focus on the real reason for getting together."

To try to seduce the two of you, Emerson thought.

"Right." Emerson led them downstairs and into the large room that included a television roughly three times the size of Jaime's, a game table, a computer room, and even a mini-kitchen. "Would you like a soda?"

"Thanks," Keira answered for the two of them. Jaime began unpacking his laptop and the microphone and headphones. While he did, Keira took the opportunity to survey Emerson's mind, as well as checking out her really stellar body. Other than the last week of the term, she hadn't seen Emerson dressed so casually elegant.

She was barefoot with carefully pedicured toenails. Her jeans looked like they'd been painted on her legs and round butt.

Angus would love that, Keira giggled to herself.

On top, Emerson wore a sweater that ended in a ribbed band tight beneath her boobs and left her belly enticingly bare. It had a neckline that allowed it to fall off one shoulder. Keira figured it would also afford some nice views down the front if Emerson leaned forward a little. Between her look and the thoughts Emerson had, Keira could tell she was braless. Her light brown hair, normally tied back or up in school, fell in casual curls below her shoulders.

I'm not going to make any moves on them, Emerson thought firmly—as if she was trying to convince herself. *If they happen to be enticed to get close to me, I just won't object.*

Two can play that game, Keira thought. She was planning to spend the day with Jaime, so she'd conveniently forgotten a bra herself. The room was plenty warm, so she removed her jacket and made sure Emerson noticed the thin T-shirt she wore. She'd chosen it specifically based on the image Jaime had shared of Emerson looking in the mirror just before she removed her T-shirt. Of course, Keira wasn't soaking wet but the points were made.

Jaime caught bits and pieces of the two girls' thoughts and did his best to ignore both of them.

"So, all you need to do is read this passage," he signed to Emerson, positioning the mike where she was seated. "I'll record it and we'll feed it into the synthesizer. Then you can work the controls to vary your tonality until you find one you like." Keira interpreted the signs as he went to make sure Emerson understood the assignment.

> *"I sat with my back against the last standing oak tree at Westwood High, a book resting on my knees. It was my favorite reading spot. I was off behind the football field, far enough away for privacy, but not totally isolated. I could still see morning practice and the members of the football team who were running around with their shirts off. I guessed even if it was twenty degrees colder, they'd still be shirtless. There was a crowd of girls on the other side of the field."*

"Did you choose this, Zip?" Emerson said, looking up from the page. "Am I really going to read a chapter from a teen romance novel?"

Jaime nodded toward Keira.

"I chose it. I looked around for something that would allow a gentle and sometimes emotional reading," Keira said. "Jaime had chosen a passage from Shakespeare! If you read Juliet's speech from the balcony, your recording would come out all stilted. It just wouldn't be natural. I thought a romance would work well."

"Right. Okay. You did say you had the computer read the entire *Dark Love* series for your voice. Do I need to read it all?" Emerson laughed.

"Not for this," Jaime signed. "Just a page to test the system. It won't have your entire vocal range captured, but should be enough for you to play with the adjustment filters." Keira interpreted.

"I'm glad you're here to interpret, Keira," Emerson said. "Sometimes Zip signs so fast I just can't catch everything. You interpret so fast, it's almost like you're reading his mind!"

«Maybe we should slow down a little,» Jaime said to Keira.

«Good idea. I didn't mean to jump ahead like that,» she answered.

Emerson went back to reading the passage and then they played back the recording in her normal voice.

"Does everyone hate the way their voice sounds when they hear it recorded?" Emerson asked.

"I had the same response when I tested mine," Keira answered. "I don't know if everyone *hates* the sound, but it's a real surprise that it doesn't sound anything like what you think it does."

"It's partly the acoustics and mechanics of digital recording," Jaime signed. He carefully fingerspelled 'acoustics.' "Now, you can play the passage and use the sliders to adjust various properties of the soundwaves."

"Okay, so I just hit play and start sliding these? Do I have any idea what they'll do?"

"Have to experiment," Jaime signed.

Emerson clicked the play button and then started experimenting with the sliders. One changed the overall pitch of her voice and ranged from a deep bass to a squeaky mouse.

"Oh, cool!" she said. She chose a vocal range that she liked, which she noted was a few intervals lower than her normal voice. "That sounds kind of smoky," she said. Then she went on to other sliders that controlled things like the smoothness of the voice. 'Gravelly' to 'buttery' was the way Jaime had labeled the ends of the slider.

Emerson continued to play with the sliders until she had a voice she generally liked.

"How do I make this the voice I want to use?" she asked.

Jaime showed how to save the settings and then had her read another passage. This time he played it back with her saved settings.

"What do you think?" Keira asked.

"I think it's amazing. I listen to it and think, 'Who is this sexy girl?' I want my voice to sound like that."

"Okay," Jaime signed. "Put on the headset." He handed her the earphones and set the computer to play as she read.

She began reading a passage and her eyes popped wide open.

"It's changing my voice as I'm reading!" she said. "It's like if I talk into the app, people hear me differently! This is really amazing, Zip!"

She reached out and wrapped an arm around him, pulling him close for a hug. Of course, he was standing and she was sitting, so that pulled his hips right against her face. Jaime dropped his hand to Emerson's bare shoulder.

«Thank you, Emerson. But we're not going to go that way.»

Emerson jerked away from Jaime and looked up at him.

"Did you…?" She shook her head. "Uh… Sorry about my exuberance. No offense for hugging your boyfriend, Keira." She reached out to hug Keira as she had Jaime, holding her breath to see if Keira was going to send her a message. Nothing.

Just my conscience warning me to back off. This isn't Paris.

Jaime and Keira

«Did you hear that?» Keira asked Jaime after they'd left Emerson's house. They'd stayed another hour, running further tests on Jaime's voice synthesizer and then Keira ran a few tests on Emerson's color picker. Jaime had left a copy of the app for Emerson to play with.

As soon as they were away, though, Keira had to talk to Jaime.

«It's the skin-to-skin contact!» Jaime said. «It has to be! She heard me!»

«She was this close to getting another surprise. As soon as you touched her, I nearly ran my hand down the front, inside her gapping sweater. I caught myself as you spoke to her,» Keira said.

«But she heard!» Jaime said.

«Yeah. But she thought she was crazy, remember. She assigned what you said to her conscience. Thank goodness! Just imagine, though, if she went to school thinking you talked in her head, or that someone else had given her a command.»

«I didn't command. I just stated a fact. We're not going that way. … We aren't, are we?»

«No! For me it was just an impulse quickly mastered. When she hugged me, I carefully did not reach out to touch her. But damn! Why does she have to be so sexy? She's a walking wet dream!»

«And we can't follow up on that,» Jaime sighed. «Can you imagine Trayce's response to catching us masturbating to images of Emerson? No, thank you. Trayce is too important!» Jaime said firmly.

«I agree. Thank you for reining it in. I was just caught so off guard, it took a minute for my brain to catch up with my body.»

«Hmm. I wonder what might happen with Trayce Friday. I'm really excited to be face-to-face with her.»

«If skin touch really is like that with a person who isn't a head talker, what we have with Trayce will be ten times that when we touch,» Keira speculated.

«I have a dozen questions. I've not connected to anyone else I touched. Except maybe my Mom. Why did I connect with Emerson? She's head deaf. Was she somehow susceptible?»

«Is it just you who can do that? Would it have been the same if I was the only one touching her?» Keira asked.

«I can imagine it being a geometric progression of some sort. When the two of us first touched without filters… in the theater with the kidnapper… it was like our individual ability wasn't doubled, it was squared. If that holds, when we touch Trayce, it could be cubed. Or even squared again. I don't even know how to measure it. But we could possibly hear everyone in the entire mall!» Jaime said.

They reached Jaime's house and decided to settle in the TV room. David was at work, so they had the house to themselves. They restrained themselves from immediately starting to make out. Then they jumped up and went to the kitchen to fix lunch before they got serious with each other.

«What are we going to do?» Keira asked.

«I think we should warn Trayce," Jaime said. He fried two cheese sandwiches and served canned tomato soup. Both considered the lunch a delicacy.

«If she was suddenly flooded with the voices of everyone in the mall, she would totally freak out. We also need to set a bunch of filters before we touch her. We could be overwhelmed, too,» Keira said.

«Just touching her threatens to do that to me, even if we were in isolation. Isn't it weird? I could have anticipated the reaction when we first touched our hands together. Could have but didn't. But I already knew we had a deep connection. I think I'd already fallen in love with you. But now, with that experience behind us, we're both expecting the same kind of connection with Trayce.»

«And we both acknowledge that even though you opened up a channel to communicate with Emerson, there was no similar response when you touched her sexy bare shoulder,» Keira said. «I mean, I know you were responding physically. I was, too. But it didn't double your hearing.»

«So, is it only because we are head talkers that our hearing is enhanced?»

«No,» Keira said. «I shook Mr. Angus's hand and didn't have any kind of increased awareness with him at all.»

«Hmm. The stalker. He doesn't know that it isn't just any combination of head talkers that can work together. We need a special connection. We should make sure we don't share that out. He thinks he needs three head talkers or more to form his gestalt for ordering people around. He might have captured my thought about skin contact, but I still don't believe he's a head talker himself. And he has no concept that our connection and the amplification of our ability is based on our emotional connection with each other.»

«Theoretically, would adding Emerson's skin to ours increase our abilities or decrease them by the amount it takes to communicate to Emerson?» Keira asked.

«I don't know. Maybe Trayce will want to run experiments someday.»

Jaime and Keira and Trayce

«LOVER, ARE YOU there? Can you talk?» Jaime and Keira called softly as they kissed each other deeply.

«Oh, God! You called to me!»

«Yes, but we don't want to disturb you if you aren't where we can talk,» Keira said.

«Meaning you're going to have sex! I must be the horniest little bitch on the planet! Let me close the door and lie down.»

«We weren't planning to get too carried away,» Jaime said. «But it is easier to talk to you while we're kissing.»

«Oh, don't back off because of me! I love to feel you kissing me. Or each other. Whatever.»

«That's kind of what we wanted to talk about,» Keira said. «You don't really listen to any others around you. But you might suddenly hear more than you're prepared for the first time we touch you.»

«That sounds weird.»

«Let us show you what happened on our first date,» Jaime said. They quickly replayed the moment they touched and the expansion of their abilities.

«Wow! What happened after the movie? Did the guy kidnap the girl?»

«He tried,» Keira said. «We broke it up. The thing is he confessed to police that he'd done it before and led them to three bodies he'd buried in a swamp.»

«He could have killed you both! And the girl!» Trayce gasped.

«We were lucky. His flight instinct took over before his fight instinct. But the point is that the first time we touch, even if it's just to shake hands, our worlds could explode into a thousand voices. We'll try to put up filters and barriers, but it might not be enough,» Jaime said. «We wanted to warn you.»

«You are the most considerate characters I've ever made up,» Trayce sighed.

«Trayce…» they began.

«I know. You say you're real. We're going to meet up on Friday for lunch,» Trayce said. «The thing is, as long as I think of you as my characters, I'm completely free to ask you to do anything I want to do in my head. Because it's all just me. Like right now, I just want you to run your hands all over my body and lick me to an incredible come while I'm licking and sucking on the two of you. If you actually show up at the bookstore, I will be embarrassed to death! I would never say things like that to real people. I mean, I'm respecting my characters' desire to tease and not go too fast. It makes for a good story. But I really want Jaime to push his cock between my legs and fuck me while I'm eating Keira to a great orgasm. Do you think I'd say that to a real couple? I'd die!»

«We're kind of even on that,» Keira laughed. «Jaime and I didn't even fantasize about each other until the night you joined us. And we shared everything we discovered about each other with you! It's Jaime's finger you can feel on my clit. It's my lips you feel sucking on your cute little nipples. Your hair is like silk beneath my fingers. I would never have imagined I could fall in love with a blonde. And a girl, at that! Oh, yeah. Now I can feel *your* fingers on my clit. I love you so much, baby!»

«Wait! That… That's Jaime's tongue on my clitty. Oh God, yes! Oh, Keira, I'm going to come with you.»

«Join me, my love. Join your joy with mine and let it flow!» Keira said.

Jaime was leaking fluids, but he was doing a pretty good job of holding back his own excitement so he could enjoy that of the two girls. When the dam burst for them, it was all he could do to keep from coming. He was glad he did. Keira pushed him back on the couch in the TV room and pulled his trousers down so she could put his dick in her mouth. Trayce moaned.

«I want you!» she said. «I want to feel you coming in my mouth. I want to come with you!»

«You're still diddling our clit!» Keira said. «I think this will be all three of us. Come, Jaime. Let me have your semen.»

«I love what you're doing, Keira. Oh, Trayce, I can feel my fingers slipping all over your pussy. I want to put my cock in you like it's in Keira's mouth. I'm going to… Oh! Here it comes!»

The job of gulping down Jaime's semen was complicated by Keira's own orgasm, multiplied by Trayce's. She coughed and sperm flew all over Jaime's balls.

«I'm choking!» Trayce coughed. She was in unison with Keira even though there was nothing in her own mouth or throat. «There's a little more!»

Keira licked up the last spurt from Jaime and cleaned his balls with her tongue.

«That's something that could broaden our sensitivity even more,» Jaime said. «I nearly passed out with the intensity of our orgasm, but I think I could hear thoughts from everyone on the block. When the three of us are actually together and making love, we might have infinite power and range.»

«Do you really think so?» Keira asked.

«No. Not really. It just feels so mammoth to me that I can't imagine anything being bigger.»

«Huh?» Trayce said. «Sorry. I wasn't with it there for a minute. It was like I was deep under water and couldn't surface.»

«That's pretty much what we were saying,» Keira said. «What time is it? Can we just lie here touching each other for a couple more hours?»

«My mom's at the mall. She got a seasonal job at Lois's Accessories. I'm going in tomorrow to get a new pair of earrings to wear when we meet. Don't peek.»

«Does that mean you can join us for a while and just let me pet your perfect body?» Jaime said.

«Touch me! I want to live in your touch.»

26
INTERRUPTION

Jaime and Keira and Trayce

JAIME AND KEIRA talked to Trayce frequently through the week, but they agreed that when they got together, they would not simply rush to bed as soon as they could. Trayce had even more of the fears regarding her first time than was typical among the other teens Keira and Jaime had listened to.

They were very different than Keira's fears. Keira—and Jaime to a somewhat lesser degree—feared being subsumed by the mind of the other and losing their own identity. Trayce had no such compunction. Her lower level of psychic activity led her to discount the idea of other voices. Her stalwart belief that Keira and Jaime were only characters she imagined made it impossible for her to consider that she might lose her own identity in their relationship.

«You haven't been, like, stalking me, have you?» she asked on Tuesday.

«The only time we attempted to see you was that afternoon after your class at Rose CC,» Keira said. «We're sorry about that one. We thought if we showed you we were real, you'd be as excited as we were.»

«I was totally freaked out! Inside, I didn't want to run away, but I couldn't help myself. But you didn't come back to the school?» Trayce asked.

«No. Never,» Jaime said. «We promised we wouldn't try to see you if you didn't invite us. Why?»

«I've just had the oddest feeling I've been watched the past couple of weeks. I mean, not just in my head. Like someone literally has eyes on me. I stayed in the classroom at Rose for an extra hour after class let out and left by a different door. But even going to school or picking Mom up at work has made me a little uncomfortable.»

«We promise it's not us,» Keira said.

«But don't take the feeling lightly,» Jaime admonished. «We know there is someone out there who is hunting for head talkers. I've encountered him twice, and Mr. Angus chased him away from the grocery store once. He isn't a good guy.»

«Wait! Mr. Angus? The old detective I wrote about?» Trayce said. «That's ridiculous. You can't possibly know about that story.»

«We don't know anything about your story, but he and his two friends often walk in the same park we do. He's a detective and also a head talker. He agreed to keep an eye out,» Keira said.

«You're making it harder to believe in you,» Trayce laughed. «He's an old man with two strippers for friends and he imagines he carries a sword in his cane.»

«It's a real sword,» Jaime said. «But hey! We don't need to discuss him. Just be careful and watchful when you're out and about. This stalker fellow is definitely out there.»

«Yeah. Okay.»

«*IF YOU SHOW* up,» Trayce said when they talked Christmas Eve, «I'm going to need some time to adjust to your physical presence. You see each other every day. I'm just out here alone with you in my head. No matter how much I desire you and imagine what it will be like to make love to both of you, bringing my physical body into the equation is going to take some time.»

«We agree, precious,» Jaime said. «It's one of the reasons we've taken so much time with each other. I mean, if desire was all that was needed, Keira and I would be naked and making love right now.»

«Well, maybe not while my parents are in the living room,» Keira laughed. «But as soon as we could get alone.»

«What I don't understand is that I want… Well, I want you as much as I want Jaime,» Trayce said. «I'm not the least bit homosexual. At least I don't think so. I've never met another woman I wanted so much. It's one of the things that makes me believe you are really just a part of me I made up. I have no qualms about playing with myself.»

«Ached for,» Keira said. «I've looked in on other girls' fantasies and enjoyed using the fantasies for myself. I've imagined myself being them, or occasionally being with them. But with you, gender seems irrelevant. I just love you and want to be with you.»

«Keira, please don't jump to that. You make my heart beat faster and I want to say I love you, too. But I really need to *see you* with my own eyes. I just can't say I love you before I know beyond a shadow of a doubt you are real.»

«I wish it was Friday,» Jaime sighed. «I want to take your hand and let you truly see inside me.»

KEIRA AND HER parents went to Jaime's house for Christmas dinner. Jaime had volunteered to cook, but was relegated to setting the table as David and Olivia took control of the kitchen. Keira had come early 'to help.' She and Jaime escaped to the TV room to kiss and wish Trayce a Merry Christmas.

«Merry Christmas to you, too,» Trayce said. «But please don't get carried away with making out and stuff today. Mom and I are going out for Christmas dinner and she insisted we get dressed up for it. Do you like my dress?»

Trayce spun in front of a full-length mirror and the other two caught their breath as they saw the beautiful girl. The only other time Trayce had given them a mirror image of herself was when she posed naked the night Jaime had been injured.

«You are breathtaking,» Jaime said.

«Girl! Where did you get that dress? And does it come in green?» Keira asked.

«Yeah… Don't you like the red?»

«It's perfect on you. It brings out the color of your eyes. I'm afraid it would clash with my hair, though. I would never in a million years imagine I'd fall in love with a blue-eyed blonde! Of either sex.»

«I'm not blond,» Jaime said. «I don't think the dress would do anything for me, though. I mean, not if I was wearing it.»

«You're so silly sometimes, Jaime. I really like that about you,» Trayce said.

«I'll keep that in mind.»

«Oops! My parents just arrived. We need to go upstairs and be sociable,» Keira said.

«Yeah. I think Mom's ready to leave for dinner. Merry Christmas to both of you. If we happen to all be in bed at the same time tonight, that would be great!»

«Merry Christmas, Trayce. If you are there, we will be, too.»

The Families

"So, HOW ARE you planning to spend the next few days of your winter break," John asked Keira and Jaime at the dinner table.

"Oh, we thought we'd just spend it in bed together," Keira shot back.

"Keira!" June exclaimed.

"How about if we're just occasionally there?" Keira asked.

"I'm trying to think of ways to ground an eighteen-year-old," David growled.

"I didn't say anything!" Jaime signed. Everyone laughed.

"Well, since you don't like that idea, we thought we'd go meet a friend at the mall tomorrow," Keira said. "Olivia, what did you do to the mashed potatoes? They are so rich and creamy!"

"Oh, secret ingredients. A parsnip and cream cheese. I'm glad you like it," Olivia said.

"Not to get sidetracked," David said. "Who are you meeting?"

"Trayce," Jaime fingerspelled and Keira said at once. "We met her online. She goes to school across town and writes fiction."

"An online friend?" John said. "How well do you know her?"

"We've known her for quite a while online and we were all talking about our love of books," Keira explained. "We decided to meet up at B&N and each of us buy a book for the other two for Christmas. It should take us out of the category of imaginary friends we talked about at Thanksgiving. We can decide if there's an IRL friendship in the making."

"You have to be careful about things like that," Olivia said. "You could be meeting a middle-aged man masquerading as a teen girl. Or a 12-year-old boy."

"That's why we're meeting in a super public place," Keira said. "With so many people around on the day after Christmas, we should be able to spot a predator. Especially in a bookstore. We aren't six-year-olds."

"Keep a line open to us," David said. "If there's a problem, I'll be cruising around."

"Want to drop us at the mall, Dad?" Jaime signed.

"I walked into that, didn't I?"

Trayce and Her Mom

"Gosh, Mom! This place is really fancy," Trayce said when they were seated at the Mayfair Restaurant for Christmas dinner. They arranged themselves at the elegant table, set with a white tablecloth and napkins and a stack of dishes and flatware Trayce wasn't completely sure how to use.

"It's a prix fixe three-course meal, but you get a choice for each course. I figured we'd both find something here we like," Lanie Lombard answered.

"Would you care for a cocktail, ma'am?" the waiter asked.

"No, thank you," Lanie answered. "I'll just have water with the meal and coffee with dessert."

"Same for me," Trayce said.

The waiter left to get their water and was back in a few minutes with their water and to take their order.

"I'll have the rutabaga and parsnip bisque and the smoked duck breast," Trayce said. "I feel adventurous."

"I'm going all seafood," Lanie said. "The scallop agnolotti starter and the seared salmon."

"Excellent choices. I'll get the starters out right away," the waiter said.

"Do you suppose there are anything other than excellent choices on the menu?" Trayce giggled. "I love being out with you, Mom."

"Between the meetings and counseling and having a job where I'm around people again, I'm feeling like a new woman. It still hurts, but I'm not going to let it ruin my life any longer."

"I'm glad. I saw a new counselor last week, too," Trayce ventured. "She specializes in teen girl problems. It was nice to… uh… just talk about life and how I respond to situations."

"She didn't give you drugs, did she?" her mother asked, alarmed.

"Oh, no. No. We just talked. I'll probably see her again next week sometime. We left it open."

"You're eighteen and have your insurance card. If you need money to help defray the cost, we have money. Just please be careful, dear. Let me know when you're seeing her again. I'd like the contact information."

"Okay. Oh, um… One of the things we talked about was me getting out a little more, too. It seems I spend a lot of time online and just in front of my computer writing and don't have much contact with real people. Most of my friends are characters in my head. So, I'm going to meet a couple of friends at the mall tomorrow for lunch," Trayce said.

"Do I know them?"

"No. They're friends from my writing group online. I don't know them all *that* well, but we're meeting at the bookstore to talk about what books we love. I feel pretty safe and confident in the bookstore, so I should be able to spot whether they're really the people I met or if I fabricated the personalities based on too little information."

"Well, be careful. I hear so many terrible things about internet friends. I know I'm a Luddite, but I just don't need to get addicted to the internet now that I'm breaking my addiction to alcohol."

"Well, you finally got a smartphone, so at least we can keep in touch like that."

The Christmas dinner was delicious and mostly lighthearted. Even the desserts of tiramisu and chocolate crunch cake was shared and was delightful. Trayce felt she finally had her mother back.

Jaime and Keira and Trayce

«I'm kind of jealous,» Trayce said later that night. «You two always get to be together and I'm kind of a remote… I don't know what.»

«Satellite,» Keira supplied. «We've always wondered what drew you into our orbit.»

«A satellite. That's not a relationship I'd have ever thought of.»

Jaime and Keira had cleaned up the dishes from Christmas dinner. John and June went home. David and Olivia went to her apartment. Keira had promised her parents she'd be home by midnight.

«When you showed up it was a complete surprise to us,» Jaime said. «We hadn't been together long and every time we touched, something new in the world opened up to us. When we kissed the first time on Keira's front porch, we both heard someone sigh and say 'Wow!' We didn't even associate it with you at first. Just thought it was the universe reflecting our own feelings.»

«I remember hearing two people in my head professing their love and then kissing,» Trayce said. «I didn't know who it was or anything about them, but what I experienced in that first kiss totally took my breath away. Will it be that way tomorrow?»

«We hope so,» Keira said. «But we're trying not to have expectations so high we can't possibly meet them. You just kept showing up as we learned more and more about each other. We worked hard at filtering out uninvited mental images and thoughts. Still, when we were absorbed in each other, you were there.»

«Sounds kind of invasive,» Trayce said.

«I think we subconsciously left a door open for you,» Jaime said. «When you joined us the first time we seriously made out with each other, we realized you were special to us.»

«Special how?»

«I believe Keira is my soulmate,» Jaime said. «I can't imagine a world without her. I care about her so much I'd die for her. And more importantly, I live for her.» Jaime and Keira kissed, bringing Trayce into the depth of their emotion. «When we heard you with us, it didn't take us long to realize it was possible for us each to have two soulmates. I don't know if it's possible to have more than that, but I don't really want to find out. I feel so complete when you are with us that I can't imagine a world without you.»

«Jaime, if I write that down, I'll cry. I thought the two of you would be the most awesome characters I could ever invent. I wanted to write a love story so big it would change the world. And then I let myself get involved in it. The more involved I became, the more real the story was. And the more frightening. I think I was really close to losing my shit all together. Dr. Schwartz told me to block you out and forget that story. He gave me a bunch of keywords and mantras to quote when you were around in my head and you'd disappear. And it sort of worked for a while.»

«How did he give you keywords?» Keira asked.

«He hypnotized me. At least he said he did. I don't remember ever going to sleep, but I could hear his voice and his lips weren't moving. Really weird,» Trayce said. «But I couldn't just quit you. So, I went to see Dr. Rose. She gave me the challenge of proving to myself absolutely whether you are real or not. I'm… really scared to meet you. If you're there or you're not there, it says something about me that I don't think I want to know. But I have to.»

«Honey, we'll be… I don't know. We'll *do* whatever you need to feel okay. We really can't do anything else. We love you,» Jaime said.

«Will you just… I know you're alone and you have a great opportunity to really enjoy yourselves. I know we'd have spectacular orgasms together. But can you just… hold me. Without getting too sexual. Just hold me like you really love me and want me to be with you?»

«Yes, love. But it's two ways. Hold us. Even though we aren't literally in your arms, hold us and make us feel how much you care about us.»

«Yes.»

It was a strange evening. Jaime and Keira embraced and shared little kisses, but in their minds, Trayce was with them. She felt their kisses and their arms around her. She imagined giving them little kisses as well. Eventually, they fell asleep.

Keira woke up a little after midnight and quietly kissed Jaime goodnight before she went home. Jaime went to bed. Both felt themselves present in Trayce's dreams.

ALL THREE TEENS were incredibly excited Friday. They wished they'd made arrangements to meet earlier in the day instead of for lunch. It seemed so silly to need a pretense for getting together.

«We told our parents we met online and were going to meet IRL today,» Keira said.

«I told Mom the same thing. She's all concerned. I told her she didn't need to worry. We'd known each other for a long time,» Trayce answered.

«Don't discount our parents' concern,» Jaime said. «They care about us and we need to respect that. We aren't driving to the mall. Dad and Olivia are taking us and they plan to circle around the area in case we need help and call them,» Jaime said.

«What would you need help for?»

«Just in case you're really a middle-aged predator or a twelve-year-old boy pretending to be a girl.»

«That's ridiculous. I'm not pretending.»

«We know that, precious. But how can we explain that to our parents?» Keira said.

«We need to get in the car now and might lose contact,» Jaime said. «Being surrounded by metal cuts down on how much we hear from outside.»

«Oh. That's why it always seems quiet when I'm driving. Okay. I'll see you there. I *will* see you, won't I?»

«We're on our way.»

The ride in the car was quiet, Jaime and Keira holding hands tensely. David thought they might be having second thoughts, and reached for Olivia's hand in the front seat. She had gladly agreed to join him and they were going to have lunch at a nearby restaurant. His own thoughts were very pleased. He'd spent Christmas night at Olivia's apartment and they'd finally gone to bed together. Jaime and Keira focused on blocking out the memories shared by the two of them.

When David pulled up to the curb to drop them off, he admonished Jaime and Keira to call if there was *any* kind of trouble. They agreed and then dashed to the door of the mall, still holding hands.

«Calling Trayce. Calling Trayce,» Jaime sent out. It was meant to be light-hearted, but they were filled with anxiety. «We've arrived and are making our way to B&N. Are you here yet?»

«Ack! I just got out of the car. I'm parked in the farthest corner of the lot. This is a zoo! And I'm so nervous, I dropped my keys. I feel like I'm building myself up to a colossal trauma!» Trayce panted.

«We're making our way across the mall. Dad dropped us at the other end. We should be there in a couple of minutes, though.»

«I can't believe we're actually doing this!» Her thoughts were tinged with anxiety. «I must be crazy! I should leave you as a figment of my imagination.»

«Please don't run away, sweetie. We'd be heartbroken.»

Hey! Stop! I won't go! Go away! Go away!! Trayce screamed out in her head.

Her thoughts were suddenly cut off from Keira and Jaime. They stopped where they were in the middle of the mall's center court.

«Trayce? Trayce, are you all right? Where'd you go? We're almost to the bookstore,» Jaime called.

«Trayce, please don't run away from us? Please!» Keira pled.

Only silence responded.

27
HEARTBREAK

Jaime and Keira

«WHAT JUST HAPPENED?» Jaime asked Keira.

«She cut us off! She screamed to go away again and slammed the door so hard my head hurts!»

«Why? Trayce! Where are you? Don't cut us off.»

«Let's go on to the bookstore and see if we can find her. I can't believe she'd just cut us off like that when we were so near!» Keira said.

The two hurried to the bookstore, but hurrying through the mall on Boxing Day, the day after Christmas, was a matter of perspective. They were going faster than others, but not nearly as fast as they wanted to go. When they reached the bookstore, the sales had the cash registers backed up and people were standing in line in the café to place their orders. Jaime and Keira split up, first checking the café for any sign of Trayce.

«I don't think she's here,» Keira said.

«It's a big store. Let's make another circuit around. She could be hiding,» Jaime said.

«She's hidden herself from me. I can't feel her at all.»

Both teens were upset, but continued their search, meeting up at last at the café once more.

«I don't feel much like eating,» Jaime said.

«Me either. Can we go to your place?»

«I'll text Dad. If he's still circling the mall, he'll be here in a few minutes.»

Jaime and Keira made it back across the mall, holding hands. Tears were near their eyes. David and Olivia were still nearby and in a few minutes were back to where he'd dropped the two of them.

"How did your meetup go?" David asked. "You weren't there that long."

"She didn't show up," Keira said.

"I don't like that," David said. "She could have been someone scoping the two of you out. Maybe not even a woman. I want you to be extra careful this week."

"We will, sir. Can you take us to your house? We just need to figure out what we'll do next," Keira said.

"Sure. How about a dip of ice cream on the way back? That always makes me feel better."

"Before lunch, David?" Olivia laughed.

"Why not?"

"Yes, please," Keira said.

Jaime and Keira sat on the sofa in the family room holding hands. They'd finished their ice cream with David and Olivia. The older couple then said they were going out to lunch. Jaime had the impression from both of them that lunch might be in Olivia's apartment.

«I feel really hurt,» Keira said. «I never thought she'd tell us to go away again.»

«I didn't think she was capable of slamming the door so tightly. Any time she's backed away from us, I could still sense her. I've never slammed a door so tightly—not without pretty much going into a coma.»

«You don't suppose *that* happened to her, do you?»

«If it happened like it does to me, we'd have had time to understand it.»

«What if she was in an accident? Maybe she was hit in the parking lot. When you were knocked out, we both lost touch with you. Then you were in the hospital and there was so much interference I couldn't reach you until I was in your room.»

«I didn't see any flashing lights at the mall. We can check the news and call the hospitals, I suppose. Something really bothers me about this.»

«Did our lover really just ghost us? I'm bothered, too,» Keira said.

«I don't know how to explain it without… at least kissing you,» Jaime said.

«There's nothing stopping you from doing that.»

The two folded into each other's arms and kissed deeply. In that moment, Jaime opened up and shared his deepest fears and desires. Keira could not help but do the same. The two were of one mind. Both were flooded with the intensity of each other's feelings.

But there was no answering thought from Trayce.

Jaime had only one experience that came close to what had just happened. It was his last moments with his mother, when she'd told him she loved him. Then there was nothing. She was gone from his life forever.

Keira gasped at the intensity of the memory and the two embraced as tears began to fall. The thought that Trayce might truly be gone forever broke their hearts.

«We're here alone,» Keira said. «Your dad won't be back for a long time. There's nothing stopping us… We could just go to your room.»

«Keira, you've just been inside my mind and body. You know how much I want you. But…»

«Yeah. Except that.»

«I just don't like the idea that we make love to each other for the first time while we're grieving the loss of Trayce,» Jaime said.

«It would always feel that way, wouldn't it? I just want us to have the joy in each other that we've always had before. I don't want a dark cloud hanging over us,» Keira said.

«I always thought it would be so much easier to have a relationship with a woman who could hear my thoughts and speak in my mind. Like, we'd always know for sure if our partner was consenting to something,» Jaime said.

«Instead, we see each other's desire, complicated by our doubts and misgivings. We don't even know our own minds and feel like we are never ready. I love you so much, Jaime.»

«I can't imagine my life without you. I would be miserable.»

«I'm miserable enough right now,» Keira said. «Wouldn't it be acceptable to comfort each other with some more kissing… and stuff?»

«Yeah. That would make me feel a lot better.»

Each wanted the comfort they found in the other's arms. They were determined not to have intercourse, but that didn't eliminate any of the other things they'd done together. It began with just a little kissing and progressed to touching and petting. Before long they were both naked and lying on the sofa together.

«So easy. It would be so easy,» Keira sighed.

«I love you so much,» Jaime said. «I know it would be wonderful. Maybe we're silly to wait.»

«Let's make sure first. It won't hurt to wait a few more days. No regrets, remember?» Keira said. «But New Year's Eve is our time, lover. New Year's Eve I want all of you.»

«I want to feel you, Keira. I want to feel your body and your mind as you come.»

«Keep doing that. Yes. Right there. Slide your finger… up… yes… in. I can feel you searching inside me. Searching for my soul. I want you so much! I'm… going…»

That was all the warning Jaime got for Keira's impending orgasm. As she began to slip back into herself, she felt Jaime ramp up for his. Both rode the waves of the other's pleasure.

They held each other and eventually dozed off to sleep.

Jaime's phone buzzed, waking them up. He looked at the text message.

"Picking up pizza. Be home in fifteen minutes," was David's message.

«It's so nice that he gave us a warning,» Keira giggled. Jaime continued stroking her body.

«He could have given us more time,» Jaime sighed. «I could continue doing this for the next fifty years or so.»

«Oh, yes. No! We need to dress.»

«I'm dressing. I love you, Keira.»

They pulled themselves together and each supported the other when sadness got hold of them.

Jaime and Keira and Emerson

"Hey, Keira, it's Emerson," said the cheerful voice on the phone. "I was just wondering if you and Jaime might want to get together this afternoon. We could run another test on our software and then maybe get a pizza. Um… Your girlfriend is welcome to come, too."

"Oh, hey. Thanks Emerson. That might be just the pick-me-up we need today. Our girlfriend kind of… rejected us Friday. It's been a real downer," Keira said.

"I'm so sorry! Really! Nothing makes the holidays suck like being rejected by someone you really like. Can you guys get over here by, say, one, to run some tests and then we can get a pizza mid-afternoon?"

«Are you up for this?» Keira asked Jaime.

«Sure. Why not. You know what she wants, though.»

«Yeah. Maybe that's okay. I'm so down, mindless sex might be just what we need.»

«Let's not go too far, okay?»

"I just checked with Jaime real quick. We'll see you at one."

"That's great! Later!"

It was about eight blocks from Keira's house to Emerson's, but they decided to walk through the falling snow. It wasn't the first snow of the season, but this one was looking like it would accumulate some serious inches. Not much chance Monday's return to school would be delayed, though.

«Is your hand too cold?» Jaime asked. They each had a glove on one hand, but were holding bare hands between them.

«I'd rather freeze than lose touch with you,» Keira said.

«I wish we were sharing this with Trayce,» Jaime said. «And that is the last thing I'm going to say on the subject of our former girlfriend,» he added with more finality than he felt.

«You need to remember to sign while we're with Emerson,» Keira said. «Based on her reaction when you spoke in her mind, she could freak out completely if she finds out we talk in our heads. We don't need to send another girlfriend to therapy.»

«Got it.»

«Look! There's a crossbill!»

«Is that what that bird is called? He sure looks bright against the snow, doesn't he?»

«His light shines.»

They walked through a mix of neighborhoods before reaching Emerson's slightly more opulent area.

"Hey! You made it," Emerson said when she opened the door to their knock. "Did you walk? I could have driven over to pick you up!"

"Thanks, Emerson. It was just so beautiful out there, we decided to walk and enjoy the snowfall."

"It's really coming down now. We usually have to go farther inland to the mountains to see this kind of snow," Emerson said. She took their coats and hung them up in a hall closet. "Not to worry, though. If we get snowed in, we have plenty of supplies. We could last a week here. Let me introduce you to the fam."

They went into the living room where Emerson's parents were sitting and reading.

"Mom, Dad, these are my friends Keira and Jaime," Emerson said.

"Happy to meet you, Mr. and Mrs. Flaherty," Keira said as Jaime signed.

"Emerson has told us so much about you," Mrs. Flaherty said. "I understand you don't speak, Jaime, but I think it's great Emerson has been learning sign language so you can work together in your computer lab. We should make sign language a mandatory course in elementary school. And make sure we have appropriate assistive technology where needed."

Mrs. Flaherty was desperately trying to make them feel comfortable, but, like so many well-intentioned people, was focusing on the disability rather than the people. Jaime and Keira could clearly read her thoughts, though, and realized quickly her good intentions. Mr. Flaherty just looked up and smiled at them, content to let his wife handle the embarrassment without him getting involved.

"We're going downstairs to the computers to test our apps," Emerson said, moving them toward the door. "You might want to investigate Jaime's text to speech app when you're looking at assistive technologies. He can speak in class like any other student."

"Fascinating," her mother said. "Have fun and don't work too hard. We're on vacation, remember?"

As soon as they were out of earshot, Emerson whispered, "Hope that wasn't too painful. Mom really tries hard, and usually she manages to get something good accomplished. Mercy has the best patient care reputation in the city. I have to respect her for achieving that."

"I'm glad she's achieving things over there," Jaime signed and Keira interpreted. "I spent a night there a couple of weeks ago when I got cut and they were afraid I had a concussion."

"Other hospitals would have stitched you and shoved you out the door within an hour," Emerson said.

"Is your sister here, too?" Keira asked.

"She's fourteen," Emerson said as if that explained everything. "She has her computer, a television, and her cell phone in her room and figures the only time she needs to come out is to eat or piss. God! Was I that much of a twerp just four years ago?"

They laughed, Jaime's odd squeak among the noises. They got sodas and sat discussing the holiday for a few minutes. They tried not to probe Emerson too deeply, but there was a definite sense of her being lonely most of the time.

"Well, we'd better run some tests so it doesn't seem like I'm just desperate to have company," Emerson said. "Look what I did with your app!"

Jaime had left a copy for her to play with on her own. She'd definitely put in some work.

"That's great!" Jaime signed when Emerson played a version of her voice that had a soft southern drawl to it.

"Very sexy," Keira added. "I might need to go live in Georgia just to listen to the belles."

"Why go so far when you have me right here?" Emerson typed as the text to speech engine spoke in the drawl. It was still identifiable as her voice, but had a completely different accent.

"I can see we are all going to need to coordinate our TTS voices and then do something bizarre in school," Keira said.

"We could put on a play," Jaime suggested. "Our synthetic voices performing *A Streetcar Named Desire* or something." Of course, he and Keira had memorized part of that play as a tool for blocking people in their heads.

"Oh, yeah!" Emerson said. She typed, "I have always depended on the kindness of strangers." The voice picked it up.

"We might have a whole new use for the app," Keira said. "Jaime, you could be an acting sensation. Just feed the lines into the computer and act them out!"

"I was kidding! Don't even think of putting me on stage or in front of a camera!" Jaime signed.

They ran several more experiments, including recording Keira's voice tests as they had with Emerson a week earlier. Then they applied the same filters Emerson had set up for her southern drawl.

"They're different!" Keira exclaimed.

It was clear that even though they had the same accent, the tone and timbre of Emerson's and Keira's voices were different and recognizable.

Jaime pulled a composition book from his backpack and started writing notes in his elegant script. Emerson looked over his shoulder.

"Not only do you have sign language that only select people understand, but you write in a way only a few people can grasp," she said. "I'm just beginning to be able to decipher it."

"You should see Mex and Cheery's wedding invitations!" Jaime signed. "They both learned at the same time I did and handwrote each invitation!"

"When's their wedding?" Emerson asked.

"The weekend after graduation this spring. The invitations haven't actually been sent yet. I just happened to know both the bride and groom," Jaime signed.

"And he's going to be the best man at the wedding!" Keira said.

"*You're* not, like, thinking of getting married right away, are you?" Emerson asked.

"Girl, we haven't even had sex yet," Keira laughed. "It's a little early to be thinking of marriage."

"They're kind of different things," Emerson said. *How about going up to my room now?* she thought.

"Um… We probably won't be virgins much longer," Keira said.

"We were waiting for our girlfriend, but she cut us off, so there isn't much reason to wait except making sure the two of us are ready," Jaime signed.

«Did you see that?» he shot to Keira.

«Loud and clear! If we said let's all go to bed now, she'd be all over it… us.»

«Are you sure we aren't just responding to a fantasy?»

«It's definitely a fantasy, but there's real intent behind it.»

«Wow!»

"I've got an idea," Emerson said.

Jaime and Keira could clearly see her idea taking shape and caught their breath.

"This is just because you should have one experience that I can help with. I, like, understand you wanting to wait for sex and you should really be alone together for that." *I could coach them through each step of the way. Maybe after their first time, I could get more involved.* "You both know I've got experience with a three-way. God, it haunts me and I can't stop thinking of Dom and Raquel. They're getting married New Year's Day. I might need to see you guys just to talk me out of despair as they're getting hitched."

"We understand," Keira said.

"I knew you would. So… What I was thinking is that I could show you, or participate with you, or something, in a three-way kiss. It's just for instructional purposes, you know. It wouldn't mean I'm your third wheel or anything. It's just…" Emerson stuttered to a stop. "I feel so alone now. And you two are so sexy. And… I really *want* to kiss you."

«Okay?» Keira asked Jaime.

«Yeah. You know. Just to see what it's like.»

«Yeah.»

Jaime and Keira pulled Emerson into an embrace that let each girl know quickly the other was braless. They just held each other for a few minutes with Emerson breathing heavily between them. It was clear in her mind that she was excited beyond words just to be held by them. She desperately wanted the kiss.

«We need to be careful,» Keira said. «It could be overwhelming for her if we share what we felt when we kissed the first time.»

«Do you think she'll feel that?»

«Definitely. Just based on the last time you touched her bare skin. That was just her shoulder.»

«Okay. I'm ready.»

Being physically in touch with a third person when they kissed was far different than being with Trayce in their heads. They could see from Emerson's memory how they needed to tilt their heads the same direction as they came together for that first electric touch of their lips. Emerson was not waiting. Her lips were parted and she touched theirs with her tongue. Then all three tongues came into play and the world shifted.

For Jaime and Keira, it was like merging themselves into Emerson, her memories and hopes. They could clearly see the difference between their thoughts and hers. She was open to them, but not really sharing with them beyond enjoying the experience of the three-way kiss together for the first time.

For Emerson, it was a new world. She could feel their growing interest in her, but also felt both her disappointment in losing her lovers in Paris and the other two losing Trayce. Still, the passion they had for their missing partners was shared completely with each other. Emerson gasped for breath and then put her hands behind both Keira's and Jaime's heads to hold them for a longer and more passionate kiss that brought tears to the eyes of each of them.

«We do care about you, Emerson,» Jaime whispered in her mind. «You are our dear friend. We just want to hold you.»

«Can we be more than friends?» she whispered, not realizing she was actually speaking with them.

«Anything is possible, but we all need time to heal. Right?» Keira asked.

«Yes. I just… I just want to kiss you some more. And everything!»

Everything proved to be hands exploring each other, eventually slipping beneath shirts to caress bare chests. The teens let the kiss deepen with more and more boundaries between them disappearing as they found each other's breasts and nipples.

Before they could let their hands slide lower, Keira and Jaime pulled back.

«We need to get control of ourselves,» Jaime said.

«Yeah. If we let this go further, we'd be screwing here on the carpet,» Keira agreed. «If you want.»

«Tempting, but I don't think we should.»

«Right.»

They stood looking at Emerson as they pulled their hands from beneath her shirt. Emerson continued to hold her position with her face upturned for the kiss, her lips parted, and her eyes closed.

"That was nothing like what I expected," she sighed. Her eyes slowly opened but she continued a glazed look into space. "I felt like… like I could feel all three of us. Like I was somehow inside you and you were in me. I… I think we should put our coats on and go get a pizza. Yeah. That's what we need. Just a pizza with pepperoni and lots of cheese."

"Sausage and mushrooms," Keira added.

"Sure," Emerson pressed her legs together. *Fuck! I think I came.*

28
COUNSEL

Jaime and Keira and Rose

"I WONDERED IF I was ever going to get a chance to meet you, Jaime. Welcome," Dr. Rose said on Tuesday when the teens went to meet with her. "Tell me what the problem is."

"We can't talk about this without asking you to suspend disbelief and just go with Jaime and me being able to talk in our heads to each other. I recognize that it sounds insane, but I know you know it's true," Keira said.

"I'll suspend disbelief for the time being," Rose said.

"We also know that you talked to Trayce Lombard," Keira said. "And then she left us."

"She left you? Okay. Obviously, I can't discuss what Trayce and I talked about, but tell me about what happened."

"Dr. Rose," Jaime signed with two taps of the inside of his wrist followed by his fingers crossed and circling beneath his nose. They were established signs for doctor and rose. "We talked to Trayce on Christmas night." Keira interpreted, though she thought her aunt probably knew exactly what he was saying.

"So, you met with her?"

"No," Jaime continued signing. "We talked in our heads. We've never met her face-to-face. She was excited for us to meet in the mall on Friday at noon. We were all there. Keira and I were crossing the mall and Trayce told us she was just getting out of her car in the farthest corner of the parking lot."

"We were all crazy excited," Keira said. "We'd only ever talked in our heads before. But as we were all heading to meet, she suddenly screamed at us. She said, 'Stop! I won't go. Go away. Go away.' And then she went completely silent on us. Like she just vanished."

"And you both heard this… in your heads," Rose said.

The teens nodded.

"You haven't heard anything else from her since?"

"Not a word," Keira confirmed.

"Hmm. You've posed an interesting problem. A person you know only as a voice in your head suddenly stopped being a voice in your head just when you thought you were going to meet her. Am I right?"

"Yes, but Aunt Rose, we know her! We've talked a lot. Yes, in our heads. We've been intimate. She's really a wonderful person and it just doesn't seem right that she'd cut us off like that," Keira said. Tears were leaking from her eyes and Jaime took her hand. The teens combined, but could not hear a single thought from Rose.

"Okay. Now I want *you* to suspend your disbelief for a moment," Rose said. "Perhaps Trayce was just a voice the two of you hallucinated together. Perhaps your own anxiety over the meeting caused you to cut her off before you could be disappointed in the outcome of the meeting."

"If we suspended our disbelief that much," Jaime signed, "we'd have to question whether Keira and I know each other and even if you are in this room with us. I understand it is hard for the head deaf to comprehend what it is like to hear other people's thoughts. But I have always been this way—from birth. I'd only once heard another person deliberately answer me until I met Keira. That was seconds before my mother died. Then she went silent like Trayce did. Two girls and an old man are the only people I've ever met who could do this. I can't stand the thought of losing one of them."

"You have always been able to read the thoughts of others? What am I thinking?" Rose asked.

"Keira warned me you were well-shielded. So well, in fact, that we suspect you can hear others, too," Jaime signed and Keira interpreted. Then he reached over to take Keira's hand and she opened fully to him. Before she could respond, Jaime reached out and touched Rose's hand as well.

«Please help us! You know we can communicate like this,» Jaime said.

Rose snatched her hand back, but it was obvious she'd heard Jamie's demand.

"You don't know the depth of what you are playing with," Rose said severely. "You should go home, make love to each other, and close yourself off to the rest of the world. Don't disclose your suspicions about your talents to anyone. Whether it is true or not, it is dangerous. I think we need to close this session. We can talk again next week."

The dismissal was so firm and so final that Jaime and Keira stood and left the office.

Jaime and Keira

«I never thought Aunt Rose would tell me to go have sex with my boyfriend!» Keira laughed in her mind.

«I think she was just telling us to distract ourselves. She knows something!» Jaime said.

«Does that mean you don't want to make love to me?»

«You think I'm crazy? Of course I want to make love to you.»

«Damn! I promised my parents I'd be home tonight and go to their friends' house with them,» Keira moaned.

«I think tomorrow night would work as well,» Jaime thought. «Maybe better. I know Dad plans to spend New Year's Eve with Olivia.»

«New Year's Eve! What a perfect way to end the old year and start the new. I'll come to your house and we can celebrate all night long!»

«Keira, I love you and the images you are sending me are making my pants uncomfortably tight.»

«I feel it. I might be… slippery the whole time between now and then.»

«I love you! I don't think there will be a moment I'm not in touch with you between now and then.»

«Just, no orgasms between now and then. Especially when I'm visiting my parents' friends.»

«Agreed.»

Rose

"KENTON! WHAT HAVE you done?" Rose barked into the voicemail of her one-time friend and lover. "I warned you to stay away from them. I warned you! Now I'm coming for you. I have a lot more credibility in the community than you do. I'll destroy your reputation. The State Board will kill your license. I warned you, Kenton. I warned you!"

Rose disconnected and sifted through her old contacts. She had a tattered business card she didn't know why she'd kept. He might not even have the same phone number after twenty years. She'd bet his address was the same, though.

And she knew the best way to get through to the dirty old man. She went home to change clothes and apply a little makeup. Even for a head talker, Angus had simple tastes. She looked at herself in a mirror and then took her bra off. Simple tastes.

Jaime and Keira

«I'M READY,» KEIRA said when she picked Jaime up Wednesday afternoon. «You are all I wanted in the first place and I want you more now than ever. Please say you'll make love to me tonight.»

«You know I'm ready,» Jaime responded. «I told Dad I'd invited you to spend the night.»

«How'd he take that?»

«More chaos in his head than you can imagine. For a while I thought he was just going to stay home. The thought of spending the night with Olivia won. He just said to be safe and not to rush things,» Jaime said.

«About the way my parents took me telling them I was planning to spend New Year's Eve with you. Mom asked if I thought I'd be home by one. I said, 'Maybe by one Thursday afternoon.' She almost swallowed her tongue biting back forbidding me to go. I think Dad saying to be careful and safe and to call if I needed anything was what settled her down.»

«My heart is going a million beats a minute!»

«I can feel it. This is it, Jaime. Make love to me tonight.»

«I will make love *with* you. I don't think there is any other possibility,» he said. «We need to pick up a few things to eat, assuming we have an appetite for anything but each other.»

«I thought we could pick up something ready made at Whole Foods.»

«Good idea.»

They went to the grocery store and tried to select something simple. They ended up just grabbing a frozen pizza and some chips.

Rose and Angus

"I KNEW I'd find you here," Rose said when she spotted Angus at the tip rail at Sassy's. "Still just a dirty old man, aren't you?"

"If it isn't one of my favorite fantasies," Angus said turning to Rose. She spun around to let him get a full look at her. "Ass good ass, I remember."

Rose sat in the chair next to Angus and he tapped the tip rail

"Two dollars a song if you're sitting here," he said.

Rose reached in her bag and pulled out a five. She tossed it over the rail. The girl dancing was having a good time displaying herself to the half dozen men gathered to watch her.

"I need to talk to you, Angus."

"After Thursday's set is over. We'll go to the patio."

Thursday had one more number during which she lost her bottoms and danced around the floor completely naked, making sure Rose got as good a view as Angus did.

"She your main squeeze now?" Rose asked as they pushed their chairs away at the end of the song and Thursday collected her tips.

"My friend. Sometimes a partner when I'm investigating. We don't fool around, so there's still room for you and me to have fun if you haven't joined the dark side." They went outside to the patio where heat lamps warmed an area around the fire pit. "Did Schwartz send you after me?"

"What makes you suspicious of that?"

"Little run-in I had with him a couple of weeks ago. I warned him to stay away from a boy and his girlfriend."

"I warned him of the same thing," Rose said. "I don't think he listened very well."

"We've been keeping an eye on the kids. Haven't seen him around since I warned him off. What's happened?"

"I think he picked up their girlfriend."

"They said there was a third. I staked out the community college and never saw a sign of her," Angus said.

"She was supposed to meet them at the mall Friday and suddenly went dark on them."

"Damn! I thought they were acting strange. Went into the mall and raced to the bookstore. They were searching all over, then took off."

"They thought she blew them off. Her signal suddenly went blank. You know what that means," Rose said as she accepted the joint Angus lit and passed to her.

"Some variety of Faraday cage. That damn bastard. I don't think he ever caught on to me being able to hear him. Unless you told him," Angus said, reaching over to put a hand on Rose's bare leg. Fortunately, the heat lamps and gas fireplace on the patio kept a limited area warm, but Angus's hand on her leg heated Rose even more. She'd always had a soft spot for Angus. If she admitted it, she'd call it a soft wet spot.

"I cut myself off from Kenton when you and I discovered what he was trying to do. Until I started threatening him a week ago, I hadn't really thought of him at all. Then Trayce, the third wheel, came in for counseling and mentioned she'd already seen him. Red flags all over."

"I'm glad you're keeping the shields up. I let mine down a little and those other two jumped right in," Angus said.

"They are incredibly powerful together. They joined hands and gave me a command. You know what that means, Angus? They projected a command through my barriers," Rose said.

"Goddess! If Schwartz knew they could do that…"

"He thinks it takes a gestalt to be able to have that much control. I think that's why he may have picked up Trayce. He figured the other two would follow her."

"Probably right," Angus said. "They don't have a lot of good sense to go with their power. We'll have to keep a closer eye on them."

"I told them to go home and have sex, cut off the rest of the world, and forget about everything."

"And?"

"I'm pretty sure they'll do the first, at least," Rose laughed.

"It's not a bad idea," Angus said as he squeezed her leg. She'd made no move to have him remove his hand.

"Angus! Does this mean you don't need me to drive you home tonight?" Thursday said when she arrived at the patio. She was dressed again and had her fur coat on.

"Thursday, honey, this is an old friend from a bygone era. We have a lot of catching up to do," Angus said.

"That's fine. I don't want to stay around much longer, though. The New Year's Eve drunks are arriving."

"Drunks already?" Rose asked.

"Drunk or will be drunk soon," Thursday said.

"Thursday helps me get around," Angus said. "I hate to drive at night."

"I can get you home," Rose said. "Is that okay with you, Thursday?"

"Hell, yes. I'm going over to Kate's house then. The two of us will wait out the old year."

"Okay, sweetie!" Angus said. "I'll be okay. Tell Kate I got delayed."

"Oh, believe me. By the time I finish describing how you've already gotten your hand under her skirt, Kate and I will be naked together. Too bad you have to miss that!" Thursday laughed.

She bent down to give Angus a kiss on the cheek and then took off. Rose looked down at her leg and verified that Angus had slid his hand up far enough to be fully under the hem of her short skirt.

"This probably isn't all that appropriate for here," Rose said, preventing Angus's hand from going any farther. "If the drunks are arriving, we should take off."

"Yes. We should definitely take things off," Angus said.

"Still have bunnies in your apartment?"

"Just one. She sleeps on my right shoulder at night."

"Anyone sleeping on the left?"

"Position's available. Don't expect a miracle, though. I'm not taking any drugs these days."

Jaime and Keira

THE TWO HAD all the usual first time jitters. They heated the oven and got the frozen pizza on the rack. Keira opened soft drinks as Jaime opened the bag of chips.

«We really chose to eat healthy, didn't we?» he asked.

«No. We chose to eat fast,» Keira laughed. «And with almost no cleanup.»

«I'd like to cook a nice meal for you sometime. In addition to the basics Dad and I usually eat, and that I fed you when you were here for dinner, I'm a pretty good cook. Just not tonight.»

«It's distracting, isn't it?» Keira asked.

«What is?»

She kissed him.

«Yes. Distracting.»

They got involved in their kissing in the kitchen with hands busily exploring each other as their tongues danced. Keira pushed him away.

"Pizza!" she gasped. The timer was beeping and neither was sure how long it had been going. The pizza looked fine, though. Keira pulled it out with mitts and turned off the oven. She slid the pizza onto the waiting cutting board and Jaime took care of cutting it into wedges.

They giggled together as if they'd been caught being naughty instead of just enjoying the contact with the other. They finished their meal and took care of the minor cleanup.

«Want to watch TV for a bit?» Jaime asked. Keira looked at him strangely.

«What's on?»

«Netflix.»

«Okay… I guess.»

«Come on. I have a TV in my room,» Jaime said.

He kissed Keira's open lips and they nearly got lost again. The prospect of watching TV sounded a whole lot better as he led her into his room.

Jaime had prepared his bedroom as well as he could. It was spotlessly clean, with fresh sheets on the bed and a stack of pillows so they could prop themselves up. Keira spent a minute just looking around. There were interesting little tidbits that gave her an insight into her lover that even their shared minds had not revealed. He had photos of his core of friends through all the years of school. His laptop was closed, but she could see it was connected to both the speakers and the television. Mex and Cheery's calligraphed wedding invitation was on his desk. And a photo of his mom sat alone on the dresser.

They propped themselves up on the bed and turned on the TV, tuning to the movie service and choosing the first one that popped up. It was different than what would have popped up on Keira's screen, based on Jaime's watching habits. He had some of the typical boy tastes for action and adventure.

Neither one really cared. As soon as the show started, they were lost in each other's arms and kisses.

There were too many marvels to rush. Had either been focused on their genitals, it would have been much briefer. But as they lost their clothes on Jaime's bed, they also lost themselves in each other. Their minds were fully opened to each other and if their bodies were meant to fit together perfectly, their minds were even better matched. They meshed together creating something much more than either had experienced before.

Jaime poised at Keira's entrance, their juices mingling. Keira pulled him steadily forward until his flesh was fully buried in hers. And there they stayed for an eternal moment, marveling at the wonder of being one as they made love.

«You… are in me,» Keira whispered in his mind. «In my mind and in my body. And I feel you. Inside you. I feel how hard you are and how sensitive. My tongue is in your mouth and our arms are wrapped around each other. If I could, I would meld my body completely into yours.»

«I feel your fullness. I know where and how to move to give you the most pleasure. I feel each twitch in your vagina and the tingling in your nipples. I've never been so completely consumed by a connection in my life. I am you. A part of you. I give you all of me.»

They moved together, automatically finding the best rhythm and the maximum pleasure for each other. They rose to their first peak and were consumed by the passion for each other. Both lost consciousness, Jaime nearly smothering Keira with his body. She gasped for breath and he fought his way back to the real world and rolled to her side, still keeping her tightly in his arms.

«I never imagined…» Both thought to the other. They smiled at each other and kissed again.

They maintained their head link as they dozed and even dreamed the same dreams. When they stirred again, Keira slowly withdrew from her lover's mind and body.

«Sorry,» she said. «I need to use the bathroom. Back soon.»

Jaime smiled and was contented with their light mental link, keeping them always in touch with each other. When Keira was finished, he used the toilet as well, and then cuddled up to his lover. A couple of episodes of the series they'd tuned in had passed and they had no idea what the storyline currently was. Jaime switched off the TV.

They were content, for the moment, just to lie in each other's arms, sharing the warmth of body and spirit. Both knew they would make love again soon—possibly before they slept and probably after they awoke.

«I dreamed of her,» Keira said in the morning.

«I think we shared the dream. She was alone and afraid.»

«I hate that. It was like we were with her but she wasn't there.»

«We *tried* to be with her. We're still going through withdrawal since she cut us off. She probably is, too. I didn't know how hard it would be to let someone go after we shared so intimately,» Jaime ventured.

They made love again, and when they woke up the next time, they went to the kitchen to make breakfast.

«I wonder if Trayce is feeling twitchy,» Jaime said. «It seems this was always the time she showed up. She's blocked us from reading her, but do you think it's as effective for her not reading us?»

«Maybe so. She never recognized that she listened to others. I think, though, that deep down, she realized we were real and not in her imagination.»

«If we were in her imagination, do you think we'd stop existing eventually?» Jaime asked.

The two were back in bed, kissing and petting. They weren't rushing toward another coupling, though both knew it was coming soon. It was the best New Year's Day they'd ever had.

«The concert. She didn't know how she could listen to music she'd never heard before if it was just in her head. I'm sorry I held on to Trayce so hard,» Keira said.

«Please don't feel guilty about that. I held on, too. And it was much stronger because it was both of us she attached to. There was always something about that attachment that was different. Like she could have broken it at any time, but we were just subject to her call. I don't know,» Jaime said. «I know that being with you makes me happier than I've ever been. I'm not going to spoil that happiness by thinking about what we can't have anymore.»

«Then come to me, lover. Fill me. I want you in me again. I want to feel you in every part of my being,» Keira said.

«How could I say anything but yes?»

Neither of them had a concept of how many times they might make love in a day, or of what they might do when they weren't making love. As they moved together again, both were aware that their bodies would need to rest and recover soon. But neither was willing to stop when they were so close to each other and so close to a mutual orgasm.

Keira could feel it boiling in Jaime as she let herself go to enjoy both their orgasms. Jaime's mind opened so wide he feared he would overload as he dealt both with all of Keira's sensations and all of his own. The explosion they shared left them floating in a suspended space neither present nor apart.

Help! Help me! Please don't! I don't want to go to sleep. Go away!

This will just relax you. Don't worry. We'll have you ready to share in no time.

Don't. Please don't! «Jaime! Keira! I believe in you. Please, help me!»

The orgasms were still pulsing in both teens as they jerked apart and sat bolt upright in bed.

«Trayce!»

29
EMERGENCY

Rose and Angus

"**M**Y GOD! WHAT was that?" Rose exclaimed sitting up in Angus's bed. She hadn't intended to spend the night with him They'd started talking about what they could do to find the missing girl. That led to talking about old times. One thing led to another and they'd had a very nice New Year's Eve.

"That was a psychic call for help," Angus said. "Was it the missing girl?"

"Yes. I'm sure of it. She called for Keira and Jaime."

"Which means those kids got the call loud and clear. Who knows how many other head talkers there are in Portland who heard her? We need to find her. Oh, goddess! The girls will hate me if I get them out of bed at this hour!" he muttered.

"It's almost noon!"

"You're right; they probably just got to bed." Angus pulled Rose down to him and began kissing his way down her body.

"You're incorrigible, old man."

"Just because I'm too old to cut the mustard doesn't mean I can't lick the pot. It's New Year's Day. Let's start it the way New Years should be started. Then we can start looking for the little lost darling."

Rose thought they should probably call Jaime and Keira, but just at the moment, she was lost in the sensations Angus was delivering to an area that had been neglected for entirely too long.

Jaime and Keira

«She was here!» Jaime gasped.

«He's raping her!» Keira yelled, jumping out of bed.

«He's…»

«Raping her mind. Giving her drugs to expand her ability. Couldn't you feel the fear?»

«Yes. That other voice. I know that voice. It's the guy who's been stalking me.»

«That must be why she shut down when we were supposed to meet. Was she trying to protect us?» Keira asked.

«Faraday cage,» Jaime said. «Like in the *X-Men*. That has to be it. Like the aluminum foil in my closet and the way it was suddenly so quiet in your aunt's office and house. He must have rigged his vehicle so it functions like that.»

«Don't tell me it's the guy we stopped after the movie!» Keira cried.

«No. It's the guy who was stalking me. Maybe Angus knows something. I'll always recognize that guy's head taste. He's evil. I just know it,» Jaime said.

«We have to do something!»

Keira and Jaime wrapped each other in a hug, their naked bodies pressed against each other, but no new messages came.

«Where is she?»

«She didn't seem to know. Trayce? Where are you, honey?»

«I don't think she can hear us now. Not sure she could hear us when she broke through while we were making love. She just managed to be heard.»

«That's a little crazy. Why is it she almost always contacts us during sex?» Keira asked.

«Probably because that's when we are most open. It's multiplied by our physical contact with each other. Remember what happened when we kissed Emerson Monday?» Jaime asked.

«Oh, God, yes! Do you think she knew what was happening?»

«I'll bet she has a suspicion. But Trayce has always contacted us from miles away. All our barriers have to be down in order to receive her.»

«And that means we're broadcasting loudly, too,» Keira said.

«How, though?»

«How do we find her?» Keira asked. «I don't know.»

«We need to start by going to her house to make sure she isn't there and just working on a new novel,» Jaime said.

«That would be embarrassing. We could, you know…»

Both snorted at the thought of just tumbling back into bed.

«I mean… we could try,» Keira whispered. «It's how we always contact our lover. I'm nervous now. More than when we made love the first time last night.»

«It's not going to work right now anyway. I'm eighteen, but I'm not superman. Sex with you is really intense. My body is depleted and our brains are drained. We were in a dream state when she contacted us. Let's spend some time brainstorming and investigating other alternatives. We need to recharge. I'm too anxious to do anything intimate right now,» Jaime said.

They agreed. It was only noon, so they both started searching the internet for information on her.

«We should have shared our social pages,» Keira said in frustration.

«It never even occurred to me. You and I didn't even do that. I mean, we were much more intimate without needing to connect online. You and I can talk to each other anytime, and we can see what other people are doing. If we want to talk, we talk. The socials are really for the head deaf,» Jaime said.

He supplied his friend info to Keira so she could connect their profiles. She proudly added, "In a relationship with Jaime Stackhouse."

"Who do we know who is really active on the socials and could help us find her?» Keira said. «We need someone we can trust.»

Jaime tried to block a name from his thoughts, but Keira picked up on it immediately.

«Do you think she'd help us?» she asked.

«Probably. She wants to spend more time with us. I mean, she's tapped into a huge network online. Not just on the usual high school socials, but professionally, as well. I think she'd help, but we would need to be clear that it isn't about anything else. Just needing her help.»

«We might have to tell her. We could do it just by touching her, I think,» Keira said.

«I've never told a head deaf person about my ability.»

«Right. There's a first time for everything.»

Keira found her cell phone amidst her discarded clothing and dialed Emerson's number.

"Hello?"

"Emerson, it's Keira. Happy New Year."

"Hey! Happy New Year to you. I'd love to get together again before school starts Monday."

"We would, too."

"I don't know what happened Monday, but I've had you guys on my mind a lot," Emerson said.

"I don't want you to have the wrong impression. We like you a lot, but this is more of a professional call, if you could call it that."

"Did Jaime make some more improvements on his app?"

"This doesn't really have to do with that… Would you be available to help us do some searches on social media? We… uh… God! Emerson, this would be a lot easier to talk about in person."

"Hey, I'm getting the impression you guys are having trouble. Was this like the… big celebration?" Emerson asked.

"Please come over so we can talk. And bring your laptop for searches."

"You're serious? I mean, don't you have all the social accounts and all?"

"Neither of us really use them. We've always had other ways of communicating."

Emerson paused to consider that statement.

"I've been getting that impression. I can help. I mean, give me the address. The snow is all slush on the streets right now. Probably freeze tonight," Emerson said. "You really just want help on the internet?" She sounded so hopeful, Keira squeezed her eyes shut.

"Oh, God! Emerson, if it was something else, we'd tell you right up front. You were really frank with us and we'd owe it to you to be just as clear. We really like you, but this is just about finding our friend. Please?"

"Yeah. Okay. Give me the address. I can get there in about half an hour."

Jaime and Keira and Emerson

"THIS IS NOT how we intended to spend the day," Keira said when Emerson arrived with a shoulder bag of equipment. "As I'm sure you can imagine."

"This was it, wasn't it? Congratulations, you two. I hope it was great."

"Oh yeah. It was. But then we got a message that made us believe Trayce was in trouble."

"Your girlfriend? Where's the message?"

Emerson unpacked her computer on the kitchen table where Jaime and Keira were already set up.

"That's a little hard to explain," Jaime typed on his computer, activating the text to speech engine.

"You know, I actually believe that's what your voice would sound like," Emerson sighed. "So, anyway, what's the story?"

"Remember the system I wanted to design that allowed people to communicate head-to-head?" Jaime asked.

"You did it! You tested it on me Monday! I felt… thoughts that weren't my own!"

"It's not quite like that," Keira said. "We didn't know that you would feel anything other than a really nice kiss. We discovered certain people have the natural ability to do that. In fact, Jaime and I have it."

"Oh, come on. I thought you guys were serious about this." *I can't believe they're trying to put this one over on me. What do they think I am? If they want to get naked and all of us screw, I'd believe that. I'm in.*

"If they wanted to get naked and all of us screw, I'd believe that. I'm in," Jaime typed into his computer. This time, the voice was the one Emerson had recorded and tested.

"That's… it's the voice I recorded. But I didn't say that!" Emerson said, pushing back from the table as if to run.

"You thought it," Jaime typed in his own voice. "It was really near the surface, so it was easy to read. We aren't trying to put one over on you."

"Oh, shit! You guys are serious. Give me a minute. I need to get my thoughts in order."

"Good idea," Keira said. "We'll give you tips on how to keep your thoughts from being read."

"You're reading them, too?"

Keira nodded. Emerson was near to hyperventilating. *They know everything!*

"It would have been easier to believe if it was only Jaime. You're, like, normal. I mean, not that you're not normal, Jaime, but you're different. Is the school full of people who talk in their heads?"

"We're the only ones we've found. In fact, Trayce and an old retired detective are the only other people we've had any conversations with in our heads," Jaime typed.

"But you think she's real." Emerson was beginning to get her senses back and control what she was thinking about.

"We're more convinced she's real than she's convinced we are. A lot of the time she believes we're characters in her head that she's writing a story about," Keira said.

"But you don't really know her."

"We were going to meet last Friday at the mall. But all of a sudden, she cut us off and never showed up. She'd been a little unpredictable about her beliefs and we thought she'd just closed her mind and decided not to meet us. Since then, we've decided someone else prevented her from getting there," Jaime typed.

"Is it possible for a person—like me—to cut off their thoughts from the outside?" Emerson asked.

"Yes, though we try to be polite and not eavesdrop on other people too much. Everybody has random thoughts that they wouldn't want anyone else to know. We try to respect that. Sometimes people just shout them so loudly, we can't help but notice."

"Like me. My thoughts weren't so random. You guys must think I'm a real slut for all the things I've thought about you." Tears were leaking down Emerson's face as she hung her head.

Jaime glanced at Keira and reached out to take Emerson's hand. Keira took the other hand.

«We are not ashamed of you,» Jaime thought to her. «We're sorry we weren't able to control our reading of you better. We didn't know until Monday that we could talk to you like this.»

"It's like I can hear you," Emerson said in wonder.

«We promise that anything you think or have thought, we have locked in the back of our minds so we don't think about it or think about you in that way.»

«You might as well think of me that way. I've sure thought of you like that,» Emerson thought.

«Privacy,» Jaime said. «Everyone's entitled to it.»

«Thank you… Am I really doing this? Am I talking to you in my head and you are actually hearing me? I'm not just imagining a conversation?»

Jaime typed one-handed and the TTS system did the rest.

"It's really happening. Apparently, we can talk to you when we are touching you. I've tried to send you messages in class before, but you didn't hear them."

"I'm going to have a million questions about all this, and I'm going to need more examples," Emerson said, pulling her hands away from Jaime and Keira. "But first, let's see if we can find your girlfriend," she said finally. She launched half a dozen social media sites on her laptop at once.

Before she could say anything, Keira pushed a piece of paper over with the vital information about Trayce they had compiled while waiting for Emerson to arrive. Emerson shivered and then started entering the data in her social search engine.

"Okay. Trayce Lombard, age 18, attends Roosevelt High School and Rose Community College. Are you seriously telling me that's all the info you have on your girlfriend??"

"Well, like concrete info about her, yeah," Keira said. "She always seems to pop in when we're… um… you know."

"I think I'd blush if I could read your thoughts," Emerson laughed. "You sure are blushing."

"Keira and I have had to learn to accept each other's thoughts no matter how embarrassing they might appear," Jaime typed. "It's just part of life."

"I'll bet," Emerson mused. *I wonder how many times they've seen me naked. God! I can't accuse them of voyeurism—especially with the way I've imagined them.*

The typing continued as Emerson concentrated on the screen; Keira and Jaime concentrated on not reading her extraneous thoughts by reciting lines from *A Streetcar Named Desire*.

"Okay," Emerson announced. "Unlike you, it appears *she* has at least five social accounts and is pretty active on all of them. Is this her?" She pointed to a profile picture.

"Yeah. Without the cat ears and nose," Keira said.

"Seriously cute! Wait! If you've never met, how do you know what she looks like," Emerson pounced, thinking she'd caught them in a contradiction.

"She once faced a mirror and… um…" Keira began.

"And let us look at her all over. It was her seeing herself," Jaime finished on the TTS.

"Oh, fuck! Have you read my thoughts while I was looking in a mirror?" Emerson exclaimed.

Jaime and Keira clamped their mouths and thoughts shut.

"You have! Oh, my God! When?"

"It was an accident," Jaime typed. "It was a rainy afternoon a month or so ago. I happened to see you in the cafeteria looking out the window, kind of daydreaming. After school, I was lying in my bed for a nap, you know, and all of a sudden you were in my mind—or I was in yours. You were daydreaming about your lovers in France, Dom and Raquel. You stood in front of a mirror and took off your wet shirt. Then I pulled away quickly."

"Except not right away," Emerson said. "I remember that. Just as I was daydreaming about Dom, your face occupied my mind. I started to kiss you and then you were gone. The next day, I asked you if you ever had random thoughts about people crossing your mind. I was more embarrassed then than I am now, knowing you'd already seen me naked and just decided against me. Shit, shit, shit."

They were quiet as Emerson stood up from the table and stretched. Then she turned quickly and kissed Jaime hard. Before he could respond, she pulled away and grabbed Keira to kiss her, too. It was all too fast for concrete images to form in their minds and the kisses were hard, but not intimate as the three-way had been on Monday.

Emerson sat down again and began typing in her search engine.

"You're accepting this whole thing rather easily," Keira ventured. "I mean that we can actually talk to each other mind to mind."

"I'm in a state of suspended disbelief. You know science says you can't just believe your eyes. You have to document proof. I've heard you talking in my head. I've felt the magic of your touch. You've answered questions I only thought. None of it is proof. Not according to science. It's experience, not experiments. It has to have independently reproducible results."

"That's where science has failed regarding telepathy over the years. Even when some know for a fact it exists," Keira said.

"Weird, isn't it? Like, I had fantasies about you two. Maybe I even shared them with you. We were talking without our voices. That was after I saw your design for a thought broadcaster, Jaime. I wondered what it would be like to make love while we were linked together mind to mind."

"It's intense," Keira said.

"Yeah. Well, I never expected to experience it. Like wondering what it would be like to have sex in the weightlessness of outer space. You never expect to actually do it."

"We didn't know we could connect like that with someone who wasn't a head talker," Jaime typed.

"I sensed something when we kissed. Not this time. But Monday. And I knew it was a glimpse of what someone could have. But I also knew it wasn't me. I could sense even then that it was all for your girlfriend, Trayce."

"Have you ever heard someone's thoughts?" Jaime typed. "Other than when Keira and I touched you?"

"Mmm. Maybe. Once or twice. I just assumed I was hearing things. You know… inner dialogue or inner monologue. That kind of thing."

"Probably. Possibly. There's a slight chance you actually do catch snippets, but don't recognize it and can't control it," Jaime typed.

"Well, here's an address. Trayce was pretty active on all her social media sites—especially the one for writers. But it wasn't only you she went dark on. She hasn't posted anything since last Friday morning when she said she was off to meet a couple of characters in her head and not to bother her," Emerson said.

"So, she disappeared," Keira said. "But why hasn't anything been reported? No police reports. No hospital reports. No missing persons report. How can she just disappear with no one looking for her?"

"Unless this is all a figment of your imagination," Emerson said. "And that would mean you were writing an in-depth backstory that goes through years of social media. There are a few messages from people asking where she is. Some not so kind about what they think she'd do. Hmm. Here's a dm from her to another person on the writer's forum. They talk about hearing voices and she says she's going to see a shrink named Schwartz. That's a possible place to start."

"Emerson, you've been really helpful. We'll go to her house first and find out if there is anyone there. Then we'll hunt down this Dr. Schwartz."

"I'll keep monitoring her social sites. Call me if you need a driver for your rescue. I can do that," Emerson said.

"You're really willing to do all that?" Jaime typed. Emerson looked hard at him.

You turned me down after seeing me naked. This girl must be something really special. We still have some experiments and testing to do on our comp lab projects. Maybe we can do some other testing, too.

Emerson didn't say anything and just hoped that Jaime and Keira really could read her thoughts. She shouldered her bag and headed toward the door.

Keira and Jaime glanced at each other, not needing any direct communication. The kind of testing Emerson was interested in was clearly written across her mind. She wanted to know if they could communicate to her while having sex. She was ready to try anytime.

30
THE HUNT

Rose and Angus and Kate and Thursday

"**AND YOU THINK,** based on a curious message you can't show us, that this girl has been kidnapped and some psycho guy has her to do nasty experiments on. Why the fuck us instead of the cops?" Kate demanded.

"Did you bring something funny instead of weed?" Thursday demanded of Rose. "Angus can't handle hard stuff anymore. It's the PTSD."

"I know, honey. I was around before you were even thinking of dancing," Rose said. "By the way, I understand why he comes to look at your cute sex garden when you dance. It's inspiring."

"Hope you had fun last night," Thursday shot back.

"Oh, we did. We certainly did."

"Quit farting at each other, my droogies," Angus said. "This is serious. Rose and I both know this guy. He's a crackpot disguised as a psychologist. He's been stalking kids he thinks have a special ability."

"The guy we sent on his way at Safeway?" Kate asked. "You mean he got one of those two kids?"

"No. He got their girlfriend. She's a client of mine," Rose said.

"What's she buy from you?" Thursday asked.

"I'm a counselor for teen girls. You should have come to see me when I could have helped. Girls don't have to endure that kind of abuse."

"Angus! Did you…?"

"Didn't say a word. She's just very perceptive." Angus scowled at Rose.

292

«Turn it off!»

«This isn't getting us anywhere,» Rose responded.

"Here's what I want us to do," Angus said. "You two visit the girl's mother. Find out when and where she disappeared and why it wasn't reported to the police. Rose and I will head to the bastard's home. We've got an address."

"You can take care of him if he's home," Rose said. "He won't be, but I know you'll have a good look around. I have a college friend who has an office near his. I'll see if she's spotted anything and find out if I can get into his office. It's not likely. His office will be locked up tighter than the house. But maybe she's seen something."

"Okay. We'd better change into different working clothes," Kate said, looking at Thursday's cheekies and crop top.

"I wore a coat over it," Thursday complained. She and Kate headed out to visit Mrs. Lombard.

"You be careful, Rose." Angus said.

"You, too, old man. Keep that sword unlocked."

Jaime and Keira and Lanie Lombard

«This is the place,» Jaime said, checking the street view Emerson sent to his phone. They still had Keira's mother's car, though they'd need to get it back soon. They hadn't yet decided how they would arrange being together the rest of the weekend.

«Yeah,» Keira responded as she managed to park behind a snowbank. «We might as well go knock on the door. If Trayce answers and screams, we just turn around and leave.»

«Otherwise, we ask whoever's there where she went.»

The two walked up to the door. Keira took the lead and rang the bell. There was no immediate response and Keira knocked. After a few moments, there was a noise and the door scraped open.

"Who are you and what do you want?" the woman demanded. "You're too young to be police."

She looked unkempt, a little desperate, and as if she hadn't slept recently. Jaime and Keira could see a bottle of vodka and a baggie of what they assumed was weed on the living room coffee table. Neither looked as if they'd been opened yet.

"Is it okay, Lanie?" a woman asked from the kitchen.

"Couple of kids," Mrs. Lombard answered.

"Mrs. Lombard, we're friends of Trayce and haven't heard from her all week. We were wondering if she was okay," Keira asked.

"Okay? I wish I knew. 'Leaving and never hear from me again.' That's what she said. The police won't listen to me. They pointed at the note and said she was eighteen and they couldn't do anything. I can't believe she just walked off with just a note on a scrap of paper left in the car. Didn't take anything!"

"She was going to meet us at the mall Friday. It was the first time we were going to meet face-to-face and she never showed up. Are you saying she left a note in the car and just ran away?" Keira asked.

"I know I've not been much of a mother. Not since her father was killed. But I've been making progress. I thought she was with me. That she understood. There's nothing left now."

The woman who had called from the kitchen came rushing to Mrs. Lombard and immediately wrapped her in a hug.

"We'll make it, Lanie. We got through last night. We can get through today," she said.

"Are you related to Trayce?" Keira said, she could see the answer, but wanted to establish the relationship aloud so she didn't sound like she was making assumptions.

"I'm Lanie's AA sponsor, Susan," the woman responded. "Why don't you come in and tell us what you know about Trayce's disappearance?"

Susan and Lanie backed up to allow Jaime and Keira to enter the living room and sit down. They looked at the unopened bottle and baggie.

"Those are our enemy," Lanie said. "They try to tell us Trayce is the enemy and they are our friends. We know. We won't fall."

"Not today," Susan said. "One day at a time. Not today."

Jaime was alarmed by the thoughts of bloody destruction Mrs. Lombard held in the back of her mind. They were filled with alternating images of a happy family and all of them lying dead and bloody. Her mind was a horror story, held together for the moment by her sponsor.

"You've told the police she disappeared?" Keira asked.

"They called me when they found her car in the mall parking lot," Mrs. Lombard said. "Told me to come and get it or they'd tow it away. Snow was coming. When I got there, I found the note in the car. I showed it to the police, but they said there was nothing they could do. We call every day and they say they haven't heard anything about her. Where could she go with nothing more than her purse? She didn't have that much money. She hasn't touched her bank account."

Jaime could see she was barely holding it together. She had images playing in her mind of drinking the entire bottle of vodka at once. If that didn't work, she'd run her car into a bridge abutment.

«We can't leave her like this,» Jaime said to Keira. «Even with her sponsor helping her.»

"Don't be too hasty, Mrs. Lombard. We believe something happened to Trayce. She disappeared on her way to meet us at the mall. We're going to find her. Don't lose hope. We'll find her. May we see the note?"

Mrs. Lombard fished in her pocket and brought out a wrinkled piece of typing paper. It had been torn, but most of the message was still visible.

> *"I can't take it anymore. You and the voices in my head are driving me crazy. I don't know where I'll go or what I'll do, but I'm leaving and you'll never hear from me again. Don't even try to find me."*

«Fuck!» Jaime shouted in their heads. «She can't have meant that. She was on her way to meet us!»

«It's typed. It's not even addressed or signed. She didn't do this,» Keira responded, grasping Jaime's hand. The world around them opened and Mrs. Lombard's thoughts clarified.

He doesn't speak. They are the voices she heard in her head. Like the voices I heard. But they're kind and aren't threatening her. They are angry at some man who… kidnapped her! We have to find her, she thought.

«She hears,» Jaime said, clamping down on his thoughts.

"Mrs. Lombard, Trayce is in danger. We're going to find her. Hang on until we do, okay?" Keira handed the note back to her and Mrs. Lombard shoved it back into her pocket.

"Tell me what I can do," Mrs. Lombard said. Her eyes were clearer than they'd been when the teens arrived. Susan was sitting up straight, observing, but mentally silent.

"We're going to her therapist's office and see if she contacted him. We're suspicious of him anyway," Keira said.

"She said she was seeing a woman counselor," Lanie said.

"She went to Dr. Edmonds after she'd seen Dr. Schwartz. Yes, you are right. We are two of the voices she heard. But we're real people, not characters she was writing about. We've already seen Dr. Edmonds. But Dr. Schwartz is a little shady. He tried to treat Trayce with hypnotism and triggers. Trayce was coming to meet us and we were all very excited. Then she was suddenly not there. We couldn't find her anywhere."

"And you are just now looking?" Lanie asked.

"We thought she just decided she didn't want us to be real and left. But, we kind of got a message from her early this morning and she was asking for help. The problem is we don't know where she is yet. But I promise you, we'll find her!" Keira said.

Yes. Find her. Bring her home safely to me.

Jaime and Keira and Emerson

"Emerson, what do you have on the quack? Anything?" Keira asked when she got their friend on the phone.

"Well, he's got a lot of reviews online. Most say things like 'So nice!' and 'Who'd believe hypnotism works? Lost ten pounds!'"

"That's not encouraging. Sounds like a nice guy."

"That's not all of them. Here's one that says, 'Don't fall for his ventriloquism act. He's not talking in your head. I recorded it.' Another says, 'I don't think I was hypnotized, but I think I got good advice.' And here's one that says, 'This fraud knows absolutely nothing about women. Go to a female counselor!' There's enough to raise red flags if I was looking for a counselor. Which I might be after this."

"Don't despair, Em. We'll work out a way to show you everything is real."

"That's the problem. Maybe it's the same problem Trayce was facing. You can convince me that it is all real, but the rest of the whole world says it's not. That's what I have to reconcile. Don't worry, though. I won't break down until we get your girlfriend back."

"Thank you. You're really a great friend," Keira said.

"So, here's the doctor's office address and a map from where you are. I don't know what you might find on a holiday like today, though. Surely, he won't be there."

"We can't wait," Keira said.

"Okay. I sent a link to the Google map to Jaime's phone. Good luck."

Jaime and Keira and Alice McCormick

«This is the building,» Jaime said.

«Underground parking. Let's take a look»

Keira pulled into the garage of the fairly new office building.

«Must be doing pretty well to afford a place here. Look. Designated parking spot.»

«It would be easier if he was here,» Keira said.

«I have an uneasy feeling,» Jaime said. «Keep an open ear. He might not be the only one involved.»

«That's spooky.»

They looked around the garage trying to spot anything that might not look right. There were only half a dozen cars in the garage.

«Emerson said suite 201,» Keira said. «Let's go up.»

The elevator did not respond.

«Holiday,» Jaime said. He tried the door to the stairway and it opened. It looked like it hadn't been closed tightly. They went up the stairs to the second floor. «The stairway doors aren't very well defended.» He started to open the door.

«Wait! Someone's at the elevator,» Keira said. They paused, peeking out the door as a woman got on the elevator and the doors closed. Keira gasped.

«Who was she?»

«My Aunt Rose. Please God, don't let her be involved in this mess. She was here to see someone, so there must be an occupied office here.»

«Maybe she was just investigating, too,» Jaime said, comforting Keira. «We practically demanded that she help us.»

«Let's go with that.»

The two listened carefully as they worked their way along the hall. A low mental hum came from an office marked 'Parent/Child Resource Center.' They couldn't make out specifics, but the woman—they could tell it was a woman—sounded upset. They moved on to the end office.

«Do you think he works alone?» Keira asked.

«I'm not sure anyone would work *with* him. I'm sure some of the anger from that other office was directed at him, not at your aunt. She might have asked your aunt here to report something.»

«I've got an idea.» Keira dialed Emerson's number and their friend picked up immediately.

"Emerson, can you send me a picture of Trayce? A recent one from her socials that doesn't include cat ears or a nose?"

"Sure thing, hon."

"Do you know who has the office next door to Schwartz? It's called Parent/Child Resource Center," Keira said.

"Give me a minute. There's a building directory. Um… 205. Alice McCormick, Parent/Child Resource."

"You're so good! I don't suppose you can hack into traffic cameras and find out where Schwartz has gone, could you?"

"Keira, I'm not a hacker. I'm on a lot of social media and I can get good search results by using different search engines. But I don't know how to hack into security cameras or traffic cameras. Sorry to disappoint you."

"Oh, you're not. Really. It was just a thought and how would we know if we don't ask. Please don't get upset with us."

"I don't know why I'm *not* upset. But I'm not. You're not mind-controlling me, are you? I really like you guys and I said it before: I'll do whatever I can to help find your girlfriend. Just be careful out there."

"We are absolutely not trying to control you! We're just so thankful you are willing to help."

"Well, give the boy a kiss for me," Emerson laughed.

"I might wait and let you do it yourself," Keira responded.

"Well, if you give him one, then he'll have to give me one and I'll have to give it back to you. Isn't that the way it works?"

"Emerson! Wow! Um… I'll check in again later."

"Be safe."

Jaime and Keira moved back to the other office.

«So, Alice McCormick? Let's see if she has information,» Jaime said after Keira gave him a quick kiss and then darted back in for one slightly more serious. If it was going to go around in a circle, she wanted it to be a good one.

They tried the door and when it opened, Keira took the lead and saw an empty reception area, complete with a toy chest and comfortable chairs.

"Hello? Ms. McCormick? Is anyone here?"

The inner door opened almost immediately.

"Hello. How may I help you. You don't look like a parent and child," the woman said. She appeared to be in her early forties—about the same as their parents. She had dirty blonde hair and was just a few pounds overweight, but not obese.

"Ms. McCormick, we're Keira and Jaime. We're looking for someone and we're canvassing the area to see if she's been seen. Do you recognize this girl?"

Keira held up the photo Emerson had sent her. Ms. McCormick took the phone and backed into her office, beckoning them in. She sat behind her desk and motioned them to chairs as she continued to look at the picture.

"What is your interest in this woman?" she asked.

"She's our girlfriend. She's been missing since last Friday. Just dropped off the map," Keira explained.

"Your girlfriend. You plural."

"How did…?"

"If she was just a friend who was a girl, you'd have said 'a girlfriend.' If she was *your* girlfriend, you'd have said 'my girlfriend.' Or, it could have been 'his girlfriend.' But you used a specific article: 'our.' The two of you share a girlfriend?"

"Um… It's complicated."

"Just go ahead and tell her," Jaime signed as he spoke in Keira's head.

"We… Yes. She is both our girlfriend. We were supposed to meet at the mall last Friday, but just before she arrived, she disappeared."

"Is your friend deaf?"

"No. He just doesn't talk. He signs."

"You aren't signing to him."

"He hears fine."

"I see. What do you hope to do when you find your girlfriend?"

"We think she's in danger. We have to help her."

Ms. McCormick sighed and sat back in her chair, handing the phone back to Keira.

Exactly what Rose said. She didn't mention the boyfriend and girlfriend. Hmm. I suppose that means I'm free to tell them what she and I discussed. The more people looking for the girl, the better.

Jaime and Keira heard her thoughts clearly.

"How strange that you would show up right after an old friend of mine asked to meet me here to discuss the same thing. She agrees that the girl might be in danger."

"You think something is wrong, too!" Keira said.

"Possibly. Schwartz—I assume that is who you really want information about—saw her a few weeks ago. When she left his office, she seemed strange—like she was in a trance. Didn't speak when I said hello. Of course, I inquired about her, but Schwartz wouldn't give out any information on his client. He's not supposed to. There was nothing more I could do."

Ms. McCormick didn't really need to say what came next. It was fresh in her mind from having told Rose. Of course, she assumed she needed to say it aloud anyway.

"He's been acting strange lately. For over a week before Christmas he didn't seem to have any appointments. Every time he was in the office he was accompanied by two… bodyguards, I think. Man and woman who acted like minions. Don't go thinking they are incompetent, though. I overheard him in the garage telling them to prepare a room. Then, last Friday morning, they picked him up and left. He hasn't been seen here since."

"A room where he could stow Trayce!" Keira said. "Do you know where?"

"Schwartz has a second home in Astoria. It's a small historic inn. It's managed by a couple who lives there year-round. I'd bet it was the same people who were with him here. He has his own suite and goes there often. The whole thing is a warren spread across two buildings and connected underground."

"How do you know so much about it?" Keira asked.

"I was invited to be a guest there a few years ago. That was long before I became suspicious of how ethical his counseling might or might not be."

"What raised your suspicions?"

Jaime was constantly signing and communicating with Keira mentally, while she asked all the questions. She took his suggestions along with her own and kept the questions coming. Jaime, in the meantime, stayed tuned into Ms. McCormick's head, reading more deeply into what she was saying.

"Schwartz revealed himself as quite the conspiracy theorist. Not about things like who shot Jack Kennedy or did we really land on the moon. He is more of the CIA spying on people using some kind of rays to extract their thoughts."

"Geez!"

"Unfortunately, he believes he is a target of such surveillance because of his research while doing his PhD at the University. You know, don't you, that psychologists are not medical doctors. That's psychiatrists. Schwartz is a neurological psychologist who studies the brain and how it functions. He ran several bizarre experiments during his time at UO before settling on a topic for his dissertation. I was one of his subjects. He wrote a dissertation on inner monologue and inner dialogue. He may be paranoid, but he is quite brilliant.

"That's where I met Rose Edmonds and we hit it off well and have stayed friends. She's always said I should keep an eye on Kenton. I guess this is why."

Jaime began signing rapidly and Keira waited until he was finished before she began to interpret.

«Are you sure?» Keira asked Jaime.

«Yes. This woman knows more about him than anyone we have access to. Except maybe Angus and your aunt. See if she knows.»

Keira composed her question.

"Are you aware that he is continuing to do research because he believes there are people who can talk in their heads and he wants to control them?"

Ms. McCormick paused while the two teens looked at her. They could see enlightenment dawn on her.

And you are two of them, aren't you? And your girlfriend is another? You must be very careful. It could be as dangerous for you as for your girlfriend.

She didn't speak, just nodding. She wrote down the address for the inn in Astoria. Jaime and Keira left.

31
RIDING TO THE RESCUE

Jaime and Keira

«SHE WAS THINKING to us, but she couldn't hear us thinking,» Jaime said as he and Keira left Ms. McCormick's building.

«I don't think she intended to think some of those things,» Keira responded.

«She thought Schwartz was awfully pleased with the way the wire mesh in the old plaster walls prevented microwaves from penetrating and reading his mind.»

«That could leave us deaf, too.»

«And it would prevent Trayce from getting a message out to us,» Jaime said. «Especially if she's in what Ms. McCormick called the basement warren. She made it sound like a whole underground complex.»

«She must have been incredibly panicked to get those few words to us when we were making love,» Keira said. «I need to get the car back to my parents. We have to figure out how we're going to get to Astoria.»

«It doesn't make sense to drive out there tonight. It's two hours out there and we don't have a place to stay. Trying to get a room at his inn gives me the willies,» Jaime said.

«I guess we'd better just go back to your house,» Keira said with a mental hug.

«Are you okay with being at my house with me while my father is probably home?» Jaime asked.

«That's a question you should probably be asking yourself about when your father has Olivia staying the night.»

«Holy shit! Well, if we get used to it, it should be easier for him. Right?»

«We should let Emerson know what we're doing.»

«What?»

«Not everything,» Keira giggled. «I'm sure she'll figure that part out. I mean about going to Astoria in the morning.»

«Maybe she'll want to go, too.»

«Oh, wow! Can you imagine being inside a car with her for two hours? We really need to clamp down on our openness,» Keira said. «You know what she's going to be thinking about, and I'm not sure I'd be able to keep from pulling into a roadside rest and doing it.»

«We can practice teaching her not to broadcast her thoughts.»

Jaime and Keira and Emerson

"What time do we leave?" Emerson demanded on the phone.

"We didn't plan it yet. It doesn't look like snow but it's cold and roads might be slick," Keira said. "You really want to go?"

"Of course. Superheroes always need a sidekick. You need a driver. A getaway car. I'll pick you up at 8:00. The sun will be up and that should give you time to… um… you know… get out of bed and get ready."

Emerson was too far away for Keira to read her thoughts, but some things were obvious without being a mind reader.

"You're the best, Emerson. I'm so glad you're on our side."

"Yeah. See you in the morning."

«She really wants to come with us?» Jaime asked.

«Yeah. I think she really wants to come.»

Jaime and Keira and David and Olivia

THAT SOLVED THE problem of transportation, but when Jaime and Keira got to his house after walking from hers, they found David and Olivia cooking dinner.

"Hi, David and Olivia," Keira said.

"Dad! What are you guys doing cooking dinner?" Jaime signed.

"Someone needed to be sure everyone was nourished. A pizza for dinner and cornflakes for breakfast? Really, Jaime? We got home about four and decided to roast a chicken," David said. Jaime and Keira could see the lie, but held their tongues.

"Don't let him fool you," Olivia said. "We bought a roasted chicken at Whole Foods yesterday and just had to pop it in the oven to reheat. It's simple fare, but who wants to spend the day cooking?"

"I'd volunteer to make up the traditional black-eyed peas and salt pork tomorrow," Jaime signed. Keira interpreted. "But we're going out for the day. With Emerson. She's picking us up in the morning for an adventure."

"I think we can wait until Sunday. I already bought all the ingredients, but I didn't want to infringe on your annual ritual," David said. "Where are you going tomorrow?"

"We're all going out to Astoria," Keira said. "Emerson said she knew of a cool restaurant out there and some fun sights to see."

"I've never been to Astoria," Olivia said. "You'll need to give us a report on the best places so we can go, too. I mean, not at the same time. I wasn't meaning to imply we'd come tomorrow or anything."

"It's okay, Olivia. We all have words to trip over while we're getting used to each other," Keira said.

"By which I assume you mean you will be staying the night here?" David asked.

"Jaime invited me. Unless you object," Keira said hesitantly. Jaime quickly took her hand as if she might flee.

"No objection," David hastened to say.

"David, why don't you spend another night with me?" Olivia asked sweetly. "I'd like that."

"I'd like it, too, honey," David said. It was the first time Jaime had heard him use an endearment aloud and it pleased him irrationally. "After dinner, we'll get things cleaned up and leave the two of you to yourselves. You say you won't need the car tomorrow for your adventure? Jaime, we should look at the possibility of getting you some wheels now that you're driving."

"Thanks, Dad," Jaime signed. "That would be great."

They got the table set and the four had a good meal with friendly conversation. They even played a dice game after cleanup, before David took Olivia home—and stayed. Jaime and Keira introduced them to their kissing rule for five-of-a kind.

Jaime and Keira

As soon as David and Olivia were out the door, they ran to Jaime's bedroom. They were naked in bed in no time. Then they slowed down again.

«She'll be okay, won't she?» Keira asked.

«She has to be,» Jaime said. «I know Schwartz kidnapped her, but I don't think he'll physically harm her. Remember, his intent is to lure us into his trap so he has all three of us. He wants to use us and we all need to be healthy for that.»

«Why? Why does he want us?»

«I got a little inkling the other day when we met with your aunt, and it got a lot clearer when we met with Emerson this morning.»

«What is it?»

«We understand head talking as listening, right? But when you and I were connected, we could talk to Emerson. She can't hear us unless we're touching her. So, we had to be projecting our thoughts to her. Otherwise she's head deaf.»

«Oh, my God! And what Schwartz always wanted was to use head talkers to command others!»

«Right. He thinks it takes three, but we've done it with two if we are touching,» Jaime said. «In fact, the other day, I took your hand and grabbed your aunt's hand to tell her to please help us. I phrased it politely, but the way she jumped back from us and sent us away—to make love—told me she received the message loud and clear, right through all her barriers.»

«Jaime, what are we going to do?»

«We're going to get Trayce back. He doesn't know what we can really do. We're going to need a plan.»

«I have a plan,» Keira said. «I plan to have you inside me and not think about this again until tomorrow,» Keira said.

Jaime was a ready participant in that plan, but the idea that neither of them would think about Trayce until morning was a non-starter. As Jaime and Keira moved together, kissing, and sharing their entire minds with each other, Trayce kept entering their thoughts. At the peak of their passion, as both were sharing the other's orgasm, they called out with one voice.

«We love you, Trayce. We're coming to find you. We'll find you. We promise.»

«Love,» was the only whispered response.

Rose and Angus and Kate and Thursday

"The kids had already been to see the girl's mother," Kate reported. "Mrs. Lombard was pacing around the room with a friend. They'd called the police again after the kids left, but you know what that's going to yield on New Year's Day. Anyway, we saw the supposed note Trayce left behind in her car. Leave it to the PDX finest to accept that piece of rubbish as real."

"What else?" Angus asked.

"Mrs. Lombard confirmed that Trayce was on her way to meet Jaime and Keira. But then she went off the rails," Kate said.

"How?"

"She said she'd gone into AA and counseling because she'd started hearing voices," Thursday said. "She pointed at the note and said Trayce was also hearing voices and that this Jaime and Keira were who she was hearing. Sorry. I know how ridiculous it sounds, but that's what she said."

Rose and Angus shared a glance that may or may not have been accompanied by an explicit thought. Rose started in on her part of the tale.

"I went to see a friend who agreed to come into her office for a while today. Her office is next door to Schwartz's," Rose said. "She suspected Schwartz of some kind of funny work, but didn't have any specifics. She just said he was acting strange the past couple of weeks with no appointments but a pair of bodyguards popping in and out. Then he just disappeared last Friday."

"That would be the couple we chased away with him," Kate said. "That's been two weeks ago."

"When we found out Schwartz was stalking the boy, we decided to send him a direct message," Angus said. "I should have shoved my cane up his ass instead of putting it against his neck. Apparently, our message wasn't strong enough."

"Well, the other thing my friend Alice said was that Schwartz owns an inn out in Astoria. She'd visited once with her husband and Kenton was inordinately pleased with the fact his inn was impenetrable to WiFi, Microwave, and Cellular signals. Chance are that's where he took her."

"Then that's where we should go," Angus said. "His house is empty and has a for sale sign in front. He doesn't plan to come back."

"Can we find a place to stake his other place out? If those kids find it, they could walk right into his web," Kate said.

"Yes. Good idea," Angus said. "I'd suggest we take Rooby, but it's a little cold for the convertible."

"I can't believe you're still driving that old car. It was old when we met twenty years ago," Rose said.

"I only use her in the summer now," Angus said. "She's been rebuilt a few times."

"We can take my car," Rose said. "The SUV has plenty of room in it. We might want to pack some supplies and a change of clothes."

"Yeah, I'm fine with this whole thing about rescuing a bunch of kids from the claws of an evil psycho," Thursday said. "But I need to know why. Why is he even interested in these kids? What's special about them? This all sounds like some sort of plot to capture somebody who is a whole lot wealthier than any of these three seem to be. I'll go help rescue them, but you need to tell me why he wants them."

Rose and Angus took a simultaneous deep breath and Angus shrugged.

"Because," Rose said, "they can talk to each other in their heads."

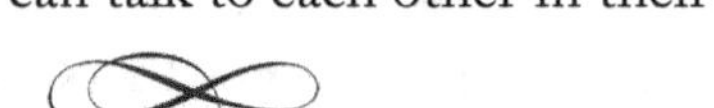

Jaime and Keira and Emerson

"Come in and at least use the bathroom," Keira said when Emerson arrived at eight a.m. "We made up bacon and egg sandwiches. Do you drink coffee?"

"Yeah. That would be great. When did you have time to make that up? I figured you'd be having sex this morning," Emerson said.

"That was at five," Keira said. "And six-thirty."

"Oh, great. I was prepared for hair still dripping wet from the shower. I didn't expect you to have been up half the day already. Bathroom?"

Emerson headed toward the door Jaime pointed out while muttering in her head: *Why am I so fucking jealous? Of both of them. Just pull yourself together, girl.*

Jaime and Keira shared a shrug and waited.

"Can we eat in the car?" Emerson asked when she emerged. "I want to get out of town before heavy traffic hits. I expect that the day after New Year's is going to be as chaotic as the day after Christmas was."

"We're with you," Keira said. Jaime locked the house and they headed toward Emerson's Kia.

"I've got a hotspot in the car, so you can bring your computers if you want. No sense wasting all the time we're driving out to Astoria. I emailed you a bunch of links last night before I went to bed," Emerson said.

"You're really a good partner to have," Keira said.

"Thanks. Um… Sorry to relegate you to the back, Jaime, but can Keira ride shotgun? I'd like to talk," Emerson said.

Jaime nodded and crawled into the back seat of Emerson's car.

"Wow! Is this a new car?" Keira asked.

"Yeah. Why do you think I'm so willing to drive?" Emerson laughed.

"We'd have taken my Dad's car," Jaime typed into his TTS app. "He says we're going to go car shopping for me soon."

"My grandfather bought me the Kia. Said he'd buy me a new one if I didn't ask for a lesbian car. I told him if I ever had a girlfriend, I'd bring her boyfriend along with me," she said.

"You already intended to have them, didn't you?"

"Yeah, but that was before I fixated on you. Dom and Raquel got married yesterday. I guess that was part of why I was so willing to bury myself in your project. I just didn't want to think about them."

"It's okay to miss them, Em," Jaime typed. "God knows we're a mess at the moment."

"Yeah. Which is another piece of the puzzle. Dom and Raq are both in the industry, you know. Raquel is a seamstress and Dom is a model. I imagined we'd be together and maybe create our own fashion house one day."

"It must be really hard," Keira said, reaching over to pat Emerson's leg. Emerson caught her breath, half expecting to hear Keira in her head, but it was just a friend comforting her.

"I really, you know, loved them." A tear dropped from Emerson's eye and she wiped it away with her glove. "I guess having that experience and feeling the emptiness afterward was part—probably a big part—of why I became so attracted to you guys."

"I can understand how that can be. I mean, Trayce entered Jaime's and my minds the first time we made out. She never initiated anything, but whenever we got intimate, she showed up. And she was sweet and fun and it didn't take long for us all to fall in love. You know, we share something that not many people do. I've been in her head when she had an orgasm! I thought I had pretty strong climaxes, you know? It's something else when you experience your own plus another person's at the same time. Then add in Jaime and it's a whole different feeling entirely."

"If you keep talking like that, I'm going to end up driving with one hand between my legs," Emerson laughed.

"I think Jaime is getting uncomfortable, too. You okay, lover?"

Keira turned in her seat to look at Jaime and he smiled and nodded.

Of course, he hadn't been uncomfortable, though if he let himself get lost in Emerson's thoughts, he might have been. She was a very sensual person and could as easily see herself with Jaime and Keira as she could with Dom and Raquel.

«Maybe you'd better describe some of the problems she'd have with the two of us and how we can help her block her thoughts from being read,» Jaime said. «Talk about a division between parties. How would she feel being left out when you and I are head talking? And how would I ever communicate with her?»

"So, you understand the problem," Keira said. "I mean, even without Trayce in the equation, it would be hard for you to be in a *ménage à trois* with the two of us—Jaime and me. And, please understand, we both think you are sexy and funny and hot and smart and everything. Did I mention you're really pretty and sexy? But Jaime and I are constantly carrying on conversations with each other in our heads. How would it feel to know you were on the outside of that?"

"I do feel that way," Emerson said. "That's why I've been thinking that—just for fun—you could sort of run some experiments on me. I'm not going to compete with Trayce. Really. I'm envious of all three of you, but I'm not going to try to displace anyone. Back a while ago, I looked at Jaime's thought machine diagram. It made me think it was a little tinfoil hat-ish. At the same time, it woke a desire to experience that. Like I did when you touched me and I could hear you yesterday. That was real, wasn't it?"

"It was real," Jaime typed.

"Maybe if you hypnotized me, I'd open up to hearing you all the time. Maybe there is some drug that might open the senses—like they used to say LSD would. I believe it would not only be a good experience to me, I think it would be valuable to you, too," Emerson said, not taking her eyes off the road as they left Portland behind on Route 30.

"Be careful there, Em. That's exactly what we think Schwartz is trying to do with Trayce—against her will. Emerson, I can't tell you how terrified she was when we heard her. He was raping her mind, taking it over and playing with it. We've just got to get her free, whether she decides she wants anything to do with us or not. It's nasty stuff," Keira said.

"Our, kind of, friend is an old guy who served in Vietnam years ago. When he came out, they treated his PTSD with LSD. He thinks that might be part of what woke him up, but it also totally messed up his psyche," Jaime typed.

"But, like, you wouldn't do bad things to me. Right?" Emerson asked uncertainly.

"Of course not," Keira said. Emerson was suddenly a little less certain.

They continued on out to Astoria, with Emerson carefully watching for icy patches on the road. They talked about other things, including the beginning of the next semester on Monday. Eventually, Emerson pulled into a shopping area on the edge of Astoria.

"What are we doing here?" Jaime typed.

"Before you go assaulting the walls of some medieval fortress, you need empty bladders. So do I. It's ten o'clock in the morning and I need another cup of coffee in order to stake out a position nearby where I can peel up and open the doors of the getaway car. Then we're going to go save your girlfriend."

32
ASSAULT ON THE CASTLE

Kenton and Trayce

"**THAT'S A GOOD** girl. Now just relax. You're getting better every day," Kenton said as he waved a medallion in front of Trayce's blank eyes.

"I don't want to," she struggled. "Let me go. I want to see my friends. Help!" she said weakly.

"Just let yourself drift. Those imaginary friends will all go away soon."

"They'll come for me."

"They have no idea how to find you. And while you are here, you can't send them any messages. 3-2-1 and sleep."

Trayce struggled to stay awake, but the hypnotic was too powerful. Kenton had laced her food with just enough cannabis to make her susceptible to his hypnotic suggestion. It had been working for three days. Now she fell into his trance quickly, no matter how she struggled.

"Now let's talk about how you send messages to your friends. Jaime and Keira, is that right?"

"We have sex."

"Can you send mental messages to anyone you have sex with?" Kenton asked, intrigued. He'd certainly participate in that. Trayce was a delectable bit of temptation. He could just imagine himself stretched out on her naked body.

"Only with Keira and Jaime. We do it in our heads."

"Not when you are physically making love?"

311

"I'm a virgin. I've never seen Jaime and Keira physically," Trayce said. In the back of her consciousness—what was left of it—she could see Dr. Schwartz's lust. She wanted nothing to do with it.

Kenton sat back to consider his options. He didn't think he'd learn any more about the command voice. He'd already decided Trayce was just an accelerator, not the real power. But she was still useful.

"What you really want," he said softly, "is to make Jaime listen to me. Make Keira listen to me—like you can hear me now. When I give you an instruction, you will pass it on to Jaime and Keira. They will do what you say. It's really all that easy. When you have accepted this instruction, you can see your friends for real. I'll bring them to you."

"I will give them your instructions," Trayce said mechanically. She still wondered if she could stop it. Not all of Trayce was under the spell. In fact, she could hear more of what Dr. Schwartz was thinking than what he was saying. That was how she knew he was thinking about sex with her. Now he was thinking he might have to have sex with all three of them together. It was a gross and disturbing image.

Kenton spent more time reinforcing his implanted suggestions, but within half an hour, Trayce began to twitch, indicating the effectiveness of the trance was failing. Better he should wake her up and let her believe he was helping her write than let her drag the suggestions into consciousness with her.

"Now, dear Trayce, when I count back from three, you'll wake up and be refreshed and ready to start the day. You have some new ideas to write about and you'll find a notebook and pen ready for you. 3-2-1." Kenton snapped his fingers and Trayce's eyes came into focus.

"Dr. Schwartz."

"Trayce, I brought you a new notebook and a new pen—the kind you like so much. You've almost filled the last notebook with your stories. You're doing so well!"

"Thank you, Dr. Schwartz. Will I need to stay here much longer?"

"Oh, no. You'll be able to leave soon. You've almost unlocked all your writing potential. I see a *New York Times* bestseller on your horizon. I'll stop back later to check in on you. 'Bye now."

Schwartz left her room and Trayce immediately opened the notebook and began to write all she could remember about her dreams. She'd had spooky dreams about Dr. Schwartz possessing Jaime. And she could almost hear Jaime and Keira as she slept.

Rose and Angus and Kate and Thursday

"They just went to the grocery store," Kate announced.

Less than a block away from the Olde Whale Guesthouse, was another small bed and breakfast. The owners were a couple of old salts like Angus and were happy to have the unusual quartet in their house. As it happened, the room they were given—actually all the second floor—looked out diagonally across the block at the back of the Olde Whale.

One person was always awake and looking out the window during the night, while the others slept. When two people had left by the back door of the inn, Kate had run to the car to follow them. It was nearly ten and she'd just gotten back.

"Since that's the only activity we've seen there, we should go around to the front to watch," Rose suggested.

"You go. It's cold out there," Kate said. "This is a nice place, Angus. Rent it for the rest of the weekend for us."

"You have the money, honey," Angus said. "You rent it."

"I'll rent it," Rose said. "Geez. Can we just pay attention to the situation?"

"You know, you're not too old to become a stripper," Thursday said. "You could be the new Gypsy Rose. I'll show you some moves."

"Movement," Angus said shortly.

"Stripper moves," Thursday corrected him.

"Movement behind the Whale," he growled. "Hmm. I wonder if he's got information we don't have. He's going in the back of the annex building."

"Who?" Rose demanded, trying to see past the trio that crowded the window.

"The boy. Jaime," Angus said.

"Just him? Where's Keira?" Rose asked.

"Smart kids," Angus said. "We can't see the front of the building. Bet they split up and she's got a distracting front while he does a rear entry." Rose groaned at the puns.

"Well, it looks to me like we need to be closer," she said.

"I agree. Lock and load, ladies," Angus said.

Thursday and Kate went to their overnight bags, pulled out small handguns and slid magazines into them. They advanced a shell into the chamber and hid the guns inside their coats. The short heavy fur seemed an incongruous contrast with the tight yoga pants Kate and Thursday wore. Rose wore heavy wool slacks and a sweater under a three-quarter length overcoat. Her earmuffs weren't stylish, but they covered her ears and that was all she cared about.

Of course, if incongruous outer wear was in question, Angus wore over-the-knee socks with his utility kilt and a leather coat and gloves. With this he carried his dragon-head cane. The temperature was in the mid-40s and none of them was enthused about standing outside.

"Kate and Thursday, take the front. Rose and I will be on the ass end."

"Somehow that was predictable," Kate snorted.

Kate and Thursday left by the front door of the B&B to circle around the block and find a place to stake out the Whale. Angus and Rose left by the back and found a place in the trees between the two properties.

Jaime and Keira and Emerson

Emerson found a place to park in a bank parking lot just up the hill from the Olde Whale Guesthouse.

"Wow! That looks rustic," Keira said.

"Old," Jaime's computer chirped as he typed. "Built in the late 1800s. It doesn't look like the front desk is always occupied. Might be able to just walk in and look around."

"It's too late for breakfast, so there might be someone in the kitchen doing cleanup," Emerson said.

"Or cleaning rooms," Keira added. "From what Ms. McCormick said, it seems likely we'd need to get to the annex just down the hill. There's a separate exterior entrance, but she said there was a tunnel passage between the two."

"It must be deep. The main floor of the annex is more than a full level below the entry floor of the main building," Jaime's computer said.

"Okay. Here's a plan," Keira said. "I'll go up to the main entrance and see if I can attract any attention. If not, I'll just start exploring and looking for the staircase down to the other building. Jaime, go to the back of the annex and see if you can get in there. We'll keep in touch, you know, mentally. Emerson, stay up here and watch. We'll call if we need anything, like police or something."

"Right," Emerson said. "I'll have 9-1-1 entered and waiting to send. You know, those two old places could look kind of romantic and inviting if we were here on a fun weekend. Thinking someone is being held underground makes them look really spooky. Gives me the willies. You guys be careful."

"Cell phones and head talk only," Jaime said through the TTS. Then he closed and stowed his computer. He reached forward and touched Emerson on the neck. She shuddered and gasped. «You're a really great friend, Em. Thank you for being part of this.»

«Yeah. Please be careful.»

«We will.»

The psychic contact was broken when Jaime withdrew his touch, leaving Emerson panting a little. Jaime got out of the car and circled the block to the back of the guesthouse. After giving him a couple of minutes to get ahead, Keira reached over and touched Emerson's hand. The touch was as electric as Jaime's had been.

«I'll text you as soon as I know anything,» Keira spoke to her. «Can you hear me?»

«Yeah. God, Keira. I'm never going to be able to let you two go.»

«We'll see how it works out, babe. Thanks for being here.»

Emerson watched Keira move directly toward the old inn. Keira paused at the steps to the entrance and waited a minute before going inside.

Jaime

«GIVE ME A minute to get inside and catch anyone's attention if they're there,» Keira said when they were in position.

«I'm ready when you are,» Jaime said.

«Okay. Here goes.» Keira entered the building. Jaime couldn't hear her as well through the walls of the building, but he waited till a count of thirty before he tried the door of the annex and pushed it open.

Everything was silent. Completely silent. Jaime shook his head.

«Keira?» There was no response. Jaime couldn't hear the thoughts of anyone in the area. He strained to hear Emerson, sitting in the car, but there was nothing.

It was so disorienting that Jaime stumbled and nearly fell in the hallway. There was always someone talking in range of his mind. The silence in his head was as absolute as if he had shut down his entire body. There was no sound coming to his ears, either. He glanced at his cell phone and saw he had no bars. Ms. McCormick had warned them that Schwartz was proud of the signal blocking in the inn. He didn't realize it would be so complete.

He nearly panicked, backing out the door slowly. In the distance, sounds and thoughts began to seep into his head again. He could hear the hum of mental voices and honed in on Emerson.

Where are they? I wish they'd text me.

Jaime checked his cell for a signal and quickly sent her a message.

"Don't worry. There's no cell reception inside. Did you hear from Keira?"

"Not a word," Emerson texted back. "Do you want me to go check on her?"

"No. We'll meet up as soon as we're in range of each other. Just sit tight. I'll try to find a place where I have reception once I'm inside. Let Keira know I'm in when she comes back outside."

"Will do."

Jaime took a deep breath and pushed his way inside again.

Keira and Kenton

"Hi. Um… My friend and I were out sightseeing and saw this old inn. Do you have a brochure and rates? We might want to come back on another trip," Keira said to the man who hurried to the front desk when she rang the bell.

"Oh, possible guests! We're always looking forward to greeting new people. I'm afraid we're booked up tonight, though."

"We can't stay tonight anyway," Keira said. "My friend just went to get us a cup of coffee for our drive back down to Salem while I checked this place out."

"Just give me a minute here. I'm not usually out here, but the hostess has gone grocery shopping. I was just vacuuming upstairs. I'm sure I have a brochure in the drawer here. Yes. Here it is," the man said.

"Wow! I didn't hear a thing. It's really quiet here," Keira said as the man opened a desk drawer and eventually pulled out a brochure and rate card to give her.

"We take pride in how quiet our buildings are. You'd hardly know anyone else is resident. We have twelve rooms in this building and another six in the annex down the hill. It's amazing how well these old buildings were constructed to baffle noise. Of course, we did some enhancing of the insulation when we got the place years ago."

"It's almost like sensory deprivation," Keira said. «Jaime, are you there? I can't hear you!» There was no response.

"Oh, I assure you it's not quite that quiet. Have you ever been in a sensory deprivation tank? Nothing like this at all. Nothing at all. Would you like to see a room?"

"Uh… sure, if it's not too much trouble. Maybe I should let my friend know I'm going to see a room," Keira said, pulling out her phone.

"I'm afraid that won't work unless you step outside. Something about the construction of the buildings prevents cell signals from getting inside. Several of the older buildings in Astoria have that problem. When you're a guest here, we give you our WiFi password which works from inside any room. It's a cable system so there's a WiFi modem in each room connected to the system. Only way we could get service inside."

"I'll just step outside and text her," Keira said, backing out the front door. She looked up the street and heard Emerson clearly.

Just text me, okay? There's no signal of any kind inside. Jaime's in the annex. I'm out here alone and I'm afraid for you guys!

"Em, it's okay. No cell service inside here either. I'm going to go look at a room and try to spot where the stairs down are," Keira texted.

"Be careful! J says he'll meet you inside when you find a place where there's a signal—or a mental or something. He's looking for the passage from that side."

"Good. I'll be back in touch in ten minutes."

Keira went back into the inn and into silence.

"Does your friend want to come in for a tour as well?" the guy asked.

"Still in line at the coffee shop," Keira laughed nervously. "Just said I wouldn't be long."

"Okay. The couple who manages the inn live here on the main floor. Out getting groceries just now, I think. All the guest rooms are upstairs. This was once the mansion of a shipping magnate who had visions of grandeur. Would you look at that dining room? We serve breakfast to all our guests. It didn't take long after his heirs got hold of the property to convert the monstrosity into an inn."

The guy had an easy way about him that relaxed Keira. The inn was a fascinating building, decorated in period fashion from the turn of the twentieth century. He indicated some of the rooms were occupied, but he'd just stripped a room that had been checked out of that morning. Aside from the unmade bed, the room appeared very attractive. Keira immediately went to the window and checked her cell phone. She had a weak signal through the glass and quickly sent a text reassuring Emerson.

"I'll be out soon." She couldn't get a clear mental contact with her friend and wasn't sure the text message went through.

"This is a lovely place," Keira said, turning to the man who was watching her carefully from the doorway. "How did you happen to start working here?"

He chuckled.

"It's a long story, but the short version is, I own it."

Keira reflexively took a step backward. The man smiled at her.

"Dr. Schwartz?" Something in the makeup of the room prevented her from reading his thoughts, even at this close range.

"Ah, so it *is* you! Keira, isn't it? I suppose your little girlfriend Trayce told you all about me. I assume it is your boyfriend… Jaime?… outside getting messages from you. You can invite him in. You've both been such a pain to poor Trayce."

"Where is she?!!" Keira shouted. Even her shout sounded muted.

"Just downstairs. Shall we go visit her?"

"You're a rapist! I won't go anywhere with you."

"What a terrible accusation. I have not molested your friend in any way," Schwartz said.

"You raped her mind. You drugged her and probed her secrets."

"Hmm. I didn't think you'd be able to contact her here. She must be stronger than I thought. I can see how you could think I was mentally assaulting her, but I assure you the treatment is all completely above board. She pled for help with her schizophrenia. The voices in her head were driving her crazy. Do you have the same experiences?"

"She's not schizophrenic," Keira growled. "She's telepathic. It's you who's upsetting her and making her doubt her reality."

"She came to me because she couldn't get the voices out of her head. Thought they were characters she was writing about and couldn't get them to shut up. They were taking over her life. I brought her here as an intervention so she could recover. Confidentially, she's not a very good writer."

A man and woman appeared behind him in the doorway and Keira backed all the way against the window as Schwartz approached her.

"SOS" she texted, but Schwartz grabbed the phone before she could hit send. Keira swung at him and hit him in the side.

"That's not very nice. I was offering a nice guided tour to go see your friend, if she is indeed your friend. Now, I'll have to insist you accompany my associates. They are not grocery shopping at the moment, it seems, but are here watching for invaders like you and your boyfriend."

The couple reached Keira and each took an arm. Keira screamed in the sound deadened room. The assistants snorted.

"Did you notice how dead the acoustics are in this old inn?" Schwartz chuckled. "You can scream your head off and no one—even in the room next door—will hear you. Trayce was quite hoarse before that finally sank into her."

"Jaime will find you and free us," Keira declared as she was escorted down the hall.

"I do hope so. He's the objective of all this research, after all. I'll leave the front door open, shall I?"

Keira closed her mind, not sure if Schwartz was a head talker or not. She couldn't hear a thing in the building mentally. She didn't want to give Jaime or Emerson away.

They went down several flights of stairs and into another silent hallway. Keira estimated they were at least two floors beneath the main floor of the inn—maybe three. Even the air pressure felt different. If her calculations were right, that would put them somewhere lower than the annex. The deeper they went into the complex, the quieter it became, if that was possible. Even their footsteps seemed absorbed by the walls and floor. She could read nothing from her three companions.

They stopped in front of a door and Schwartz opened it cautiously. Inside was a nicely appointed hotel room, similar to the one she'd toured in the inn. It had a large bed, a table and two chairs, and a window with a view of the harbor. Keira shook her head and squinted at the window, realizing it was a projection against the wall in a window frame. At the table, Trayce looked up from what she was writing. Her eyes got big.

"No! No! Go away! Don't bring her in here. I don't want her here!"

"Trayce! Please don't send me away. We've come to get you out of here. We'll take you home."

"Liar! You aren't her. If you were, I'd be able to hear you in my head. You are just someone he's testing me with."

"Test yourself with her," Schwartz said. "Probe her and see if any of what you thought was true. Send mental head messages to each other. I'll just leave you here to get acquainted."

Schwartz and his two assistants backed out of the room and the door latched behind them. Keira ran to the door and tested the handle. Schwartz hadn't used a key from the outside, but the inside was securely locked.

She turned and faced Trayce.

33
THE RESCUE

Emerson

IT HAD GONE on long enough as far as Emerson was concerned. She really had no proof that Keira and Jaime were talking in each other's head, reading her thoughts, or talking to her. It could all be something she just wanted to believe. It could all be coincidences. It was possible their 'girlfriend' wasn't even real and wasn't at this inn anyway.

It was her own foolish fantasy that got her involved with them. They certainly read that right. She hadn't felt this way about anyone since she left Dom and Raquel. And that was a disaster. She was just a training wheel on their bicycle, not a tricycle at all. They'd gotten married the day before without her.

She knew in her heart that any involvement with Jaime and Keira would end the same way. She was a third wheel, no matter who she was with. When school started up in two days, she was going to come back a changed woman. The couple of outfits she'd worn so far were nothing compared to the other things she'd purchased in Paris. It was too cold for some of the skirts, but she had enough great form-fitting clothes to knock their backwater school on its ass.

But it probably wouldn't be enough to win a long-term place with Keira and Jaime. They'd go off someplace together and she'd… She supposed she'd still go back to Paris. She'd made good contacts there over the summer and could pick up that part of her life, at least. If her software project worked even a little, she was sure she could interest one of the houses in bringing her on while she continued her studies at the *Academe Internationale.*

Keira had said she'd be out in ten minutes. That was nearly half an hour ago. Emerson got out of her car, locked the door, and headed toward the inn. Leave it to her to clean up the mess. She'd go find them herself.

The front door of the guesthouse was unlocked and she walked in to look around. No one was in the foyer and she couldn't hear anything from the direction of the kitchen. She glanced at her phone and saw she'd lost service as soon as she entered the inn.

No sense calling attention to myself, she thought. *I'll just start looking for the stairway down.*

The stairway leading up to the rooms was obvious, but she figured the most likely place for a staircase down was behind it, in the kitchen. She headed toward the kitchen and found a huge walk-in pantry behind the stairs. She supposed the original family had a ton of servants living in the building. She was pretty sure Oregon never had slaves. It was admitted to the Union just before the Civil War as a free state. But rich people always had a way of getting around that. If someone owed you money, for example, they could be bound to you to work off the debt.

This Schwartz character was a descendant of the shipping magnate who built the original house. She'd found a lot of information about him, including his published research on inner monologue and inner dialogue. He'd let a few things slip into it regarding the manipulation of weaker minds. If she accepted that Keira and Jaime had communicated with her telepathically, it seemed possible they could influence her thinking. They could exert outright power over another person's mind if they didn't let them know they were talking to her. It was confusing and made her head hurt.

She heard a noise from the pantry and quickly hid behind a door to the next room.

Schwartz and two others emerged from the pantry.

"Check up and down the street. Teenage boy. You know what he looks like from the photos I took. He'll probably be trying to find a place where he can observe the inn. Clever kid. Sent his girlfriend in instead of coming himself. We don't want him bringing cops. Find him and bring him in. I'm going up to the cupola and will monitor the cameras."

"You got it. Shirley, go out the back. I'll go out the front," the other man said.

Emerson heard the back door close and footsteps retreat toward the front of the house. They faded quickly. She ducked around the pantry door and found the stairs downward she'd been looking for.

He's so casual about leaving doors open and unlocked, she thought. *It's almost as if he's inviting intruders. Shit!*

She was only a step down the stairs when lights came on. She froze and listened, but nothing seemed to be approaching. She caught her breath and kept going. Acoustically, the passage was muted. She could barely hear her own breathing and footsteps. The door at the bottom of the stairs was a heavy-duty steel door, but it was unlocked. It had an old and faded sticker on the door that had three yellow triangles in a black circle. Under it were the words "Fallout Shelter."

Handy if there's a nuclear attack and they all have to get underground. I wonder if it's still a fully stocked bomb shelter.

She went on into the hall and the heavy door closed behind her. The hall immediately branched into two and looking down each, she could see they branched again a little way on. She remembered Jaime saying the child services lady said the place down here was a maze.

Okay. So, you're supposed to keep one hand on the wall and just keep following that wall until you get out or return to the start. I'll use some lip gloss to mark this door so I know it's the one I came in by. At least it's not dark down here.

She marked the door, put her hand on the left wall, and started following the hall. Each time she came to a door, she opened it, looked, and then continued. She soon lost track of how many turns she'd taken in a quiet that even muffled her thoughts. She was getting tired, checking every door to see if it was the one she came in by.

Suddenly, she sensed a change in the atmosphere. It was as if her ears were unstopped and she could hear again. She hummed and could hear her own voice. When she walked in the hall, she could hear her footsteps on the carpet and the brush of her fingers against the wall. She took a deep breath, unaware that she'd been holding it.

And then she heard a voice.

Rose and Angus and Kate and Thursday

"WHAT THE FUCK, Angus? Another girl just entered the front door," Kate said into her cell phone. "Is the missing girl trying to track down her friends?"

"Another girl?" Angus said, looking at Rose. "No. We don't know of any other girls. Rose, do you think they brought more people with them?"

"It's possible. I told you they could command someone. Or it could be another of Kenton's goonies," Rose said.

"Speaking of goonies, the woman he had with him just came out the back door," Angus told Kate on the phone.

"Shit! Here comes Tweedle-Dumbass," Kate said. "He just bounced out the front door looking up and down the street."

"He see you?"

"No. I don't think so. We're behind a car on the other side of the road. You want us to take him out?" Kate asked.

"Don't. Wait." «Did you get a read on her?» Angus asked Rose.

«Yes. They're hunting for Jaime. They don't know he's inside.»

"Look, Kate. I think they're out hunting for the boy. The farther afield they go the better we are. That means we let them go and get ready to enter the building."

"Christ! Watch your ass!" Kate snarled. "The baddy is up in the cupola with a pair of binocs scanning around."

"I see him. We've faded back to avoid the woman, so I don't think he spotted us. Are you safe?"

"My bunny-tail is wet from the pavement. We don't dare move, though. We'll try to find a spot where we can see when he's looking a different way and we'll take a stroll farther down the hill."

"I'll make it my mission to dry your ass when we're done," Angus said. "Buzz me if you see anything else. And stay away from the guy. You know he's packing."

"Right-o, pops. Talk to you later."

«What do we do now?» Rose asked Angus.

«Well, we've got the goonies in the street and Kenton's on the roof. That means Keira, Jaime, and Miss X are inside, maybe being held and maybe on the loose. I think we should get ready for an assault.»

«If we go now, the lower level should be undefended,» Rose said.

«Watch for the woman. We'll make for the back door when it looks clear.»

Jaime

JAIME INVESTIGATED EVERY doorway and passage in the annex as he came to it. He used a Sharpie to mark an 'x' on any door he couldn't open and a 'y' on any door he could. The lights in the rooms came on automatically when the door opened. Jaime didn't go into any of the rooms, but looked to see what was there.

That was how he found the stairway to the lower level. It was a heavier door than the others with a 'Fallout Shelter' sticker on it. It opened just fine and Jaime checked to be sure it wouldn't lock when he walked through.

Schwartz apparently depended on secrecy and archaic stickers on blast doors to guard his facility instead of security. With the noise blocking acoustics, Jaime couldn't even hear himself. He'd fought down his panic when he entered the annex, becoming mentally and physically deaf. He'd found nothing so far, but the next door proved to be a bonanza.

It was a small room and Jaime blocked the door open to keep from being locked in. The door had been labeled 'Janitor,' but inside was an array of electronic equipment. It was on the lowest level of the building, at least as far as the stairs were concerned. Jaime wondered what the effect of the dampening tech would have on those who were already head deaf.

The equipment was an elaborate sound panel. Jaime had studied sound engineering when he was developing his TTS and fine tuning it to the voice he wanted. One of the topics he'd looked at was noise-cancelling, and upon close examination, that seemed to be the major function of this system. The entire complex was divided into segments that could be dampened or not. He decided the most expedient course of action would be to simply turn the whole thing off.

He hit the master switch and the building came to life.

He left the sound room and closed the door again. While the atmosphere was more alive than it had been, it still seemed soft and muted. There was obviously a passive system in place as well as the active system, including the carpet and soft, spongy walls. Unfortunately, removing the noise dampening did nothing to unblock his mental hearing. That had to be something embedded in the walls.

I'm running out of time, he thought. *How long have I been exploring? Keira will be angry and Emerson will be in a panic. This calls for desperate measures. Shit!*

He couldn't hope to keep from being discovered forever, but he hadn't yet reached the stairs going up into the inn. He was sure they must be ahead, but he hadn't found a door that revealed any captives. He needed to do something he'd sworn never to do. He wasn't even sure he could, but he had to try.

"Keira!" he rasped out, forming the word in his mouth and letting his vocal cords vibrate. It hurt. He knew *how* to talk. The mechanics of it. He just prayed no one would die because he used his out-loud voice. The sound was weak and didn't travel far. He closed his eyes and inhaled deeply.

"Keira! Trayce! Where are you? It's Jaime. Where are you?" he called out. He winced and fought nausea. It wasn't loud like he'd heard others yelling, but the sound seemed to carry.

Keira and Trayce

"Trayce, it's really me. Keira," Keira said as she moved slightly toward where Trayce was cowering.

Trayce held a finger to her lips. "Shh!"

She ran to the door and pounded on it.

"Let me out! Don't trap me in here with her!"

"Please, Trayce. Don't do this to me. To us!" Keira pled.

Trayce hushed her again and then turned to advance on Keira.

"Why can't I hear you? If you were really her, I'd hear you and you'd hear me."

"I don't know what he's done. The walls in this entire building prevent the penetration of sound, cell signals, and brainwaves, even in the same room. Walking in here is like becoming head deaf," Keira explained.

"I don't trust you," Trayce said. "He's using you to trick me into something. He tries all the time."

"He's been raping your head!" Keira cried. "I'm the one you cried to when Jaime was injured. You were there when we made love. We were going to the café to meet you for lunch last Friday. Then he kidnapped you. And yesterday morning… we heard you say you believed in us and to please help you. That's why we're here."

"We? He's here, too?"

"We split up. He's looking for you, too."

"You were making love."

"Yes."

"What day is it?"

"It's Friday after New Year's."

"Mommy!"

"We went to see her yesterday. Schwartz went so far as to leave a runaway note in your car telling her she'd never see you again. That doesn't mean she hasn't tried to find you. The police just didn't believe her. We convinced her to hold on while we came to find you."

"Was she drunk and alone?" Trayce whispered.

"No. She's resisting. Her AA sponsor, Susan, was with her."

"Are you really Keira?"

"Yes, honey. And as soon as we get out of this building, you'll be able to connect with us again."

Trayce started crying.

"Don't take me with you. Tell him you don't know me. He's done horrible things and I might… I don't trust what I might do. He wants us all together. He wants to drug you and Jaime, too. He wants us to tell people to do things."

"We won't let him."

"But *I* might. He's been drugging me and hypnotizing me every mealtime. I might do something terrible! I might betray you! You have to run and leave me behind!"

Keira finally got close enough to catch Trayce by the shoulders and hold her facing her.

"We will never leave you behind, Trayce. We love you."

Keira pressed her lips against Trayce's. It wasn't the world-opening jolt that they had experienced with Jaime, but it was still electric. Trayce collapsed against Keira.

"I always knew. I tried to deny it, but I always knew," she whispered.

There was a shift in the atmosphere of the room and her whisper seemed suddenly loud. They still didn't have head talk, but it felt like wads of cotton had just been pulled from their ears.

Then they heard the voice.

"Keira! Trayce! Where are you? It's Jaime. Where are you?"

Keira rushed to the door and began pounding on it and yelling. Trayce backed away.

Emerson

EMERSON FROZE. JAIME calling out loud? As far as she knew, Jaime had never spoken. And the voice was nothing like his voice on the computer—the voice she associated with him. This had to be a trick by Schwartz to flush them out of hiding. She backed around a corner and watched the passage ahead.

Of course, Jaime doesn't have his computer with him, she thought. *I locked it in the car when I decided to launch this stupid rescue. Now we're all in here.*

She could hear so much more now. Air vents circulated heat. There was even a low 60-cycle hum from the power. How amazing that she could hear her own breathing and heartbeat now that it was no longer being dampened. She looked around the hall and spotted speakers carefully concealed in the walls and ceiling, as well as what she thought were tiny microphones. Now that she had her hearing, her visual acuity seemed to increase and let her focus.

If it's you, Jaime, I'm ahead around the corner. Emerson, I mean. I'm thinking at you. God, I feel like an idiot.

No answer came, either in her head or by voice. Now she really felt like an idiot.

"Keira! Trayce! It's Jaime. Answer me or pound on your door or something. I don't know where you are!"

That same squeaky voice. She wondered if it could be heard through the doors that were spaced about thirty feet apart. Then she heard pounding from the nearest door.

"Let us out! Jaime!"

Emerson rushed to the door and opened it from the outside. Immediately, she was face-to-face with Keira.

Rose and Angus

WHEN KENTON DISAPPEARED from the cupola windows, Rose and Angus ran across the back yard to the door. They paused outside long enough for Angus to send a text to Kate.

"We're going in the backdoor. One of you come around to the back and keep watch for the woman. Don't let them re-enter the house."

As soon as he pressed send, he and Rose darted inside.

Both were immediately affected by the deafness inside the building. Angus looked at his phone and then shoved it in his pocket. Rose glanced at her phone and did the same thing. There was no signal. The two walked through the kitchen and glanced out into the foyer.

Angus unlatched the sword from his cane so it was ready to draw and they moved into the living quarters on that level. They heard the change in acoustics when it shifted and Angus dug in his ear for a moment before he realized it wasn't in his head.

"Someone shut off the noise dampening," Rose said. "Something is happening."

Angus looked out a bedroom window in the caretaker's suite and across the yard toward the B&B.

"We need to move," he said. "The woman just came cutting across a block over, moving fast. Thursday is in pursuit."

Just then, they heard footsteps pounding down the main stairs. Four steps across the foyer and the front door crashed open. Angus and Rose headed for the kitchen door and out into the brisk air.

34
COMMAND VOICE

Everybody

"EMERSON!" KEIRA BREATHED as she hugged her friend. She caught the door just before it closed behind her.

"You brought *her!*" Trayce screamed. "You didn't want me at all!"

"That's not true, hon," Keira protested.

Emerson stalked across the floor to Trayce as Keira shoved pillows to block the door open.

"Listen here, you little bitch!" Emerson growled. "You have no idea what these two have gone through to find and rescue you. If they had to call in a friend to help them, you should be thankful they had a friend to call. Did you have a friend? Or are you only bitching about what they did?"

"Emerson, please. Not now," Keira said. "Where's Jaime?"

Just then they heard the repeated squeaky call from the hall.

"I don't know if that's him or not," Emerson said. "I've only ever heard his voice on the computer."

"Schwartz has some kind of brain-wave dampening mesh surrounding all the surfaces in here. None of us can use our head voice," Keira said.

"Either that or head voice doesn't really exist," Trayce declared. "It was a figment of my imagination. None of you are real. They were just characters in a story I'm writing."

"Are all creative types this stupid?" Emerson asked.

"Jaime! We're here. You're getting closer," Keira yelled out the door.

Jaime came running to the door and into the room.

"Keira! Trayce! I found you," he squeaked in his out-loud voice. "Emerson! What are you doing in here?"

"I came looking for you after you'd been out of touch for forty-five minutes. We need to get out of here. Schwartz and his two cronies are searching outside for you. They don't know I'm in here."

"Let's go, Trayce. Bring your manuscript. You'll want to finish it later. But we are taking you out of this dungeon," Keira said.

"I don't believe you. I'll go outside just to prove you are a test the doctor set up for me to show it's all imaginary," Trayce said, gathering her notebooks.

"We've been trying to find you ever since you screamed for help yesterday morning," Jaime said. "This way will get us up the back stairs and out of the annex. I marked the walls."

They followed Jaime with Emerson bringing up the rear as Keira wrapped her arm around Trayce and guided her through the hall. Soon, they reached the stairs and Jaime went ahead to check that the coast was clear.

«Let's move to the car,» Jaime said in their heads as soon as they were outside.

«Right,» Keira answered.

"No! I didn't hear that. It's just what I think you'd say," Trayce said. "You didn't hear anything, did you?" she demanded of Emerson.

"I never hear anything unless it's spoken out loud or one of them has a hand on me. I can't head talk. If you think you just heard something, you probably did."

"It's ridiculous," Trayce said.

"Guys, head downhill," Emerson said. "I'll go up to get the car and meet you at the bottom of the hill where there's a park with trees. Phones should work again now, so I'll text you when I'm on the way. They won't be looking for me and I have to go the other direction to get to the car. They know all three of you."

Emerson went to the front of the annex and crossed the street. Jaime led Keira and Trayce down the alley.

«I don't think they've seen me,» Jaime said.

«But they're looking for you,» Keira said.

I need to spice up the dialog a bit. These guys are boring, Trayce grumbled in her mind.

«You can spice things up when we get you home,» Jaime growled. Trayce gasped. They crossed behind the guesthouse and the next street, heading for the trees in the park.

"Perfect!" Schwartz yelled as he jerked the passenger door of Emerson's Kia open. He plopped in the seat and grinned at Emerson. "Now, you will take me to the pickup point. Are you one, too? It's quite a bonus to get a fourth."

"You don't have any!" Emerson growled, opening her door to get out. A gun faced her.

"Get in and drive," the thug growled. "Your friends don't have a ride if you don't go to pick them up."

Emerson closed the door and started the car. The thug got in the back seat, making sure she knew he still had the gun on her.

"I don't need to take you to find them. All I need to do is drive around a while and they'll be gone. You'll never get to them."

"Don't try it," Schwartz said. "You're too young to die. Besides, Shirley is on their tail and she won't let them get far."

Emerson floored the Kia and squealed out of the parking lot, but soon let up on the accelerator when she felt the gun barrel against her neck.

* * *

Jaime, Keira, and Trayce came to a stop beneath the trees near the road. They were panting as much from the adrenaline rush as from exertion.

«Is it true?» Trayce said when Jaime and Keira wrapped their arms around her. «Are we really talking to each other in our heads?»

«Yes,» Jaime answered. «Trayce, we won't let him try to drug and block you.»

«He'll use me to hurt you. I tried to resist. He gave me something in my food that made me sleepy and then hypnotized me. I tried to resist. But I know he told me I had to obey,» Trayce said.

«You know the keys of what he'll try to do. You can resist with us to help you. Hold our hands, honey. You'll see how much stronger we are than when we're alone,» Keira said.

«We've got a problem,» Jaime said. «Schwartz carjacked Emerson. He and one of his thugs are arriving with her. The woman is coming up behind us.»

Emerson's blue Kia skidded to a stop a few feet away. She jumped out of the car and ran to Jaime. He took her hand and felt the gestalt forming among the four of them. It was almost enough to knock him out. He could feel power flowing, even from Emerson.

Schwartz and the thug got out of the car to face them.

"So, I finally have you all! This is wonderful," Schwartz said.

"You don't have us," Keira growled, feeling the support from Trayce, Jaime, and Emerson. "And there are enough of us that we can make a pretty big stink before you can kidnap anyone again."

"I don't want to *kidnap* anyone. I want to save you!"

"From what? So far, you are the only threat," Emerson said. "You and your goon held me until I drove here. That's carjacking."

"Let's not be picky," Schwartz said good-naturedly. "It's the government we need to worry about. Why do you think I went to so much trouble to dampen audio and psychic waves and microwaves? Whoever found the control room and shut down the ANC system was very clever. Of course, we knew as soon as we saw this one run that you'd reached the honey in our trap."

"Trayce is not honey in a trap," Keira said. "Step aside and we'll be gone."

"No, no, no! If the government finds out about you, they'll want to experiment on you, just as they did on me," Schwartz said.

"The government didn't find anything of interest in you, Kenton," Rose said, stepping past the thug. Angus stepped up from the other side with his sword drawn and pressed it against Schwartz's side. "They tossed you aside and you haven't been able to stand it. You wanted so desperately to be a cool kid and talk in people's heads. Nothing you can do can make it better. You're a fake and a charlatan."

"Rose! My dear sweet girl. How I've missed you. I haven't missed you, Angus. Still running around with a sword? We have guns, you know," Schwartz said, seemingly unfazed. "Now, Trayce, tell your friends about Kalliope."

«We're supposed to go back in the building. I'm sorry. I have to take you back,» Trayce said, exerting mental force on the other three. Jaime gathered the reins of the gestalt and cut her off.

«DROP YOUR GUNS!» Jaime sent to the group.

Four guns hit the ground.

"What the fuck?" Thursday yelled. Schwartz's two guards spun on Kate and

Thursday, who had slipped up behind them. Fists began flying, showing that both the strippers were as skilled at martial arts as Schwartz's guards seemed to be.

«STOP IT!» Jaime commanded. The four combatants froze. «YOU TWO. GO HOME!» he directed at the two goons. The girls joined their out-loud voices to his mental voice. The two thugs started backing away.

"This is wonderful! It's wonderful! It's just like I said it would be. You commanded with your mind and people obeyed!" Schwartz nearly jumped for joy. "With me to guide you we'll be unstoppable! How I wish I'd had you when we were experimenting at the university. Of course, you weren't yet born, were you? And when I first spotted you, you were much too young. But now, look at you. All grown up and testing your power. I'll show you how to use it."

The two goons were now running flat out toward the guest house. Kate and Thursday bent to scoop up all four guns, now being free from the command.

"You're paranoid," Rose said. "You don't have anything to offer them. Even your inn is a detriment to them. You've been feeding Trayce drugs, haven't you? And attempting to hypnotize her. You can see it didn't work."

Jaime sent some hints to Keira, still holding the force of their gestalt.

"Here's what you need to do," Keira said. "You need to retire from counseling. Forever! Do not *ever* attempt to investigate head talk or head talkers again. Make a happy business for yourself with your inn and never bother us again."

"You can't imagine that I'm just going to give up my life work," Schwartz said. "I'll…"

"GO AWAY AND LEAVE US ALONE!" the four said in unison, three with out-loud voices and Jaime in his head.

«OBEY!» Jaime commanded.

Schwartz straightened as if he'd been struck. He looked around at the eight others still in the park.

"I'm getting too old for this," he muttered. "I was going to retire anyway. I'm going to live up there in my apartment at the top of the world and watch the ships come sailing in. You kids don't need me. I don't need you. It's all a bunch of nonsense anyway. Talk in people's heads. That's pretty stupid when you stop to think about it. Have a nice life."

Schwartz turned and wandered back toward his guesthouse as Jaime increased the pressure on him to forget all about the kids from Portland.

Then Jaime collapsed in a heap on the ground.

Emerson and Kate and Thursday

"WHAT THE FUCK just happened?" Thursday fumed. She, Kate, and Emerson had been left in the living room of the B&B while Rose and Keira carried Jaime to their bedroom, trailed by Angus and Trayce.

"We were just mentally hijacked," Emerson said. "Fuck. I'd experienced Keira and Jaime talking in my head before, but never anything like that. It was him. He was issuing commands and we were just sucked up into it."

"You know Angus did it, too," Kate said.

"What?" Thursday asked.

"I suspected it a long time ago. He's always been half a step ahead of the crooks, even when he was drugged half out of his mind up in the Idaho. He's a mind reader," Kate said.

"Unreal," Thursday said.

"I didn't think it was real. It can't be scientifically proven. You can't run repeatable experiments with different subjects. But that doesn't mean it isn't real. You just got a command to drop your guns," Emerson said. "I felt what it was like to issue the command. It made me rethink my life."

"Hmm. You're pretty cute. No tattoos? No unusual piercings? You could make a bundle on the stage," Kate said.

"What stage?"

"Sassy's," Thursday said. "I might retire from the detective business myself. Except I promised Angus I'd drive him around after dark. My degree's almost finished."

"I don't understand," Emerson sighed.

"Become a stripper, like us," Kate said. "Thursday and I can show you the ropes and make sure no one takes unfair advantage of you when you're starting out."

"You mean take my clothes off on stage?" Emerson asked in disbelief. "I don't think so."

"We won't pressure you," Thursday said. "But if you decide you'd like to try it—even on a lark—let us know. We'll help."

"Thanks. I just need to figure out what I'm going to do about Jaime and Keira. And Trayce, I guess. Can't have one without the others."

Jaime and Keira and Trayce and Rose and Angus

«Oh, geez, my head hurts,» Jaime moaned to himself.

"For good reason," Angus said aloud. "You're dangerous. I've told you before that you need to control your volume."

"Angus, honey. That might not be the best way to handle this," Rose said.

"I can't believe you really exist, too!" Trayce said touching Angus on the shoulder again. "Is every character I write about someone who is a real person?"

"Probably not. Some might be inspired by real people, but I know the stories are all yours," Keira said. She held Jaime's hand. Trayce hadn't decided yet if she should join them.

"The thing is that you used a command voice, Jaime," Rose said. "You used it on me when it was just the two of you and I found it compelling. Not quite a command I had to follow, but something I needed to consider. But I'm a head talker, like you suspected all along, Keira. What worries us is that you commanded everyone around you and they all obeyed. First, the four who were armed with guns. They didn't even consider what was demanded! They dropped them."

"I'm thankful you didn't command weapons down. I don't like to drop the sword," Angus said.

«I'm sorry. It was… he was trying to hurt us,» Jaime said.

«I'm not saying you didn't have a right to defend yourselves,» Rose answered. «But you need to decide what kind of person you are going to be. What you did was what Kenton always wanted to do. He was convinced that he could control other people with the right number of head talkers. Is that what you're going to do?»

«No.»

"Are we really holding a conversation in our heads as well as with our mouths?" Trayce asked. "Unreal!"

"I know you are newer to this than the rest of us," Rose said. "You haven't had time to get used to it like Jaime and Keira have."

"I don't think I'm ever going to get used to it."

"We can teach you ways to block it. It's been eighteen years and Keira never got a signal from me," Rose said.

«We'd like you to give us a chance to know you first,» Keira said. «We'd be pretty devastated if now that you know it's true, you decided you didn't want anything to do with us.»

«Yeah, I guess. You… already made love.»

«I guess that's how we managed to find you. It was strong enough that you heard us and answered,» Keira said.

«What kind of person are you going to be, Jaime?» Angus asked, not letting go of the real issue in the room.

«I wanted… At one time, I wanted to help other people hear thoughts. I believed it would have saved my mother. I would never have spoken with my out-loud voice. Then Keira told me how there were people who would misuse that and she used the example of giving someone driving a car an instruction to run a stop light. I thought that was horrid. I didn't want to ever force anyone to hear my thoughts again. I didn't know how potent that could be, though, until today. Did he really… Are we safe from him?»

"Based on what I read, we're all safe. That doesn't mean there aren't others who will want the same thing. Mind control has been on the government's list of things to use in battle for a hundred years," Angus said. "If they'd understood what they were doing to my brain back in the sixties, you can bet they'd have had me locked up in a laboratory kennel deep underground."

"You experienced the worst of the awakening experiences," Rose said. "Most of us progress to it naturally—often with the onset of menses. Jaime was born with the gift."

«Gift? Ha! If I'd been normal and not all confused as hell, my mother would still be alive!» Jaime shouted at them.

«But think of what we have, love,» Keira said. «It's not a fair trade, but it would be terrible to live without my soulmate.»

Both Jaime and Keira looked at Trayce.

«Can you have two soulmates?» she asked. «Can I?»

«We think so,» Jaime said.

"There is a lot you need to work out among yourselves," Rose said. "But you should have some counseling, too. I'm not promoting my business. And I don't want to control you like Kenton did. But you need a safe space where you can examine your feelings and talk about the difficulties."

"I need that," Trayce said. "Um… can we go home now? I'm worried about my mother."

"I agree," Keira said. "Do you feel fit enough to travel, Jaime?"

Jaime nodded his right fist up and down rather than try to send any lengthy messages.

Rose and Angus and Kate and Thursday

"So, ARE YOU two going to hook up and start controlling the universe like those kids did?" Kate asked over dinner that evening. They'd booked the B&B for one more night and didn't feel like abandoning the lovely room to follow the teens back to Portland. Besides, they still wanted to keep an eye on the guesthouse across the back yard, just to make sure people stayed put.

"No." Rose answered promptly. Angus sighed. "Angus and I are old friends and sometimes lovers. We have a talent. But we don't have what those kids have."

"Soulmates," Angus said softly. "I never even believed in that before. Bunch of new age hooey. But it was obvious with them. It isn't just that they are strong telepaths. They are unique in the world."

"Well, they spooked the hell out of me," Thursday said. "I think I'll move back to Texas."

"Don't forget to take your passport," Angus said. "You might want to come back to the United States one day."

"Ha ha," Thursday said disgustedly.

"You guys have been able to do that mental telepathy stuff for a long time, though, right?" Kate asked.

"All telepathy is mental," Rose said. "Yeah. I started as a pre-teen and made the connection between acquiring the ability and menses."

"I went through a period back then," Thursday said. "I kind of went crazy. Didn't understand what was happening. Tried sex, drugs, and rock and roll. The craziness eventually abated some, but at least the sex and rock live on."

"We can talk if you want to," Rose said. "I don't exclude women just because they've survived. Sometimes it helps to understand what happened."

"Uh… Yeah, maybe," Thursday said cautiously. "We'll see."

"I'm going to want to keep an eye on those kids," Angus said.

"You don't trust them?" Kate asked.

"Not that so much. They're good kids and they'll always *try* to do what's right. I just want to be sure there aren't any other Kentons around. Until they learn to corral their broadcasts, they might still be a target."

"That's what I'll work on with them most," Rose said. She turned to the two strippers. "What we've known since Angus and I met during Kenton's college research is that telepathy is limited to hearing with the brain. We're huge signal receptors. It's what drives people crazy. They hear people, but they can't respond to them. On the other hand, everyone broadcasts their thoughts. Some are really loud and some are timid. Some are verbal, some are pictorial, and some are strictly emotional. But for almost everyone, there is some leakage of what they are thinking. It's always been up to the head talkers to limit what they hear, respect others' privacy, and block out all the mental noise around them."

"What we've never seen before… the holy grail for assholes like Schwartz… is the ability to force someone to hear who doesn't have the gift." Angus said. "The girl who drove the three gifted teens is head deaf. She doesn't normally hear others' thoughts. But let Jaime and Keira touch her and she's an open receiver, able to hear whatever they think to her. Still, that's nothing compared to the command voice the kid used on everyone this afternoon. You didn't even comprehend you'd received a command, but you immediately dropped your guns."

"Yeah. I'm not happy about that. Dropping it scratched the pink powder coating on mine," Thursday said.

"And by the time the two goons were a hundred feet from us, they were running back to the guesthouse as fast as they could go. And Kenton completely accepted the command to retire and leave all his research behind. That's power I never speculated about. In fact, when Angus and I read Kenton during his study and discovered what he wanted to do, we resigned from the study because it was just one more fraud," Rose said.

"So, are we done with this shit?" Kate asked.

"You are," Rose said. "I'll counsel the kids and Angus will keep an eye out for other baddies."

"Ass I always say, my droogies, I'll let you know when the game's afoot," Angus said.

35
COMING TO GRIPS

Jaime and Keira and Trayce and Emerson

"WHAT HAPPENED BACK there?" Emerson asked as the four teens drove out of Astoria and headed toward Portland. "I mean what really happened?"

"We linked our minds together and sent Schwartz packing!" Keira said. "We didn't know we could project our head voice like that." She sat in the back seat with Trayce and handed Jaime his computer so he could use the text to speech engine. Jaime launched the app, but didn't type anything.

"Who were those other people?" Emerson continued.

"Angus is a detective," Keira said. "The two strippers are his sidekicks. The other woman is Dr. Rose. In addition to being a psychiatrist, she's my pseudo-aunt. Not really related, but I've called her 'Aunt Rose' ever since I started talking."

"And they just happened to show up? How convenient," Emerson said. She wasn't sure just how much of everything that just happened she was buying. She couldn't hear anyone's thoughts now. She was trying to guard her own thoughts so no one else could read them.

Jaime reached across the console to touch her hand on the steering wheel.

«Just like you happened to be with us,» Jaime said to Emerson. «They all had a purpose.»

«Fuck! Stop talking in my head! And stop mindreading me!»

Jaime withdrew his hand and things went silent for Emerson again. She couldn't tell if he was still reading her mind. She focused on the road instead of the conversation in the car. It was just Keira talking to Trayce, so Emerson decided to work on her color scheme software design. If she could.

"Dr. Schwartz theorized about needing a number of people tied together in order to control other people's minds. I guess, in a way, we just proved him right. We linked minds and gave him a command to retire and quit pursuing head talkers. It took all four of us linked together, though," Keira said.

"I still can't believe it," Trayce said. "I'm hearing a complete muddle of you three in my head. I need to go back to a doctor. My mother has started hearing voices in her head and her doctor gave her some pills that help her. I don't want to be schizophrenic. When I was there, at the inn, everything was quiet and peaceful."

"Schwartz was drugging you and hypnotizing you. Have you forgotten that?" Keira asked.

"I can't think straight," Trayce said. Emerson was feeling some empathy for the girl.

Jaime reached into his computer bag and pulled out a folded-up sheet of aluminum foil which he handed to Keira.

«Wrap it around Trayce's head. She'll get a little relief,» he said to Keira.

Keira told Trayce what she was going to do and then proceeded to wrap the top of Trayce's head in the foil, crimping it down so it would stay in place, then smoothing it out against her scalp.

"You've got to be kidding me!" Emerson laughed at the image in her rear-view mirror. "An honest-to-God tinfoil hat?"

"Jaime has a closet lined with aluminum foil," Keira explained. "It's the same principle that Schwartz used in the walls of the inn to block microwave, RF, and brainwave transmission. This isn't as effective as that, but it should help to lower the volume for Trayce."

Trayce snorted.

"Now I really feel like a lunatic."

"Imagine you're getting a perm. Is that better?"

"Kinda. I still hear voices, but not as loud."

Keira reached over to take Trayce's hand and helped to guide her into a quiet space, blocking out the voices she heard. Keira was surprised to find that the only voices she seemed to be receiving were hers and Jaime's. Emerson was not actually in Trayce's head.

"Are we going to have sex now?" Trayce asked sleepily.

"I don't think we're quite ready for that, do you?" Keira responded.

"But you already had sex with Jaime. Without me."

"We wished you were with us. And then, all of a sudden you were. Except you were crying for help. So, we came to find you."

"Thank you, I think," Trayce said, squeezing Keira's hand. She was flooded with calm and reassurance. "I'm going to sleep for a while now. I just want to go home to Mommy."

"We're on our way, love," Keira said.

«Are you okay, love?» Keira whispered in her mind to Jaime. «You're awful quiet.»

«I used my out-loud voice,» Jaime whispered back. «I'm afraid someone will die.»

«Oh, honey. There isn't a correlation between those two things. You don't cause people to die with your out-loud voice.»

«I know that in my head. But my inside voice was so loud people obeyed me. I could have killed Schwartz. Or made him kill himself.»

«It was all of us together. We don't know how powerful you actually are,» Keira said. «We need to run a lot of experiments.»

«No!» Jaime shouted. Trayce jumped in her sleep and Keira quickly comforted her back to sleep.

«Honey? What's wrong.»

«I don't want to know what we can do. You and I are strong enough to see the entire world in our heads,» Jaime said. «What will happen if we make love to Trayce? I mean really. Physically as well as mentally. She has no discipline and I had to fight off the commands Schwartz put in her. It could blow up any time.»

«Is she that strong?» Keira asked.

«No. She's that weak. She truly is a satellite. She gets drawn into people's orbit for a while and then wanders off. We are apparently the strongest gravitational pull she's encountered. Think about it. The characters she says she's written about are all people we connected her to. Angus and the strippers. The woman and her daughter in the theatre. The depressed woman who felt she was ugly and unloved, even though she was beautiful and her fiancé adored her. They were all people we showed her. I don't think she is actively hearing anyone else.»

«Oh no! What are we going to do?» Keira cried. Jaime sighed.

«Continue to love her and provide the channel for her. All we've done is provide characters, not stories. No matter what Schwartz said, she's a very talented author.»

They both calmed themselves and the car continued to be quiet for a while. Emerson glanced over at Jaime with a raised eyebrow, but Jaime didn't try to respond.

«What about Emerson?» Keira asked. «Is she part of our family?»

«Emerson is a catalyst. That's the only way I can think to describe her. When she was brought into our link, she was like glue that stuck us together. She has no innate head talk ability. But I don't think we could have commanded Schwartz without her.»

«Aunt Rose…»

«I didn't tell her. I don't think we should. Right now, that's something that only you and I know. If Emerson leaves us, we'll no longer have the command voice,» Jaime said. «At least, not like we just did.»

"Um… Could you talk to me a little?" Emerson said just then. "I mean with your TTS. I think the adrenaline has left my veins and I'm having trouble focusing on the road."

"Of course," Jaime typed into the TTS. "I understand what you mean. Trayce is asleep and Keira is nodding. I feel pretty drained, too. I was thinking that the color scheme tool part of your app could be a standalone and would have a wide range of uses. Take house paint, for instance."

"You're actually thinking about my color picker?" Emerson asked.

"Yeah. I still think it's the coolest thing in our class. Imagine picking a paint color for your bedroom and having an accent and trim color suggested. Or three or four options for a scheme."

"That *would* be pretty cool. And it's a more slowly changing environment than fashion. Do you think I could actually scan an entire paint company's color palette? Then I could plot all the colors on the HVC scale and interpret the color schemes with the company's paint names or numbers," Emerson said. She glanced over at Jaime. "You really are a great computer lab partner. It's not just your sex appeal.”

“Well, you know the old Amish saying,” Jaime typed. “Kissin’ wears out. Cookin’ don’t.”

“Okay. I’ll make the stretch to apply that to what I said,” Emerson laughed. “Um… I don’t know if I’ll be able to continue with the fantasy. I mean, it all sounds so neat when I think it, but when I say it out loud, it doesn’t seem as practical.”

“I think we’re all going to be evaluating our place with each other in the next few days and weeks,” Jaime typed.

“Some of that is going on right now,” Emerson said.

She nodded toward her rearview mirror and Jaime turned to look at Keira and Trayce. They were leaned toward each other across the empty center seat. Trayce had her head on Keira’s shoulder with Keira’s head leaning against her. They each had a hand clasping the other. Both girls had beatific smiles on their faces.

Trayce and Lanie

“Mommy!” Trayce cried out when they got her home. “Mommy, hold me!”

Lanie ran to the door and wrapped her daughter in her arms. Susan stood across the room and smiled at them. Keira and Jaime stood in the doorway. Emerson had chosen to stay in the car.

“You’re back! Oh, thank God, you’re home,” Lanie said.

“I didn’t want to go, Mommy. I didn’t want to leave you,” Trayce said. Lanie looked up at Keira and Jaime.

“Thank you,” she said. “Whatever you did to find her and bring her home, thank you.”

“Mom, this is my boyfriend and girlfriend, Jaime and Keira. I know that isn’t a usual kind of situation, but I think I love both of them,” Trayce said. “We’ve got a lot of things to work out yet, but you’ll probably be seeing them around.”

“They found you and brought you home,” Lanie said. “I’ll reserve judgment on anything else.”

“We’ll leave you to talk and tell about the adventure,” Keira said. “We’ll talk later. Okay, Trayce?”

"Yeah. Thank you, Keira and Jaime." She let go of her mother long enough to softly kiss each of them. All three sighed. "You know how to reach me."

Jaime and Keira left to rejoin Emerson.

"Yes, we know who it was and where he is," Trayce told her mother at dinner. Susan had gone home once the family was reunited.

"We should call the police," Lanie said. "Though I don't have much faith in them at the moment."

"I don't think it's necessary," Trayce said. "He's really pretty pathetic. Jaime and Keira had a heart-to-heart talk with him and showed him the error of his ways. I don't think he'll ever try anything like that again."

"Were you… sexually abused?" Lanie asked.

"No. If I had been, I wouldn't have left before he was arrested. He wanted to run hypnotism experiments on me. Somehow, he decided I was an easy candidate if he kept me in isolation for a week. Not only was he not a very good kidnapper, he wasn't a very good hypnotist either."

"Are you… still suffering from hearing voices?" Lanie asked. "I mean, that's what the note said."

"I didn't write a note," Trayce said. "That was part of the ruse he was using to keep the police from looking for me."

"Well, that part worked."

"I do still have some imaginary friends, you know," Trayce giggled. "They show up in my stories. That's all. I've got a bunch of story ideas I wrote down while I was there. I think second semester creative writing is going to be fun."

Jaime and Keira and Trayce

«Are you there, love?» Jaime whispered to Trayce over the distance.

David and Olivia had decided to stay another night at her apartment after checking in with the kids. Jaime and Keira had reported a 'fun' time in Astoria. They were all too happy to have another night of the house to themselves, and after checking in with Keira's parents had gone to Jaime's house. After David and Olivia left, the couple went to bed, and just slept.

When they woke up and had scrounged dinner from leftovers in the fridge, they watched a movie and then decided they'd waited long enough. This time when they went to bed, they were naked and kissing with intent.

«I'm here. Mmm. Kiss me again?» Trayce murmured.

«We always have kisses for you,» Keira said. «Are you doing okay?»

«Yeah… I think so. It's funny, I didn't really hear any voices in my head until you called. It was almost as peaceful as the inn, but there's out-loud noise. He blocked ears as effectively as thoughts at the inn,» Trayce said.

«You might not be able to hear anyone else inside for a while,» Jaime said. «Maybe that's a good thing for you. I can see you're still struggling to accept us.»

«Yeah, a little. Now that I've seen you and touched you, you seem more real to me. But it's still hard.»

«Keira and I… We're in bed,» Jaime said.

«Yes. I can feel it. I can feel your skin touching mine… or hers, I guess. Are we going to make love?»

«Do you want to?» Keira asked. «Jaime and I didn't want to make love in our heads until we were ready to do it physically, too. I guess we pushed the limits of that.»

«I think I pushed your limits,» Trayce laughed. «Can I ride along? Is that too much like just being a voyeur?»

«No, it isn't,» Jaime said. «We really feel like you… belong with us when we're making love. But just like we didn't rush together, we don't want to rush you, either.»

«I think I might be a little oversexed,» Trayce giggled. «I didn't know there were other real people doing all the things I was doing in my head. I just found how great it was and wanted more all the time. Still do.»

Jaime and Keira kissed, inviting Trayce to join them. They didn't hold back from that point on. They folded Trayce into their caresses and oral stimulation. When Jaime went down on Keira, Trayce burst out.

«Yes! I can do this! I love it! Keira, I will never hesitate to go down on you. I didn't know if I could, but I love your taste, your texture, and the way you smell. Thank you, Jaime, for letting me experience this!»

«It will be even better when you are on the receiving end,» Keira gasped. «Oh, lovers! Just a little more.»

Trayce was near an orgasm, but chose to float along with Jaime's joy in having given their girlfriend such pleasure.

How could I ever have thought they were anything but real? Trayce thought.

«It's hard to imagine we have such a deep connection that other people don't know or understand,» Jaime said. «Oh, yes. I still can't believe you do this to me!» He settled back as Keira sucked on him. Trayce imagined more kisses with Jaime as they both mounted to his climax.

«Oh! Why am I not in bed with you? Now especially! He's going to do it, Keira! He's going to put his penis in our vagina. It feels so good!»

The excitement of the three experiencing everything from each other as well as their own arousal kept them all ready for another round. Having just come, Jaime was less likely to speed ahead, but sliding into Keira gave him a weird double image as he saw both Keira and Trayce in his vision. He was in both, though physically he could only be in Keira.

«You rub me in all the right ways,» Keira said. «Trayce! You're rubbing our clit while Jaime is in us. Oh, God! I love the way you make us feel.»

«Oh, yes! Don't stop. I'm coming. I'm coming,» Trayce said. Keira peaked with her, but Jaime didn't stop. «Yes! More!»

«More!» Keira joined. It was only a minute before they were pulsing together in orgasm, this time bringing Jaime along with them. They could feel the power of his spurts in Keira's vagina.

Jaime stayed in Keira as long as he could, but ultimately, he softened and slid out, still holding and kissing his lovers. His thoughts expanded, listening deep in both Keira and Trayce. Worlds of possibilities opened before him as the three silently committed themselves to each other.

«Order Dr. Rose and Detective Angus away like you did Dr. Schwartz,» came a command from deep inside Trayce. Jaime and Keira had nearly raised their hands together when Jaime exerted control over the subliminal command.

«Schwartz doesn't have that power over you any longer,» Jaime said to Trayce. «Let him go and all the suggestions he made to you. You are free of him now.»

«Did… Did I do something?» Trayce asked. «We were all together and then I was separate. Don't leave me!»

«We're not leaving you, lover,» Keira said. «We knew Schwartz left some nasty triggers in you. It's not you. Jaime just had to stop one.»

«He's still controlling me?» Trayce cried. «Will I never be free? There's this part of me, deep inside that is joyful over the… power we have. Are we ever going to use it?»

«Not if we can help it, sweetheart. I never want to need that kind of power again. Don't try to force our will on anyone,» Jaime said gently.

«I'm not safe, am I?» Trayce said. «I mean you're not safe with me. I can't risk hurting you because of what he did to me.»

«We can take care of that,» Keira said. «You won't hurt us. You love us as much as we love you.»

Trayce was not fully mollified, no matter how much Keira and Jaime reassured her.

«I don't think I should sleep with you tonight,» Trayce said. «I mean, while we're connected. I'm afraid I'll transfer something while we're dreaming. I need to withdraw. I can't sleep like this.»

«You don't need to worry, Trayce,» Jaime reassured her.

«Hate to… you know… come and go, but goodnight. We'll talk more this weekend. Can we get together IRL? Good. Let me know.»

Trayce faded out of their connection.

"THAT KIND OF hurt," Keira said aloud.

«She's been abused by that quack and left with post-hypnotic suggestions,» Jaime said. «We just need to be patient and dismantle them when we find them.»

«What was that one?» Keira asked.

«One of Schwartz's most fundamental. He couldn't predict that Dr. Rose and Detective Angus would be a threat. So he left a suggestion that she should disable his enemies.»

«That would include us.»

«I don't think she or he realized that. In fact, it was how I fought the suggestion. She weakened the link by attacking his enemies,» Jaime said.

«Are we unsafe?» Keira asked. Jaime pondered the question, taking Keira with him in his analysis of the problem.

«I don't think so. When it comes down to it, Trayce has very little power. She doesn't hear everyone around her,» Jaime said. «Even in Angus's room, she was listening to you and me. We heard Angus and Dr. Rose, so she heard them. When she's in a creative mode, she hears snippets from around her that fit in with what she wants to write. But lately, she's been getting all those snippets from observations we've made. The mother and her daughter in the theater. Angus, Kate, and Thursday. The depressed woman at the play. They are all people we observed and she got through us. She is really a satellite.»

«You mentioned that before. We should be careful about how much of Emerson we expose to her.»

«Emerson would not be happy to be featured in a story. But at least, Trayce knows who that is and I don't think she'd write a story about her without telling her.»

«What are we going to do about Emerson?» Keira sighed.

«That's a million-dollar question.»

36
CONVERSATIONS

Jaime and Keira and Trayce

TRAYCE PARKED HER car and walked to where Jaime and Keira were waiting for her in the park. The three didn't say anything, though surface thoughts were clearly readable. All were excited to be physically together, but were also cautious. They met with cheek-kisses.

"Hey, Jaime and Keira. Fancy meeting you here. I feel like I know this place already."

"Yeah. We walk here frequently. Even when it's freezing cold like today," Keira said. "How are you doing?"

"Okay, I guess. Mom really didn't want me to leave the house unaccompanied today. We had a bit of an argument. I got a new phone this morning, so I can give you my number and we can text, you know," Trayce said. She looked at Jaime.

«Hi, Trayce. I'm really glad to see you,» he said.

"Why did you do that? It makes me uncomfortable. Just talk to me."

«I don't talk out loud. Sorry.»

"I heard you yesterday. I know you have a voice."

«You're one of only four people who have ever heard it. One of them is dead.»

"Shit! I don't know if I can do this head talk thing. Seriously. I mean it was sort of okay when we were miles apart, but we're standing right in front of each other," Trayce said, shifting from foot to foot.

"Trayce, honey, head talk is part of who Jaime and I are. I can use my out-loud voice because I had it before I had my head voice. Jaime didn't. Even as I'm talking to you, I'm talking in your head as well as your ears. Otherwise, you'd know if I wasn't saying what I meant. Jaime forced his out-loud voice yesterday because we needed to rescue you. You were the only reason," Keira said.

"I'll try to understand that, but I really can't just do head talk right now. I suppose you can read everything I'm thinking, but I don't want to talk that way," Trayce said.

Jaime and Keira began putting up filters so they couldn't read Trayce's thoughts nor talk to her with their heads.

«Do you really think this is the right thing to do?» Keira asked.

«We have to respect what she wants,» Jaime said. «I'll sign to you if I need to talk.»

"Wait! Where did you go?" Trayce asked, alarmed.

"I've withdrawn so I'm not reading your thoughts or sending you mine," Jaime signed. Keira interpreted.

"I've done the same thing," Keira said. "Honey, we don't want to do something that makes you uncomfortable. We've learned to limit our communication to just each other. It's a bit of a strain at the moment because we didn't used to know anyone else who could hear us, but we're getting better at it."

"It's like… You've always been there, haven't you?"

"We don't know exactly when it started, but circumstantial evidence suggests it was significantly before you joined us in kissing," Keira said.

"What kind of evidence?"

"Um… People we met started showing up in your stories before we knew you were there," Keira said. "Like Angus, Kate, and Thursday. We met them just over there. But that was while we were still figuring out if we could hold hands."

"My characters! I haven't been writing my stories at all, have I?" Trayce appeared truly distressed.

"I don't think that's true. It seems the only thing you've picked up from us is the general scenario. The old detective and two stripper sidekicks. A woman trying to tell her daughter her father was dead. A depressed woman who didn't look like it to the outside world. Once you had those characters, you brought them to life in amazing stories," Keira said.

"You've read them?"

"When we make love, we sink really far into each other. We saw them in you," Keira explained.

"I don't know if I'm relieved or terrified," Trayce said. "Jaime, I'm sorry I kicked you out of my head—or whatever happened. I really do like you. I even told my mother I loved you—both. Maybe we can do a little trial at a time when we're together. Would that be okay?"

"We'll take it at whatever pace you want," Jaime signed and Keira interpreted.

"I should learn sign language, shouldn't I?"

"It's easier when Jaime is telling you inside what the signs mean. He's been signing since kindergarten."

"Yeah. Maybe. Um… I'm so mixed up at the moment," Trayce said. "Like I want to just drop all my barriers and preconceived notions and be one with you both. But I'm scared that Dr. Schwartz left some suggestions buried in me that will hurt you. I'd die if I hurt either one of you. And as sexual as we've been in our heads—and I really loved it—I've never even had a real kiss. I mean, not counting the quick one we each had at the door yesterday or on the cheek. And I'm panicked to think I'm actually going to get naked with you and really have sex. It seems like it will be so different that I should go slow on that."

"Exactly what Keira and I were determined to do," Jaime signed. "At each stage, something new and a little frightening opened up for us. The first time we held hands was for only a minute and we almost passed out from it. It was even more dramatic the first time we kissed. It was like the world just exploded."

"But you do it all the time now. Does it get less?" Trayce asked.

"We've learned to control it more," Keira said. "We call it filtering so we can enjoy touching each other without opening ourselves to every input within a mile."

"We could… um… if you're willing… we could try a kiss. Can you protect me from being overwhelmed?"

Jaime and Keira communicated with each other before Jaime responded to her question.

"We think so. Trayce, we love you." He invented a name sign for her, pretending to hold a pencil and write. "We'll try to hold back how much we open up, but it could still affect you more."

"Or less," Keira said. "We don't have much experience."

"You've both kissed… her… Emerson," Trayce said.

"We've been exploring and experimenting like any two people," Keira clarified. "It was easy to do. But Emerson is not a head talker. She can only hear us if we are in skin-to-skin contact."

"Okay. I guess. I don't want to talk about her right now. I just… I really want to kiss you. You aren't pushing me to do that, are you?"

"Absolutely not!" Jaime signed.

"Come here, precious," Keira said holding out an arm to embrace Trayce. Trayce stepped forward and put an arm around Keira and one around Jaime. "Now, tilt your head a little to the right. It's so we don't break any noses when we come together."

"Both? Both at the same time?"

"We can't stand to be first or second to kiss you," Keira laughed. "This is remarkably easy once you touch."

"Yeah," Trayce sighed as she closed her eyes, tilted her head, and moved forward.

The touch of lips was tentative at first, but those nerve endings sparked an opening of the senses to each other. Trayce felt the flood of warmth and love that came from her lovers and they could feel her joy in their touch. When their tongues came into play, the senses opened further. Jaime and Keira struggled to keep some filters in place, but Trayce was completely unfiltered and both gave and received anything available. They began to hear voices of others in the park: children, dog walkers, and even a power walker who was caught up in the music he was listening to as he strode down the path.

Jaime pulled back before they let the kiss get too overwhelming.

«Wow!» Trayce thought to them. «I really love you both. Thank you for protecting me. I know now that I'll get better if you are patient.»

«We love you,» Jaime said, then withdrew from her mind.

"Maybe it would be better if we don't… um… make love for a while," Trayce said. "I mean with me. I wouldn't stop you two from loving each other. I just mean I should start to focus on the actual physical part of our relationship instead of staying in the virtual world. You can still text me or call, though."

"We will, hon. And we probably won't be making love for a little while either," Keira said. Jaime made a sour face but nodded. "It's not like we have our own place where we can spend the night together. If we're lucky, David will spend the night with Olivia again next weekend. Believe me, it's not because we wouldn't be headed for bed if we could."

"I wondered," Trayce laughed. "I just know so little about how life really works."

"Welcome to our world," Jaime signed.

"Well, I should go now or Mom will be panicked. She just sent me a text asking when I was coming home. Um… I'll talk to you later, okay?"

"We'll see you soon," Keira said. They gave each other an air kiss and Trayce went back to her car and left.

«Are you okay?» Jaime asked Keira when Trayce was gone.

«Yeah. It's going to be a long path, but I'm okay with it. You won't withdraw from me, will you?»

«Absolutely not!» Jaime affirmed. «You are the love of my life, Keira. I think Trayce could be the other love of my life, but we all need to grow into that. And it will be difficult, but not impossible.»

«We should have a regular date next weekend if she's willing. One where we go officially pick her up and promise to get her home at an agreed-upon time. Then go out and practice opening up a little at a time while we do something teens do all the time. Like something… I don't know.»

«We'll figure something out. I love you, Keira. I'm getting cold. Can we go to your house and get warm before I go home?»

«Silly. Of course we can. I'll ask Mom if I can borrow her car to take my lover home.»

«And then somewhere along the line, we'll need to figure out how to tell our parents about Trayce,» Jaime said.

«That should be a fun conversation!»

The two walked back to Keira's house and sat at the kitchen table while they drank cocoa and were polite to her parents.

Keira and Rose

"You've always been able to read my mind, haven't you," Keira said when she sat at Rose's kitchen table Sunday evening. Rose had made chocolate sundaes instead of their usual cup of tea.

"I have never invaded your privacy," Rose said. "I simply understood what you were going through and tried to help you."

"Oh, you did! Really! Even if you'd been reading my deepest inner thoughts, I'd have still appreciated what you did to help me. I guess this weekend just made me reevaluate everything I've always believed and experienced."

Keira became absorbed in her sundae for a minute. Rose simply waited for her.

"Like now. You say something innocuous and then just wait for me to talk out what's on my mind," Keira laughed. "Well, I came here to talk, so that's okay. There isn't really anyone else I can talk to. It's just that there are things that hurt. Like Trayce."

"Is she okay?"

"Yeah. I think so. And I think we're going to eventually become the three-some we all thought we were before she believed we were real. That's really exciting. I mean, Jaime and I have only been lovers since Wednesday night. And there was no place we could go on Saturday and Sunday, so we have the typical problems high school lovers have. And we're both equally excited about having Trayce with us. But it's going to take a long time. Which is strange because Jaime and I would have taken longer if it wasn't for Trayce pushing us forward. Now we're trying to be sure we don't push *her* too hard or too fast."

"That seems wise. You need more time to truly know each other as well."

"Yeah. We think we'll invite Trayce on, like, a normal date so we can get to know each other better. In a way, we're all kind of messed up. Trayce lost her father in a drunk driver accident and her mother is struggling to stay sober so she can recover their relationship. That was a pretty terrible time for Trayce. Jaime lost his mother when he was not quite five. He's never spoken aloud, having the ability to hear people's inside voice since he was born. He learned sign language in kindergarten and he gets along just fine in school. He can hear, and he invented a text to speech application so he can participate in class. It's cool."

Keira and Rose both finished their sundaes and Keira picked up the bowls to rinse and put in the dishwasher. She sat back down at the table.

"And you?" Rose prompted.

"Yeah. I'm, like, the normal one. Isn't that a laugh?" Keira said, shaking her head. "I had you to help me understand what was going on and to help me limit my exposure. But in eighth grade, some boys planned to rape me."

"You've never mentioned that before," Rose said, concerned.

"No. I got warned by the first head talker I ever met that I knew about. He was struggling to come to grips with it and thought I could help. He heard the boys making their plan and warned me. I went home by a different route and he walked the direction I normally took. The boys beat him up. Badly. I told Jaime he moved away. He's in a nursing home. I don't know if he can still hear people's thoughts or not. He is just a little more than a vegetable."

"Oh, dear. How terrible. How did you find out?" Rose asked.

"I went to visit him once. I talked to him, but I didn't hear anything in response. I've been so afraid something terrible would happen if I met another head talker. Then I met Jaime and I couldn't help but fall in love with him."

Tears were running down Keira's cheeks.

"I'm so afraid something bad will happen to him or to Trayce like what happened this weekend. I'd die. I'd really die."

"Honey, fear is usually something we make up in our minds. What we are afraid of is something we *imagine* might happen."

"How do I not be afraid?"

"We don't. We learn to live with the knowledge that the fear is not real. We live past the fear and don't let it interfere with what is important. Like love. You know that in your heart."

"Yes. I've even told Jaime his fear is not of something real. It's hard to convince myself."

"Maybe you should suggest Jaime pay me a visit, too," Rose said. "In the office."

"I'm sure he would. I think he would. I'll talk to him."

"In the meantime, let's give you a few exercises that will help you get through the scary times."

Jaime and Emerson

"CAN WE KEEP all our conversations out-loud?" Emerson asked when Jaime arrived in the computer lab.

Jaime had been a little worried about his friend and had not spoken to her since Friday's adventures. The first day back in school after the winter holidays was filled with surprises. Jaime was eager for the day to end so he could meet with Keira. He handed Emerson her earbud and launched his TTS app.

"Is this good?" he typed.

"Great. Just, you know, stay out of my head for now, okay?"

"Of course. How are you doing?"

"Not really ready to talk about it, okay? Let's just focus on the progress we made with our apps over the break. I love the voice manipulation module. Do you think you could release it without your TTS adaptation? Like as a plug-in for other apps?"

"That makes a lot of sense. I really developed it separately. You know even this one with my voice is really a plug-in to an established program. I like the idea."

They progressed through class with no further questions regarding the weekend. Jaime noted that Emerson had returned to her former look of baggy clothes and no makeup. She'd also abandoned her contacts and wore black-rimmed glasses, enhancing her studious nerd look. Jaime found he was more comfortable with this look on her than with the Paris look.

Jaime and Keira

«HOW WAS SHE?»

«Okay. Not ready to talk about it. Asked me not to look inside,» Jaime said.

«We're getting pretty good at that. Did you get a text from Trayce this morning?»

«Yeah. Sounded fine, but also not ready to talk.»

«Aunt Rose suggested you might want to come in to talk to her. I met with her last night and she was helpful.»

«I might do that, but I can't right away. I got asked to sort of be in the school play,» Jaime said.

«What? Are you using the TTS?»

«No. The request came through my ASL class. Three of us were asked to be sign language interpreters. The play is *Blithe Spirit*. It has seven characters and only one is a man. The two girls who will sign will play all six other roles,» Jaime said.

«Sounds like fun! When does it start?» Keira asked.

«Now. Or in fifteen minutes. We were all asked to be at auditions this afternoon so the cast could get used to working with interpreters.»

«So, no sneaking off to make out after school?»

«Afraid not.»

«Maybe I should audition.»

«Sure. Come ahead.»

«I'm kidding. It just seemed like the only way I'll see you for the next… How long will you be working on it?» Keira asked.

«Six weeks. It will be on Valentine's weekend.»

«Oh,» Keira sounded disappointed. «I guess we won't be having a hot date with our lover on Valentine's day then.»

«Crap! I'll tell them I can't do it.»

«No! You committed to it and we don't have a commitment for a Valentine's Day date. Maybe Trayce and I will come and watch you in the show. Quick kiss and I'll see you tomorrow.»

They had a quick kiss and Keira headed home while Jaime went to auditions in the auditorium.

37
LIFE GOES ON

Jaime, Miss Thompson, and the Cast

"JAIME, SARAH, AND Lynn will be sign language interpreters for our production of Blithe Spirit," Miss Thompson said. The bright and energetic young director was only a year out of college and was directing her first student production. "Since I expect them to be an integral part of the production, I've asked them to audition with you. So, when you are called to read, one of the interpreters will be called upon to sign for you."

"Wild," Tony Lamonte said. "So, are they deaf?"

"No," Miss Thompson said. "They have to be able to hear you in order to interpret. However, they won't be saying anything. Right?" she asked the three interpreters. As one they raised their right hands and nodded a fist, then looked at each other and laughed silently.

Sarah and Lynn were in the advanced ASL class with Jaime, so they knew he never said anything and they agreed they'd simply adopt the same persona in the theatre.

"Let's get started," Miss Thompson said. "Grab a script and turn to page one. Liselle, read Edith. Maura, read Ruth, and Tony read Charles. Interpreters, there is a music stand for each of you with a script on it, but I hope that after a read-through, you'll be able to focus more on the actors and interpret from them instead of the book. Ready? Doria," she said turning to her student assistant, "Read the stage directions for them. And go."

"The scene is the living room of the Condomines' house in Kent," Doris began. The actors started pacing out the scene on stage. The interpreters quickly agreed on which actor each was interpreting and the audition was underway.

It was a little confusing at first. One of the actors stumbled a lot and Sarah finished interpreting her lines significantly ahead of her actually getting them out. Miss Thompson had them run the scene again. It smoothed out significantly. The third time, the interpreters left their music stands and followed the actors around, signing over their shoulders. The actors didn't notice since they were still focused on the book.

Miss Thompson called three more actors to read the lines. It soon became obvious that Jaime, Sarah, and Lynn would know and possibly memorize the entire play before the production night. But they might also have more fun than any of the other actors, no matter who was chosen for which part.

«I can't believe how much fun being in this show will be,» Jaime said when he was home making dinner and could connect with Keira. «When I've seen sign language interpreters at theatrical performances, they have always been off to one side where all the deaf people were seated. They follow the script and just sign for that small section of the audience. Miss Thompson plans to have us actually on the stage and following the actors around. The girls will have a time of it. There's only one guy in the show. Each girl will need to sign for three characters, and not always the same ones.»

«It sounds complicated,» Keira said. «Will I ever see you?»

«Yes. Rehearsals are scheduled Monday through Thursday right after school until the last week when we go every day, including the weekends for dress rehearsal and technical rehearsals. That's the first time anyone will actually see the set,» Jaime said.

He finished chopping a pepper and tossed it in the skillet with the onion. He was making a basic stir fry and was timing it with David's expected arrival at home.

«I talked to Trayce after school,» Keira said. «On the phone. We had a little mental hug at the end, but she's still pretty confused. She's going to see Aunt Rose Thursday. If that goes well, she said she'd be interested in a date this weekend. We still haven't decided what, though.»

«There must be something we could do together. A gallery or museum?

There's a rock climbing gym. There's even a place where we could do axe throwing,» Jaime said.

«Wow! Rock climbing and axe throwing are a lot more active than we have been on *our* dates.»

«I was thinking we should do something that required us to move instead of all sitting in one place holding hands and trying to communicate slowly or not at all.»

«True that. Bowling. Basketball game. Trail Blazers are playing basketball this weekend,» Keira said.

«Isn't there a basketball game at school Friday?» Jaime asked.

«I doubt she'd want to go to one of our school's games, but I'll see who we're playing.»

«Dad's home. I need to start stirring.»

«Talk to you later, love.»

Trayce and Rose

"You had quite an ordeal, Trayce. How are you doing?" Rose asked when the teen visited her Thursday evening.

"Yeah. Well, I'm pulling things together a little. It's slow going. I'm constantly looking over my shoulder, you know. Just in case Dr. Schwartz and his hoods come for me again."

"I can understand how you'd feel that way. Are you doing anything extra to protect yourself?" Rose asked.

"Yeah. I'm staying in groups when I'm out, like leaving school and all. I look around a lot. Classes at the community college start next week. The bus stops right in front of my class building, so I won't have far to run to get inside. I'm thinking of taking a self-defense class."

"Okay. Those are all good measures. It's important, though, not to let the fear rule you. You need as normal a life as possible. Schwartz wants you afraid. As firmly as he was put down last week, I doubt he'll make another play. And Angus is keeping an eye on him."

"That's good to know. I… um… think I'll go out with Jaime and Keira tomorrow night. It's just to a school basketball game and then burgers, but... I feel safe when I'm with them."

"You had quite an experience."

"I still don't understand it. I can't hear anyone else in my head. Like I can't hear you and you're right in front of me."

"Don't count that as a standard. I've learned over many years to block being read. Is that what you want?"

"Um... No. I don't think so. I mean, linking up with Jaime and Keira is really... oh, wow! It's so overwhelming, though, that I'm trying to go slow. And I'm still afraid Dr. Schwartz left post-hypnotic suggestions in my head that will hurt them. Can you, like, remove them?" Trayce asked.

"I can help *you* remove them, if there are any. The combination of drugs and hypnotism he used leaves you in a vulnerable state. But now that you are out from under the direct influence, you have the power to fight those impulses. It is when you take control and deny their power that you will truly be free. It's not something I can do for you."

"Yeah. I think when the three of us are together, I can do that—or Jaime can. He pulls me out of the trance real quick. I guess what I'm thinking about now is when we become intimate. I mean... just when we kissed, it felt like the whole world opened up to us. I could see and feel everything they could. It was so intense."

"And that's when you feel most vulnerable?"

"Yes. But also most powerful. With Jaime and Keira guiding me, I know I can fight off his suggestions unless we get so involved in each other that at least one of us isn't being watchful. And it's really easy to get that involved in each other. There's just so much to look at and share."

"You're excited about it."

"I guess I am," Trayce laughed. "I'm just... Even though the three of us have been linking together for a couple of months, Friday was the first time I'd ever physically been in the same room with them. And, like, they're lovers who have been together all this time and I feel like I need to catch up with them, but I'm not sure I want to go that fast. That's why we're going on a normal high school date this weekend. So, I can get to know them in real time before I just crawl into bed with them."

"I'm glad you're taking it slow," Rose said. "And I know Jaime and Keira will respect that. I think they reached that point sooner than they wanted to. I don't think any of you will feel pressured to go more quickly."

"Yeah. I think… That's one of the reasons I think I'm in love with them. They always respect me and don't try to rush me. Which makes me want to hurry up and get there, you know?"

"A real conundrum," Rose agreed. "How about if we meet again next week and you can tell me about how your date went and how your class at the college progresses?"

"Okay. Thank you."

Jaime and Keira and Emerson

JAIME AND KEIRA were at their usual table for lunch on Friday when Emerson caught up with them.

"Hey, guys. Can I join you?"

"Hey, Em. Of course you can. You're always welcome," Keira said. "How's your week going? It seems like forever since we got to talk."

"Oh, Jaime and I meet every day in class to work on our projects," Emerson laughed. "But we don't discuss anything… important."

"Is there something you'd like to discuss now?" Jaime signed. Keira started to translate, but Emerson waved her off.

"I got it," she said.

Jaime reached in his bag for the ear bud and his computer, but she waved that off as well.

She bowed her head, staring at the unidentified mass on her plate as though she could turn it into a steak and potatoes just by the fierceness of her gaze. Then she darted out and caught Jaime's and Keira's hands in hers. «Tell me it's real—this talking in people's heads,» she thought to them.

«It's real,» Jaime answered. A second later, Keira spoke the out-loud words. Emerson drew her hands back and heaved a few heavy breaths.

"I knew it was. I think I knew back when we kissed… um… at my house. That was pretty powerful."

"We've been on the receiving end of that surprise," Keira laughed.

"Yeah. But you already knew the head talk part of it. Maybe not how deep it could go yet, but you could talk to each other. Unless I'm touching you, I'm as head deaf as a brick. I've even tried touching some other people to see if I could connect with them, but there was nothing." She pushed the food on her plate around and then pushed the plate aside.

"What's got you bothered, Em?" Keira asked.

"How much does Trayce know about me?" Emerson blurted out.

"Oh, wow! That's hard to say," Keira said. "Um… She knows we're attracted to you because she caught us fantasizing about you one night. She got really mad and said she wasn't going to let her characters run away with the story. Obviously, that was when she thought we were just characters in her head. I think she suspects that you are also attracted to us."

"Yeah. I'm still trying to deal with that. It's obvious I don't stand a chance with you when Trayce is around and I don't think a foursome is a workable *ménage*. But does she think… know I was part of a *ménage à trois?* I don't know why, but somehow it matters to me," Emerson said.

Keira waited for Jaime to speak to her and then summarized for Emerson.

"We don't think so. These things are a little hard to find out without asking a direct question, which would then give away the answer," she said. "We… Trayce isn't quite the same as Jaime and me. As far as we can tell, we're the only ones she actually hears. When she's connected to us, she can hear what we hear, but mostly that's just surface things. She picks up details about characters that are defining characteristics, like that Angus is a detective and Kate and Thursday are strippers. Beyond that, she makes up her stories. We've already asked her not to write any stories about you."

"I guess that's a relief. But if she only hears you, then she's more like me, right?" Emerson asked.

"It doesn't require a touch to connect with Trayce. She is actually capable of listening, but she's filtered out almost everything else. We refer to her as a satellite because she seems to be caught in our gravitational field, or something like that," Keira explained.

"I see. Have you seen her since the rescue?"

"Last Saturday she came to walk in the park with us for a while, but her mom is kind of paranoid about her being out yet, so it wasn't long. We've talked a few times—you know, on the phone," Keira said. Jaime mimed texting. "But we'll see her tonight. We're taking her to the ballgame. Our school is playing hers tonight."

"Oh! Well… um… maybe I'll see you all there. I go to all the girls' games and they play before the guys most of the time," Emerson said. "Anyway, thanks for answering my unending questions. See you in class, Jaime."

She dumped her mostly uneaten lunch in the garbage and left the cafeteria.

«We need to keep Trayce and Emerson on opposite sides of us if we see her tonight,» Jaime said. «It could get nasty.»

Jaime and Keira and Trayce and Emerson

THE BALLGAMES PROVED to be a good idea for a date. The environment was noisy, so no one could really tell they were talking in their heads to each other. And somewhere along the line, Trayce slipped her hand into Keira's and felt the rush of voices from the gym that Jaime and Keira could hear when they held hands.

Washington was ahead of Adams nearing the end of the girls' game, when Emerson spotted them and came up to sit beside Jaime.

«Did you tell her to do that?» Keira whispered without alerting Trayce.

«No. Just worked out that way. Thankfully,» Jaime said.

"Hi, guys! Hi, Trayce. How are you doing?" Emerson asked.

"Um… Pretty good, I guess. I'm just on a date with my boyfriend and girlfriend." She sounded a little possessive, but Keira didn't notice any real animosity.

"Is this like all the girls' games?" Jaime signed. "It's exciting."

Emerson shook her head, then reached over to take Jaime's hand. He slipped his other hand back into Keira's. They could all feel the gestalt forming around them. Jaime exerted control and kept it low.

«Ask again?» Emerson thought.

«Is this like all the girls' games? It's exciting,» Jaime thought to her, letting the other two hear him as well.

«Yeah. Pretty much. Amy Dotson, number 15, is a friend of mine from French club. I always come to cheer her on,» Emerson thought.

«Do you cheer on the boys, too?» Trayce asked. It seemed like a fairly neutral question.

«Sometimes. Usually, I just hang around until the girls get showered and dressed, then Amy and I go get a burger. I don't really date,» Emerson said.

«Cool. I've never dated much either,» Trayce said. «We're going out for a burger after the boys' game.» *You can go away.*

There was a note of dismissal in Trayce's thoughts. Jaime quashed the thought and note of command in Trayce's inner voice. Emerson was no longer of interest and Trayce latched onto the thoughts of a player on the bench that Keira drew her attention to.

«Well, that answers that,» Emerson said, attempting to limit her thought to just Jaime. Jaime assisted by filtering Keira and Trayce.

«What were you searching for?» Jaime asked.

«Answers of course. I'll write the questions down this weekend. I'm going to see that counselor, Dr. Rose, Tuesday evening. I just need to sort out the right questions and then go hunting the answers. I'll see you Monday," Emerson said.

Her friend scored and Emerson jumped up to clap and shout. She did not rejoin hands and when the game came to an end, she bid all three of the others goodbye and left the stands.

Jaime and Keira and Trayce

The Adams boys' team got revenge on Washington for their girls' loss. The evening was a split decision. The three teens headed out for Keira's car, borrowed for the night from her mother. Trayce clutched a hand of both Jaime and Keira, asking them to scan the area for danger before they left the building.

They let her see what they could see and hear what they could hear. Then they left for a burger joint not far from the school. While they ate their food, they practiced communicating with sign language, Keira interpreting whenever necessary. Trayce was picking up the language very quickly, partly because Keira shared her knowledge with her girlfriend.

"Are you sleeping with Emerson?" Trayce asked bluntly.

"No!" both Jaime and Keira responded.

"I could see she wanted to," Trayce continued, supplementing her signs with her voice. "And she's very pretty."

"Trayce, we don't know what to do about Emerson yet. She's a very good friend and she kind of latched onto us as possible partners, you know?" Keira said.

"Like I did," Trayce declared.

"Different," Jaime signed. "She has imagined everything we might do. You've participated. You are part of us. She's… She wants to be part of us, but there's a big divide. She's head deaf."

"Unless she's holding your hand. She can hear you just fine then," Trayce persisted.

"That's a big difference. We don't know what causes that and I'm not interested in investigating. I'd like her to stay my friend," Jaime continued. Keira was interpreting as fast as Jaime was signing. Trayce was getting the message in her head at the same time.

"Well, I'm just saying, you might have to sleep with her. Just leave me out, okay?" Trayce said.

"Honey, Jaime and I are a couple. With you, we are a trio. One thing I can be sure of is that neither Jaime nor I is going to cheat on either of our partners. If we *ever* invited Emerson to be with us, it would with all of us. We don't think you're interested in that and we really don't think Emerson is. So, it won't happen," Keira said.

"Okay. It's just… I know I'm a little backward when it comes to being physically intimate and I can tell she's experienced. I don't want you to feel like I'm holding you back."

"*We* are holding us back," Jaime signed. "We are waiting for what we truly want in our lives."

"I'd, um… be willing to make love with you in my head tonight," Trayce ventured.

"And we'd be willing to have you, but it's getting late, we all need to get to our own homes, and we have a better opportunity tomorrow," Keira said.

"Tomorrow?" Trayce asked.

"We thought we could go do something fun tomorrow afternoon, like bowling," Jaime signed and mimed.

"Bowling? I've never been bowling!" Trayce said.

"Neither have we," Keira said. "Want to try?"

"Sure!"

"Afterward, we can talk over dinner at my house," Jaime said. "Keira and I learned some great games we could play that kept us learning more about each other but didn't let us go too far."

"Holy cow!"

38
DISCOVERY

Jaime and Keira and Trayce

AFTER JAIME DID the grocery shopping with David Saturday, he dropped his father at Olivia's apartment and was invited in to see where she lived.

Please like me, Olivia thought. *I'm falling in love and I don't want to stop.*

"This is a cool place, Olivia," Jaime signed. "I see why Dad likes to visit here. And Keira and I appreciate the time alone, too. You don't need to feel like you can't spend time—or the night—with Dad at our place. I'm cool with it."

Olivia crushed Jaime in a hug.

"Thank you. We won't interfere with you and Keira," she said. "It's okay for us to be here when you and Keira want to be together." *At least until we move in together.*

Jaime could clearly read that Olivia had another five months on her lease, so the idea of her living with them wasn't a big deal. He left his father with Olivia, went home to put away the groceries, and headed out for his date with Keira and Trayce.

"I NEVER EVEN considered bowling!" Trayce said. "It's kind of fun!"

"Neither of us have ever been bowling," Keira answered. "It really messes up your manicure, though, doesn't it?"

"Well, my nails are kind of short from chewing on them," Trayce sighed. "Maybe we could do each other's nails after we're done here."

«That would be cool,» Jaime said to the two girls. «Maybe you could do mine, too!»

«That sounds like the kind of thing two girls would do with their boyfriend,» Trayce shot back. «Maybe we could do your makeup and dress you up, too!»

«Let's… like… not take it too far. Okay?» Jaime said to the image of himself in lipstick and a dress that was floating in Trayce's mind. Keira just started laughing.

"We could get into a lot of trouble together, Trayce," she said. "I always knew you were a bad influence."

"Not too bad! Look! Jaime knocked them all down."

"We have a rule," Keira said. "Anyone who makes a strike gets a kiss from each of the other two."

She quickly caught Jaime and gave him a sound kiss. Jaime turned to Trayce and they realized she had not kissed him without Keira at the same time before. He pulled her into his arms and they kissed like lovers, letting himself flow into her and receiving her images of herself and her love. He filtered the surrounding sounds in the alley so they weren't too overwhelming, but Trayce was still stunned by the ability to see a little inside everyone in the alley.

It only lasted a few moments. Keira nudged Jaime to not take too long and draw attention. A child on a nearby lane pointed at them. Jaime and Trayce pulled away from each other. Trayce instantly blushed and hid her face against Keira's shoulder.

"Hey! It's your turn," Keira said. "Just wobble over there and get your ball. Maybe you'll get a strike."

"Oh, Lord! Wobble is right. That was… awesome."

She did not get a strike, nor did either of the other two for the remainder of the game. Jaime paid for the game and they left to go to Jaime's house. On the way, they stopped at a drugstore to pick up some nail polish and an emery board.

«I didn't get to kiss you,» Trayce whispered to Keira as they cuddled in the back seat and Jaime drove.

«We can remedy that,» Keira said.

She pulled Trayce into a warm and passionate kiss, opening herself fully to her girlfriend and drawing Jaime into the experience as well. Jaime had to filter in order to keep his attention on the road.

Trayce felt much of the same openness and expansion with Keira as she had with Jaime, but she could only read her girlfriend and boyfriend.

"Were you preventing us from hearing everyone else?" Trayce asked.

"No. We're in the car. Between the metal walls and the movement, it filters out most of what would reach us from outside," Keira said.

"It was nice to be able to focus just on you and Jaime," Trayce said. "The bowling alley was a little overwhelming."

"It takes a little practice before you learn to filter out things yourself. Jaime just let it flow. Well, I did, too, but he was the only other person in range," Keira said.

"I liked it. I mean, I could really feel what I'd been imagining for so long. I could feel the love. I want to do that with Jaime, too. With just the three of us," Trayce said.

"The TV room at his house is on the lower level and is pretty sheltered from the outside. You are the only one we've ever connected with from down there."

"Good!"

AFTER JAIME'S SPECIAL meal of breaded porkchops, mashed potatoes, and lima beans, Keira led the way to the TV room. She and Trayce had done each other's nails while Jaime cooked. He insisted they not try to help him since he had the system for this meal down pat.

In the TV room, Keira and Trayce each took one of Jaime's hands and began filing his nails and pushing his cuticles back, then rubbing lotion into his hands as they rubbed it into their own. It was a sensuous experience and with the skin-to-skin contact of holding hands, they'd shared with each other mentally.

«You're so petite,» Keira said.

«Is that good?» Trayce asked, bashfully.

Jaime read that she was very uncertain about her looks and tended to discount what people said about her. Somewhere along the line she'd been called a runt and was made fun of in elementary school for being so tiny. Of course, as an adult, being petite was looked upon as a desirable trait but Trayce still carried the stigma of the elementary school taunts.

«We aren't in grade school, Trayce. We aren't making fun of you. You are a beautiful young woman and I'd bet those who made fun of you for being small truly regret it when they see you now,» he said.

«It *is* silly to carry around that grade school mindset, isn't it? I just always felt like I was too small to do any of the big kid stuff. I was terrible at sports. I'm still challenged if I enter an adults-only business or try to go to an R-rated movie. Maybe I'll always see myself as that runt.»

«It won't be because we ever mention it again. I think you are perfect!» Keira said. She leaned in and kissed Trayce on the lips. It didn't become passionate, but in that contact, Trayce could see the pure joy her partners had in having her with them. She turned to kiss Jaime in the same way and reveled in his love.

"I think some of my creativity came from being small," Trayce said aloud while Jaime got the dice game out. "When you don't have a lot of friends, you sort of make them up. It started with my dolls and stuffed animals and then I started writing down stories about them with dialog that just sort of popped into my head."

"That would explain why you didn't identify what was happening," Keira said. "You know how to play this game?"

"Yeah. When my dad was alive, we played family games. This was a favorite."

"We have one new rule," Keira went on to explain. "Five of a kind gets a kiss from the person of your choice. Who's playing the game, I mean. So, if you get five of a kind, you can choose whether you want to kiss Jaime or me."

"But I want to kiss you both!"

"Have to roll another five of a kind," Keira laughed.

«Don't forget that the same applies to Keira and me. If I roll five of a kind, I have to choose whether I kiss you or Keira.»

"Oh, but you have to kiss Keira! You're a couple. You can't choose me!"

«We are a triple. All I *have* to do is kiss *one* of my two girlfriends.»

«Okay. I'm ready.»

They began the game and were only five turns in when Trayce rolled five of a kind. She looked back and forth between Jaime and Keira, almost frantically trying to decide which to kiss. Then she threw herself at Jaime and quickly lost herself in his embrace.

«Oh, wow! Oh, God! That was ten times the way it felt when I was home and you were kissing Keira,» Trayce said. «Keira, is it that different for you, too?»

«Oh, yeah! But being here with the two of you, the experience for me was better, too. I could feel your tongues together with mine. And my breasts were…»

«Yeah,» Jaime said. «Before we get carried away, we need to agree on the other rules. I almost lost it there.»

«Rules?» Trayce asked.

«We all agreed earlier that we weren't all three going to make love tonight— at least not all physically together. I fully plan to make love to Jaime physically, but you'll be with us in our heads.»

«Yeah. I'm not really ready for the physical part of that yet, but I bet you could get me ready pretty fast.»

«While we're all together, we should abide by the same rules Keira and I used when we were trying to go slow. Hands stay above the waist and clothes stay on,» Jaime said.

«You were touching my breast! I thought I was remembering you touching Keira!»

«Part of doing this is trying to be aware of what is happening. We don't want to become so lost in the emotion that we don't know what we're doing. It will take a little practice,» Keira said.

«Practice,» Trayce agreed. «Whose turn is it?»

They continued game until Jaime rolled five of a kind. He didn't hesitate to pull Keira into a kiss, but he held Trayce's hand during it. They plunged into each other, taking Trayce with them. When they parted, all three were panting.

"Wow!" Trayce said. Jaime and Keira just nodded, still gasping for breath.

It was the second game before Keira rolled a five-of-a-kind and she pulled Trayce to her as Jaime held the two girls in his arms. The combined sensation of the two girls touching each other's breasts while they kissed was almost more than Jaime could bear.

«Do we need to roll the dice in order to have a kiss like the three of us had in the park?» Trayce asked.

«I don't think the game is needed,» Keira said. She pulled at Jaime without letting go of Trayce and soon the three were darting in to kiss the lips of both partners and then to touch their tongues. Jaime kept a lid on the input coming from the rest of the community. He could clearly hear the thoughts of people as much as a block away. He let Keira and Trayce sink deeper into the experience while maintaining vigilance over them and still enjoying all the sensations of kissing and caressing the two girls.

«Your hand is in my shirt,» Trayce sighed. «Keira said I'd love it when you slipped inside my clothes. This doesn't count as taking them off, does it?»

«Not as long as you're happy with it,» Keira said. She slipped her hand beneath Trayce's blouse to caress her breasts. Jaime had already pushed Trayce's bra above her breasts. Trayce had a hand inside each of Jaime and Keira's shirts. Keira hadn't bothered with a bra.

«Is it… Is it okay… to come like this?» Trayce asked as an orgasm swept through her body. *Too late to ask now.*

«As long as we stay above the waist with our touches,» Jaime said. The climax rolled through all three teens and then made a second circuit. When they finally came to their senses enough to break the kiss, they flopped back on the sofa and all three lost conscious thought for a minute.

«We should pull ourselves together and end our date,» Jaime said. «I don't know if I could stay within the rules if we did that again.»

«I want so much more,» Trayce said. «But I need to absorb what just happened. I was… I was you… and you… and me… all at once.»

«One of the things we have to be careful of is not to lose our individual identity when we are sexually involved like that,» Keira said.

«I've heard you say that before, but I didn't know what it meant,» Trayce said. «I didn't even care if I never came back to myself. I was in a completely different world. Love… Yes, I love you. But that doesn't even begin to describe what I felt when we were together. If you could take me home, I'd like to crawl in bed and just be with you in our heads tonight.»

«After what we've just been through, that might be all we're capable of tonight. In the morning, though, we might wake you up by licking your clit. Virtually,» Jaime laughed.

There was a shared orgasm in the morning and a walk in the park Sunday afternoon, but the three teens had their climaxes and didn't go any further over the weekend.

Emerson and Rose

MONDAY, EMERSON WAS not in school and Jaime was curious as to why.

Emerson had cut school to prepare for her visit with Dr. Rose. She was out of school again on Tuesday and found herself in the doctor's office at four-thirty, after pacing in her room all day.

"Hello, Emerson. I'm glad you decided to come in for a visit."

"Mom says our insurance covers counselling, though she wanted me to stay in-system for it," Emerson said.

"After the experience you and your friends had a week ago, I would not deny you counselling even if you were completely uninsured. The weekend might have been harder on you than any of the rest of us," Rose said.

"I guess. Are you reading my thoughts?"

"No. I built effective barriers against inadvertently reading people or being read by them. And much like what Schwartz did in Astoria, I enhanced the psychic dampening characteristics of my office. I want people to feel safe here, even from psychic probing."

"Whoo! I guess that's a relief, though I don't know why. I know Jaime and Keira can read me anytime they want, and I carried on a conversation with Trayce at the ballgame Friday night. I think Keira and Jaime facilitated that, though. I don't know that I could have that kind of conversation with just Trayce," Emerson said.

"They have a unique relationship. I can't answer that question."

"Well, that's not really important anyway. I only know Trayce through Jaime and Keira, really. I'm only actually interested in them. I mean, Trayce is a nice girl and I can see what Jaime and Keira see in her. But I'm kind of obsessing over Jaime and Keira. I just don't see any way it can work out."

"Why don't you tell me about what you *want* to work out?"

"Yeah. Well, it started with Dom and Raquel," Emerson said.

"Do I know them?"

"Um… No. And it isn't fair to lay it on them anyway," Emerson sighed. "It's me. I was sick of being the mousy chick no one noticed. I want to be free and be a little wild. When I went to Paris for seven months on a study exchange, I decided to try on the persona I really wanted to be. I had enough money to buy clothes and do interesting things. Not drugs or booze. Even Paris has a few laws governing seventeen-year-olds. But I'm really into clothes and being sexy and daring. That's when I met Dom and Raquel. We just fit together, you know? It seemed so right. We were lovers—all three of us. We talked about a future together and that I'd be back in the spring. But I had to come home for senior year. And as soon as I left, Raquel got pregnant and Dom married her on New Year's Day. And then I was no longer part of that *ménage à trois*. I was alone."

"You miss them, don't you?"

"Yeah. But I'm too mad at them to miss them much. We were supposed to be all together when I went back to Paris. Now, they're married and I'm invited to 'visit this summer.' But I have this really nice computer lab partner helping me on my project as I helped him on his. And then I found out he had a girlfriend and I thought, how convenient. I could have what I had in Paris, but with two really nice kids here. And then there was Trayce and I kept getting shuffled in and out of the relationship. I mean, I was never really in the relationship. Except in my head. And when Jaime spoke to me in my head the first time, I about shrieked."

"How did that happen?"

"I invited him and Keira to my house to test our apps and I hugged him. He just said we weren't going to go there. But, of course, I tried again a week later when they thought they'd been rejected by Trayce. That time we kissed— the three of us together—and I saw something a lot more than that they talked with each other and with me in their heads."

"What did you see, Emerson?" Rose expected most of the first part of the story, but the idea that Emerson might have seen something different than the rest of them experienced was a curiosity.

"I could see how they were connected," Emerson said. "Like, how their molecules intertwined with each other. I tried to fit myself into that link, but I couldn't find the path. Then when we were in Astoria and the four of us did that thing to the bad guys… *Shit!* That was some strong juju. But I still think I saw something different from what the others saw. I saw where everyone was linked together and I could build bridges between them. Like Jaime and

Keira and Trayce had never met physically before and Trayce was being a bitch about it. I saw where they were linked, though, and I sort of reached in and put myself on their bridge to hold them together while Jaime took control and ordered that guy to leave and never come back. And then it was over."

"Have you had any repeat of this experience?"

"Sort of. I saw them at the basketball game Friday night. They were pretty cute. It was like their first real date. I couldn't help myself. I sat down and took Jaime's hand. I was linked in with the three of them again. I could talk to them and answer questions in my head. But I could also see how they were linked together and the bridge I saw in Astoria was still there and getting stronger."

"That's an amazing thing, Emerson. Might I suggest it is not the kind of thing you want to tell a lot of people about? It could be that you subconsciously did the same thing with Dom and Raquel. It might not be limited to people who talk in their heads."

"Wow! Really? Yeah. I see it now. I thought what I saw with Dom and Raq was about how the three of us worked so well and so easily together. It could have been something else. Of course, that would involve another whole level of believing in this whole head talk kind of thing. I still have trouble believing any of it is real. But you've given me some interesting things to think about."

"As you have for me," Rose said. "Let's talk about what you want to happen from here on out."

Rose continued to ask probing questions and Emerson considered the answers carefully, moving closer and closer to what she needed to do.

39
THE WINTER BALL

Jaime and Keira and Emerson

THINGS CONTINUED TO progress well for Jaime and Keira with Trayce. They had a fun date the next weekend, continuing to explore physical activities by trying axe-throwing. They were all surprised that Trayce proved to be the champion.

"Wish I could carry one of these around with me," Trayce said, hefting the axe. "I'd feel safer!"

"It might not work as well in close quarters," Keira warned. They went on talking about self defense and the pros and cons of having a weapon.

They also agreed to attend the winter ball at the school the next Saturday.

On Monday before the ball, Emerson found Keira and Jaime at lunch.

"Can I join you today?" she asked.

"Of course! You're always welcome," Keira said.

"We made some good progress on the apps last week," Jaime signed.

"Yeah, we did. Mr. Perkins said he thought I could sell the app as is to a paint store, but encouraged me to do a scan of their paint chips first and test the app on real data. I guess you know what I'll be doing for the next few weeks," Emerson laughed.

"That's exciting," Keira said.

"Yeah, but that's not what I wanted to talk to you about," she said. "Can I hold your hands?"

Jaime and Keira looked around the cafeteria and nodded.

"It will just look like we're praying and no one will bother us," Emerson said. «I want you to be able to look inside me and I want to see in you while I say this,» she continued in her head. «I've managed to fall in love with another couple who can't love me back the way I love them. Yes, I'm talking about you. You can look in me and see everything about me. I'm standing here naked in front of you. I have a powerful lust for you and I'll probably be seeing you in my dreams as I masturbate for weeks.»

After a silent agreement, Jaime and Keira agreed to show themselves to her as well.

«Fuck! Now I know I'll see you in my fantasies,» she said. «Wow! Thanks for that. But I need to tell you that I know there isn't a real future for us. I'm even further outside you two since Trayce is in the picture than I was with Dom and Raquel. I'm in such serious lust that I'd literally strip off my clothes right here if you'd both fuck me. But I'm not part of your *ménage*. I won't ever be. There's no sense in trying to kid myself about it. You have something very special with Trayce and I wish you the utmost of happiness.»

«Thank you, Emerson. I hope you aren't saying that you won't be our friend any longer,» Jaime said.

«No. Not at all. We've got some real work to do on our projects together. And… if you, like… need a fourth for your… you know… crime fighting? I'll be available. We did good in Astoria. Yeah. That's all.»

Emerson withdrew her hands from Jaime and Keira, though she could still feel them lurking in her mind.

"Thank you, Emerson," Keira said. Then she started channeling Jaime as he began signing. "We hope we will never need to do that again. We don't want to be mental crime fighters. We have a long way to go before we are comfortable even with the powers we have. Nonetheless, I've been referring to you as the glue that held our gestalt together in Astoria. I could feel it and I don't understand it, but I know it's there."

"Well, if you just want to run some experiments, I'm up for it. I'm just beginning to understand what happened out there and could use your help on it. And Trayce. Everything has to include her now. I'll see you in class later, Jaime." Emerson left their table and the cafeteria.

Jaime and Rose

"I MUST ADMIT, I didn't really expect you to come in to see me," Rose said. "You seem very independent."

"As long as you don't mind my computer voice, I'd like to talk a bit. I might not be as independent as you think," Jaime typed into his TTS.

"It's fascinating. It should be easy for me to suspend my focus on the technology once we get going. You've never spoken aloud?" Rose asked.

"My mother died when I spoke aloud," Jaime said.

"Oh! Do you blame yourself for that?"

"Yes. If I'd been normal, she wouldn't have been surprised and fainted. It was my fault."

"That's a heavy burden for a child to bear. You know, don't you, that you're not to blame for it? You didn't know what would happen. People were pressuring you to speak aloud, I'll bet. It was expected and hoped for."

"Not being intentional doesn't mean there wasn't cause and effect," Jaime said.

"Are you confusing cause with sequence?"

Jaime just shook his head.

"Is this what you want to talk about today?"

"Sort of," Jaime typed. "I'm concerned about the possible results of Keira, Trayce, and me linking our minds."

"I see. Do you think you might give someon-e orders just because you are linked together and have that ability?" Rose asked.

"It's less about controlling our ability than about controlling our impulse. We're eighteen. We want to save the world. But our idea of what makes a better world might not conform to other people. What right would we have to interfere?" Jaime typed.

"Back in college, we had a Buddhist monk come to give a guest lecture to our ethics class. He was a quiet and unassuming man, as you would expect. He started his talk by saying, 'Everyone wants to make the world a better place, but no one wants to help Mom with the dishes.' It stuck with me—possibly the only specific thing I remember from that class," Rose said.

"I like that," Jaime agreed. "I don't think Keira or Trayce or I would have any problem with that. Of course, we should all become more aware of helping those closest to us. I just don't want to get enthused about something, like Keira and I did with the kidnapper at the movie, and just start shouting commands about it. I'm not even sure it would work."

"You had no qualms about giving me a command when you and Keira came to see me."

"Impulse control. That's what I'm talking about. We never should have done that. Thank you for helping. It could just as easily have gone badly."

"I had already decided on a course of action before you jumped on it," Rose said. "I didn't know you had already contacted Angus."

"He stopped them from grabbing me a week before they got Trayce."

"They're quite a team," Rose laughed.

"Yeah. I guess what I'm looking for is a way to restrain ourselves when we're… being intimate and happen to discover something wrong someplace. I'm worried about Schwartz's post-hypnotic suggestions being triggered by something."

"Has it happened?"

"Yes. We were sharing a fantasy. Long distance because we didn't want to rush things physically and we'd been sharing fantasies for a long time. Just when we were all relaxed and basking in the afterglow, a command came from deep inside Trayce to order you and Angus to go away like we did Schwartz. I recognized it just in time. It was a command to protect him from his enemies. But when she used the command, it weakened our ability, too, since we're his enemies. I was able to dismantle that one."

"My oh my, Jaime. You surprise me at every turn. First of all, you must realize how unique that ability is. And I can't help but think it is ultimately *your* ability, supported and bolstered by your girlfriends. Our… or *my* understanding of our gift has been that it was all one of hearing. You have a gift of speaking, and that is scary. I think for you as well as for me. I've never heard of someone able to dismantle a subliminal command without either drugs or hypnotism."

"Like Schwartz used to plant them in Trayce," Jaime typed.

"Yes, but you have a better method, in my opinion. You are gentle and non-invasive. You will need to keep a part of yourself aware of the possibility at all times, but that is the best way to discover any triggers. I don't believe you need to worry *directly* about Schwartz, but there could be some landmines," Rose said.

"Okay."

"There's something else."

"Yes."

Jaime hesitated with his hands above the keyboard. Rose was experienced enough to just let him think without interruption. Finally, he started typing.

"I spent all my life trying to make other people hear me. I thought I was a bad person because no one would respond to my head talk. Then, in kindergarten, I learned to sign but I still didn't open my mouth. And then it became so much a part of me that I never considered out-loud speaking again. Mostly. But then Keira found me and she could speak in my head. And we found Trayce… or she found us. Then, I discovered that if I was touching Emerson, she could hear me if I wanted her to."

"Your world is growing."

"But what if… if Trayce and Keira only love me because I *want* them to? Am I controlling them? I don't want to force them to love me!"

"Oh, Jaime. It's so hard, isn't it? I think you would know if you were influencing their feelings toward you any more than any one person influences how others feel about him. Be conscious and be vigilant. You *control* how you influence others. If you were truly controlling Keira and Trayce, you would have included Emerson in your group. But you've accepted her decision to not be a part of it. I believe you would accept Keira's and Trayce's decisions as well. You influence them through your love for them. Not through your ability to control their minds. Trust your love, Jaime."

Jaime and David

After grocery shopping on Saturday, David had Jaime drop him at Olivia's apartment so the teens would have the house to themselves that night.

"Dad," Jaime signed before David got out of the car. "I need to tell you something."

"What is it, son?"

"There might be more than two of us spending the night tonight," Jaime said.

"No parties, son. That's just too dangerous."

"No. Not like that. Remember when Keira and I intended to meet our online friend after Christmas, but it never happened?" Jaime signed, wishing he'd taken care of this while they were home and he had his computer. This was complicated to sign.

David nodded.

"She didn't meet us because she'd been kidnapped. When we went to Astoria the day after New Year's, it was to rescue her. She managed to contact us. We brought her home and we've been dating her when Keira and I go out. We think we're ready for that next step."

Oh, Lord, Nola! How am I supposed to deal with this?

"You mean you are planning to become a threesome?" David asked.

"Yes."

"Do Keira's parents know?" David asked.

"Trayce is at Keira's house to get ready for the dance tonight. They're talking to Keira's parents," Jaime signed.

"I can't say I understand this. Oh, I understand the mechanics, but not the emotional content. I really thought you and Keira had something special."

"We do, Dad. It's so special we can share it with Trayce and not lessen any of it between the two of us."

"Okay. Well, thank you for letting me know. We'll probably stop by tomorrow morning—not too early—to meet your other girlfriend. Just… Good luck, son."

David hugged Jaime and then got out of the car. He glanced back, but kept going resolutely.

Jaime and Keira and Trayce

The Winter Ball was a formal dance and the threesome decided to treat that traditionally. The idea of formal wear had evolved into a wide range of dress. It was mostly boys who eschewed the rental of a tuxedo. The school had banned jeans and all forms of denim, but they couldn't possibly cover all the variations that guys could come up with. One guy had a tuxedo printed on a long-sleeve black T-shirt. There were a few who wore dark slacks with cowboy boots, a bolo tie, and a western jacket. A few miles east of them in Idaho, that would have been the standard mode of dress. There were a few plain suits, a couple of white dinner jackets, and even a bright pink full set of tails.

On further examination, it was revealed the pink tails belonged to one part of a lesbian couple. Her date was dressed in an outrageously daring formal gown.

Jaime wore a traditional tuxedo and picked up the flowers for his two dates. They'd had to figure out the tickets for the dance. Jaime registered Trayce as his guest and Keira attended as a solo. A number of students who had no date but simply wanted to attend the mid-winter party got solo tickets. Some, who were forbidden by parents to date, bought solo tickets and met their partners at the dance.

Once they had presented their tickets and were inside, no one thought twice about seeing Jaime with two beautiful girls—a redhead and a blonde. They worked hard at screening thoughts from the people around them and caught only a few derogatory remarks from people. Everyone was required to arrive between seven and eight o'clock, and the event would end precisely at ten.

Soon after they arrived, Mex and Cheery caught up with them.

"Hey, Jaime. Hi, Keira. Um…" Mex started in.

"Juan and Letitia, I'd like you to meet Keira's and my girlfriend, Trayce," Jaime signed. The mouths of both his friends dropped open. "Trayce, these are my friends Juan and Letitia. We've known each other since kindergarten."

"Wow! That's a great friendship!" Trayce said.

"It's nice to meet you, Trayce," Cheery said. She turned to Juan. "Don't get any ideas, buster."

"Not on your life! You are my everything," Mex said. Cheery beamed.

"We'll see you later," Mex said. He and Cheery headed toward the refreshment buffet.

«Well, that… went okay,» Keira said. «Why don't we just go dance for a while?»

Like most high school dances, the early music was mostly contemporary and fast-paced rock. The idea of dancing to the music was a matter of perspective. They had a pretty good DJ who kept the music rolling and hopping from song to song without more than a minute or two of each number unless the crowd was really into it. The dancing was mostly bouncing up and down and screaming.

The last half hour of the dance, the music slowed down some, allowing couples—or triples, as the case was—to at least hold hands as they danced. The first touch of skin-to-skin with the three teens after two hours of rave-style music was a shock to all of them. Just as the first hand-holding of Keira and Jaime had opened their senses to everyone in the theater, taking each others' hands as they danced opened their senses to everyone in the room.

Trayce's eyes went wide as the overwhelming number of thoughts poured into her. Jaime tried to quickly suppress some of the noise, but Keira was caught up in the mass emotion of the dancing students. To her, it was almost like becoming a part of the music as she was borne upward by the vibe. It took only a moment for Trayce to follow with her. Jaime could feel it and joined with the girls, but stayed grounded, ready to pull the two back to earth if needed.

They gradually regained their individual identities as the music continued, pressing themselves closer and closer together. As they focused more and more on each other, lips were raised to lips and they found themselves isolated in a corner of the room kissing.

"Here now!" a chaperone said, approaching them. "That's not within the bounds of acceptable behavior at school, no matter what event. Pull yourselves together or you will have to leave at once."

Jaime jumped back and Keira spoke.

"We're sorry! We didn't mean to make a spectacle. We got caught up in the music and just lost track of what we were doing."

«Tell her to just go away!» Trayce commanded. «I want more kisses.»

Jaime clamped down on the thought immediately and Trayce snapped to him with a surprised look on her face.

«Did I…?»

«It's not a problem, love. I took care of it.»

«I'm a real bitch!»

«No you aren't,» Keira said. «We just all got caught up in the moment.»

«It's time to gather our things and get ready to leave anyway,» Jaime said. «The dance is over.»

They found their coats and joined the exodus into the night air.

"I'm sorry," Trayce said as they got into the car. Jaime drove but Keira and

Trayce sat together in the back seat. "I don't know what came over me. I'm not usually that way."

"It's okay," Keira said. «We were just excited to be together.»

«I don't think it was a suggestion from Dr. Schwartz,» Trayce said, switching to her inside voice. «I think it's because I'm not used to controlling my thoughts. It was an instant thought that I had and just let it out. I might not be able to control that.»

«That's why we'll all help each other,» Jaime said. «Three minds are better than one, I guess.»

«My mind wasn't much help,» Keira giggled. «Wow! When we all touched and the room opened up, it was like surfing on a giant wave of emotion. Everyone was caught up in the music. I didn't really feel any individual thoughts.»

«I did at first," Trayce said. «Then I saw you out there and I just wanted to be with you. I think Jaime was the only one of us with a foot in reality.»

«A tenuous foot,» Jaime said. «I wasn't sure where we might end up if we just rode the wave.»

«I'm glad you kept us grounded. Please show me what you did so I can keep from just being swept along next time,» Keira said.

«It's decision time,» Jaime said. «Trayce, we don't have to go home yet. We can go get a burger or wings or something. And even then, you don't have to go with Keira and me. We can take you home. We'd love to have you stay the night with us, though.»

«It really is time. I feel so crazy in love with you both, I can't think straight,» Trayce said. Then she switched to her out-loud voice. "No. I do know what I want and I'm ready for it. It's my excitement that's scrambling my brain, not my desires. Jaime and Keira, please take me home with you and make love to me!"

40
WHAT GREATER THING AWAITS

Jaime and Keira and Trayce

BOTH GIRLS HAD overnight bags in Jaime's car and immediately went to his room to change out of their formal wear. Jaime figured he would get his turn later and just tossed his jacket and tie on the living room sofa. He went to the kitchen to get sparkling water for them.

«God, she's gorgeous!» Keira said in his mind. He looked out of her eyes at Trayce standing naked in front of her.

«Hey! If he gets to peek at me, he gets to peek at you, too,» Trayce laughed, looking at Keira standing naked in front of her.

«I'm sorry I have nothing of interest to share,» Jaime said. The view was quickly closed down and a few minutes later, the girls came out in pajamas.

"We'll use the bathroom while you get ready for bed," Keira said.

They ran into the bathroom and Jaime went to his bedroom. The girls had not been overly neat. Their gowns lay across the back of Jaime's desk chair and their hose and underwear were piled on top. He spent a moment just looking at the assortment of things they'd taken off. Then he realized they'd put pajamas on! He scrambled to look in his drawers and finally found a pair of boxers and a T-shirt. That was as close to pajamas as anything he owned. He scrambled out of his clothes, piling them on top of the girls' gowns, then put on his makeshift pajamas. He stepped out of the bedroom as the girls came out of the bathroom. They went to the kitchen and he brushed his teeth.

«Thank you for getting unflavored water,» Trayce said. «I can just imagine what grapefruit flavored water would be like after minty toothpaste!»

«Ooh, yuck!» Keira joined.

«I didn't figure you'd want sodas after brushing teeth,» Jaime said, joining them in the kitchen. He stood just looking at them for a moment. «Wow!»

«Yeah. We're really here,» Trayce said.

«Here's to love!» Keira said raising her glass.

As soon as they'd had a drink, they moved together to kiss. The correct tilt of the head seemed automatic, even at their uneven heights. The kiss deepened and each of the teens opened further to each other, wrapped up in their discoveries.

«There's no reason to stay in the kitchen,» Jaime said.

«Yeah,» Keira said, taking Trayce's hand and leading her back to Jaime's bedroom. They all crawled onto the bed and sat facing each other.

«I love you, Jaime,» Keira said. «I love you, Trayce.»

«I love you, Keira,» Trayce picked up immediately. «I love you, Jaime.»

Jaime hesitated a moment as if struggling over the thought and the girls began to worry.

"I love you, Keira. I love you, Trayce," he squeaked out in his out-loud voice.

"Jaime!" Keira said. Trayce just stared open-mouthed.

«I had to say it with my out-loud voice, before I could say it in our heads. I love you both so much. Please don't die!»

«It hurt!» Trayce said. «I didn't know it actually hurt you to use your out-loud voice! Oh, Jaime! I'm so sorry!»

«It's okay, baby. I did it for you. I'd do it again.»

All three understood his reference to calling out for them at the inn when they couldn't use their inner voices. It was what Trayce had connected to instantly.

«I didn't know! I didn't know!» Trayce cried. «You never have to use your out-loud voice again! I didn't want to hurt you.»

«I didn't know, either,» Keira said. «I thought it was just a choice you made because of… you know… your mother. Jaime, I didn't know it hurt you to speak.»

«I wasn't sure. It hurt each time I did it, but I don't know why.»

«It's okay! Don't do it again!» Trayce cried. «I can't stand to have you hurt like that. Just kiss me and make the hurt go away.»

Jaime pulled Trayce to him and kissed her. She opened herself fully to him and wrapped him in mental arms for a long hug. Perhaps she had been withholding a part of herself from him because she thought he was withholding his voice. Now she let go of all her fears and preconceptions and let Jaime flow through her as they kissed.

«I'm… Oh, Jaime… I'm going to…»

«Yes, come!» Keira said, holding Trayce from the other side.

Neither Keira nor Jaime had their own orgasm at that moment. They joined in Trayce's and let it wash over the three of them.

«Just from a kiss,» Trayce whispered. «Is it even *safe* to have sex?»

«It was more than 'just a kiss.' We could feel your whole being open to us. It was so wonderful,» Keira said.

Trayce turned to her and opened herself in a kiss with her girlfriend. As the kiss deepened, both girls got more and more turned on. Jaime, holding them from behind, read their reluctance to dip into another orgasm so quickly, so he lent his strength to tempering the emotional effect a little.

They still sighed and were glassy-eyed when they parted.

«I… Have you… Has it been like that for the two of you all the time?» Trayce asked.

«When I kiss Keira, my world folds into hers. We've definitely both come just from kissing.»

«Kissing and the shared feeling of love,» Keira said. «That's what I felt from you, Trayce. Such a deep wonderful love.»

«I do love you both. Kiss each other and let me share in that,» Trayce said.

Jaime and Keira were only too glad to follow that instruction. Jaime had accurately described it as his world folding into hers. He gave up everything in himself to Keira. When they parted, having fended off an approaching orgasm for each of them, they found Trayce with tears dripping down her face.

«Honey? It's okay, baby. We love you just as much,» Keira said.

Trayce nodded and smiled through her tears. She sniffled a little and Jaime reached for a tissue for her.

«I'll never be able to write about this,» she said. «I don't have that many words. When we were sharing, a thousand emotions opened in me and I don't know words for a quarter of them. Our contact was in color and pictures and emotions. How could I ever *write* that?»

«Well, you experience it over and over,» Jaime suggested. «You manage to isolate one thing each time and then find a word for that one thing. Then the next time, you capture another image or feeling. You work on finding a word for that.»

«It will take forever!» Trayce laughed.

«What are you doing for the rest of your life?» Keira asked. «I hope it includes us.»

«The rest of my… Oh, God! Yes! We'll have lots of time to experience every one of those emotions and colors and pictures! I'm so much in love!»

The three teens began to focus on the process of getting to the next stage without being so overwhelmed they couldn't move. Their previous make-out sessions had the strict rule of keeping clothes on and hands above the waist. Those rules no longer applied. The cute pajama tops joined Jaime's T-shirt in a pile on the floor.

They were caught up in discoveries as they tried to touch every bit of bare skin. A ticklish spot. A tiny birthmark. A dimple.

And then the bottoms joined their tops in the pile as they continued to explore each other with their fingers and their lips. Breasts and nipples were touched and licked and sucked. Cock and pussies were stroked. Both the girls and Jaime were giving and receiving the many touches and kisses.

And each touch took them deeper into each other. They lost track of whose sex was being licked or touched or penetrated. Having had some deep experiences when kissing, they were able to simply revel in the experience of sex. Of love. When Jaime entered one girl, both felt the union. When a girl licked the other, Jaime tasted her on his tongue. And after building and restraining themselves for what seemed hours, when one finally reached a peak, orgasm washed over all three.

The experience was so intense that they simply held each other and tried to let their brains process the experience as their bodies gave in to sleep.

Sleep was in intervals of shared dreams and waking was in pairs. Trayce awoke with Jaime and invited him into her. They experienced a deep joining of their spirits as Keira followed along with them in her dreams. Keira and Trayce made love as Jaime watched in his dreams in wonder at the beauty of his girlfriends.

And when Jaime and Keira made love, Trayce was with them, not taking her own pleasure, but riding in the intense love the two had for each other.

They stumbled out of bed in the morning and showered, washing each other, and continuing their explorations before dressing in casual clothing to have breakfast.

«My soulmates,» Jaime said as they prepared bacon, eggs, and toast. They were all famished and drank half a quart of juice while they were preparing. «Dad will be here in half an hour or so. I'm pretty sure he'll bring Olivia. We need to tell our parents.»

«I think they know after we spent last night in the same bed,» Keira laughed.

«I mean we need to tell them about our connection. The two of you opened more to me last night than I ever imagined possible. And I could hear my dad worrying about me. And your parents, too.»

«I thought I heard my mom,» Trayce said. «I kind of thought to her, 'It's okay. I'm okay. Please accept us.' That wasn't too much was it?»

«Pretty much the same as what I thought to my parents, but I never considered they might actually hear me. That's still so new,» Keira said.

«I think they deserve to know how deep a connection we have, what went on between Christmas and New Year's, and why we are all three together. Maybe I've been wrong keeping it from my dad all this time. He deserves to know what happened with my mom. I just always felt so guilty and isolated before and now I feel so connected I need to heal what I can.»

«It's going to be hard with my mom,» Trayce said. «She's worried about hearing voices and has some drugs her psychiatrist prescribed to keep them away.»

«Aunt Rose says the drugs don't actually silence the voices, they just help you ignore them. The idea is that you ignore them for so long, eventually you don't recognize they're there at all.»

«Yeah. The problem is that she'll want me to go on them, too and I don't want to lose you.»

«We're actual people you see and hear,» Jaime said. «Not just voices in your head anymore.»

«Mmmhmm. You sure were real last night!» Trayce grinned. «And this morning.»

«Dad and Olivia are almost here,» Jaime said. «Help me, okay?»

Jaime and Keira and Trayce and David and Olivia

"I WANT TO use the TTS app for a conversation because Olivia doesn't know sign language and it would be hard to get what I'm going to say across even through an interpreter as good as Keira is," Jaime typed into his computer.

"Okay, son. You are still all three here, so I'm going to assume the night was good for you. We don't need to go into it in detail."

"Yeah. We're all good. That isn't exactly what we want to talk about. This is really hard to put in words," Jaime typed. "I'll start by saying, Keira, Trayce, and I are psychically linked. It isn't about three kids being physically attracted to each other. Which we are, too."

"What kind of psychic link? You're telepathic?" Olivia asked. She seemed more open to the possibility than David did.

"Yes. In a word. We can talk to each other in our heads. But it goes deeper than that. I've been able to read other people's thoughts from the moment I was born. That's what overwhelmed my body and almost killed me. I didn't figure out that was what happened until it happened again."

"When I found you in the closet in a coma," David said. "I told the nurse on 9-1-1 that it was like what happened to you when you were born," David said.

"Yes."

"Wait! You don't talk because you communicate mentally?" David asked.

"I've spoken aloud three times in my life," Jaime said. Tears were beginning to form in his eyes. "It hurts. Mentally and physically. The first time… I'm so sorry, Dad. The first time was when Mom wasn't paying attention to me and I wanted a drink. So, I asked her aloud. I'm sorry."

"She never mentioned that," David said.

"She died. She was so surprised that she fainted and fell on the broken glass. I killed her!"

The shock appeared on David's face for only a moment before he launched himself toward his son and wrapped him in his arms.

"No! No, son! You didn't kill her! That was an accident. It's not your fault. You were four years old! Jaime, you didn't kill her! You didn't! The doctor said she had an aneurysm. It wasn't you at all!"

Jaime was overwhelmed with the information. He began crying and hugging his father.

Keira and Trayce put their hands on Jaime's head and he reached out to touch his father's face.

«Dad, I swore I would never use my out-loud voice again, and I kept that vow until a month ago.»

"I… I heard you," David said, backing up to his chair. "I heard you in my head!"

"Our psychic gift is one of listening," Jaime returned to typing. Keira grabbed a tissue and wiped his eyes. "When Trayce and Keira and I are together and we touch a person… at least some people… we can cause them to hear us."

"That's amazing," Olivia said. "Would you give me a message?"

Jaime smiled, but figured that might be the response of most of the parents. He nodded and Olivia scooted closer.

Will Jaime accept me as a stepmother? she thought loudly enough that all three teens picked up on it immediately. Jaime put his hands on Olivia's.

«When are you and Dad going to get married? It would be really nice to have you around. Yes, I'll accept you as my stepmom.»

"Oh! Oh, thank you!" Olivia said, sitting back. "I'm a believer, David."

"I don't know how I could not be," David said. "Jaime is my son. He wouldn't lie to me. Uh… When else did you use your voice?"

"A month ago," Jaime typed. "A weird psychologist had kidnapped Trayce. That's why we went to Astoria. She was being held in an old inn that prevented cell, microwave, RF, brainwave, and about everything else from penetrating. I had to out-loud yell for her in order to find her. Yeah. It hurt. But I had to do it."

"Did you call police? We need to make sure this guy doesn't try something again."

"That's another aspect of the whole thing we only found out that day," Jaime typed. "There were four of us. Emerson isn't psychic, but she connected with us when we were all four holding hands. We were able to give Schwartz a psychic command to abandon his practice and his research. And he obeyed. He won't trouble us again."

"That's a little frightening," Olivia said.

"We're not going to go around giving orders to people," Jaime typed. "We might not even be able to under ordinary circumstances."

"And when was the third time you used your out-loud voice?" David persisted.

"Last night. I had to tell Keira and Trayce I loved them aloud before I could tell them in my mind. It hurt, but it was so worth it!"

Trayce and Keira both kissed Jaime on his head.

"I'm inclined to just accept all this, though I know I'll have a ton of questions when it settles in," David said. "Forgive me if I don't always get it. I might need more explaining and… and help accepting in the future. I'd say I'm remarkably calm about it all, but my hands are shaking, so I know that's only a surface feeling. What's next?"

"We figure we need to go explain all this to my parents and Trayce's mom. I think it's going to be a long day," Keira said.

"I can imagine. If you want us along for support, we'll come. Won't we, Olivia?"

"Of course, David. Jaime, it's a little like a fairy tale or a science fiction story, but I am, by God, going to accept it and all three of you. Anything I can do, I will," Olivia said.

Jaime and Trayce and Keira and John and Julia

Telling Keira's parents involved calling in Aunt Rose. Without admitting that she too was a head talker, Rose indicated she had done several tests that confirmed what they said was true. She also said she had counseled all three kids on their relationship and felt it was healthy and mutually supportive.

"I just knew there was something more to it all than it appeared," John said. "And Rose, we need to talk. Just the three of us. All three of these kids are eighteen, so aside from withholding affection and making life difficult for them, I don't see anything we could do about their relationship. And I am not inclined to do either of those. So, kids, if not our blessing at the moment, you at least have our tolerance. And our love. Never be afraid to come to us when you need a hug or advice. We are really on your side."

They breathed a sigh of relief at that and headed to Trayce's house to talk to Lanie.

Jaime and Keira and Trayce and Lanie

"Mom, life's been hard on us since we lost Dad," Trayce said as they sat together. "I know you've talked about some of your problems and what finally got you to seek counseling and AA. I had a lot of the same problems. I didn't abuse substances, but I was feeling and acting a little crazy. Then I met and fell in love with Jaime and Keira. Yeah. Both of them."

"I could tell there was a special bond among you when they came and swore to find you and bring you home. Are you… um… all three…?"

"Yes, Mom. Jaime is my boyfriend and Keira is my girlfriend and we are all three together. I honestly never considered how I would tell my mother that I'm no longer a virgin, but there you have it," Trayce said.

"Please, just tell me it was good and you are happy," Lanie said.

"Oh, yeah! Really *really* good."

Lanie hugged Trayce and then turned to hug Keira and Jaime.

"Three children instead of just one? How blessed I am," she said.

"There's something else we need to tell you about and it will be harder to accept, I'm afraid. I fought against it for months," Trayce continued.

"You're not pregnant!"

"No! I'm sure of that. But… you mentioned that you heard voices and that was part of what motivated you to get counseling."

"Not just voices. Evil, nasty voices telling me to do terrible things," Lanie said. "They wanted me to hurt myself and you. They filled my mind with blood and terror. They told me that if I wasn't happy, no one should be happy. No. It wasn't just voices. It was the sound of my nightmares."

"Oh, Mom. I'm so sorry you went through that. I… um… hear voices, too. But they aren't evil and nasty. They're the voices of my boyfriend and girlfriend," Trayce said.

"Well… I guess I don't understand."

"Jaime and Keira and I can talk to each other in our heads. Not just when we're together, but even when we're miles apart. When I was kidnapped, I cried out to them from Astoria and they *heard* me. I'd still be there, drugged into a stupor, if they hadn't heard me."

"So, it's not just that you are mute, Jaime. You don't actually need your voice. I see."

«Is she okay?» Keira asked Jaime and Trayce. «She seems like it isn't anything out of the ordinary.»

«She doesn't want a demonstration,» Trayce said. «She thinks it's enough to accept that we are a family. I think we should let it drop.»

«I agree,» Jaime said.

They wrapped up the conversation with Lanie and then went out to dinner. They chose to at last go to the café in the bookstore.

Jaime and Keira and Trayce

«It's a real relief to have told our parents, even if they are skeptical," Keira said.

«Yeah, but did anyone notice that we don't have any place to all three go together and make love tonight?» Trayce thought with a giggle.

«That's only one of the hurdles we've got to cross,» Jaime said. «Our parents accept that we are all three together, but they aren't going to make it any easier to be sexually active than any other teen's parents are going to do. We have four more months of school. We need to figure out if we're all going to the same college. We need to figure out how much time we want to spend together and apart. We need to deal with all the things everybody needs to deal with in a relationship, plus our individual privacy and mental sharing.»

«We can do it, though, right?» Keira asked. «Please tell me you both think we can really make this work.»

«You called us soulmates,» Trayce said, holding Jaime and Keira's hands. «I just found you and I never want to give you up.»

«Then we'll work it all out,» Jaime said. «We just need to take it one step at a time.»

«You've had something else bubbling in the back of your mind, love,» Keira said. «Something we should be aware of?»

The three joined hands in a circle.

«I still think we need to be really careful. Did you notice how easily our parents all accepted us as a threesome? Last night or early this morning, we were all joined together basking in our mutual orgasms when we each whispered a little prayer to our parents. I know we each thought nearly the same thing. "Please accept us." I'm not saying we commanded them, but I believe we might at least have influenced their acceptance of us. That's great. That's what we wanted. It kept harmony in our families. But we need to be really careful about things like that if we really *can* influence other people with our minds. Maybe it's not like commanding Schwartz to abandon his career and his research, but it's still wielding unfair influence.»

«I didn't consider that,» Trayce said. «It just seemed like a normal thing to say—like anyone would have said it.»

«It was,» Keira said. «But anyone else couldn't have affected the actual result of saying it while we were linked so deeply. I guess we still have a lot to learn.»

«Here's to years and years together to learn it,» Jaime said.

A SIGNATURE COLLECTION INTERVIEW WITH DEVON LAYNE

We investigated the background of the author and what was going on when writing this novel. The Signature Collection asked author/editor/publisher Nathan Everett to dig in and get the hard answers. This is the result.

NE: Devon, you are online with different names. Care to clarify?

DL: Sure. Back in 2008 or so, I decided to join Stories Online as a reader. Of course, everything was very discreet at the time. I needed to choose a screen name. I wasn't sure what to use, but my faithful greyhound Valsora was lying next to my desk chair. I just reversed the letters of his name and became 'aroslav' online. In 2012 I started writing stories and posting them as aroslav, but I soon decided to publish them for the general public. I needed a good author name. I went down the shelves in the local bookstore and ultimately arrived at 'Devon Layne.'

NE: But neither is your real name?

DL: No. Further details withheld at this time.

NE: Okay. Let's talk about *Soulmates*. You are known for writing very fast. When did you write *Soulmates?*

DL: This defied the usual. I came up with the idea of a kid who was a telepath from the moment he was born back in February of 2015. I called the story idea "From Birth" and wrote about 700 words, then stuck the file in my "Ideas" folder and forgot about it. In October of 2020, I pulled it out of my idea file and started filling in some details, including the relationship with Keira. I got about 7,000 words into it and once again decided I wasn't ready for this.

I look in my ideas folder fairly regularly, and in July of 2024 I reviewed the work I'd done thus far and decided the time had come to actually pursue the project. I wrote out a beat sheet and shared it with my editors who liked the concept and had some good ideas, including that it needed to be told from at least two characters' perspective—Jaime and Keira.

The beat sheet went through several revisions and I made pages of notes before I finally set pen to paper on July 31, 2024. This time, recognizing the importance of other characters to the story, I called the draft "Head Talkers." I was on a cruise to Alaska when I started the draft and then wrote daily as I drove from the Pacific Northwest back to my winter home in Las Vegas over a three-week span. I didn't finish the draft until October 28, 2024. Almost three months of writing. It was 85,000 words and 26 chapters.

NE: That's not what it ended up at.

DL: No. I handed it off to my editor for comments and launched my November project, which took me until mid-December before I went back to rewrite it. With the time to let the story gel and the advice of my editors, I started pumping out the draft of the retitled **Soulmates** the first of December, while I was still pumping out my November WIP. I started posting the pre-release serial chapters on December 8. Then as the edited version kept coming back to me, I revised the posted serial chapters. I released the public serial on January 26 and the public eBook and Signature Collection paperback on Valentine's Day, February 14.

NE: Ten years in the making and now 139,000 words and 40 chapters. I didn't realize that. So, what was the impetus? Why this story?

DL: I've always been interested in telepathy, but I got to wondering if we weren't just approaching it all wrong. Everything I'd read was about how a person could *send* a message telepathically. I got to thinking that maybe it was all about hearing other people's thoughts. That wasn't an unheard-of concept, by the way. Just one I latched onto. But my brain said, "What if we are all born telepathic, but it's so overwhelming to our little brains that we shut it down? Like all except one little kid who didn't shut it down and was telepathic from birth?" It just took a while for the idea to really take shape.

NE: So, what's next? Will there be a sequel? A series?

DL: That's always a good question. I have some characters I really like (as do most of my readers) and they have a particularly unusual talent. There must be more to their story. The thing is, as Trayce is constantly asking, "What's the story?" When I can answer that question—which I will be trying to do—then I'll start plotting a sequel. Even my editors have asked for it.

NE: Congratulations on this release and on the launch of the paperback Signature Collection. We're looking forward to more.

DL: Thank you to all my readers for your support.

LANCE